BULLET FOR
A STRANGER

BULLET FOR A STRANGER

A RED RYAN WESTERN

WILLIAM W. JOHNSTONE

and J. A. Johnstone

PINNACLE BOOKS
Kensington Publishing Corp.
www.kensingtonbooks.com

PINNACLE BOOKS are published by

Kensington Publishing Corp.
119 West 40th Street
New York, NY 10018

PUBLISHER'S NOTE

Following the death of William W. Johnstone, the Johnstone family is working with a carefully selected writer to organize and complete Mr. Johnstone's outlines and many unfinished manuscripts to create additional novels in all of his series like The Last Gunfighter, Mountain Man, and Eagles, among others. This novel was inspired by Mr. Johnstone's superb storytelling.

All Kensington titles, imprints, and distributed lines are available at special quantity discounts for bulk purchases for sales promotions, premiums, fund-raising, educational, or institutional use. Special book excerpts or customized printings can also be created to fit specific needs. For details, write or phone the office of the Kensington sales manager: Kensington Publishing Corp., 119 West 40th Street, New York, NY 10018, attn: Sales Department; phone 1-800-221-2647.

PINNACLE BOOKS, the Pinnacle logo, and the WWJ steer head logo are Reg. U.S. Pat. & TM Off.

ISBN-13: 978-0-7860-4436-8

ISBN-10: 0-7860-4436-5

First printing: September 2020

10 9 8 7 6 5 4 3 2 1

Printed in the United States of America

Electronic edition:
ISBN-13: 978-0-7860-4437-5 (e-book)
ISBN-10: 0-7860-4437-3 (e-book)

Chapter One

"So, tell me," Patrick "Buttons" Muldoon said, "when we reach Fort Concho, what do you calculate the Limey coward will look like?"

Shotgun guard Red Ryan's gaze was fixed on the vast sweep of the Texas prairie ahead of the Abe Patterson and Son Stage and Express Company coach. Without turning to look at Buttons, he said, "I have no idea. But I guess he'll look like anybody else."

Buttons had slowed the six-horse team to a walk, and the only sound was the steady fall of the horses' hooves and the jingle of harness. The sky was bright blue, with no clouds, but the wind blowing from the north held an edge, a harbinger of the coming fall.

Buttons spat over the side of the stage, the ribbons steady in his gloved hands, and said, "I mean, will he be scared of his own shadow? One of them rannies who wear white drawers because they'll never know when they'll need a white flag?"

"You mean is he kissin' kin to Moses Rose?" Red said.

Buttons grinned, "Yeah, that's exactly what I mean."

"Then I don't know," Red said.

Buttons seemed disappointed. "Hell, Red, you don't know nothing."

"I don't know the answer to a conundrum that don't make any sense," Red said. "How do I know what the hell the coward will be like?"

"Yeah, well, we're taking him all the way to New Orleans, so I guess we'll find out, huh?" Buttons said. "Hell, we might find out the hard way. Maybe he'll try to stab us in the back."

"Sure, and maybe along the trail he'll haul off and do something cowardly," Red said.

"Man, that's something I'd surely like to see," Buttons said. "I ain't never seen a coward do coward stuff, especially a Limey coward."

Red nodded. "Me neither. Now, quit talking for a minute and study on what that there blue thing is ahead of us."

"What blue thing? Oh, wait, I see it." Buttons was silent for a few moments, peering into the distance. Then he said, "It's blue and white, but I can't make it out. A tent, maybe?"

"Maybe. Whip up the horses," Red Ryan said. "Let's go find out."

"Keep the Greener handy," Buttons said. "It may be some road agent trick that we ain't seen yet."

"I reckon we've seen them all," Red said. "But you never know."

Buttons snapped his whip above the team, and the horses lurched into a fast trot. "You've got younger eyes than me, Red, he said. "Can you make out what it is yet?"

"Not yet. But I guess we'll know soon enough."

A large circle of blue and white striped canvas, much torn, spread across the prairie grass. Beside it were piled several leather trunks. A man and woman stood beside a battered wicker basket large enough to accommodate two people, and as Buttons Muldoon drove the stage nearer, the woman raised a hand and waved.

"Hell, Red, it's a gal and a Chinee with her," Buttons said. "In all my born days I ain't never seen the like."

"And she's a right pretty gal at that," Red said. His tanned cheeks bore a three-day growth of rusty beard and he wished he'd shaved.

Buttons reined the team to a jangling halt and then raised his hat. "Well, howdy, young lady," he said. "We weren't expecting to meet company on this run. Nothing as far as the eye can see but grass, and even more grass."

Red smiled, showing his teeth. "He's Buttons Muldoon, and my name is Red Ryan. We're representatives of the Abe Patterson and Son Stage and Express Company, and we're at your service."

The girl nodded. "Of course, you are. I'm Hannah Huckabee, and by profession I'm an adventuress. My companion is Mr. Chang." Then, as though she thought an explanation necessary, "I saved his life from a street gang in Shanghai and he followed me home." She had a very pleasing English accent.

Hannah Huckabee, who looked to be in her late twenties, was a tall, slender woman with well-defined breasts and a narrow waist. She wore a tan-colored dress with plenty of flapped pockets that was short enough to reveal lace-up brown leather boots that were scuffed from hard use. A cascade of glossy black hair fell from under a pith helmet that sported a pair of dark-lensed goggles above the brim. Belted around her waist was a blue, short-barreled Colt with an ivory handle and on the opposite side a sheathed bowie knife of the largest size. A pair of expensive brass field glasses, probably of German manufacture, hung around her neck. Her eyes were a lustrous brown, the black lashes thick and long. When she smiled, as she was doing now, her teeth were very white . . . and Red Ryan thought her the most beautiful woman he'd ever seen in his life.

Buttons Muldoon, ever a gentleman when he was around the ladies, said, "Beggin' your pardon, ma'am, but what are you and the Chinee gent doing all the way out here in the wilderness?"

"Right now nothing, except being lost," Hannah said. She smiled her dazzling smile. "And, of course, I'm also talking to you, driving man."

"He means how did you get here?" Red said.

The girl pointed to the tattered canvas on the prairie grass. "Hanging from that in a basket is how we got here." Then, reading the question on Red's face. "What you see here are the remains of a hot-air balloon. It was my intention to explore the Caprock Canyons for signs of the culture that existed there ten thousand years ago. I mean pottery, spear points, and the like. You know, the usual archaeological stuff. Mr. Chang and I were also getting in some long-distance practice for our coming around-the-world balloon trip."

"Oh, I see," Buttons said, trying to look wise, but he didn't see at all.

Neither did Red.

"The Caprock Canyons are in the Panhandle country," he said. "How come you ended up here?"

Hannah Huckabee shrugged her slim shoulders. "We left the New Mexico Territory three days ago and then got hit by a most singular thunderstorm with a strong north wind and were blown off course. The balloon was ripped up, and Mr. Chang and I came down here. We landed pretty hard and were lucky to escape with only a few cuts and bruises. We could've been killed."

Mr. Chang bowed, then smiled and said, "We very lucky. Miss Huckabee very lucky lady. She prove that time and time again."

"Well, I'm glad you made it. Nice to meet you, Miss Huckabee," Buttons said. He touched his hat brim and gathered the ribbons in his hands. "Now we got to be on our way, a schedule to keep and all that."

"Wait, where are you headed?" Hannah said.

"East, to Fort Concho, ma'am. Got a coward to pick up from the army," Buttons said.

"A coward?" Hannah said.

"Yeah, an Englishman."

"And where are you taking him, this coward?"

"To the great city of New Orleans, ma'am, where we're meeting up with a British warship that will take him back to London town to face justice for his cowardly deeds."

"I declare, it must be an important kind of coward that merits his own warship," Hannah said.

"I don't know about that, ma'am, since I never picked up a coward afore," Buttons said. Then, "But yeah, I guess he's important enough."

"And he has this Abe Patterson and Son Stage and Express Company coach reserved just for him," Red said. "Takes a mighty big auger to merit that kind of attention."

"Mr. Ryan—"

"Call me Red."

"Red, Mr. Chang and I have had nothing to eat or drink for three days," Hannah said. "Do you have any food to spare? We'll be grateful for a few crumbs."

"Buttons?" Red said. "What do you say? Can we spare some grub?"

"Ma'am, it's against company regulations, but I guess we could spare some cold bacon, sourdough bread, and water," Buttons said. "It ain't much, but you're welcome to make a trial of it."

"Right now, any food would be most welcome," the woman said. "I can pay you in American money for what we eat."

"No payment needed," Red said. "It's the official policy of the Abe Patterson and Son Stage and Express

Company to feed the hungry and clothe the poor and needy."

"I'll get the grub," Buttons said. He gave Red a sidelong look. "I never heard of that official policy."

"Neither have I," Red said. "But I'm willing to bet that ol' Abe Patterson has it wrote down in the rules somewhere."

Ignoring Buttons's reminder that they were burning daylight, Red spread a blanket on the grass and laid out a meager lunch, including a wedge of seedcake that his plump driver had seen fit not to mention.

Hannah and Mr. Chang ate with an appetite that only three days of fasting can create, and to his chagrin Buttons watched the devouring of the bacon and bread and then the seedcake vanish to the last yellow crumb.

"Ah, that was quite sufficient to restore me to good health," the woman said, dabbing her lips with a scrap of handkerchief. "Once my balloon is replaced, Mr. Chang and I are off on our greatest adventure, but perhaps you will allow me to treat you gentlemen to dinner before we leave."

"Suits me just fine," Red said. "And then you'll head back to the Caprock Canyons, huh?" Red said.

"Oh, dear no," Hannah said. "That was to be just a side trip for the experience. I have something much more interesting in mind."

"Miss Huckabee have only interesting adventures," Mr. Chang said. Then, smiling at Red, "That is her official policy."

"And what might that adventure be?" Buttons said. He looked sour, the sad fate of his seedcake nagging at him.

"Mr. Muldoon, I've already told you. It's our balloon flight around the world," Hannah said. "I'm sure you've read the book, *Le tour de Monde en Quatre-Vingts Jours*, by Mr. Jules Verne."

Buttons shook his head. "Lady, I don't even know what that means."

Hannah laughed, a sound like a ringing crystal bell, and Red Ryan thought it must be the sound the heavenly angels make when they hear a good joke. "It means Around the World in Eighty Days," the woman said. "It's about a gentleman called Phileas Fogg and his valet who travel around the world in a balloon, and it's very popular both in this country and in Europe. I'm told Queen Victoria is fond of it and has read it through several times."

"Miss Huckabee meet Queen Victoria and like her very much," Mr. Chang said. "And Queen Victoria like Miss Huckabee very much."

"We met only for afternoon tea," Hannah said. "I didn't attend one of her balls or anything like that, but she baked one of her special sponge cakes for the occasion."

"Queen Victoria very good baker," Mr. Chang said.

"And now you want to go around the world like that Fogg feller?" Red said.

"Yes, I do. I don't have a valet like Mr. Fogg, but I have Mr. Chang." Hannah smiled. "Of course, I doubt that I'll make the trip in eighty days, since a balloon depends on the vagaries of the wind, and I will also need to employ other means of travel, like steam train and ship, but I'm an adventuress and I'm willing to give it a try. I do very much wish to sail in a balloon above the pyramids of Egypt and the temples of India and pay a return visit to Cathay and fly over the Great Wall."

Buttons looked confused. "Don't that take a lot of money? I mean, to go gallivanting around the world like that in a flying machine?"

"Oh, yes it does, Mr. Muldoon," Hannah said. "But a late uncle left me a considerable fortune in his will, on the condition that I don't agree to be some man's dutiful little wife and stay home and become a drawing-room ornament. Uncle Chester was an adventurer who became rich pearl diving in the Philippines, where the pearls are said to be the finest in the world. Though he later went into the iron and steel business, it pleased him that I followed in his shoes and became an adventuress."

"Miss Huckabee's uncle was very rich man, knew many powerful people," Mr. Chang said. "President of America shake her hand, and Czar of Russia give her a kiss on the cheek."

"Yes, President Grant and uncle Chester were very close, as was millionaire Andrew Mellon," Hannah said. "And of course, he counted the Czar of Russia among his friends, and he and the Chinese emperor corresponded regularly. Uncle Chester had a good singing voice and was very popular."

Hannah took a sip of water, slowly lowered the canteen, and said, "Red, stay right where you are. Don't move a muscle."

Red sat with his arms behind him and didn't have time to move a muscle because three events followed very fast . . .

Hannah dropped the canteen, splashing water. An ominous rattle sounded close to Red's right hand. And the girl drew her Colt and fired.

Red yelped and jumped to his feet, his eyes wild. "What the hell?" he shouted. "Why did you shoot at me?"

"Snake," Hannah said. She held her revolver alongside her head, the muzzle pointing at the sky, trailing smoke. "I hate snakes. All adventurers hate snakes. They're the bane of our existence, sly, slithering creatures that they are."

Red looked down at the big, headless diamondback coiling and uncoiling on the grass where he'd been sitting. "Damn, that son of a bitch could've killed me," he said.

"It could've killed something, depending where it bit," Hannah said.

She punched out the spent round from the Colt cylinder and replaced it with a cartridge from her belt. "Snakes and I just don't get along. I once got bitten by a cobra in Macau and like to have died. Only the presence of a Portuguese army surgeon saved my life, but it was a damned close thing." Her beautiful eyes lifted to Red's face. "Are you all right? You had a nasty scare."

"Yeah, I'm all right," Red said. He picked up his derby hat, rammed it onto his mop of unruly red hair, and then, his masculine pride exerting itself, he added, "I don't scare real easy."

"Yes, I'm sure you don't," Hannah said, smiling slightly.

"Miss Huckabee don't scare worth a damn, but she very afraid of snakes," Mr. Chang said.

"I think we've already established that, Mr. Chang," Hannah said, frowning. "Sometimes you will belabor the point. I'm sure it's a Chinese thing."

She rose and picked up the still-writhing diamond-back and held it high for Red and Buttons to see. "Even minus the head, he's a good four foot long," the girl said. "Anyone want the rattle? No?" She tossed the snake away and smiled. "I think that's enough excitement for one day, don't you?"

"Hell, it's more than enough for me," Buttons said. "I don't cotton to snakes, either."

"And I second that," Red said. Then, "Buttons, let's cut a trail."

"Suits me just fine," Buttons said. He climbed into the driver's seat and picked up the reins of the resting team.

As Red gathered up the blanket and the food that hadn't been eaten, Hannah stepped beside him and said, "I'd be most grateful if you'd take me and Mr. Chang to Fort Concho with you. Our balloon is ruined, and the burner was lost overboard during the storm."

"Well, we can't leave you here to starve," Red said. "I was about to suggest that you come with us as far as Fort Concho."

Buttons looked down from his high perch and said, "Miss Huckabee, it's the policy of the Abe Patterson and Son Stage and express Company that passengers may be picked up along the route if there is room within and said passengers have the necessary coin for the fare."

"I can pay," Hannah said.

"Buttons, she saved my life," Red said.

"I know she did. But company policy is company policy, Red. You know that, because you're always quoting it. Miss Huckabee, the fare to Fort Concho will be fifty dollars for you and half that for the Chinee, since he doesn't take up much room. Meals for the next two days included, of course."

"That will be quite satisfactory," Hannah said. "Red, if you would help me with my trunks?"

"Of course," Red said. "And please excuse Buttons. He's a die-hard company man."

"Takes one to know one," Buttons said.

Mr. Chang stepped in front of Red, bowed, and said, "Lady saved gentleman's life. Gentleman must repay with life for a life."

Red grinned. "Well then, I reckon taking Miss Huckabee to Fort Concho is payment enough."

Mr. Chang nodded, unsmiling. "Perhaps. Perhaps not."

Chapter Two

The man at the open door of the Pink Pearl saloon in San Angelo turned to the patrons inside and said, "Well, Brack Cooley is on the street."

"The fun begins," a brunette girl in a short, scarlet dress and fishnet stockings said, as she and two dozen other men and women crowded into the doorway.

The sun was high in the sky, and the dusty town was oppressively hot. A yellow dog, sensing trouble, slunk from the boardwalk and crawled under the saloon.

"Where's Frank Pickett?" the bartender yelled. "Did he show?"

"Not yet," a man answered. Then, after a pause, "But ol' Brack is standing outside the hotel, and he's called Frank out. Man, he looks like he's loaded for bear."

A tall, slender man, expensively dressed, a diamond stickpin in his cravat, rose from a table, leaving two young companions, and stepped to the bar. In an exquisite English accent, he said, "Tell me, my good man, is Brack Cooley as dangerous as his reputation claims he is?"

The bartender, a florid-faced Irishman with no love for the English, looked his inquisitor up and down with considerable distaste and then said, "He's a known man-killer. How dangerous is that?"

"I don't know," the Englishman said. "You tell me."

The bartender ignored that last and his eyes moved to the door. "Is Frank in the street yet?"

"No, Tom," a man said. "I'll tell you when."

His hands busy polishing a glass, the bartender said to the Englishman, "Brack Cooley has killed two dozen men, or so they say. Me, I think he's probably done for more than that. He killed the three Simpson brothers that time in San Antone, picked them off one by one as they came at him in a hallway of the Red Garter cathouse. Shot a whore by mistake as well, but she recovered."

"In Texas, Mr. Cooley is what's called a bounty hunter?" the Englishman said. "Isn't that the case?"

"Bounty hunter. Hired killer. Lawman. Brack does it all. He's what you might call a jack of all trades."

"And who is Frank Pickett?"

"A local hard case and sometimes cattle rustler. He has a reputation as a gunman here in Tom Green County, but I don't know that he's shot anybody. He's got a two-hundred-dollar bounty on his head for lifting cows, and that's why Cooley is here."

The Englishman smirked. "Not much of a bounty, is it?"

"Times are hard," the bartender said.

The man at the door yelled, "Tom, quick! Frank's walked out of the hotel. And he's wearing both his guns."

The bartender quickly crossed the floor and walked onto the porch. The Englishman followed.

Brack Cooley raised his left hand, palm forward, as though fending off Pickett. "Frank," he yelled, "I'm taking you in for the reward on your sorry hide. What's it to be? Will you come quietly, or do we go to the gun? State your intentions."

To the delight of the onlookers, Pickett, a short, towheaded man missing his two front teeth, stepped off the hotel porch and opened fire as soon as his boots hit the street. He got off three fast shots, all of them wild, one round so errant that it splintered into the saloon doorway and precipitated a lively stampede back inside by most of the spectators. The Englishman and the bartender were among those who remained, and they saw Brack Cooley raise his revolver to eye level and fire. At a distance of twenty yards, the bounty hunter needed only one shot. Pickett dropped dead without a sound, a bullet hole blossoming like an opening rose smack in the middle of his low forehead.

As Pickett hit the dirt, Cooley holstered his gun and then looked around him at the people on the boardwalks. "He was notified," he said. "Anybody here say he wasn't?"

A man with a gray hair and a town marshal's star on his vest stepped into the street and said, "It was self-defense. I seen it all, Brack."

"Just so you know it was legal and aboveboard," Cooley said. He scowled at the frightened lawman. "Who pays the bounty? Speak up, now."

"County sheriff, Brack," the marshal said.

"Where is he?"

"I don't know. He's gone fishing, but he said he'll be back before nightfall."

Cooley thought that through and then said, "I'll wait."

A tall, black-haired man with eyes the color of a winter mist, Cooley grabbed the dead man by the collar of his coat and dragged him to the front of the hotel, where Pickett's paint pony stood hipshot at the hitching rail. Displaying considerable strength, Cooley threw the little man across his saddle and then tied the horse beside his own waiting mount outside the Pink Pearl.

He looked at the crowd on the saloon porch and said, "You heard the marshal. It was self-defense. Anybody see it different?"

"Marshal Lewis called it as he saw it, Brack," the bartender said. "Pickett fired first and missed with three shots. Nobody is blaming you."

A mixologist being a highly respected member of any western community, there were no dissenting voices.

"So be it," Cooley said. "Now, who will buy me a drink?"

"I'd be honored, sir."

The gunman turned and saw a tall, thin man dressed in a black cutaway morning coat, claret-colored vest, and high-collared shirt and cravat. He wore a top hat and a bemused expression, as though the rough-hewn Cooley was an exotic creature beyond his understanding.

"And who are you?" the gunman said.

The tall man smiled. "Someone with your well-being in mind who wishes to place you in his employ. But first a private word with you, Mr. Cooley, if you will."

Cooley shrugged. "Sure." Then, "Are you heeled?"

"No." The tall man didn't elaborate. But he was obviously a gentleman, and his word was enough.

Cooley stepped closer to the Englishman. "Talk," he said. "I want to hear about my well-being an' all."

"I want you to kill a man, Mr. Cooley."

"I've done that before. Who's the man? Is he a gun?"

"I presume you mean has he practiced with arms?"

"I mean is he a gun?"

"Yes."

"Then it will cost you more for the kill. If the mark is a shootist, I run a higher risk, and in my profession high risks don't come cheap."

"The mark, as you call him, is a yellow-bellied coward, Mr. Cooley. Does that make a difference?"

The gunman thought about that, his black eyes on the Englishman's face. Then he said, "Hell, mister, if he's a coward, why don't you shoot him your own-self?"

The tall man's face stiffened. "Because I don't want to dirty my hands."

"But you want me to dirty mine?"

"You can wash your hands later. No matter how many times I washed my hands they would always be stained with a coward's blood, and I could not live with that. I assure you that you'll be paid well for your trouble, Mr. Cooley."

"How well?"

"Five hundred dollars now. Another five when the job is done."

The gunman whistled through his teeth. "Around these parts, that's top dollar."

"Around these parts, you're supposed to be the top man. Top dollar for the top man, Mr. Cooley."

"There's no supposed to be about it. I am the top man, the fastest and best there is, around these parts or around any other."

"Then do we have a deal? Speak up now, or I'll be forced to find someone else."

"Deal," Cooley said, sticking out his hand.

The Englishman pretended not to see it. He said, "My name is Captain Rupert Bentley-Foulkes, formerly of the British army. You will meet my associates inside, former lieutenants Granville Wood and John Allerton. You will accompany us with all due haste to Fort Concho."

"When?" Cooley said.

"Why, now, of course."

"Well, maybe tomorrow," Cooley said. "I've got a bounty to collect tonight."

Bentley-Foulkes reached inside his coat and produced his wallet. He took out some bills and said, "Five hundred dollars, Mr. Cooley. Now."

The gunman looked at the money, shrugged, and tipped Pickett's body out of the saddle. The corpse thudded onto the ground, and Cooley said, "I saw a livery stable close. I'll sell this here hoss and saddle, and then we'll leave."

"As you wish," the Englishman said. "Just don't haggle too long, there's a good chap."

Chapter Three

"I'm an adventuress, Colonel," Hannah Huckabee said. "I have places to go, a balloon to fly. The last thing I want is to kick my heels around at Fort Concho for the next month."

Colonel Ben Grierson was apologetic but firm. "I'm sorry, but providing you with room and board is the best I can do. We just battled an Apache outbreak and the telegraph lines are still cut in dozens of places. Wiring your accountants in New York is out of the question, at least for a while."

"Maybe you can get the stuff you need right here in San Angelo," Red Ryan said. "I know for a fact they have a good hardware store."

Hannah shook her head. "Red, I don't think you understand. I need a new balloon, burner, hydrogen cylinders, and most of all, money," she said. "I can't find that in San Angelo."

"Lady, you couldn't find that in all of Texas," Buttons Muldoon said.

"Mr. Muldoon is right, and I don't know what to suggest, Miss Huckabee," Grierson said. "I'm at a loss."

He rose from his chair and walked to a map of the state that hung on a wall. "And there's a further complication." The colonel looked at Red. "This will interest you, Mr. Ryan, and you too, Mr. Muldoon."

"Not more Apaches, I hope, Colonel," Buttons said. "I had enough of them the last time."

"Worse than that, or at least just as bad. The word I get from the Texas Rangers is that Dave Winter has moved up from the border." Colonel Grierson swept his hand across the map, taking in the country to the southeast of Fort Concho. "He's currently operating in this area and already playing hob."

"Hell, Colonel, that takes in most of my stage route," Buttons said.

"Indeed, it does," Grierson said. "And the ranger here at the post says Winter has about twenty hard cases with him and he's on a rampage. Homesteads have been looted and burned, people murdered, and a posse out of Houston was ambushed with three dead and five wounded before the survivors broke off the fight. A deputy U.S. Marshal was among the dead. From what the ranger said, there were no casualties on Winter's side."

"But I was told that the ranger has two prisoners in the stockade, Colonel," Buttons said. "Any chance that those are a couple of Winter's boys?"

"No such luck. They're poor Mexican farmers from a village to the southwest of here," Grierson said. "The ranger arrested them after they crossed the border from the New Mexico Territory."

Hannah Huckabee said, "Good heavens, Colonel

Grierson, what did they do in the territory? Steal somebody's chickens?"

A slight smile touched the colonel's lips. "They stole a Madonna from a mission chapel on the Pecos. Caught red-handed with her, I'm told." It was obvious from the girl's expression that she was drawing a blank, and Grierson said, "During the recent Indian troubles, the Mexicans fled their village and the Apaches then burned their adobes and killed off their livestock, leaving them in even greater poverty, if that was possible."

"So, a couple of farmers stole to make ends meet," Hannah said.

"It's not quite that simple," the colonel said. "Ranger Tim Adams told me that a preacher passed though the village and told the people that just across the New Mexico border the peons were prospering and that they should go there with their families. He happened to mention a village on the Pecos that was particularly thriving, thanks to their black Madonna, Nuestra Senora del Alba Luz."

"Our Lady of the Dawn Light," Hannah said. She smiled. "I have some Spanish. I once had a sword-fighting adventure at the Castle of Catalina in Cádiz."

"You must tell me about it sometime," Grierson said. "Well, our two farmers decided that stealing such a powerful Madonna and bringing her back to their own village was a good idea, because she would bring prosperity. They left with a few tortillas and a donkey for hauling the statue and did what they set out to do."

"They stole it," Red Ryan said.

"Yes, they stole it out of a chapel and now the New Mexican villagers want their Madonna back and the two thieving Texas peons hanged," the colonel said.

"Where is the Madonna now?" Hannah said.

"Miss Huckabee always interested in the Madonna," Mr. Chang said. "She want to get to the bottom of things."

"Is that so? Well, Ranger Adams has her in custody. He says she's evidence." Colonel Grierson put his hand on Buttons's shoulder and said, "And now I have bad news for you, Mr. Muldoon."

Buttons raised a hairy eyebrow. "I hate bad news, Colonel. But lay it on me."

"Ranger Adams plans to commandeer the Patterson stage to transport the Mexicans and the Madonna to Austin, where his prisoners will stand trial for theft and possibly sacrilege," the colonel said.

Buttons was indignant. "He can't do that, it's against company policy."

"Yes, he can," Grierson said. "But to ease your pain, Buttons, he'll book himself and his prisoners as passengers."

"How does he plan to pay?" Red said. "It's two hundred miles to Austin."

"And every mile of it out of our way," Buttons said.

"My guess is that he'll give you a ranger IOU," the colonel said.

"Colonel, have you ever tried to collect an IOU from the Texas Rangers?" Red said.

"No, but I understand it's difficult."

"Difficult?" Buttons said. "It's impossible. The rangers never have any money. They spend it all on ammunition."

"You'd better speak to Ranger Adams about that, I'm afraid," Grierson said.

"And what about the coward?" Buttons said. "What's his name? John Latimer."

The officer's face stiffened. "What about him?"

"The Patterson stage company was contracted to carry only one passenger . . . and he's the coward," Buttons said.

"Yes, I know that," Grierson said. "As far as I'm aware, that bill will be paid by the British legation in Washington."

"They're paying for the whole coach and one coward, Colonel," Buttons said. "They won't want a couple of Mexican Madonna thieves in there with him."

"That's a matter you'll have to take up with the British government, Mr. Muldoon," Grierson said. "I'm sure they'll be understanding."

Buttons shook his head. "Well, if this don't beat all. And here I thought driving a yellow-belly was bad enough. Now I'm stuck with a ranger and two Madonna thieves."

The colonel said, "Have you read about the troubles the British have had in India, fighting Afghan bandits, Mr. Muldoon? Have you, Mr. Ryan? It's all-out war along the Northwest Frontier, with heavy casualties on both sides."

Red and Buttons exchanged glances, and then Red

said, "Can't say as we have. We read plenty about the Apache war that almost cost us our scalps, but nothing about them bandits."

"Then I have some dispatches in my office concerning that conflict if you wish to read them," Colonel Grierson said. "You may discover that the line between hero and coward in any war is very fine indeed, and both options are open to interpretation."

Buttons smiled. "Well, you lost me there, Colonel."

"All I'm saying, Mr. Muldoon, is don't be too quick to pin the coward label on a man until you know all the facts."

Chapter Four

Red Ryan and Buttons Muldoon stood at the counter of the sutler's store eating cheese and crackers with Hannah Huckabee and Mr. Chang.

"Perhaps Colonel Grierson thinks that Captain John Latimer is not a coward," Hannah said. "If that's the opinion of a brave man, then it bears weight, but in Latimer's case his sympathy might be misplaced."

"Miss Hannah, have you heard of this man Latimer before?" Buttons said.

"Yes. He fought in the Afghan war in India, or didn't fight as the case may be."

Red said, "The colonel mentioned that war to Buttons and me. It must be when Latimer turned yellow."

"It would seem so," Hannah said. She used the tip of her left pinkie finger to remove a cracker crumb from the corner of her mouth. "The rumor is that Captain Latimer ran away from a fight to save his own skin and left his soldiers to die. His command was wiped out to a man."

Mr. Chang tutted and then said, "Fortune turns a

deaf ear to the prayers of cowards. Better for the man Latimer that he'd never been born."

"I rather fancy that's what he's thinking about now," Hannah said. "He can be thankful that Colonel Grierson elected not to throw him in the stockade."

"Where is he?" Red said.

"He's confined to quarters."

"Isn't the colonel afraid he'll escape?" Buttons said.

"The colonel said Latimer gave himself up willingly, so I hardly think he'll try to escape." Hannah yawned behind her hand. "I'm all in," she said. "I'll read Mr. Verne for a while and then to bed."

"It's dark out. I'll walk you to your quarters, Hannah," Red said.

The woman nodded. "As you wish." She smiled. "Red, you are very gallant."

A well-worn path led from the sutler's store to officers' row, a gray ribbon in the moonlight that wound around the parade ground and across the front of the headquarters building. The shadows cast by scattered buildings were dark and deep, and exploring fingers of mist clung close to the ground, drifting in from the grasslands. The cool air smelled of the day's as yet unsettled dust and of the strong coffee, black as mortal sin, that simmered constantly in a sooty pot in the cookhouse.

Hannah Huckabee in moonlight was a thing of beauty, and Red Ryan kept sneaking looks at her face and hair as they walked. She was a lithe, slim girl who moved well, her full lips moist and slightly parted as she breathed the cool night air. Hannah called herself an adventuress, but in Red's opinion, goddess would be a more apt description.

It was Hannah who saw the three figures . . . or was it four . . . before Red Ryan did. But they both heard the frightened cry of a girl and then an angry male curse, followed by what sounded like a violent slap.

"Red, what's going on over there in the dark?" Hannah said. "Can you see?"

"No, I can't, but I intend to find out," Red said.

"Maybe it's just a lovers' quarrel?" Hannah said.

"It didn't sound like that to me," Red said. "Hannah, go find some soldiers and bring them here."

He quickened his pace, but Hannah kept up at his side. Ahead of them came another cry, stifled this time as though someone held a hand over a woman's mouth.

"Hannah, there's something going on over there. I think you should stay back," Red whispered. His hand was close to his holstered Colt.

"No, I'm coming with you," Hannah said. "This could be an adventure, and after all, I'm an adventuress."

"Then stay behind me, adventuress," Red said, smiling despite the clutch of tension in his gut.

Now as he drew closer, Red saw what was happening, and it didn't look good. The shadowy figures of three men stood around a smaller person lying on the ground. One of the men had dropped his pants and drawers, and his bare butt was a white moon in the uncertain light.

A hiss of alarm and then a man's voice said, "Somebody's coming!"

Now Red saw what was about to take place and he drew his revolver. "Here," he said, "that won't do. I am a representative of the Abe Patterson and Son Stage and Express company, and I order you to cease and desist."

A tall, lanky figure took a step toward him and the man said, "She's only an Apache squaw. Now, beat it. We ain't in the mood for sharing."

Red turned his head slightly and said, "Please, Hannah, get away from here. Go get help."

But the woman, the brim of her goggled pith helmet low over her eyes against the moon glare, had other plans.

"I know what you are!" she yelled. "You're a bunch of damnable rapists."

The tall man stepped closer. He wore a gun and a savage expression. "Shut your trap, girlie, unless you want to take her place," he said. "Hell, now I get a good look at you, you *will* take her place."

"I will do no such thing, you sorry piece of trash," Hannah said.

The tall man said, "We'll see about that." He drew his gun. "Do you want to step over here, or do I come for you?"

Hannah Huckabee's answer was short, sharp, and to the point . . . a bullet from the Colt she'd pulled from her skirt pocket that slammed into the man's chest and dropped him.

"Damn, lady!" Red yelled.

A bullet split the air inches from his head, and then events occurred very fast.

Red thumbed off a shot at the man who'd fired at him, missed in the gloom, and then he felt another bullet tug at his sleeve. He fired again and a third time. At least one of his shots took effect, because his opponent shrieked and dropped to his knees, then fell flat on his face. While this happened, the third man was hopping around on one leg, trying to pull up his pants. As Hannah would say later, "He should have gone for his gun, not his drawers." She fired twice, two shots very close, and the would-be rapist staggered, got tangled in his pants, and fell. He didn't rise again.

Acrid gray gunsmoke drifted, men yelled, and booted feet pounded, coming from all directions.

Red quickly took stock of the three men sprawled on the ground, realized there was no fight left in them, and lifted a young Apache girl to her feet, her bruised, swollen face revealing the beating she'd taken.

Grierson and other officers and soldiers arrived. The colonel had pulled on boots, breeches, and his blouse but still wore his nightcap. He looked at the girl and the three dead men and said, "Mr. Ryan, do you have an explanation for this?"

Red opened his mouth to answer, but Hannah Huckabee cut him off. "Colonel, those three men were about to rape this poor girl before Mr. Ryan and myself intervened," Hannah said. Her face flushed with anger. "I will not stand idly by when I witness the most singular violence leveled against the weaker sex. I was bound by my honor as a woman and an adventuress to intervene, sir." She thrust out her hands. "Here, clap me in irons, but I'd do it again if I had to."

Grierson shook his head and, in a resigned voice, said, "All right, Mr. Ryan, who shot who?"

Again, Hannah was quick to answer. "Both myself and Mr. Ryan fired at the miscreants in the dark, but I could not determine which of us did the most execution."

"Ryan?" the colonel said.

"That sounds about right," Red said. "It was dark and hard to see anything but moving shadows, but one of them had a gun in his hand."

"For two people who couldn't see, it seems that you both did very well," Grierson said.

"Colonel, come see this," a voice said from the gloom.

Grierson took a step forward, realized that the tassel of his sleeping cap dangled down his cheek, and irritably pulled it off his head. "What am I looking at?" he said.

"The man with his pants down," Ranger Tim Adams said. "A couple of years ago, I saw him down old Fort Mason way. He didn't have a beard at that time and he was in chains, but as I live and breathe, that's Boone Marker."

"I've never heard of him," Grierson said. As though suddenly aware he was holding his nightcap, he sourly shoved it into his pocket. "Who the hell is he? Or was he?"

Red had been listening, and now he said, "Boone

Marker was a gun out of the Brazos River country. For a spell, he ran with Mannen Clements and that hard crowd, and then hitched up with Dave Winter and them."

"He was a bad one, Colonel," Tim Adams said. "A killer, rapist, and bank robber who was sometimes confused with his older brother Brink. Before he got hung, Brink was a bad man to the bone, but he wasn't a patch on Boone."

"Mr. Ryan, do you recognize the other two?" Grierson said.

Red shook his head. "No, I don't."

"Me neither," Ranger Adams said.

"Excuse me, gentlemen, but what about the victim here?" Hannah said. She had her arm around the trembling Apache girl's shoulders and held her close.

"Oh, yes . . . yes, of course . . ." Grierson said. "Was she . . . I mean . . ."

"You mean, was she raped?" Hannah said.

"Ah . . . yes . . . quite . . ."

"No, she wasn't. Mr. Ryan and I saved her just in time."

The habit of command reasserted itself, and Colonel Grierson said, "I'll have the post doctor treat her wounds."

"Who is she?" Hannah said. "Have you seen her before around the post?

"No, I can't say I have," the colonel said. "There are some Apaches camped close to the fort, and I'll have enquiries made there. Someone must know who she is."

"I know who she is," Hannah said. "She can't

speak English, but she pointed to herself and said, 'Dahteste.'"

"I'm pretty certain that in the Apache tongue that means Warrior Woman," Ranger Adams said.

Hannah smiled. "Good. I like that name very much. Dahteste will be an adventuress." She said to Grierson, "I'll take her to the doctor and then reunite her with her parents."

"Be warned, Miss Huckabee," the colonel said. "There are many orphans among the Apache. You may not find her parents."

"Please, Colonel, don't build houses on a bridge I haven't crossed yet," Hannah said, frowning.

Red smiled. "Colonel, if there are parents, Miss Huckabee will find them."

"Damn right I will, Mr. Ryan," Hannah said.

Colonel Grierson said to Ranger Adams, "Do you think that Miss Huckabee and Mr. Ryan should in any way face criminal charges?"

"No, I don't," Adams said. "I think they probably did us all a favor."

"My sentiments entirely," Grierson said.

Hannah made a face and said, "Charges? I should think not."

Chapter Five

The three dead men were buried just after dawn in the post cemetery. Apart from an army chaplain, there were few mourners, but among them were Red Ryan and Buttons Muldoon after Hannah Huckabee insisted that it was their Christian duty to attend.

"I already judged these men and found them wanting," Hannah said after she tossed a handful of dirt on each unmarked grave. "Let us hope that God will be more forgiving and give them eternal rest."

"Amen," Red said, because he couldn't think of anything else.

But Buttons rose to the occasion. "They say Boone Marker was a fair hand with a gun and a mighty successful outlaw. May he rest in peace."

"Amen," said the chaplain, who couldn't think of much to say, either.

Buttons's words weren't much, but they were the only obituary Marker would ever receive.

As they walked away from the cemetery, Hannah

said, "I'm going now to see if I can find Dahteste's family. I hope her parents are with the other Apaches."

"They didn't exactly come looking for her," Buttons said.

"No, and that doesn't bode well," Hannah said. She thought for a minute and then said, "Gentlemen, here is something most singular that you might wish to ponder. Adele Cole, Lieutenant Cole's wife, told me that four men are hanging around the fort, and she says that three of them have the bearing of army officers."

"Not surprising," Buttons said. "This is an army fort."

"British army officers, Mrs. Cole says," Hannah said. "Judging by their accents."

"What about the fourth gent?" Buttons said.

"A rough-looking character. Mrs. Cole says he has the look of a professional gunman or perhaps an outlaw."

"Plenty of those kind in Texas," Buttons said.

Hannah nodded. "That is so, but I wonder if the three Englishmen, if they indeed are or were officers, have any connection with Captain Latimer."

"Here to rescue him?" Buttons said. "I doubt it."

"No, not to rescue him," Hannah said. "After all, Captain Latimer surrendered voluntarily, so there's no rescue involved."

"They could be here on army business," Red said. "Englishmen here to see how things are done on the frontier."

"Possibly," Hannah said. "I'll ask Colonel Grierson."

"And I got to talk with him my ownself," Buttons said. "He told me I can't take the coward until all the paperwork is completed. That was yesterday morning. How much paperwork could there be for one man?"

"That's the army for you," Hannah said, smiling. "Everything in triplicate."

"Well, the Patterson stage is standing over there by the livery doing nothing, and that's costing me and the company money," Buttons said.

"And lost wages are costing the shotgun guard," Red said.

"Yeah, you're right about that," Buttons said. "I'm going to see the colonel. Red, are you coming with me?"

"No. I reckon I'll escort Hannah to the Apache village," Red said. "You never know, there might still be some of those Winter boys around here."

"You're being gallant again, shotgun man," Hannah said, smiling.

Red's face fell. "You don't want me to come with you?"

"Of course, I want you to come with me," Hannah said. "Red, after last night, you're my knight in shining armor."

"You could've gotten your damned fool heads blown off," Buttons said, turning in the direction of the headquarters building. Then, over his shoulder, "Rescuing an Apache woman, no less. Red, what did the Apaches ever do for you?"

"They gave me a paint hoss, remember that time?" Red said.

Buttons waved off that comment and stalked away, intent on business. Then he turned and hollered, "And nearly lifted your scalp. Remember that time?"

Red watched his driver go and said, "Buttons

sure does get worked up about things. One time he brooded for six months after his cat died. He called him Dynamite and he rode in the stage with us and he must have bit me a hundred times. He was the meanest animal God ever put on earth, but Buttons set store by him."

"How did Dynamite die?"

"He just upped and died. Old age, I guess."

"Poor kitty," Hannah said.

There were around sixty Apaches camped outside Fort Concho, most of them old men, women, and children. They lived in canvas army tents and depended on handouts from the local Indian agent, who shorted them on food so that they constantly teetered on the edge of starvation. At first, no one admitted to even knowing Dahteste, their natural distrust of white skin made worse by the recent Chiricahua outbreak that was put down with considerable cruelty. But finally, one old woman, who'd lost an arm years before to the saber of a Mexican cuirassier, said through an interpreter that the girl was Mescalero, that she'd fed her and let her sleep by the fire. She said that the night before, some white men had stolen her and that was fine because she couldn't afford to feed her anymore and cast-off clothing was getting scarce. Hannah gave the old woman five dollars and told her she'd look after Dahteste herself. The old woman said she didn't care one way or the other.

"So now what?" Red said as they walked back to the post. "Seems like the girl is an orphan."

"So now I take care of her, like I told the old lady. I'll be a mother to Dahteste."

Red smiled. "A mother? Hannah, you're not much older than she is."

"A sister then." After a moment's silence, Hannah said, "Red, what do you know about Apache women?"

"Not much."

"Tell me what you do know. It might help me understand Dahteste better."

Red turned that over in his mind and then said, "Well, Mescalero women are desert dwellers, and they can find water where others like you and me would die of thirst. They prepare meat and skins brought home by their menfolk, and while the men hunt, they look after the young 'uns and gather plants and nuts and seeds."

Red fell silent, and Hannah said, "That's all you know?"

"Yeah, that's about it. I did hear tell from army scouts that Apache women gather the fruit of the yucca cactus and pound its roots in water to make a soap that makes their hair shine. They also bake a kind of bread from the mescal plant, and that's why the old Spanish men called them Mescaleros, the people who eat mescal."

"And what else?"

"Hannah, I'm not an expert on Apaches. Just about any soldier at the fort can tell you more than I can."

"I want to hear it from you, Red."

"Then what else do I know? I understand Apache women, and men, are kind to their children and they teach them good manners, kindness, fortitude, and obedience. And that's me all used up. Oh, and there's a ceremony all Mescalero girls go through when they become women. It's in honor of a goddess they call White Painted Woman, the gal who gave the Apache people the gifts of a pleasant and long life. I've never seen it, but I'm told it's a right pretty ceremony. I'm sure Dahteste has gone through the White Painted Woman thing."

"I'm sure she did, when her parents were alive," Hannah said. She smiled, "See, Red, you know more about Apache women than you thought."

"I could tell you more about Apache warriors," Red said. He grinned. "None of it good."

On their way back to officers' row where Hannah had left Dahteste, she and Red met Buttons Muldoon, who'd just stalked out of the headquarters building, his face like thunder.

"Well, you look about ready to pit your bird," Red said.

"Yeah, well I'm as mad as hell. We can't leave until tomorrow," Buttons said. "The colonel says he'll have the coward's paperwork finished by then."

"We can make up time on the trail," Red said.

"No, we can't," Buttons said. "Not with them young wheelers in the team. They don't have a lick of sense between them."

"What are wheelers, Mr. Muldoon?" Hannah said.

Instantly somewhat mollified, as he usually was when someone took an interest in his profession, Buttons said, "A six-horse hitch like mine has three pairs of horses, Miss Huckabee. The smallest pair weigh about a thousand pounds and lead the team. Naturally, they're called leaders. The center pair are called swings and they weigh about eleven hundred pounds. The big boys are next to the coach. They weigh about twelve hundred and fifty pounds and they understand the jerks I make on the lines. We call them wheelers."

"That's very interesting, Mr. Muldoon," Hannah said.

"Yes, it is, and thank'ee for asking, Miss Huckabee." Buttons gave Red a look. "There are some shotgun toters I know who never ask."

"Will you let me drive your team sometime, Mr. Muldoon?" Hannah said. "It would be an adventure."

"I'd like to, but it can't be done. It takes years of study to become a driver. Just learning how to show-boat with the whip when you enter or leave a town is a rare skill all by itself."

Hannah smiled. "Ah well, driving a horse team is something I must learn someday."

Flattered by Hannah's question, Buttons had taken time to answer her, but now he had a more urgent matter on his mind.

"Red, guess who killed a man in San Angelo last night and is now strutting around like the cock o' the walk here at Fort Concho," he said.

"Brack Cooley," Red said.

Buttons was disappointed. "You mean you know?"

"Saw him at the sutler's. He's renting a room at the back."

"And don't it bother you none that he's here?"

"No, it don't bother me. Brack's a bounty hunter. He's got no interest in us."

"Red, Brack Cooley's always been a finger looking for a trigger," Buttons said. "He ain't planning to rob the stage, is he?"

Red smiled. "What's he going to steal? A coward? And a wooden Madonna?"

Buttons saw the logic in that and said, "Well, I guess not, but mark my words, trouble follows Cooley around like his shadow."

"We've got nothing he wants," Red said. "Trust me."

Chapter Six

The evening before the Patterson stage was due to leave Fort Concho, Brack Cooley had been two things . . . half-drunk and bored. Taken together, they made him irritable, unpredictable, and an almighty dangerous man.

Cowboy Bob Walker should have read the signs and left Cooley the hell alone. He didn't, and it cost him his life. As a contemporary San Angelo newspaper account would later have it:

A SHOOTING IN THE ALAMO

*Gunman Brack Cooley
Again Kills His Man*

Bob Walker Left Weltering
In His Own Blood

Cooley Claims Self-Defense

Last night, a little before ten, Bob Walker died with his beard in the sawdust of The

Alamo Saloon. He gasped out his last breaths with three bullet wounds in his chest that bartender Luke Arnold later covered with an ace of spades playing card, to the amazement of a large crowd of onlookers. Better for Bob, a cattle drover and well-known face around town, if he'd given Cooley a wide berth. This was Cooley's second victim in just two days. Ere he braced Walker, he had already gunned down small-time thief and all-round nuisance Frank Pickett for the $200 reward on the man's head. Cooley is known to the law as a desperate character, one of that new breed of Texas drawfighter they're all talking about, though THE GAZETTE sees nothing admirable in the species. We consider six-shooter men like Brack Cooley who love the bark of the festive revolver a blight on the landscape and a threat to civilization itself. We hear from Mr. Arnold that Cooley is about to embark for New Orleans and pastures new, and all we can say is, "Good riddance." The State of Louisiana is more than welcome to him.

The events leading to the shooting scrape began when Cooley refused an invitation from Captain Bentley-Foulkes to join himself and Lieutenants Wood and Allerton for a late supper.

"I've got five hundred dollars burning a hole in my pocket," Cooley said. "I reckon I'll have a drink or two and see if I can find myself a woman."

"I'm reliably informed that the Patterson stage is due to leave the fort tomorrow morning," Bentley-Foulkes said. "It would not do to lose sight of it, don't you think?"

"I'll be there when the stage leaves," Cooley said. "When it comes to agreeing to kill a man, I keep my word."

"Then see you do, Mr. Cooley," the Englishman said. "The where and when of the deed, I'll leave to your discretion."

"Did you find out who's up in the seat?" Cooley said. "I'm talking about the guard, not the driver."

"Yes, I found out, and there's a complication," Bentley-Foulkes said.

"I don't like complications," Cooley said.

"It seems that a Texas Ranger by the name of Tim Adams has commandeered the stage and is taking a couple of prisoners as far as Austin."

"I never heard of him, but any ranger is bad news."

"I'm paying you to handle bad news, Mr. Cooley."

"Like I asked already, who's the messenger?"

"A man named Muldoon is the driver."

"Hell, give me the name of the shotgun guard."

"His name is Red Ryan."

"I've seen him around. Wears a fancy buckskin shirt and a plug hat? Carries a Greener shotgun and a Colt on his right hip?"

"I can't answer that question," Bentley-Foulkes said. "I haven't seen the man."

"If it's the Red Ryan I'm thinking about, he has a reputation of being pretty slick with the iron."

"He's a shotgun guard, so I rather fancy that

he'd need to be something of a crack shot," Bentley-Foulkes said.

Cooley nodded. "Ryan's been in a few shooting scrapes."

"Goes with his chosen profession," the Englishman said. Then, a frown gathering on his well-bred, handsome face, he said, "Mr. Cooley, I hope you're not having second thoughts. Perhaps the job is too much for you?"

The gunmen's anger flared. "No job is too much for Brack Cooley. I can handle Ryan and the ranger as well, if I have to."

"Then I'm glad to hear it," Bentley-Foulkes said. "You've set my mind at rest."

"When do we pull out tomorrow?" Cooley said.

"About thirty minutes after the stage leaves. Be ready."

"I'm always ready," Cooley said.

But the Englishman's words had rankled him, and Brack Cooley was on a slow simmer when he walked into the Alamo Saloon and filled the place with his brooding, menacing presence.

There were no women available at The Alamo that night, and Cooley sat at a table by himself and steadily drank rye whiskey that did nothing to improve his mood. He was aware that a man kept looking at him, open hostility in his eyes, but already half-drunk and planning to work on the remaining half, the big gunman kept to himself and avoided a stare-down.

But the belligerent man's eyes never left him, and Cooley, a man who'd been a willing participant in a score of saloon fights, drank his rye and prepared for the inevitable.

The bartender, plump and jolly Luke Arnold, missed nothing in The Alamo and his restless eyes read the crowd like a book. He saw that Bob Walker was on the prod and he decided to act as a herald. On the pretense of offering Cooley a cigar, he whispered, "His name is Bob Walker. Watch your step."

The gunman smiled. "I see him."

A moment later he saw Walker within spitting distance.

The drover was a nondescript man of medium height, dressed in a shabby gray ditto suit and collarless shirt. He had a Colt revolver on his hip, the finish badly worn, possibly a pawnshop purchase. A spade-shaped brown beard gave his narrow, unprepossessing face a tad more character, but his dull black eyes showed little intelligence. Walker wore a gambler's silver signet ring on the little finger of his left hand, an adornment that Cooley dismissed as an affectation.

In all, there was little about Bob Walker to impress, but the man seemed to harbor the belief that he was bulletproof. A fatal mistake.

Cooley's cold eyes lifted to Walker's face and he said, "What can I do for you, mister?" At that point, he didn't want to get into a fight that would further jeopardize his already complicated relationship with Bentley-Foulkes.

"Killing Frank Pickett was a dirty trick," Walker said, loud, aggressive. He waved a hand. "And I want all present to hear me say it."

"The fight was of his choosing, not mine," Cooley said. "He could have given himself up."

"Damn your eyes, Frank was a friend of mine," Walker said, pushing it, pushing into mighty dangerous waters where treacherous shoals lurked in the shallows.

"Then you should choose your friends more carefully," Cooley said. He was calm, amused, at that point still willing to let things slide.

But Walker, who'd never been in a shooting scrape, knew gun reputations were won by putting the crawl on named men like Brack Cooley. He fervently wanted to be recognized as a bad man, to be mentioned in the same breath as draw fighters like John Wesley Hardin and Clay Allison.

The Texas Rangers, no strangers to dangerous men, would later describe Cooley thusly: "The fast draw, the spin, the border shift . . . he did them all with what amounted to magical precision and a cool nerve."

What Walker didn't know, or chose to ignore, was that Hardin and Allison would have stepped around Brack Cooley and only gone to the draw when their backs were to the wall and there was no other way out.

Bob Walker had already made a major mistake in bracing Cooley, and now he made another that would have fatal consequences.

Cooley stretched out his foot and pushed a chair from under the table. "Sit down, man, and have a drink and a ceegar," he said. "Frank Pickett was a fool, and let it end there. I have no quarrel with you."

Had Walker been sober, he might have seen it as an honor to be invited to drink with such a famous shootist and gladly taken the chair to be seen hobnobbing with the great man. But that night he was drunk, belligerent, and incredibly stupid.

"I won't drink with you and be damned to ye," he said. Then, a note of exasperation in his voice, "Git up on your feet and apologize to all present for killing Frank Pickett, the best friend a man ever had."

"Go to hell," Cooley said.

Now there was no going back. Walker had called the tune and had to face the consequences.

The drover's hand dropped for his Colt, and at the same time Cooley rose behind the table like a wraith, his gun flaring. Three shots triggered in the space of a single heartbeat sent three lead bullets slamming into Walker's chest. The man staggered back, his face registering shock and horror. *No . . . this can't be happening . . . I can't be dying this way . . .*

Bob Walker carried that thought into eternity.

Brack Cooley, his smoking Colt in his hand, looked around the saloon.

"He drew down on me," Cooley said to the gaping crowd. "You all saw it."

"I saw it, but I don't believe it," bartender Luke Arnold said.

His diamond stickpin glittering in the lamplight, he stepped from behind the bar, picked up a playing card from a table as he passed, and hurried to the dead man. He looked at Walker's wounds and then placed the card, the Knave of Spades as he later noted, on the chest of the corpse.

"The card covers all three wounds," Arnold said. "Damn it all, folks, that's good shooting!"

For a moment, the late-night sporting crowd, now

joined by several saloon girls, was stunned. Then one rooster, drunker than the rest, yelled, "Three cheers fer good ol' Bracky!"

In the West, notorious gunmen were feared, but also admired, and the hearty cheers that went up for Cooley's prowess with the pistol attested to that fact.

Basking in the limelight, Cooley realized that now was the time for a grandstand play. The crowd expected it, something to later add to the legend when it came to the retelling of the saga of the Gunfight in The Alamo Saloon. The bounty hunter tossed a handful of coins on top of Walker's body and said, "Bury that decent."

Again, the crowd cheered. This was theater at its best.

Cooley didn't disappoint. He grinned, crossed the floor in a chime of spurs, and grabbed one of the saloon girls by the arm. He pushed her toward one of two curtained cribs at the far end of the room, and he and the giggling woman vanished inside.

Luke Arnold, something of a philosopher, nodded and smiled as he stepped back behind the bar and to the excited throng said, "To the victor belong the spoils."

And the crowd's huzzahs were even louder than before.

Chapter Seven

On the afternoon of the day that Brack Cooley killed Bob Walker, Hannah Huckabee received permission from Colonel Grierson to visit Captain John Latimer's quarters.

"I suppose a visit from a fellow English countryman will cheer him up," Grierson said. He smiled. "Or should that be English countrywoman?"

Hannah returned his smile. "The latter, I suppose," she said. "Does he need cheering up?"

"He's facing a court-martial and possible death sentence," the colonel said. "I'd say he's is not in an optimistic frame of mind."

"Colonel Grierson, you're an experienced soldier. Do you think John Latimer is a coward?"

"I know the British army does. Cowardice in the face of the enemy is a very serious charge, and for that reason it's rarely used."

"Colonel, I asked what you think of John," Hannah said. "Is he a coward?"

Hannah's use of Latimer's first name puzzled Grierson, as did her apparent interest in the man. "He's not a relative of yours, Miss Huckabee, is he?"

The girl was quick to answer. "No. He's not a relative."

Hannah had changed out of her tan dress into a plain, blue afternoon gown with white collars and cuffs, and in place of her pith helmet and goggles her hair was tied back with a scarlet ribbon. She had left her Colt and bowie knife behind in her room.

Grierson thought she looked very young, very beautiful, and very formidable.

He smiled. "A glass of sherry with you, Miss Huckabee? The sutler assures me that its original cask came all the way from Spain by steamship."

"You are most kind, Colonel. Yes, a glass of sherry would be very welcome."

Grierson was silent as he busied himself with a decanter and glasses, and Hannah did not interrupt, knowing that he was also busy with his thoughts. Finally, he handed Hannah her glass and waited until she'd taken a sip and then another. "The wine is to your liking, Miss Huckabee?"

Hannah nodded. "It has a honey and nut aroma and a simple, balanced palate. I detect flavors of caramel and sugared pecan." She took another sip. "Ah yes, the finish is as I expected, a mix of mushroom, coffee, pecan, and toffee, pleasant but sticky." She smiled. "The sutler did not steer you wrong, Colonel Grierson. It is indeed a Spanish sherry, not of the finest quality, but quite acceptable."

The colonel was surprised. "You are very knowledgeable about wine," he said. "I'm impressed."

"When one is an adventuress, one learns about many things, Colonel," Hannah said. "As you have learned much about soldiers and soldiering."

Grierson smiled and said, "To answer your question, no, I do not think Captain Latimer is a coward. I read the report the British army sent me, and at the very worst, he was remiss in stopping to brew coffee in what he knew was enemy-occupied territory. If he'd been one of my officers, I would've reprimanded him and sent him away with a flea in his ear."

"Coffee? His court-martial will be about coffee?" Hannah said.

"Not quite. Captain Latimer led a scouting patrol of nine men of the 51st Lancers, including a young lieutenant of good family named Thomas Bentley-Foulkes. That officer had dismounted in an abandoned village when Afghan bandits suddenly attacked out of a stand of thorn trees. According to Latimer, his sergeant, without orders, immediately led his eight lancers into a charge, and they fought well but were quickly overwhelmed. Latimer later said that he saw Bentley-Foulkes and the lancers fall, and then, firing his revolver at the enemy, he made his escape."

Hannah was silent for a while, then whispered, her voice breaking on each word, "John should've charged with the others and died like a British officer and gentleman."

This girl had an amazing capacity to surprise him, and Grierson looked at her and said, "And that is why he was branded a coward. Captain Latimer decided not to throw his life away in a vainglorious last stand."

Hannah nodded. "Yes, that was John's decision." She laid down her glass and said, "Colonel Grierson, I withdraw my request to visit Captain Latimer."

"Miss Huckabee, have I said something that—"

"You told me the facts of John's actions on the Indian Northwest Frontier. I asked, and you told me, and for that I am most grateful. Now, if you will excuse me, I feel a headache coming on and must rest awhile."

Hannah Huckabee gathered her skirt and walked quickly to the door. She stopped, her back stiff, as she heard Grierson say, "Miss Huckabee, why did you change your mind so suddenly?"

Without turning, Hannah said, her voice firm, "Captain Latimer should have died with his men. He abandoned them and fled to save his own skin. I find that unforgivable."

"Miss Huckabee, did you know him?" Grierson said. "I mean . . . before."

"Yes. Captain Latimer and I were engaged to be married, but I thought him lost at sea when the ship bearing him to England sank."

"And then you heard that he was here at Fort Concho," Grierson said.

"Yes, the Patterson stage driver told me. He called him, 'the coward.'"

Hannah turned, her face very pale. "And now I realize that John Latimer is exactly what the British army says he is . . . a coward."

After Hannah Huckabee left, Colonel Ben Grierson felt a little guilty . . . he hadn't told her that earlier in the day he'd spoken at some length with John Latimer and he'd decided that the man was no coward.

Grierson poured himself a drink, sat in his favorite chair beside the fire, and remembered the conversation that had taken place at his request . . .

"To give you a little background, Colonel, in the summer of 1879 the British army was in dire need of heroes. In Zululand, South Africa, the bodies of the fifty-five officers and eight hundred British regulars slaughtered by a Zulu army at the Battle of Isandlwana had been a month in their graves when I was ordered to lead a nine-man detachment of the 51st Lancers and a pack mule on a scouting patrol on the Northwest Indian Frontier, where I'd been stationed for three months.

"I was twenty-six years old that summer, the son of an impoverished country parson who always said that the Lord would provide, though He never did. I joined the army as a boy and rose from the ranks. My fellow cavalry officers were all the younger sons of aristocrats, and I believe they considered me a competent soldier, but I was not a gentleman born, and they treated me as such."

"And how did that manifest itself?" Colonel Ben Grierson said.

"Well, I was reserved to the point of shyness, and I was not popular in the mess. Back in England I played little part in the social activities of the regiment, the endless cycle of balls, fox hunts, and parties at great houses with ivy on the walls and fifty-year-old brandies in the cellars. By contrast, when I left on patrol that day, the young officer who rode beside the guidon, Lieutenant Thomas Bentley-Foulkes, the youngest son of a belted earl, was the darling of the 51st. He was possessed of a fine singing voice, and he was rich, handsome, dashing, irresistible to women, admired by officers and enlisted men alike . . . and in my estimation, fatally flawed. Bentley-Foulkes made no secret of the fact that he would not return to his father's estate without a medal on his chest. Several times already, he'd been reprimanded for chasing headlong after Afghan rebels whenever he saw them. Colonel David Gray, the commanding officer of the 51st, delivered those reprimands with great good humor, taking care to compliment Bentley-Foulkes on his gallantry, calling him 'a young scamp who would be a general one day.' I considered my second-in-command a glory-hunting fool and predicted that yes, Bentley-Foulkes could be a general one day . . . if he lived long enough. As events would soon show, it was a bunch of Afghan rebels who decided which of those prophecies came true."

Colonel Grierson, a strict disciplinarian, but a kindly man at heart, prodded Latimer gently. "The Afghans were rebelling against British rule. Was that the case?"

"Yes, sir, they deeply resented the British being in India and Afghanistan at all. Remember, the British government was rocked by the embarrassing defeat of their modern army at Isandlwana by a rabble of spearwielding natives, and even their victory at Rorke's Drift a day later did little to assuage their humiliation. The government's orders to the army were both blunt and brutal . . . destroy the Afghan rebels, occupy their lands, and drag their leaders to Whitehall in chains."

"And what was the purpose of your patrol, Mr. Latimer?" Grierson said. He lifted a cut-glass carafe and said, "A brandy with you?"

"Please," Latimer said.

After he accepted his drink and the cigar that went along with it, Latimer said, "I was to scout ahead of the main army column and immediately report back if I sighted the enemy in force. I'd been in the field for some three hours when I came across a deserted Indian village. Judging by the pots and baskets that were scattered all over the well-trampled ground, I decided that the peasants had fled in some haste and that the rebels must be close. It was a barren, desolate, poverty-stricken place, and God knows how those people had managed to survive. Adjoining the village was an extensive thicket of thorn trees and heavy brush and beyond that a vast, desolate, desert wasteland, broken only by patches of scrub."

Colonel Grierson smiled and said, "It sounds like some of the posts I've known."

"Indeed, Colonel," Latimer said. "I'm sure it does."

"Sorry for my interruption, please proceed," Grierson said. He had an inch of gray ash on his cigar.

Latimer nodded and said, "Lieutenant Bentley-Foulkes kneed his horse next to mine, his handsome young face a mask of disappointment. 'The damned rebel scoundrels found the village deserted and scampered,' he said. 'They're probably miles away by now.'

"For once I was in agreement with Bentley-Foulkes, and I told him if we left then we could rejoin the column before dark and I'd make my report, such as it was. But my young lieutenant was having none of it. He wanted to boil up some coffee before we started back. He said, 'I'm positively dying for a cup.'"

Colonel Grierson refilled Latimer's glass and then said, "Go on."

"Well, just then a flock of alarmed sandgrouse burst out of the thorn trees, rapidly gained height, and then veered to the south," Latimer said. "I followed the flight of the birds and then turned my head as my sergeant, an old solder named Bill Haycock, quietly said, 'Sir . . . '

"Colonel, it was but one word. One syllable. But it held a volume of meaning. I heard . . . as I remember it, surprise, alarm . . . a voice spiked by sudden fear."

Grierson nodded. "In the field, I've heard that voice many times. It's hollow, as though a man is speaking in a tunnel. I've probably used it myself."

Latimer said, "By now, Bentley-Foulkes had dismounted and slowly walked his horse toward the village. I yelled to him. 'Lieutenant, mount up. We're getting out of here.' Bentley-Foulkes stopped, turned, and grinned. 'Not without my coffee, Captain.' Those were almost the last words he ever uttered.

"About fifty Afghan rebels, sand falling from their drab robes, burst out of the thorn tree thicket armed with British Martini-Henry rifles and that terrible curved knife they call a *peshkabz*. Bentley-Foulkes saw the danger and tried to remount. He got a foot in the stirrup, but his frightened mount shied away from him, and he stumbled and fell. I saw him jump to his feet, holding the reins of his horse in his hand. He drew his revolver, fired into the running Afghans, and dropped one in mid-stride. I fired my own weapon . . ."

"Which was?" Grierson said.

"A .450 Adams revolver. I shot into the rebel ranks and one fell, and then another. Bentley-Foulkes staggered as he was shot several times, but still kept his feet.

"The rebels were closing fast, and my command was in danger of being enveloped. I opened my mouth to order a retreat . . . then disaster struck."

Latimer swallowed hard. He stared out the window, not at the dusty Fort Concho parade ground, but once again seeing a mean Indian village and a horde of Afghan tribesmen screaming for British blood.

"And what was it that happened then, Mr. Latimer?" Grierson prompted.

"Then? What happened then?" Latimer said. He looked haunted, like a man waking from a bad dream. "Then Sergeant Haycock, for a reason that he'd never live to explain, called out, 'Forward the Fifty-First!'

"No!" I yelled.

"But it was too late. Led by Haycock, my eight cavalrymen set spurs to their mounts, lowered their lances and charged into the melee. They hit hard at a gallop, their steel lance heads driving into the sweating bodies of several rebels. Colonel, I remember the blood, bright scarlet, fountaining into air that was thick with dust. The Afghans wavered and fell back from my lancers and their battle-crazed horses. For a moment, it looked like we would prevail and rescue

Bentley-Foulkes, who had lost his revolver and was now on his knees, slashing around him with his saber.

"But it was a forlorn hope. What followed was swift, bloody, and brutal. A bullet to the throat killed Haycock, and one by one the other lancers were pulled from their saddles and died under the rise and fall of bloodstained knife blades. I didn't see Bentley-Foulkes fall, but I heard the young officer cry, 'God save the queen!' followed by a scream that could only come from a man with a foot of steel rammed into his gut.

"Now the Afghans had tasted blood, and they came for me. For a few moments I stood my ground and emptied my Adams into the oncoming ranks and then swung my horse around and with only seconds to spare galloped out of danger. Behind me, my men lay sprawled in death . . . and for Captain John Latimer, a living death had begun."

"What happened after you retreated from the field?" Grierson said.

The colonel could have said, "Fled the field," but he didn't. And for that, John Latimer was grateful.

"When I made my report, Colonel Peter Anderson, the commanding officer of the 51st, said, 'You did not ride to Lieutenant Bentley-Foulkes's aid, Captain? Is that what you're trying to tell me?'

"I told him that the Afghans came on at the run, and Lieutenant Bentley-Foulkes was surrounded before I could act. 'Yet Sergeant Haycock and the rest of your command made a gallant attempt to save the officer, did they not?' Colonel Anderson said.

"I said, 'Gallant, yes. But foolhardy. They charged

into a much superior rebel Afghan force and threw their lives away.'

"'But you held on to yours, Captain. You managed to save your own skin, did you not?' the colonel said.

"I knew the question and what it implied was unfair and that I was being stabbed in the back. But it was obvious that Colonel Anderson's mind was made up, and nothing I could say would change that. The disaster of Isandlwana had hardened attitudes, and the British public demanded revenge and they wanted heroes. The army had obliged by handing out eleven Victoria Crosses to the defenders of Rorke's Drift and was eager to award more. What it very much didn't need was to brand an officer of the empire a coward. But justice, as the army saw it, had to be done.

"Finally, I said, 'I did what I believed to be right.'"

"'Then it seems that your version of right and the British Army's version of right are two very different things,' the colonel said. 'You rose through the ranks, so you are not a gentleman, but damn it all, man, you should've tried to rescue Lieutenant Bentley-Foulkes and died with your command. I don't like the idea of officers escaping on horseback while their men on foot are being killed, and for that reason you will take no further part in this expedition. You will be returned to London to face court-martial.'

"Sir, may I ask what I am to be charged with?" I said.

"'You may,' Colonel Anderson said. 'The charge is cowardice in the face of the enemy.'"

Grierson shook his head. "Mr. Latimer, you had a hard go of it, and no mistake."

"Worse was to follow," Latimer said. "As I opened

Colonel Anderson's tent flap, but before he could step outside in the heat of the African morning, his voice stopped me. 'Captain, it's not too late to do the honorable thing,' he said. 'That's why I did not take your revolver.'"

Latimer managed a wan smile. "It seemed that every officer and private soldier for miles around had lined up to see me walk to the detention tent. As I passed, one by one they turned their backs on me, making obvious their contempt for the coward who had brought such disgrace to the 51st Lancers and to the entire British army in India."

Chapter Eight

"Why should we go talk with the coward now, Buttons?" Red Ryan said. "We'll see him in the morning."

"I want him to know what I expect from the time he leaves his quarters and I walk him to the stage," Buttons said. "And I'll make sure he knows what I expect thereafter. I realize that he's a yellow-belly, but I will not tolerate uncivil behavior from him. When it comes to a coward, to be forewarned is to be forearmed."

"Did you tell Colonel Grierson about this?" Red said.

"Of course I did. He says if the coward wants to talk with me, that's fine by him."

"By the way, his name is John Latimer," Red said.

"What?"

"The coward's name is Captain John Latimer."

"So?"

"I'm just thinking that he's an Abe Patterson and Son Stage and Express Company passenger. Maybe it would be civil of company employees to call him by his name."

"Is that so?" Buttons said, stocky and belligerent in the brass-buttoned sailor's coat that gave him his nickname.

"Yes, it's so," Red said.

Buttons thought about that for a spell, then said, "All right then, I'll call him Latimer. I mean, when I'm within his hearing."

Red nodded. "That will do, I guess."

"Right, let's go talk with the coward," Buttons said. He saw Red's frown and said, "Hell, Red, he can't hear me."

There was no sentry outside John Latimer's quarters, a vacant, junior officer's accommodation, but an oil lamp burned to the right of the door, its guttering flame surrounded by fluttering white moths. The lamp cast a dancing halo of orange light that did little to banish the darkness, and the night smelled of prairie grass, men, horses, and leather.

Red rapped on the door, and a male voice from within called out, "Enter."

"Remember, be polite, Buttons," Red said, opening the door.

"I'll be as civil as an undertaker at a twenty-dollar funeral," Buttons said.

As Red and Buttons entered, John Latimer rose from his chair by the fire and laid aside the book he'd been reading. He was a tall, lean, earnest-looking young man with thinning black hair and expressive brown eyes. Gone were all traces of his 51st Lancers uniform in all its scarlet and gold glory, replaced by a sober and frayed gray suit and a shirt with a celluloid collar but no tie. The casual observer could easily mistake him for his country parson father.

"What can I do for you, gentlemen?" Latimer said. Then, pointedly, "At this late hour."

Buttons, never the soul of discretion, tried his best. "Let's make sure we got it straight. Are you John Latimer, the coward?" he said.

Latimer's face didn't change. He didn't even blink. "Yes, I am he."

Buttons nodded. "Good. You can call me Mr. Muldoon. I'm the driver of the Patterson stage, and this is my associate, the shotgun guard, Mr. Ryan. Be warned, neither of us take any sass or backtalk, and we don't take kindly to cowardly acts."

Latimer had an open smile that reached his eyes. "That's good to know."

"Damn right, it's good to know," Buttons said. "Now listen up. Tomorrow when you step on the stage, you'll be our prisoner and you'll do as you're told without complaint. Savvy?"

Latimer nodded, "Yes, that's perfectly clear. I'll conduct myself like a prisoner. Will you use shackles?"

"That won't be necessary," Red said. "Your word that you will not try to escape is good enough."

"Then you have it, Mr. Ryan. I will make no attempt to escape."

"Now," Buttons said, "if'n you want to do something cowardly on the trail, why then, you have my leave to go right ahead, just so long as you don't put the other passengers in danger. Is that clear?"

Latimer was surprised. "There are other passengers?"

"Sure are," Buttons said. "Two Mexican thieves who stole a Madonna and a Texas Ranger as far as Austin town. And a young lady adventuress and her Chinee servant and an Apache gal all the way to New Orleans."

John Latimer looked like he'd seen a ghost. "Is the Chinese called Mr. Chang?"

"Yeah. Anyways, that's what the young lady calls him," Buttons said.

"Hannah," Latimer said.

"Hell, that's right. Hannah Huckabee," Buttons said. "You know her?"

Latimer nodded. "We were once engaged to be married."

Buttons shook his head. "Nah, that can't be right, must be another Hannah Huckabee. The Hannah I'm talking about wouldn't marry a coward."

"I wasn't a coward then," Latimer said.

"Like Buttons said, the Hannah we know is an . . . adventuress," Red said, stumbling a little over the unfamiliar word. "Are you sure she's the gal you're talking about?"

"Yes. Yes, I'm sure," Latimer said. "In India, Hannah hunted tigers with the Maharaja of Mysore and shot a man-eater that had killed at least four hundred people. She flew the length of the Great Wall of China in a balloon, waltzed with the Czar of Russia in his winter palace during a blizzard, and on her eighteenth birthday, when the paddle steamer taking her to Siam was attacked by Burmese pirates, she organized the defense of the ship and later hanged three of the corsair ringleaders."

Buttons Muldoon was incredulous. "But . . . but she's only a youngster. Did she really do all them things—"

"And more," Latimer said. "Saving Mr. Chang's life among them."

"But she ended up with you?" Buttons said. "I just don't get it."

"Hannah didn't end up with me, Mr. Muldoon. I haven't seen her since the evening before I left for India with my regiment. That was three years ago."

Red said, "Colonel Grierson said you fought Afghans, whatever the hell they are."

"Yes, I did," Latimer said. "And what Afghans are . . . well, they're first-rate fighting men."

Buttons laughed. "You fought them or ran away from them?" He caught the hard look Red angled at him and said, "Hell, I was only making a good joke."

Latimer smiled. "To answer your question, I did both, Mr. Muldoon. I fought Afghan tribesmen and retreated from them."

"What were they like, them Afghan bandits?" Buttons said.

"Incredibly brave men armed with a good knowledge of battlefield tactics. In mountainous terrain they had no equal, as the British quickly learned. It was only when the army fought out in the open that it was able to defeat them."

"They sound like Apaches," Buttons said.

"Yes. But the Apache were always few in number. The Afghans came at you in their hundreds and sometimes thousands." Latimer smiled. "Just imagine you and Mr. Ryan driving your stage across the prairie and a thousand well-armed Afghan fighters suddenly rise out of the long grass and charge you at the run. What would you do?"

Buttons shrugged. "Ask Red. He's the shotgun guard."

"I'd get the hell out of there," Red said.

"A very wise choice," Latimer said.

"Here, Latimer, how many of them Afghan fellers put the crawl on you?" Buttons said.

"I'd say about a hundred. But I rather fancy that there were a few more than that."

"And how many men did you have?"

"Nine mounted lancers."

Buttons thought that through for a moment, then said, "Hell, I would've run my ownself. A man can't buck them kind of odds. That there is a heap of Apaches . . . or Afghans."

"My offense was not about retreating from a superior force," Latimer said. "It's because I didn't choose to die with my men." He saw the confusion in Buttons's face and said, "To die like a gentleman is what's expected of a British army officer. I was never considered a gentleman, so perhaps that's why I acted differently."

Red Ryan said, "Captain Latimer, how did you get separated from your lancers in the first place? Wait, let me tell you this first: One time, down Sonora way in Old Mexico, I saw what was left of a troop of Mexican lancers after they'd been bushwhacked by Comanches. I said to this American feller who was standing next to me that using lancers to fight Comanche was pretty stupid. The feller said, 'In these modern times, using lancers to fight anybody is pretty stupid.' It seems he was right."

"I think the person you spoke to in Mexico didn't know what he was talking about," Latimer said, bristling a little. "In South Africa, lancers were very effective against Zulus, and they were also a force to be reckoned with in India. Colonel Grierson says there's talk in military circles that the new Maxim machine gun and steam-powered iron wagons armed with cannon will render all cavalry, including lancers, obsolete. But I agree with him that such idle prattle is irresponsible nonsense. For centuries to come, the horseman will always dictate battlefield strategy."

Buttons said, "Even though you're a coward, you're right about that, Latimer. We'll always need horses. So, as Red said, how come you got separated from your men and showed yellow?" Buttons was a blunt, down-to-earth man who was never noted for his tact. In later years the *Strand* magazine, recounting in serial form the daring exploits of Miss Hannah Huckabee, adventuress, would mention Buttons Muldoon in passing as a "boorish frontiersman who drove a stagecoach."

Even Red Ryan, who had a lot of respect for Buttons, would not disagree with that assessment.

Latimer said, "Acting without my order, my sergeant ordered the charge, and the men followed him. The lancers were quickly surrounded by Afghans and killed. For a while I stood my ground and emptied my revolver into the enemy ranks, but then, seeing that nothing could be done, I fled the field."

"And then they pinned a yellow badge on you," Buttons said.

"Something like that," Latimer said. "I was sent back to England for court-martial, but the ship sank in a storm and I was rescued by an American clipper, named of all things, *Hero*. I spent the next couple of years before the mast as a crewman on the old *Hero*, then was paid off and headed west. I ended up in Texas and decided to stop running away and surrender to the nearest military authority. I want to travel back to England to face trial and be cleared of a coward's name."

"Hell, don't you reckon that by now they've forgotten about you?" Buttons said.

"No, I don't think that, Mr. Muldoon. The British army has a long memory, and the Afghan war was only three years ago, just a moment in time in its two-hundred-year-history."

Buttons hung his head as he always did when he was deep in thought. Then he looked up and said, "You telling us the truth about what happened with them Afghan Apaches?"

"Mr. Muldoon, as a general rule I don't lie," Latimer said.

"Good," Buttons said. "Then all I'm gonna say is this . . . behave yourself when you're on my stage. Where we're going, there ain't no Afghan bandits for you to worry about, just hundreds of miles of grass."

Red Ryan smiled. "And Dave Winter."

Chapter Nine

"Did I hear somebody use my name?" Dave Winter said. "I don't like men talking my name behind my back."

"Boss," Frank Tucker said, "I only allowed how Dave Winter is a name folks won't soon forget in this part of the country. There's a hell of an excitement going around."

Winter, tall, thin, dressed in black, grinned in the light of the campfire. "Is that a fact now, Frank. If folks won't forget it, neither will you, and maybe you'll get it into your head to talk it to the wrong people. Get my drift?"

"I would never do that," Tucker said. "I'm as loyal as the day is long. I ride for the brand."

Winter sneered. "Ride for the brand? You've never done an honest day's work in your life."

"Well, since I met you, Dave, I've put in plenty of dishonest ones," Tucker said, grinning.

Some of the men around the fire laughed, but softly and nervously, and for a moment the whiskey bottle stopped its rounds.

"Was that meant to be a good joke?" Winter said. A man with rust-red hair and beard, he wore two guns, butt-forward in stiff, canvas holsters buckled over his frock coat. "I don't like good jokes about me, and I don't like the men who tell them."

Bean Gosford, a gray-haired, careful man who'd been with Winter for three years and was acknowledged to be the gang's fastest gun, looked across the fire at Tucker and said, "Frank, shut your trap. You talk too much, so don't say another word."

Gosford knew two things about his friend Winter that Tucker didn't.

The first was that Dave had spent eight years in an insane asylum and during his escape from the place had killed two doctors, three nurses, and a female secretary, all six of them savagely bludgeoned to death. The second was that Winter was a dangerous madman, a homicidal powder keg ready to go off when any number of different fuses were lit. Teasing, even good-natured teasing, was one of them.

Some people never learn, and Frank Tucker was a prime example.

Stupidly, unbelievingly, instead of pulling in his horns and keeping his mouth shut, Tucker grinned and blew Gosford a noisy, wet raspberry.

For a few moments a gasping silence fell on the camp, broken by Winter's soft-spoken words, "Was that another good joke, Frank?"

Young, reckless and good with a gun, Tucker said, "Gray hairs in a man's beard don't give him the right to tell me what to do."

"Truer words was never spoke," Winter said. He

settled by the fire and, a man who seldom drank whiskey, poured himself coffee. "Bean," he said without turning his head, "you got no call to be giving another man advice."

"I'll bear that in mind, Dave," Gosford said.

"See you do," Winter said. "Now, how close are we to the San Saba?"

"I'd say half a day's ride," Gosford said. Then, anticipating Winter's next question, "At this time of year it's easy to ford."

"And the trail to Fort Mason?"

"After we cross the river, there's a stretch of rolling hills, some of them rocky, but then the trail evens out into flat country and there's plenty of water. It's an easy ride, and we'll make good time."

The army had abandoned Fort Mason in 1871, but the rumor persisted that in 1880 the outlaw Len Blackburn had buried thirty thousand in gold and silver coins there, the proceeds of a train robbery. A year later, before he could recover his loot, Blackburn was killed by a Mexican bandido for his boots, silver saddle, and fancy Smith & Wesson revolver.

Gosford said, "You think the treasure is still there, Dave?"

Winter shrugged. "Maybe so. It's worth a look on account of how there's slim pickings around this country since the Apaches emptied it of white folks."

"Might involve a heap of digging," Gosford said.

"Digging? Yeah, a heap of digging if that's what it takes."

Frank Tucker then dug his own grave deeper. "I don't use a damned shovel for anybody, Dave. My pa was a laborer, and I seen him work himself to death with a shovel, and I swore I'd never do the same. And I never did after I got this." He tapped his holstered Colt.

Winter smiled and nodded. "You won't have to, Frank."

"But if we find the treasure, I still want my fair share," Tucker said. "I'm the top gun in this outfit, remember?"

"You'll get what's coming to you, Frank," Winter said. "Don't worry about it."

Seventeen men sat around the campfire that night . . . but only two of them, as they stared through the scarlet-flickering gloom at Tucker, knew they looked at a dead man. One was Bean Gosford and the other was Dave Winter.

Gosford built a cigarette, listening to Tucker, who didn't know when the hell to shut up.

"Dave, if we find the thirty thousand, you maybe think about retiring?" Tucker said. He was a twenty-five-year-old towhead with cold blue eyes, a ladies' man who abused whores and had killed three men, none of them in a fair fight. He was fast, but shooting down unarmed men was a shaky foundation on which to build a reputation as a dangerous hombre with a gun.

"I haven't studied on it any, Frank," Winter said, his face composed. "Why do you ask?"

"I reckon I'm destined for great things, Dave, and when you decide to retire, I aim to take over the business," Tucker said. "I got a lot of good ideas and new ways to do things."

"Business? What business, Frank? We're a gang of outlaws," Winter said, drawing a laugh. "We're not businessmen."

Tucker didn't like that. He didn't like it one bit.

"I'll make it a business, Dave," he said, irritated. "Maybe we've been doing too many things the old-fashioned way for too long. We got to move with the times."

Gosford, his own annoyance niggling at him, said, "I walk into a bank and order the teller to fill a sack with money. If he does what he's told, I leave him be. If he don't, or gives me sass, I put a bullet in his belly and fill the sack my ownself. If that's old-fashioned, how would you do it different, Frank?"

Tucker was silent for a few moments and then said, "Well, I can't say right off, but I'll think of something, you can depend on that, Bean."

Winter said, "If and when I retire, I'll leave it to a vote by all present to decide who takes over. I can't say any fairer than that."

"Fine by me," Tucker said. He grinned and tapped the holstered revolver on his hip. "But Sam Colt here will have the casting vote."

Bean Gosford, who would not be intimidated by any man, rose to his feet, his hand close to his gun. His eyes were on Tucker as he opened his mouth to speak. But Winter didn't want a shooting, at least not that night.

"Bean!" he said, louder than he'd spoken before, almost shouting the tall gunman's name. "Tell me about that settlement south of Fort Mason."

Gosford unwound slowly, one piece of him at a

time. When his breathing and heart rate went back to normal, he said, "You mean Fritztown?" His eyes were still on Tucker, who studiously ignored him.

"Yeah, where the squareheads live," Winter said.

"There ain't much to tell, Dave, just a bunch of Germans who brew beer and make wine. They also call the place Fredericksburg."

"Farmers?"

"For the most part."

"I was thinking . . . if the payroll thing doesn't pan out, we could hit their bank on our way back to the border."

Gosford considered that and said, "I don't recommend it, Dave. The Texas Rangers love Fritztown, and they're always riding in for a beer and a sausage. Last time I was there, a few years ago, five rangers were in town, and one of them was John B. Armstrong, who arrested Wes Hardin in Florida that time."

"He busted up Wes pretty good, they say."

"Bent a six-gun over his head."

"I liked Wes," Dave said. "Real good on the draw and shoot."

"Fast."

"Yeah, fast, and then he'd usually hit his mark." Winter rose to his feet and stretched. "Getting late. I got to spread my blankets."

"What about Fritztown?" Gosford said.

"The hell with Fritztown. I don't want no truck with rangers. We'll ride around it," Winter said.

* * *

Dave Winter and his gunmen woke with the dawn to a mist that ghosted the grass country for miles around and smelled of raw iron. Sour, grumbling men, last night's whiskey punishing them, boiled up coffee, and a few, hardier than the rest, broiled bacon over the fire and ate it with sourdough bread that had turned stale days before.

One of these was Frank Tucker.

"Hey, Dave, how are you feeling this fine morning?" he said, talking through a full mouth. He wore his gun, and his saddle lay at his feet. "You got a touch of the rheumatisms maybe?"

"Nah, I can't complain," Winter said, blowing across the boiling-hot coffee in his cup.

"Just as well," Tucker said. "Nobody would listen anyway."

"About the size of it," Winter said. "A man complains, and nobody listens or cares. That's always been the way of it."

Tucker had a habit of standing hipshot, his right hand resting on the butt of his Colt, a sneer substituting for a smile. Some said Bill Bonney had a mocking smile like that . . . until the year before these events when grim, unsmiling Pat Garrett had wiped it off his kisser permanently.

The same thing would very soon happen to Frank Tucker.

Sneer firmly in place, the youngster said, "I've been thinking about what you and Bean Gosford was saying about Fritztown," he said. "I got something to say about that my ownself."

"Then say away, Frank," Winter said. "We're all listening."

And all of the outlaws were. They stood in silence, attentive, steaming coffee cups to their faces, wondering if Tucker was about to challenge the mad old bull for leadership. The morning mist drifted among them like sacrificial smoke from an altar, as though waiting for the drama to unfold and create a new god.

Tucker began, "It seems to me—"

"Is this about a modern way of doing things, Frank?" Winter said.

"No, not modern, just sensible," Tucker said.

"Then go right ahead, Frank. Sorry for horning in."

"Listen up, Dave. Sodbusters don't drink, they don't whore, and if they ain't walking behind a mule's ass, they're a-readin' of their Bibles. That's why clodhopper banks are always stuffed to the rafters with money."

"You know that for a natural fact, Frank, huh?" Winter said.

"Yeah, I know it, and so did the James boys, and that's why Jesse and them done such great things."

"Jesse's dead, Frank," Winter said.

"And we can take his place."

"All right, then let's hear it," Winter said.

"Well, look around you, Dave. We ain't pick-and-shovel men. I say forget Fort Mason and a buried treasure that's sure to be nothing anyway, and head straight for the Fritztown bank."

"And then?" Winter said. He poured the dregs from his cup and then let it drop.

Tucker missed the clue.

"We rob the bank, load up, and head for the Rio Grande and ride into Old Mexico," Tucker said. He grinned. "And, man-o-man, then we have us a time."

A few of the outlaws made approving noises but kept them low and quiet. Dave Winter's gun hand was free and there was no telling which way the pickle would squirt.

Winter didn't keep them guessing for too long.

He smiled as he talked. "You heard what Bean said, the squareheads have a liking for Texas Rangers and feed them sausage and beer, so robbing their bank may not be as easy as you think. And even if you did, it's near three hundred miles from Fritztown to the Rio Grande and you'd have lawmen that were pulled away from their sausage supper dogging your trail every step of the way. A hungry ranger is an angry ranger, and an angry ranger is a man you don't want to mess with if'n you don't have to."

"Can I believe my ears? You ain't turning yellow on us, Dave?" Tucker said, sneer firmly in place.

A spare, dry wind thinned the mist, and out in the long grass a coyote yipped its hunger to the emerging sky. Around the outlaws, the air carried the good smells of horses, burning wood, and coffee . . . and something else. Death maybe.

"Time we saddled up, moved south for Fort Mason," Winter said.

"You got nothing to say to me, Dave?" Tucker said, his grin somewhere between a smirk and a grimace.

He knew he was fast on the draw and shoot, but he'd never drawn down on a named shootist. That unfortunate gap in his education would very soon kill him.

"Nothing much, Frank," Winter said. "Only that you're the dumbest son of a bitch I ever knew."

Tucker's face stiffened.

"That's hard, Dave. Mighty hard."

"The truth sometimes is, Frank."

Tucker knew he'd been called out, and the circle of unshaven, expectant faces around him knew it too. Time stood still. Tucker's life tick . . . tick . . . ticked to its end.

The youngster looked around at the other men. A few revealed concern, but most showed open contempt. The damned kid had gotten too big for his britches and was overdue a slap down.

Tucker read the faces. Read the derision. Read what would have to be his next move.

"Damn you, Dave!" he yelled.

His hand dropped for his gun.

Dave Winter didn't move.

But Bean Gosford did.

He was faster than Tucker, faster by the split second that wins gunfights. The younger man's Colt hadn't cleared his fancied-up holster when Gosford's first bullet hit him dead center in the chest. Another shot missed as Tucker fell. But when the young man landed on his back, Gosford scored two more hits, both an inch below the left collarbone.

Dave Winter looked at Tucker, shook his head, and stepped to the young man, looming over him like the angel of death. He stared into the youngster's terrified eyes and said, "Why, Frank, you ain't even nearly dead yet." Winter triggered two shots into Tucker's face. "Now you are," he said.

Winter turned to Gosford. "Good shooting, Bean," he said. And then, "Throw Frank's saddle on his horse and bring it along with us. I've always admired that Palouse."

"Hey, Dave, can I have his boots and his gun?" an outlaw said, a lank man with green, reptilian eyes. He looked around at the others. "I spoke first."

"Sure, Sam, take them," Winter said. "Poor Frank no longer has any use for them."

Chapter Ten

Colonel Benjamin Grierson and two junior officers escorted John Latimer to the Patterson stage, under the watchful, baleful eye of Buttons Muldoon, who looked as if he expected the prisoner to at any moment make a run for it and head for higher ground.

Red Ryan stood with Hannah Huckabee, who wore her tan dress, boots, and pith helmet with the goggles above the brim. She had belted on her revolver and bowie knife, and in the amber light of the dawn she looked breathtakingly beautiful . . . and desperately unhappy.

"Here he comes," Hannah said. Then, as though all she had left to her was defiance, "I won't ride in the stage with him."

Red played along. "It's strictly against the policy of the Abe Patterson and Son Stage and Express Company for a passenger to ride up top, but I think I can talk Buttons into making an exception."

Hannah's eyes lifted to his. Red saw that they were red-rimmed, as though she'd recently shed a tear or two. "You're most kind," she said.

John Latimer didn't look like a British army officer. He didn't look like any kind of army officer. Tall, thin, almost frail, in his ill-fitting suit and collarless shirt he looked like a junior countinghouse clerk who hadn't been eating well. By comparison, the two manacled Mexican thieves were short, stocky, and strong. Ranger Tim Adams walked behind them, his Winchester at the ready. Following Adams and his clanking prisoners, a couple of cavalry troopers carried the stolen Madonna, one of the men with a length of rope looped around a shoulder to lash the statue into the boot at the rear of the stage.

But Red's eyes were no longer on this melancholy procession. Rather, he watched the four men now riding toward the sutler's store. Three of them sat tall in the saddle and had a military bearing, but what caught and held Red's attention was the fourth rider, the grim Brack Cooley, who gave Red a murderous scowl as he passed.

Hannah Huckabee noticed and said, "Red, I don't think that man likes you very much."

Mr. Chang agreed and then said, "Looks like bad man to me. Gunman, I think."

Red smiled. "His name is Cooley, bounty hunter, lawman, and sometime stage robber. I'm a shotgun guard, so what is there about me for him to like?"

"Do you think those four plan to rob us?" Hannah said, with a little spike of alarm in her voice.

"Buttons Muldoon said that very thing, and I'll tell you what I told him . . . we're not worth robbing . . . unless . . ."

"Unless what?"

"Nothing. Forget I said it."

"Unless they want a woman. Was that what you were about to say?"

Red nodded. "Out here on the frontier, females are in short supply—there's always that."

Hannah shook her head. "Red, neither robbery nor a woman is why they're here. John Latimer is the reason."

"How do you figure?" Red said.

"Did you get a good look at the three men with Cooley? Red, if I don't miss my guess, they're army officers, British army officers."

"You sure?" Red said. "I'd say that's a tall heap of guess."

"Not really. I've been around army officers all my life and I can spot them anywhere," Hannah said. "British, American, Russian, Prussian, and French, no matter, they all have the same air of authority about them."

"Then maybe those British boys are friends of Latimer's and aim to spring him somewhere between here and Austin, and that's why they need Cooley's gun backing them," Red said.

"Or maybe they plan to kill him," Hannah said. Then, giving Red a sidelong glance, "John Latimer has a lot of enemies and no friends."

"Well, as far as I'm concerned, he's a paying passenger of the Abe Patterson and Son Stage and Express Company, and anyone who plans on doing him harm will have to go through me," Red said. Then, parroting a company line, "The Patterson passenger has a pal in Abe."

Hannah's smile was as faint as baby breath. "For men like John, sometimes death comes as a welcome release," she said. She frowned. "I'm rather surprised he hasn't shot himself by now. It would be the honorable thing to do."

It was then that an openmouthed John Latimer stopped in his tracks like a man who'd just run into a solid wall of memories. "Hannah!" he cried out, breaking into a delighted smile. "It's you! It's really you!"

"Steady, Captain Latimer, steady," Colonel Grierson said, but he made no attempt to stop the young man's dash across what was soon to be an impassible distance between himself and Hannah Huckabee.

The woman stood stiff-backed and still and she said just two glacial words that froze Latimer in place. "Hello, John."

He stopped, confused. "Hannah . . ."

"Miss Huckabee, if you please."

Latimer's stunned face revealed his mental turmoil, and he stammered, "I . . . I thought . . . I thought you'd come . . . I thought . . ."

Then Mr. Chang, who'd been watching from a distance, hurled himself in front of Latimer and said, "No! Enough talk. You go away now, leave Miss Huckabee in peace."

Latimer looked over the top of Mr. Chang's head. "Hannah, can we talk? I have so many things to say to you, things I should've said years ago and didn't."

"We have nothing to say to each other," Hannah said. "You chose the coward's path and betrayed our country and betrayed me, and now you must live with it." Tears sprang into her eyes. "You are dead to me, John. You died that day in India when you fled the field, and as far as I'm concerned you're now in a coffin six feet under the ground." Hannah dashed a tear from her cheek, turned away, and smiled. "Dahteste! How pretty you look in your new clothes. That blouse and skirt become you so."

Hannah took the girl's arm and walked quickly away from Latimer, who stood and stared after her, thinking how lucky was the man that dies only one death. He had just died too many to count . . . and those deaths were only the beginning . . . not the end.

As Mr. Chang said to Red later that day, "It is destined that some men die scores of times before they take their final breath. John Latimer's is a cruel death . . . the death of a thousand cuts."

Buttons Muldoon shook his head and said to Red Ryan, "We've had some strange ones, but this crowd is the strangest ever."

"I'm inclined to agree with you," Red said. "Seems we never get normal passengers. Maybe it's Texas, maybe it's us. What do you think?"

"The hell if I know, Red," Buttons said. "But it is mighty peculiar. And when I'm on the subject of peculiar, who gave Hannah Huckabee permission to ride on top?"

"I did. But I told her you wouldn't mind."

"Ordinarily, I would mind, I'd mind a lot, because it's strictly against company policy, but on this run . . . it seems like anything goes," Buttons said.

Inside the Concord Stage Line coach, Dahteste sat between John Latimer and Mr. Chang, facing front. Opposite them, the two Mexicans clanked their chains and alternately bemoaned their cruel fate. Buttons told Red that he was sure the pair expected to be hanged without benefit of clergy since they'd stolen a holy Madonna and committed a great sacrilege. But since Buttons understood little Mexican, Red doubted that was the case.

Ranger Tim Adams swung into the saddle and took up a position at the rear of the coach. "Any time you're ready, driver," he said.

Red waved a farewell to Colonel Grierson, and then Buttons turned his head to Hannah Huckabee, whom he considered a promising student should she ever decide to take up the stage-driving profession.

"Watch close now, Miss Hannah, and I'll teach you how to cut a dash," he said. "I'm gonna do some show-boating fer the colonel and them other folks standing around. Hold on to your hat!"

The whip-cracking departure of a stage was a magnificent sight and one much appreciated by everyone at Fort Concho from small boys to soldiers to mature matrons. A finely tuned instrument, Buttons's whip was a work of art made by a white-haired craftsman in Galveston. The stock was of tough hickory, long, slender, and supple, the heavy butt end decorated with silver rings. The whip was made from plaited strips of ox leather, the cracker at its tip cut from a bolt of the finest sewing silk. The stock was four feet long, the lash ten, and to crack the whip near the ears of the team leaders was a feat that could only be mastered by the most accomplished driver. Buttons stood in the box, six in hand, and leaned forward, his right arm extended and his whip crack, crack, cracked with amazing rapidity, like a string of exploding fire-crackers. In his blue sailor's coat with its double row of brass buttons, he was a splendid sight, and Hannah, caught up in the moment, clapped her hands and cheered him on with loud huzzahs and bravos.

As the speeding coach rumbled, rattled, and clattered out of the fort, its yellow wheels spinning, churning up dust, the Madonna bound with heavy leather straps in the boot jumped up and down on her wooden rack as though she, too, was enjoying the ride.

Red Ryan, his right foot braced, sat beside Buttons in the high seat, and even though he'd seen it hundreds of times before, as he always did, he grinned at his driver's derring-do and spectacular display of Western dash.

Chapter Eleven

"I've changed my mind, Mr. Cooley. We execute him in Austin or in New Orleans," Captain Rupert Bentley-Foulkes said. "After he has a court-martial with me as judge, Lieutenant Wood as trial counsel, and Lieutenant Allerton acting for the defense."

"Very much under protest," Allerton said. "How do I defend a coward who brought such disgrace to the British army?"

"Justice must be seen to be done, Mr. Allerton," Bentley-Foulkes said. "I'm sure you'll think of something, insanity perhaps."

"Damn it, my way is better," Brack Cooley said. "I ride up to the stage, smiling like I'm kinfolk, and shoot Red Ryan out of the guard's seat and the driver too if he makes a play. Then I shake Latimer's hand and put a bullet between his eyes." Cooley smiled, his hand sweeping in the direction of the grassland ahead of him, scarred by the passage of the Patterson stage. "Just like that, the job is done, and I ride away."

Bentley-Foulkes's horse tossed its head, irritated

by an errant fly, and its bit chimed. "What about the outrider, Mr. Cooley? You saw the outrider."

"Yeah, I know, a Texas Ranger by the name of Tim Adams. He's a nobody. I can take care of him."

"And there's yet another complication," Bentley-Foulkes said.

"Damn, mister, you ain't making this easy," Cooley said. "You keep coming up with your complications."

"A woman, I hesitate to call her a lady, by the name of Hannah Huckabee is on the stage. I am sure she harbors some idea of helping Latimer escape."

"So? Hell, I can gun her too," Cooley said.

"No, I don't wish her harmed, at least just yet," Bentley-Foulkes said. "I want no accusing fingers pointed in my direction. Miss Huckabee is known as an adventuress, and she has made some powerful friends, and I mean the likes of Queen Victoria, Czar Alexander of Russia, and your own President Arthur. It was only when I saw her at the post that I remembered she was once engaged to be married to John Latimer. Thankfully, she didn't recognize me or Lieutenants Wood or Allerton. That might have been awkward, to say the least."

Cooley said, "Ben . . . Bent . . ."

"Bentley-Foulkes."

"The hell with it, I'll call you Ben," Cooley said.

"Captain will do nicely when we're alone."

The young day was already hot, the prairie breeze still, and in the distance the grasslands shimmered.

"Well, Cap'n, when I'm paid to do a job, I do it right. What do you want done with the woman?"

"You'll make her disappear without trace and

without witnesses," Bentley-Foulkes said. "As I said, she styles herself an adventuress—"

"Damned impertinence," Granville Wood said, a not-too-bright young man with pale blue protruding eyes and the vague features that three hundred years of inbreeding produces. "A woman's place is in the home."

Cooley said, "I'll make sure she stays home, all right. At least until I tire of her, and then"—the gunman drew his forefinger across his throat—"farewell, my lovely."

"Please, Mr. Cooley, I don't want to know the details," Bentley-Foulkes said. "When the time comes, just get rid of Miss Huckabee quietly and without fuss. I don't know how many there are in the world, but I rather fancy that adventuresses die without a trace all the time. No mercy now, Mr. Cooley. Any woman who would knowingly drink from the matrimonial cup with a coward like John Latimer must be dealt with harshly."

Wood grinned. "Perhaps we should teach dear Hannah a lesson or two with a horsewhip before we hand her over to Mr. Cooley."

"No, Mr. Wood, throughout all this unpleasant business we must remain officers and gentlemen. I admit that Miss Huckabee is a coward's intended, but remember, she's a white Englishwoman, not some native belly-warmer one amuses oneself with in an African hut. Let's not forget that, shall we?"

Cooley laughed. "In other words, Lieutenant, leave the rough stuff to me. I'm not a gentleman."

"No, Mr. Cooley, you're not," Bentley-Foulkes said. "And that's precisely why I hired you."

Chapter Twelve

Buttons Muldoon had decided to take the route to Austin that had been mapped by Captain William O'Connel of the 4th Cavalry in the spring of 1869. The trail had good grass and water, and Buttons intended to ford the San Saba River by sundown, a distance of ninety miles southeast of Fort Concho, and spend the night at Kline's Station . . . if the Apaches hadn't burned it down during the recent outbreak.

The team was eager for the trail, but Buttons reined them to a distance-eating trot under the blue bowl of the sky where a few white clouds drifted like waterlilies on a pond. Once Red saw a couple of mounted men in the distance before they vanished into the heat shimmer and he dismissed them as punchers riding the grub line. But he kept his Greener close because in this part of Texas road agents were always a possibility.

"Did you see them?" Red asked Buttons.

"Yeah, I saw them," the driver said. "I never thought I'd see riders out this way, unless they came up from the border country."

"Winter's men?" Red said.

"I sure as hell hope not," Buttons said. He cracked his whip over a lagging horse. "The last thing we need on this trip is trouble from crazy Dave Winter."

After an hour or so riding on top of the stage, Hannah Huckabee squeezed into the tiny space between driver and guard, much to a frowning Buttons's annoyance at this breach of the rules and a smiling Red Ryan's eternal gratitude. Now she pointed to the southeast and said, "What's that? A prairie fire?"

Red followed the girl's finger and said, "Yeah, looks like smoke, but it's too dark to be a prairie fire."

"Wind's from the north," Buttons said. "If it is a grass fire it will head away from us."

Red shook his head. "It's not a fire, Buttons, and it isn't dust. I don't know what it is."

"Hell, it's moving fast, but not away from us. It's headed our way, Red," Buttons said. Then, "Does the ranger see that?"

"I don't know," Red said. He picked up his shotgun and rested the butt upright on his thigh, his gaze reaching into distance. "Looks like it could be a locomotive."

"No railroad tracks in this neck of the woods," Buttons said.

"Hear that?" Hannah said. "It does sound like a steam engine."

Buttons drew rein on the team. "We'll wait here and see where that thing is going, whatever it is," he said. "The horses need a rest, and over there I see the pond the army captain marked on his map. If it is a fire, I'll drive right into the water."

The stage was fifty miles out from Fort Concho and a few miles south of Kickapoo Spring, on good grass relieved by a few stands of hardwood and pine.

Buttons leaned forward in the seat and told Hannah and Red to get closer to him. Then, his voice dropping to a conspiratorial whisper, he said, "Listen up, a few years back, right on this very spot, the 9th Cavalry had a battle with a bunch of Kickapoos who'd camped near the pond. As I recollect, a couple of Indians were wounded in the fight and they lost fifteen horses." Buttons's voice dropped lower. "That's between us, you understand. Don't tell the coward. I don't want him getting upset about them Kickapoos and maybe trying to run away."

Red nodded. "Not a word of this from me."

Hannah said nothing. She turned her head and stared at the approaching column of smoke. Buttons reckoned she was so ashamed of Latimer that she'd been struck dumb.

As Buttons and Red unhitched the team to allow the horses to graze for a while, Ranger Tim Adams rode up on the stage, his rifle at the ready. "What is that thing in the distance?" he said. "Is it a fire?"

Buttons shook his head. "Hell if I know . . . some kind of locomotive, looks like."

"There's no railroad around here," Adams said. He put his field glasses to his eyes and scanned the distance. After a while he passed his glasses to Red. "Here, shotgun guard, take a look. Tell me I'm seeing things."

Red put the glasses to his eyes, studied the object for a while and then said, "It looks like four gents sitting in a wagon. The wagon's moving, but I don't see any horses."

Hannah Huckabee had her own binoculars to her eyes. Without lowering them, she said, "The wagon is powered by steam generated by wood. That's why it's smoking."

"Like a locomotive?" Adams said.

"Yes, only it doesn't run on rails," Hannah said. "It's got wheels."

Red used the field glasses again and then said, "It's coming right at us." He handed the binoculars back to the ranger, who was still mounted. "Outlaws in a horseless carriage?"

"I don't think so," Adams said. "Way too slow. Try to escape in that thing after robbing a bank and it would take you ten minutes to reach the town limits." He grinned. "And only if it's a mighty small town."

"Then what are these boys doing?" Red said.

Hannah didn't hesitate. "I think they're adventurers."

"Adventurers?" Red said. "There haven't been any adventures in this part of Texas since the Apaches called it a day and went back to the San Carlos."

"Then they're explorers," Hannah said. "Yes, they could be explorers."

"Then they're fools," Buttons said. "What's out here to explore?"

"Grass," Adams said.

"And more grass," Red said.

Buttons left his team to drink at the pond and stepped beside Red. "Good water in that pond, muddy, but good." He shaded his eyes with his hand and scanned the distance. "Now what's that thing up to?" he said.

Red was about to say that he had no idea, but

changed his mind when four riders, coming on fast and kicking up dust, bore down on the horseless wagon. "Damn it all, they're shooting," he said.

The flat statements of powerful hunting rifles racketed across the prairie followed by a sharp Crack! Crack! Crack! as a couple of men in the wagon returned fire and the pursuing riders drew rein and then pulled off a ways out of the line of fire.

"I was right," Red said. "Looks like the rannies in the steam wagon are being chased by a posse or a bunch of road agents."

"Or something," Adams said. "Well, there's one way to find out. Ryan, get up behind me. I may need some help here."

Red handed his Greener to Buttons, vaulted onto the ranger's horse behind the saddle and then regained the shotgun. "Ready when you are, lawman," he said.

Adams turned his head and said, "Any shooting to be done, I'll do it."

"Suppose they drill you?" Red said.

"Then I'll leave it up to you, Ryan. I don't want to sound like a sore loser, but if they do for me, kill them all."

Chapter Thirteen

Although a Texas Ranger didn't wear a lawman's badge, a few carried stars from their past employment as cow-town peace officers, and Tim Adams was one of them. When he was within hailing distance of the horseless wagon, he held aloft a silver star in a circle and yelled, "Hold up there, in the name of the law!"

Red Ryan thought it unlikely that Adams's voice could be heard above the hissing, belching, clanking din of the steam carriage, but up front a woman wearing goggles worked a series of levers and the machine ground to a shuddering halt.

The strange vehicle was made of blue-painted steel plates and was about fifty feet long from the flagpole at the front to the rear of its towed wood tender. For all the world it looked like an elongated and broadened wagon, but with six massive wrought iron wheels driven by a steam boiler and its attached firebox. A tangled maze of brass and copper tubes carried steam through the system, and a tall chimney, painted bright red, expelled smoke and soot. Toward the rear of the vehicle was a blue pagoda that looked large enough to afford sleeping accommodation for four.

In all, it was a contraption that moved Ranger Adams to say that he'd never, in all his born days, seen such a sight. And Red readily agreed with him.

Three men and a woman rose from throne-like seats and bowed. The men, alike as peas in a pod, each sported white hair and beards and wore safari clothing of tan-colored canvas, breeches of the same color shoved into the tops of black, knee-high boots. Like Hannah Huckabee, all wore pith helmets with goggles and field glasses hung on their chests. Red pegged the men as adventurers, though they looked decidedly elderly to engage in such a pursuit. The female driver was tall, shapely, dressed like the men but looked thirty years younger. Red thought her a handsome woman, though her black eyebrows were a shade too thick and her eyes too fierce to be pretty . . . until she smiled at him and winked and his heart almost stopped beating. Like her male companions, the woman awkwardly held a light sporting rifle that she obviously had no idea how to use.

Red slid off the rump of the ranger's horse and then waited as one of the men, spryer than he'd expected, climbed out of the wagon, held up his hand in a peace gesture, and said to Adams, "My name is Professor Sir Richard Owen of the British Paleontological Society. Are you a member of the local constabulary?"

Behind him the steam carriage hissed and groaned like an angry dragon.

"I'm a Texas Ranger, name is Tim Adams. And this here is Red Ryan, he's a shotgun guard."

"For the Abe Patterson and Son Stage and Express Company," Red said.

"What was all the shooting about?" Adams said.

Owen pointed to the horsemen, who kept their distance and seemed to be observing the proceedings with keen interest.

"I'll tell you what all the shooting was about, Texas Ranger," Owen said. "We were set upon by yon scoundrels. Yes, I say scoundrels, sir, but they're worse than scoundrels. Knaves, jackanapes, villains, blackguards, thieves, the lowest of the low . . . dash it all, sir, words fail me."

"Outlaws?" Red offered.

"Yes, that too. Their leader is Professor Edward Drinker Cope, and he's trying to steal from me, the rapscallion."

"What does he want to steal from you?" Adams said.

"I assure you, something more precious than silver or gold," Owen said.

The ranger jerked his chin in the direction of the steam carriage. "That thing?"

"No, sir, not that thing. He wishes to steal my reputation as a paleontologist, sir!" Owen said.

"Your reputation as a what?"

"As a paleontologist."

Red Ryan was as puzzled as Ranger Adams. "What is that?" he said. Then a light went off in his brain. "Oh, hold up for a second. I know. You and them other boys collect butterflies, huh?"

Sir Richard Owen was outraged, and his florid face turned purple. "Butterflies? Butterflies! My dear sir, my colleagues and I hunt thunder lizards. Dinosaurs, sir. In 1841, that's the name I bestowed on those terrifying monsters of the ancient past."

"Hell, Professor, I've never seen one of them in Texas, or anywhere else come to that," Adams said. "Do you mean Gila monsters?—because if you do, there's none of them out here."

"Of course, I don't. I mean dinosaurs, sir, dinosaurs. And if you haven't seen any it's because the terrible lizards died out millions of years ago, and now their bones lie buried deep in the ground," Owen said.

Adams said, "Then why are you and what's-his-name—"

"Professor Cope," Owen said.

"—shooting at one another?"

"Because we're at war, sir," Owen said. "The newspapers of the more sensational sort call it the Bone Wars, and I suppose that name is as good as any. It's a war between the righteous, myself and my colleagues, and those who would try to steal credit for our fieldwork . . . black-hearted Professor Edward Drinker Cope and his evil band of acolytes."

"So, all that shooting is about bones?" the ranger said.

"Not just any bones. Dinosaur bones," Owen said. "Make the distinction, man."

Tim Adams shook his head. He nodded in the direction of the four horsemen and said to Red, "Take my bay and bring those birds in, Ryan. I want to talk with them."

"Suppose they don't want to come?" Red said.

"Then tell Cope I'll arrest him for disturbing the peace, and I can guarantee him six months at hard labor in Huntsville."

"I guess that ought to do it," Red said.

He swung into the saddle and headed for the mounted men at a trot.

"Are you an emissary from that damned rogue, Sir Richard Owen?" said the man who rode out to meet Red Ryan and had introduced himself as Professor Edward Drinker Cope of Yale University and the leader of the expedition.

Red shook his head. "No, I'm an emissary from Texas Ranger Tim Adams. He says to put those guns away and go talk to him."

"And if I don't choose to?" Cope said. He was a good-looking man, younger than Owen, and his clean-shaven face held a tight, obstinate expression.

"That's the very question I asked Ranger Adams," Red said.

"And what did he tell you?"

"That if you don't do as he says he can guarantee you six months of breaking rocks in Huntsville." Red smiled. "Huntsville is the state penitentiary, Professor, and it's nothing at all like Yale."

"Edward, better do as he says," a gray-haired man said. "The treacherous Owen has led us into a trap. You go with this fellow, and I'll fetch up the pack-horse."

"Then it seems that I have no alternative but to put

my head into the noose," Cope said to Red. "Tell me, fellow, are you a police officer?"

"No. My name is Red Ryan, and I'm a shotgun guard with the Abe Patterson Stage and Express Company." Then, since the four men were well-dressed and obviously of more than sufficient means, he added, "You can trust the Patterson stage line for all your future travel needs."

Cope introduced the men with him, all of them graybeards: Professor Thomas Anderson of Yale, Professor Algernon Makepeace of Oxford, and finally Doctor Oscar Turner of Princeton, who'd left to fetch the packhorse.

"And I'm right pleased to meet your acquaintances," Red said. "Now case those rifles and come with me." He believed a warning was in order. "No sudden moves, gents. Texas Rangers are not the most trusting of men, and we don't want any unfortunate accidents."

Chapter Fourteen

"I'm not a trusting man," Dave Winter said. "Give me your information and I'll tell you what it's worth."

"I can do that, but only if you be Dave Winter," the stranger said. "If you be somebody else, then I'll bid you good day and ride on."

"I'm Winter. What do they call you?"

"Shem Pollard, and this here is my brother Jethro. Me and him, we're out of the Crockett County canyon country, born and raised."

"I don't give a damn where you're out of," Winter said. "You two are the sorriest-looking saddle tramps I ever seen this side of the Rio Grande. Don't you ever bathe?" He shook his head. "Stay the hell downwind of me when I'm drinking my afternoon coffee."

Bean Gosford said, "How did you know we were here?"

"Beggin' your pardon, your honor, but we didn't know you was here," Shem said. "Oh, we was told that Dave Winter was north of the border again, and when we saw your camp, me and Jethro put two and two together."

"How much is two and two put together?" Winter said.

Shem looked confused. "I don't know," he said.

"I took you for an ignorant son of a bitch," Winter said. "What information could you possibly have to sell me?"

The man looked sly. "Well, your honor, we seen a purty woman, the purtiest woman in Texas, maybe so."

"Is that all you have to tell me?" Gosford said. "That you saw a pretty woman."

"There's more, Mr. Winter," Jethro said, like his brother a short, bearded man with lank strands of filthy hair falling over his shoulders. He also smelled like his brother, a cloying stench akin to that of a gut wagon. "We got more to tell."

"Tell me more," Winter said. "So far, you ain't doing so good."

"The woman was riding on a stage with a shotgun messenger and an outrider," Shem said. "Now, study on that, Mr. Winter. Why would a stage have two guards unless it was carrying something mighty valuable?"

Despite himself, Winter was interested. "Where was the stage?" he said.

"We last saw it north of the San Saba and headed this way," Shem said. "When me an' Jethro was in this country a few years back, there was a stage station on the river owned by a man named Ira Kline. We know, because he ran us off his property, accused us of being trash. Seems to me the stage could be headed there."

Winter said, "Bean, what do you think?"

"I think you got a choice to make, boss," Gosford

said. "Do we rob a stage or dig for Len Blackburn's buried treasure?"

"Me and Jethro can help with them things," Shem interrupted. "We're good workers and we ain't afraid to get our hands dirty. An' we'll slit a throat, if'n it comes down to a need for some cuttin'. Yes, sir, we cut and backstab just as nice as you please."

Winter ignored that and said, "Bean, I'm not partial to stage holdups. You mind that time near Nogales when we held up a Butterfield and got into a shooting scrape with the guard and a couple of passengers and when the smoke cleared our haul was a bag of Arbuckle, a nickel watch, and seven dollars and forty-seven cents? You recollect that?"

Gosford smiled. "I should say. I took a load of buck-shot in the ass in that damned fight, couldn't sit a saddle easy for a three-month."

"Yeah, I remember it, too, and I ain't likely to ever forget," Winter said. "All right, here's what we do. We ride on into Fort Mason and deal with the stage when the time comes, rob it or leave it the hell alone. Looks to me it's headed for Austin and it's bound to pass this way."

"Dave, we've learned a lot since the Nogales holdup," Gosford said. "I reckon we can take it any time we want."

"Yeah, I guess you're right about that," Winter said. He threw the dregs of the coffee on the fire and said, "Mount up, boys. We're headed for old Fort Mason."

"Mr. Winter, what about us?" Shem Pollard said.

"Jethro don't talk much, but he's a-wondering as well. Ain't you, Jethro? Ain't you a-wondering?"

Jethro gave a slack-mouthed nod. "That's right, Shem. I'm a-wondering."

Winter hesitated, his foot in the stirrup. "What the hell are you wondering about?"

"Well, see, we're kinda curious what our telling you about the stage is worth?" Shem said. "We think maybe ten dollars."

"It's worth nothing," Winter said. He swung into the saddle and smiled. "I got other plans for you boys."

Shem's bearded face lit up. "We can throw in with you, Mr. Winter? Me and Jethro are salty, mighty salty, the kind of men you need."

"Nope," Winter said. "You can't throw in with me."

"Then what?" Shem said, looking disappointed.

"The thing is, if I let you fellers go, you'll know where we're headed and what we plan to do, and that's information you could sell to an interested party, like the Texas Rangers as an example."

Suddenly Shem Pollard felt fear stab at him. "We ain't the kind to do that, Mr. Winter. We ain't squealers. You can trust us."

Winter snorted. "Trust a pair of sorry pieces of trash like you? You'd sell out your own mother to Judge Parker's hangman if someone paid you twenty dollars."

He drew his Colt.

"No, Mr. Winter, not that," Shem said. "It's Jethro you can't trust. He's the squealer, not me."

"Damn you fer a lying swine, Shem!" Jethro yelled, suddenly talking for his life.

"You shut your trap, Jethro," Shem said. "I'm telling Mr. Winter how things are with us."

"I ain't never squealed to the law, not once," Jethro said. "And you know it."

"He's a damned liar, Mr. Winter," Shem said. "You want to gun somebody, gun him."

"Shut your mouth, Shem," Jethro said. "The hell with you, I'm gonna shut it permanent."

Jethro scrambled for the gun belted over his old army greatcoat, drew, and fired. At a range of just five feet, Jethro hurried the shot and missed. Shem, unlimbering a Remington with rust freckles on the cylinder and barrel, got his work in, and his bullet smashed into his brother's right thigh, breaking bone. Jethro screamed, staggered back, and triggered his gun. Click! The hammer fell on a dud round.

Winter roared with laughter and yanked his horse aside. "Watch out, boys!" he yelled. "Give them shootists some room."

Bean Gosford and the other riders pulled back, grinning, enjoying the fun.

Shem cursed and advanced on Jethro, who was down on one knee, his wounded leg stretched out in front of him. "Damn you, you've killed me, Shem!" Jethro said. He pulled the trigger, and this time his old Colt fired, a gut shot that entered an inch below Shem's navel and should've ended the fight. But after the initial shock of receiving what he knew was a death wound, Shem shrieked back his pain and rage and staggered in front of his brother. He pushed the muzzle of the Remington into Jethro's shooting eye and dropped the hammer. Click! Old, mildewed brass cartridges produced yet another dud.

Winter and his men were laughing so hard at the pathetic gladiators that they had trouble controlling their horses. Then Winter yelled, "Wait . . . hey, boys, what's this . . . what's this?"

Shem had dropped his gun and pulled a huge, bone-handled knife. He grabbed Jethro by the hair, cried out as another of his brother's bullets slammed into him, and then plunged the blade deep into the left side of his brother's neck. Blood fountained from a terrible wound as Jethro, his eyes wild, let out a thin, bubbling scream and fell on his back, dying hard and in pain when he hit the ground.

"Oh, well done, old fellow," Winter yelled, applauding Shem as his cohorts clapped and cheered. "You won the fight fair and square."

Shem staggered back and sat heavily on the ground, silent, his face ashen.

"Let's go, boys," Winter said. "Seems like the show is over."

Shem turned his head, the blue death shadows already gathered in his cheeks and eyes. "Get me to a doctor," he said. "I'm shot through and through."

"Hell, he wants a doctor," Winter said, fighting his restive horse. Then to Shem, "Don't worry. One will be by directly."

To the cackle of more merriment and like a flock of ravens taking flight, Winter and his men left that place . . . and Shem Pollard's dying eyes watched them go.

Chapter Fifteen

"Edward Cope, be damned to ye for a scoundrel," Sir Richard Owen said. "You tried to drive me away from my dinosaur, but you failed, and now the law will deal with you."

"If there's a scoundrel here, it's you," Cope said. "The lizard is not yours, it belongs to the world. What a pity a man so talented as you should be so dastardly and odious."

"And a pity that you are such a vile schemer, a disgrace to the British Museum that funds your shameful deeds," Owen said.

"If you boys don't simmer down right quick, the law will deal with both of you," Texas Ranger Tim Adams said. He pointed to the others in Owen's party. "Were you all shooting?"

"I must confess that we all were," a tall, overweight man with an impressive beard said.

"Identify yourself," Adams said.

"My name is Professor Othniel Charles Marsh of Yale." He turned to the man on his right. "And this is Professor Edwin Harcourt, also of Yale."

"And you, ma'am?" Adams said to the handsome woman.

At that moment Red Ryan decided that her eyebrows were just fine, her abundant, glossy chestnut hair finer, and the beautifully sculpted curves of her body finest of all.

"My name is Blanche Carter," the woman said.

The ranger smiled. "Of Yale?"

"No, of New York City."

"Are you mixed up in this Bone War, Miss Carter?" Owen said.

"No, she's not! A woman doesn't have the mental capacity to be a paleontologist," Owen said. "The profession hasn't sunk quite that low." He glared at Cope. "Yet."

"I drive *Aurora*, the land ship," Blanche said, ignoring the man's remark. "The army was to meet my father, the inventor, and I in Fredericksburg to do some test runs but postponed until next month. Then Papa took ill and is confined to bed. Sir Richard asked if he and his colleagues could rent the ship for a trip north. I readily agreed, because *Aurora* needs her engine tested and Professor Owen's terms were most generous."

"But you took part in the shooting," Adams said.

"Of course, Miss Carter took part in the shooting," Hannah Huckabee said. She stood beside Blanche, her hands on her hips and a frown on her pretty face. "Desperate men were firing at her and she had the right to defend herself." She gave her name to Blanche and then said, "Would you teach me how to drive *Aurora*? She's the Roman goddess of the dawn, isn't she?"

"Yes, because the land ship marks the dawn of modern, steam-powered transportation . . . and of course I'll teach you to drive her."

Hannah let out a little squeal of delight and said, "Oh, thank you. How fast do you think she can go?"

"I haven't given her full throttle yet, but I think on level ground *Aurora* will be as speedy as a cannon-balling locomotive," Blanche said.

"Then we must give her full throttle," Hannah said. "And soon."

"After we find and catalog the terrible dinosaur, not before," Owen said.

"You won't find it," Cope said. "I'll find it and I'll find all the other lizards in Texas and be damned to ye for a fraud and a trickster."

"Dinosaurs. Damn you, Cope, I gave them a name. A giant lizard is now and ever will be a dinosaur . . . dinosaur . . . dinosaur," Owen said.

"Lizard!"

"Dinosaur!"

"Hold on there!" Buttons Muldoon strode between the warring professors and said to Ranger Adams, "I can't wait here any longer. I want to reach Ira Kline's station before dark."

Red Ryan said, "Adams, you already got two prisoners in the coach . . ."

"And a coward," Buttons said.

"Do you plan on adding eight more?" Red said. "If not, what are you going to do with them?"

"If I leave them here, they might start shooting

again, and the prairie could be littered with dead professors," Adams said. The ranger fell silent and after a few moments Buttons said, "Well?"

"I'm studying on it," Adams said. Then, "All right, all of you consider yourself under arrest until we reach Kline's Station. I'll see if I can sort things out there. Miss Carter, fire up that tin can and follow us with Professor Owen and his party. Professor Cope, you and your friends ride ahead of the stage."

"And no funny stuff," Buttons said. "I'm primed and ready to cut loose."

"Miss Huckabee, do you want to ride with me?" Blanche said. "There's a spare seat."

"I'd be delighted," Hannah said, her face glowing. "This will be an adventure indeed."

Owens and his companions stashed their rifles in the land ship and Red Ryan figured that things had finally settled down . . .

. . . but then one of the Mexican prisoners decided to make a run for it and everything went downhill fast.

His name was Juan Perez. He was twenty-five years old, married with three children, and a curandero, or healer, by trade. He had failed to bring the good-luck Madonna to his village and she now rode in disgrace at the rear of the godless gringo stage. From the window of the coach, he'd heard shooting and then watched graybeards in black frock coats gather in heated discussion. Juan, who spoke no English, knew it was about him . . . whether to execute him or not.

Men in black frock coats always meant trouble, and he knew now that stealing a Madonna from a church was a serious offense, one that even God might have a problem forgiving.

Juan told his fears to his friend Roberto, the carpenter, and said they must make a run for it while the frock coats were still talking. But Roberto was feeling ill, and he was very afraid of the ranger with his pistol and rifle and said he would not go and he said that Juan should not go either but remain in the coach.

But Juan did not listen. The gringo in the coach and the strange little yellow man did not understand what had been said, but the Apache girl did, and she held Juan's arm and tried to hold him back, uttering some kind of warning in her own tongue. But Juan knew now was the time to make a run for it, and he broke free of the girl's hand and opened the door. He leaped onto grass that was warm under his feet and ran.

"*Alto, o disparare!*" Texas Ranger Tim Adams yelled, his blue, long-barreled Colt up and ready.

Halt, or I'll shoot!

Juan Perez kept running, the sound of his breathing in his ears, his eyes on the bouncing horizon where the way back to his village and freedom lay.

"*Alto!*"

Adams had leveled his revolver, holding it in both hands for a shot at distance.

But Juan kept on going. He was a fine runner, the

fastest runner in his village . . . and he was seconds from death.

Red Ryan saw the danger and pushed a startled professor aside. He jerked the reins from the man's hand and mounted his horse. Red kicked the surprised animal into a gallop and went after the fleeing Mexican.

"Adams, no!" he yelled. "Don't shoot!"

Red swung himself between the ranger and the running Mexican, half expecting a bullet in the back. It never came. As Juan Perez faltered, Red's mount, a leggy American mare, hit her stride. The big horse closed the distance rapidly, and when Red judged the timing was right, he threw himself out of the flat English saddle and landed squarely on top of the fugitive. Both men hit the grass hard and, after the initial shock of their collision wore off, sprang to their feet.

Juan Perez was small and thin, but he was game.

The Mexican swung a looping right at Red's chin. Wrong move. Red Ryan had spent his early years as a traveling booth fighter, taking on all comers, and he'd learned the pugilist's trade well. He slipped the wild right, stepped inside, and unloaded a left to Juan's chin, followed by a straight right. The little man dropped to the ground, moaned once, and lay still.

Red looked down at the unconscious Mexican, shook his head, and said, "Better dusting your pants than getting shot, I reckon."

Ranger Adams stepped to Red's side, holding a plug hat. "Here, this is yours," he said. "It blew off."

Red turned the hat around in his hands and smiled. "No holes. I guess you didn't shoot it off, huh?"

"I could've blown your fool head off, Ryan, not your hat," Adams said. "That was a dangerous play. Don't ever pull a prank like that again, you hear?"

"The Mexican is your prisoner, but he's also a passenger of the Abe Patterson and Son Stage and Express Company, and I am its representative," Red said. "It is therefore my duty to ensure this man's safety and well-being until he reaches the depot in Austin."

He kneeled beside the Mexican and slapped him lightly on the cheek. "Wake up," he said. He looked up at Adams. "Would you have shot him?"

"Yes, after a fair warning I would've killed him as a fleeing felon," Adams said.

"Hard, ranger, almighty hard," Red said.

"I'm in a hard business," Adams said.

Hannah Huckabee looked down at Perez, her face concerned. "How is he?" she said.

"He's a little groggy, but he's coming to and he'll be fine," Red said. "I didn't hit him too hard."

"You did a noble thing, Red," Hannah said.

Red smiled. "Nice to hear you say it."

Hannah frowned at Adams. "You had no need to shoot him."

"I didn't shoot him," the ranger said.

"But not for the want of trying," Hannah said.

"Adams has a job to do, Hannah," Red said. Then echoing the ranger's own words, "He's in a hard, unforgiving business."

He helped the dizzy Mexican to his feet, and the ranger grabbed the man's hands. Both were bruised.

"Slipped his cuffs," he said. He shook his head. "Big wrists but small hands. I should've noticed that."

Adams returned the Mexican to the stage, and Buttons, in the highest state of agitation, was waiting for him. "Can we leave now?" he said to the ranger. "Or are you and my shotgun guard planning on a few more grandstand plays?"

"As soon as I tighten this man's manacles, we can leave," Adams said. He tossed Perez into the stage and chained him up again. He looked at John Latimer and said, "You could have stopped him."

"I was about to warn him not to make a run for it, but the Apache girl did it for me," Latimer said.

"You might have stopped him. You didn't even try," Adams said.

Mr. Chang said, "Mexican man very fast. Surprise us all."

"And besides, it wasn't our job," Latimer said.

"From what I've heard, it seems you think that nothing is your job, mister," Ranger Adams said.

Chapter Sixteen

Under a sky ablaze with stars, the side lamps were lit on the Patterson stage when Kline's Station came in sight across the darkening prairie.

Professor Edward Cope and his three colleagues were already dismounted, talking to short, stocky Ira Kline when the stage jangled into the courtyard.

Buttons halted the team and looked around and when Kline stepped toward him, he said, "You've been through it, Ira."

The man nodded, his blue eyes suddenly clouded with remembered violence. "Apaches burned down my barn, my smokehouse, and ran off my stock. Buttons, I don't have a fresh team for you." He nodded to Red Ryan. "How you doing, Red? It's been a while."

"I'm just fine, Ira." He looked at the bullet pockmarks all over the adobe cabin. "Stood the Apaches off for quite a spell, huh?"

"Yeah, me and my wife and my son. We fit them for three days before cavalry from Fort Concho arrived. We'd three rounds for the Winchesters and six in my revolver by then. After all that shooting, maybe we winged one Apache, but I don't know."

"Abby and young Ben all right?" Buttons said.

"Yeah. Benjamin got scratched by an arrow, but he's fine. Abby is taking it hard though, wants to go back east to live with her sister well away from Apaches." Kline shrugged. "We'll see."

"Got a full house for you, Ira," Buttons said. "Five in the coach, one of them an Apache girl, and another four you've already met. Five more are on their way in some kind of steam contraption, two of them ladies."

"And you also have me, Mr. Kline," Adams touched his hat. "Texas Ranger Tim Adams."

"You're all welcome," Kline said. "I have bacon and beans, cornbread, and hot tea if that's to your taste. And maybe the ladies you're bringing can whip us up some bear sign."

Buttons shook his head. "I don't think they're those kind of ladies, Ira."

The man smiled. "Well, then hopefully I can persuade my Abby to make us a batch."

"There's treachery afoot, mark my words," Professor Edward Drinker Cope said. "They should have been here a full two hours ago." He shook his head. "I smell a rat."

Red Ryan ate the last forkful of beans on his plate and dabbed his mouth with a blue and white checkered napkin. "Seems like," he said.

"Maybe that steam carriage thing exploded," Buttons

Muldoon said. "I always said that it was a dangerous contraption."

"When did you always say that, Buttons?" Red said.

"Well, I don't know exactly when. Plenty of times."

"I assure you, the machine did not blow up," Cope said. "Sir Richard Owen is involved, and when he's involved, three of his mistresses—perfidy, deceit, and deception—walk hand in hand with him. The man is a scoundrel of the first order."

"You sound mighty sure about that, Professor," Tim Adams said.

"And I am sure. Ten miles north of where we forded the San Saba is a terrible lizard, or as Owen, in his abysmal ignorance calls it, a dinosaur. That is why my colleagues and I were in hot pursuit of the bounder."

"Shooting at him, you mean," Ranger Tim Adams said.

"Warning shots, that was all, just warning shots." Cope removed a fragment of corn bread from the lapel of his frock coat and said, "Do you know what it means if Owen digs up that lizard? Have you any idea of the great loss to science it will be? No? Then I'll tell you. Will the lizard end up in a museum or an institute of higher learning like Yale? I say, no sir! Not a chance."

That last was loud and accompanied by a fist-pounding on the table that made Buttons jump and spill hot tea over the front of his shirt.

"Damn it all, Professor, there are lizards all over Texas," Buttons said. "There's horny lizards, spiny lizards, desert lizards, canyon lizards . . . hell, I could round you up a hundred in a day and put 'em in a sack for you to take back to Yale or wherever you want."

"But they're not terrible lizards," Cope said. "Mr. Muldoon, I'm talking about the skeletons of monsters millions of years old, some of them as large as your coach and horses combined."

Buttons whistled through his teeth. "Big lizard, for sure."

"Professor, why don't you just let Owen find the big lizard?" Red said. "End this Bone War before somebody gets hurt."

"I'll tell you why, sir," Cope said. "Because the thunder lizard will end up in Owen's personal collection, locked away from the world of science. And worse, oh, much, much worse, he'll assemble it wrong, the hamhanded knave."

"You mean, put the skeleton's bones in the wrong place?" Red said.

"Yes, that's exactly what I mean. Everybody knows that the giant lizards crawled through the primordial swamps on their bellies, dragging their tails through the muck and mire, and that's how they should be put together. But high-and-mighty Sir Richard Owen says that his dinosaurs stood upright and that some of them were fast and nimble hunters." Cope shook his head. "The fool, the unspeakably misguided fool." He slammed his hand on the table again. "My mind is made up. I'm going after him and putting an end to his perfidiousness. I will take possession of the lizard before he makes arrangements to abscond with it, the villain."

"No, you're not," Ranger Adams said. "There will

be no more shooting from you and your friends. As Mr. Ryan said, somebody is going to end up with a bullet in him."

"Then I'll leave my rifle behind," Cope said. "If I need must, I'll use my bare hands on a rogue masquerading as a man of science."

"And if that happens, I'll charge you with assault," Adams said. "There will be no more violent encounters between you and Owen, and that is final. If need be, I'll arrest the whole damned lot of you, and Yale will be missing a bunch of professors for a year or two."

"I'll go look for them," Red Ryan said, standing. "I'll need to borrow your horse, Professor Cope."

"You've no call to take a hand in this game, Ryan," Adams said.

"Yes, I do, I've got a stake in it," Red said. "Miss Hannah Huckabee is a passenger of the Abe Patterson and Son Stage and Express Company, and if she is harmed in any way, I will be held responsible. Her safety is my concern, and that makes me the obvious choice to go look for her." He glared at Cope. "Do you have any objections?"

"None. But report back to me on whatever mischief Sir Richard Owen has gotten up to," the professor said.

"Damn it all, Red, it's pitch black out there," Buttons said. "You'll get lost."

"I'll follow the stage tracks. They'll guide me even in the dark."

Adams said, "Well, it's free country and I can't stop you. We'll wait here at the station until noon,

Ryan. Bring those pilgrims back here . . . at gunpoint if necessary."

"Owen and his cohorts have picks and spades with them, and it wouldn't surprise me if they have some kind of steam shovel hidden in their infernal machine," Cope said. "Confiscate all of it."

Red smiled. "I'll see what I can do."

Then, a surprise question that left Red without an answer . . .

"Mr. Ryan, may I come with you?" John Latimer said.

Buttons regained his tongue faster than Red. "Hell, you heard what I said, it's dark and scary out there. The prairie at night is no place for a coward."

Latimer, his brown eyes earnest, ignored that and said, "Hannah may have lost her regard for me, but I still love her." He shrugged. "Mr. Ryan, I'm concerned about her, and that's the way of it. I would really appreciate it if you'd let me help find her."

Red gave Adams a questioning look.

The ranger shrugged and said, his bemused smile slight, "Hell, I don't know. It's your call, Ryan."

"No, Red, don't do it," Buttons said. "You get into some kind of shooting scrape out there with them eggheads, Latimer will let you down. He'll turn tail and light a shuck. You know he will."

Red shook his head. "No, Latimer, I don't think—"

"I'm begging you, Mr. Ryan. And I'm not a man who begs easily. Let me go along with you."

"He's a coward, Red," Buttons said, his alarmed voice ringing a warning note. "You can't trust him."

Ranger Adams had talked with Colonel Grierson at

Fort Concho and was aware of Captain Latimer's Mark of Cain and, like Buttons Muldoon, cowardice was a concept alien to him. But there was something about the man that impressed him that night, his obvious sincerity maybe . . . or the fact that his cowardice was an accusation. It had not yet been proved.

Adams said, "Sometimes a man deserves another chance to redeem himself. I've seen it happen a time or two, a man turns and runs at the first sight of danger, but the next day leads the charge. I say let Latimer ride with you, Ryan."

And then yet another surprise, this time from Abby Kline. She pointed at Latimer and said, "That man needs a second chance. There's so much pain in his eyes I can hardly bear to look at him." She turned to Buttons and her voice rose. "And as for you, sir, you are a *nudnick.*"

Buttons was taken aback. "A what?"

Ira Kline laughed. "An irritating, annoying person, Buttons. And Abby means it. When my wife really means a thing, she says it in Yiddish."

As Buttons spluttered his affront, Red Ryan made up his mind.

"Cope, now I need two horses," he said. "Latimer is nobody's prisoner, and until we reach New Orleans, I guess he can do as he pleases."

The professor and his colleagues were confused by what had passed, believing that Latimer was just another passenger, but Cope readily agreed to the Englishman accompanying Red. "Two of us will ride in the stage, if need be. Just make sure you end Sir Richard Owen's depredations. He's a robber knight if ever there was one. Unhorse him with your lance of justice, Mr. Ryan. Lay the bounder low."

Red Ryan and John Latimer saddled their horses and were about to mount when Buttons Muldoon came out of the cabin. He hesitated for a few moments, but when Latimer swung into the saddle he stepped beside him and held up his Colt, the cartridge belt wrapped around the holster.

"Here, Latimer," he said, "you may need this. I will send no man out into the wilderness unarmed."

Latimer's eyes asked Red a question.

"Take it, Latimer," he said. "I don't think you'll have any need for it, but you never know."

"Thank you, Mr. Muldoon," Latimer said. "I'm much obliged."

Buttons harrumphed and dug at the ground with the toe of his boot before he finally managed, "I set store by that hog leg. Make sure nothin' happens to it, hear?"

Latimer said. "I'll take good care of it, I promise."

"Then see you do," Buttons said. "Sometimes a coward—"

"Buttons," Red said.

"What?"

"Don't be a *nudnick*."

Chapter Seventeen

Neither Red Ryan nor John Latimer had anything to say to one another, and they rode north in silence, following the coach tracks that were easily discernible in the opalescent light of a waxing moon. Once Red spotted what he thought was the steam wagon, but it turned out to be an upthrust shelf of limestone bedrock. Sir Richard Owen would later write in *The New York Times* that "the rock in this area of Texas is Cretaceous and the most fossiliferous in the state. Tracks of dinosaurs appear in many places and remains of terrestrial, aquatic, and flying reptiles have been collected by myself and lesser paleontologists."

Red didn't know it then, but he'd just ridden into a Bone War battlefield.

After two hours of riding John Latimer, a far-seeing man, said, "Lights ahead."

Red nodded. "I see them. Looks like oil lamps to me."

"Then we've found them," Latimer said.

"Looks like," Red said. He drew rein, and his eyes probed the darkness. After a while, he said, "All right, we ride in easy. And keep your hand away from the iron Buttons gave you."

Latimer smiled. "You don't trust those learned professors, Mr. Ryan?"

"I don't trust Hannah Huckabee," Red said. "She's the only one that knows how to use a gun." Then, "You still sweet on her, Latimer?"

"I love her. I supposed that just by being here I had already answered that question."

"She doesn't speak to you," Red said. "She doesn't even look in your direction."

"She can't love a coward."

"Are you really a coward, Latimer?"

"I don't think so."

"Say yes or no."

"No. I'm not a coward. If Custer had fled the Little Big Horn battle, would you have thought him a coward?"

"And left his men to die? Yeah, I guess I would."

Latimer said, "I didn't ride away and leave my men to die. When I fled the field, my lancers were already dead. I engaged the Afghan enemy with my revolver but could not save my men."

Red shook his head. "Hell, Latimer, I don't know what you are. Come to that, I don't even know what I am. I might've done the same thing." Then, a spontaneous gesture he could not later explain, he put his hand on Latimer's shoulder. "Let's ride," he said.

At a steady canter, the two men covered ground, and when they were within hailing distance, Red drew rein again and yelled, "Hello, the camp."

He knew the professors wouldn't understand why

the hell he called out before riding closer, but Hannah might, and indeed it was her who answered.

"Come right ahead," she said. Then, "Is that Red Ryan?"

"Yup, me and John Latimer."

A silence. And then a man's irritated voice from the gloom. "My watch is stopped. What time is it, Mr. Ryan?"

"About two in the morning," Red said, kneeing his horse into motion. Beside him Latimer rode straight in the saddle like a soldier and seemed tense.

"Where did the time go?" the man in the darkness said.

"You burned it all," Red said.

The huge steam wagon was parked a distance from the campsite where a fire flickered and a white tent had been set up, as though Owen had decided to stay a spell. In the fire glow, Red made out the other two professors and Hannah Huckabee and Blanche Carter, the women looking prettier than they had a right to be in this wilderness.

Sir Richard Owen, a trowel in his hand, stepped forward as Red dismounted. "Coffee in the pot if you'd care to make a trial of it," he said. Then, his bearded face alight, "I found it, Ryan. I found the terrible dinosaur just where I was told it would be."

"Who told you?" Red said.

"The dinosaur's location has been rumored for quite some time," Owen said. "As far as I know, the first sighting was made by buffalo hunters and then a few months ago a couple of cowboys reported to the authorities in Austin that they saw a gigantic skeleton near the San Saba river. Their account was published in the *Austin Telegraph* newspaper and was picked up by all the eastern papers, and as soon as I read about it, I immediately fitted out an expedition." Owen's mouth tightened. "Then that charlatan Edward Cope got wind of my plans and tried to beat me to it."

Red stepped to the fire and availed himself of Owen's invitation, pouring coffee for himself and Latimer.

Hannah watched the Englishman, her beautiful eyes glittering in the firelight. She was pale under her tan and appeared to lean on Blanche for support.

Red tried his coffee, welcome at this hour of the night when sleep was not an option, and said, "Well, where is the skeleton now, Professor?"

"In the tent," Owen said. "Or at least its head is. Bring your coffee and come see. You too, Latimer, it's a sight you can tell your grandchildren about. No, wait, what is today's date?"

Blanche said, "August tenth."

Owen smiled. "Ah yes, August tenth in the year of our Lord eighteen hundred and eighty-three. A date for us all to remember." He picked up the oil lamp at his feet. "Now follow me and prepare yourself to be amazed."

The canvas tent was large enough to accommodate the three tall men who stepped inside. Professor Owen held his lamp just above ground level and said, "Behold, gentlemen, many millions of years old, but soon to be a wonder of our modern age."

Red was puzzled. "Professor," he said, "I don't know if you've noticed, but that's a rock."

Owen smiled, most of his face in shadow. "Look closer, my friend."

Red did as he was told, then said, "It's a rock. A big rock, but still a rock."

"It's much more than a rock or a boulder or whatever geological object you wish to call it," Owen said. He took a piece of white chalk from his pocket, and his knees creaking, squatted down beside his discovery. His chalk moved across the rock. "There, see, the outline of the skull. And here, the mouth." The chalk scraped again. "The teeth. Do you see the teeth? Each of them three inches long. Look, gentlemen, look with your eyes and your imagination. See the monster as it was, a savage giant that once reigned as the emperor of the earth."

The chalk worked a miracle, and now Red Ryan saw, not a chunk of bedrock, but a massive skull. And so did Latimer. "My God, Professor Owen," the Englishman said, "what kind of animal was that? A dragon?"

"Of a sort," Owen said. "It was a flesh-eating dinosaur, a terrifying predator that ripped its prey apart and bolted down the steaming, bloody meat in chunks the size of beer barrels."

Latimer shuddered, or pretended to. "I wouldn't like to see that thing crawling toward me."

"The creature didn't crawl," Owen said. "It ran on legs the size of tree trunks and was fast as a racehorse."

A prairie wind sprang up, and the tent canvas flapped with a sound like wings. The oil lamp guttered and cast moving shadows. Owen grinned, showing his teeth. "The rest of the monster is still under the ground. I'll return soon to free him from his ancient grave."

The dancing lamplight glowed yellow in the massive skull's visible eye socket, bringing it life, as though the great animal had just devoured its prey and had lain down to take a sleep. Red imagined gobs of quivering flesh stuck between the sickle teeth that would soon decay and stink like rotten meat. Had this monster been one of God's creatures or had it been created in hell?

Suddenly Red felt that the tent was closing in on him, and he found the air thick and fetid and hard to breathe. He opened the flap and stepped outside into the clean darkness.

After a few minutes, Latimer joined him.

"Ancient death is still death," the man said. "That thing gives me the shivers."

Red nodded. "And me too. Owen thinks it's a thing of beauty."

"He's a scientist. Scientists don't think like the rest of us mere mortals."

"We'll move these people out at first light. Adams may still charge them," Red said. "Texas Rangers don't think like the rest of us, either."

"I get the impression that he's likely going to charge them with something," Latimer said.

"Disturbing the peace probably," Red said. "A judge in Austin will fine them two dollars each, warn them to be on their best behavior in future, and that will be the end of it."

"I don't suppose he'll throw four learned Yale professors and a woman into jail," Latimer said.

"Not if he wants to remain a judge, he won't," Red said.

Latimer nodded, but he was looking beyond Red to Hannah Huckabee. He stepped around Red and said, "Hannah, can we talk?"

"John, we have nothing to say to each other," the woman answered.

"There's a lot standing between us that's unsaid. Maybe it's time to say it."

"John, we were lovers once in another time and place," Hannah said. "But we can't pick up the pieces and go on, after . . . after what happened."

"You still think I'm a coward."

"John, brave men died that day in India, your men. You chose not to die with them. What does that make you?"

"It doesn't make me a coward, Hannah. Yes, they were brave, but they were also foolish," Latimer said. "I stood my ground for as long as I could, and you're right, I watched them die. I saw no point in throwing myself on Afghan knives to die with them."

Hannah shook her head. "You were charged with cowardice in the face of the enemy, John. That's what your fellow soldiers thought of your actions that day, and I can only agree with them. All that's left for you now is to do the honorable thing and face your court-martial. Just don't expect me to be there when the verdict is read."

"It's been a long day," Blanche Carter said. "Hannah, I think you should get some sleep now."

"Yes, of course, Blanche, we both should," Hannah said.

"Yeah, that's a good idea," Red said. "We'll move out and head back to Kline's Station at dawn." Then to Blanche, "Do you have enough wood to get that . . . whatever it's called . . . to Fredericksburg?"

"I don't know that we're going directly to Fredericksburg," Blanche said. "Though I do badly want to see my ailing father."

"Yes, we are headed to Fredericksburg," Professor Othniel Marsh said. "Sir Richard needs diggers and dynamite, and perhaps we can find both there."

"Then your answer is no, I don't have enough fuel to get us to Fredericksburg," Blanche said. "But I'm certain that Mr. Kline has a good supply of firewood. I'm sure he'll sell us some."

Two hours later as the others slept around the fire, Blanche Carter rose and lay down beside Red. He woke with a start and then smiled. "What are you doing here?" he said. "Not that I'm objecting, mind."

"Nothing. It's just that it's been a while since I slept beside a handsome man," Blanche said. "Or any kind of man."

"Given where we are, not much we can do about it," Red said.

"I know," Blanche said. "You smell of woodsmoke, horses, and leather, Mr. Ryan, a good man-smell. For tonight at least, that's all I need."

Red closed his eyes. "Enjoy," he said.

"I already am enjoying," Blanche said, her head on his buckskinned shoulder.

When Red woke up with the dawn light, Blanche Carter was gone, and he smiled to himself in the gloom, thinking that indeed, there was a first time for everything.

Chapter Eighteen

"That Professor Cope feller was all for waiting to see if Professor Owen found the big lizard you were all talking about," Ira Kline said to Red. "But your driver and the Texas Ranger decided to push on to Fredericksburg."

"Mr. Ryan, I sense Cope's perfidy at work here," Sir Richard Owen said. "He knows if I'm to remove the dinosaur I'll need pick-and-shovel laborers and he'll try to turn the town against me."

"Begging your pardon, Professor," Kline said, "but that wasn't the reason. Last night one of them Mexican prisoners of the ranger's took sick and was in a bad way. He needs a doctor, and that's why they decided to head for Fritztown without delay."

"Cope will take advantage of that," Owen said. "He'll take advantage, mark my words. There's treachery afoot."

Kline smiled. "Professor Cope and the other professors said they were already saddle sore, so they insisted on riding in the stage. Then Buttons said he'd have to charge them full fare from Fort Concho, and there was a big argument, but Buttons won in the end because them professors didn't want nothing to do with climbing on horses again."

Then, his face changing, Kline said, "What in God's name is that noise?"

The roaring, hissing, clanking racket became louder, and Red said above the din, "It's the steam wagon firing up, Ira."

"The lady took half of my woodpile," Kline said, yelling. "And she said that will only get her as far as Fredericksburg."

"And that's why it will never replace the horse," Red said, shouting directly into Kline's ear.

After a few minutes the sound settled down to a steady thump-thump-thump of pistons and the hiss of escaping steam. Blanche Carter stepped into the cabin and said, "We're all ready to go, Professor Owen."

Red thought the woman looked wonderful that morning. Her pith helmet with its goggles was tipped back on her chestnut hair and the black smudge of soot on her right cheekbone only added to her charm. Red smiled, glad he'd slept with her.

"I'm ready," Owen said. "Professors Marsh and Harcourt, are you ready to board *Aurora?*"

Harcourt, a slender man with striking hazel eyes, smiled. "I look forward to seeing Professor Cope's face when we tell him we found the dinosaur."

"And a carnivore at that," Professor Marsh said. "In nature there are many herbivores but few meat-eaters. We were very lucky."

Owen nodded. "That's what Cope lacks . . . luck. He's devious and crafty and treacherous but unlucky."

He smiled. "I've even heard it said that he's unlucky in love, but I don't want to speculate on that subject."

The ensuing laughter accompanied the professors out of the cabin door, where Hannah Huckabee stood close to the throbbing steam wagon. She held a half-eaten beef sandwich, forced on her by Abby Kline, who'd declared her "too thin by at least twenty pounds."

"All aboard!" Blanche Carter yelled.

Hannah bolted what was left of her sandwich, and still chewing, she climbed into the steam wagon beside Blanche, who worked levers and got *Aurora* rolling. Red stepped into the saddle and took up a position at the rear of the machine. The wagon lurched forward and gathered speed, smoke belching from its exhaust pipes. With their tall son between them, Ira and Abby Kline stood outside the cabin and watched them leave. "Good luck," Abby called out. "Good luck, everybody."

Red waved his farewell, ahead of him a vast expanse of grassland that seemed to have no beginning and no end. The sun had risen higher in the sky, and the heat of the morning was making itself felt.

Three hours later, the *Aurora* forced its way through underbrush that grew around the pecan, oak, and cedar on the north bank of the San Saba River and, despite the presence of rapids, forded its shallows without difficulty.

"Miles of good grass ahead of us," Blanche yelled to Hannah above the racket of the engine. "*Aurora* is running well."

"This is quite an experience," Hannah said. "So different from riding in the stage."

"Better?" Blanche said.

"No, not better, just different."

"*Aurora* is the future, Hannah."

"I can't make up my mind if that's a good thing or bad."

"Both," Blanche said. "I imagine it's both."

A few minutes later, borne on a warm south wind, came the stench of death.

"My God, what happened here?" Sir Richard Owen said. He stared at the fat black flies buzzing round the faces of the two dead men and looked as though he wanted to be sick. Professor Harcourt had already done that, and Professor Marsh stood apart and nervously tugged at his beard. John Latimer had seen violent death before and seemed unmoved.

"Looks like they got into a fight and killed each other," Red Ryan said.

"What did they fight about?" Owen said.

"What do men usually fight about? Women, money, a casual insult . . . who knows?"

Owen ordered the women back, but Hannah Huckabee stepped up and said, "I've seen dead men in the past, and I've seen them covered in flies and worse." Then to Red, "There were other riders here."

"Saw that," Red said. "Judging by the tracks, at least a dozen booted men, and I'd say they stood around and watched these two fight it out."

"But . . . but who would do such a thing?" Owen said.

Red's smile was grim. "Plenty of renegades in this

part of Texas, but the name Dave Winter springs to mind. He's known to have recently moved north from the border country with a bunch of hard cases, and that came as bad news to just about everybody."

"Is he a bandit?" Professor Harcourt asked. He seemed nervous.

"Yeah, he's a bandit," Red said. "And he's a man who enjoys killing for the sake of killing. I've heard Winter isn't right in the head, but I don't know the truth of that."

"I hope I never meet him," Harcourt said. "He sounds like a desperate character."

"Uh-huh, he's all of that," Red said.

"The stagecoach must have passed this way, Mr. Ryan," Latimer said.

"Yeah, it did, and close, over in that direction," Red said. He walked about thirty yards from the bodies, turned, waved, and yelled, "The stage tracks are here."

When Red returned, professor Owen said, "Do you think the ranger saw the bodies?"

"He sure as hell must have smelled them," Red said.

"Then why didn't he stop and bury them?" Owen said. "After all, he's an officer of the law."

Red's eyes never left the grass around and ahead of him. "I guess he figured he'd let the coyotes play undertaker," he said. He walked off a few yards, took a knee, and plucked some blades of grass and then examined them closely. "Or maybe he got shot."

"Shot?" Hannah Huckabee said.

"Look," Red said, taking the woman's hand. He dropped the grass into Hannah's palm and said,

"That rust-colored stain you see is dried blood, and there's a lot of it around. Buttons would have bled into the coach and so would the passengers. The only one who could've spilled his blood over the grass was Tim Adams."

"Or maybe he or Buttons shot somebody else," Hannah said. "That could be."

"Yeah, it could be," Red allowed. "But to me, it just doesn't stack up that way. The horse tracks tell the tale. When the stage passed this way, the team was in a flat-out gallop. Buttons never runs his horses that hard, unless he's in trouble. He was being chased."

"Highwaymen?" John Latimer said. He'd just joined them and already Hannah looked uncomfortable to be around him.

"If you mean road agents, then yes, it could be," Red said. "But in this neck of the woods I'm willing to guess that Dave Winter has a hand in it. Let's go talk it over with Blanche Carter and the professors."

Chapter Nineteen

"Then we must turn back, Mr. Ryan," Sir Robert Owen said. "I am not lacking in courage, and neither are my colleagues, but we're hardly of an age to fight bandits and gunmen."

"I'm aware of that," Red Ryan said. "And as a representative of the Abe Patterson and Son Stage and Express Company, I am duty bound to do all I can to safeguard my driver and my passengers."

"Then what do you suggest?" Owen said. He seemed tense.

"I need to think this through," Red said. "I was going to keep this to myself for a while, but you all might as well know. The way I read the tracks, a bunch of riders chased the stage and shot Tim Adams out of the saddle. They probably caught up with Buttons south of here, and he and the passengers are captives."

"Or dead," Owens said.

"Depending on who did the chasing, that's a real possibility," Red said.

"What about *Aurora*?" Blanche Carter said. "She's

fast, and we can use her to track down the attackers, whoever they were."

"If it is Winter and his bunch, they'd hear that pile of metal coming from a mile away and light a shuck," Red said. "And they might kill Buttons and the passengers out of spite before they left."

"They'll have Dahteste," Hannah said. "I don't want any harm to come to her."

Red didn't even pretend to be optimistic. "If it's Winter, then she's fallen in with a bad crowd," he said. Hannah's stricken face said it all, and he added quickly, "I think she'll be all right."

Hannah knew it was threadbare consolation, and she said nothing.

Red took himself off, hunkered down, and built a cigarette. He smoked that one and another and then spoke into the uneasy silence that surrounded Owen and his professors.

"Come sundown, I'll scout ahead in the dark and see what I can see," he said. "There's a chance that the bandits, whoever they were, are camped close by and we can attempt a rescue. But if I'm not back by first light, all of you pile into that there heap of scrap iron and head back to Ira Kline's place."

"No, that's not going to happen," Hannah said. "If you're not back by dawn, we'll come looking for you."

"Count me in on that, Red," Blanche said.

"If the ladies are so determined, then I suppose that goes for the rest of us," Owen said. He turned to his colleagues. "Does that set well with you gentlemen?"

"I doubt that I'll do much good, but count me in, Sir Richard," Professor Harcourt said.

"Professor Marsh?" Owen said.

"I'm a bit too old for all these adventures, but I'll join you," Marsh said, looking unhappy. "I suppose we owe it to Professor Cope and his colleagues to find them."

"Rescue them, you mean, Professor Marsh," Owen said.

"Yes, of course, liberate them from their captors. That's what I meant," Marsh said.

"Then it's decided," Hannah said. "We'll wait here until dawn."

"No one asked me," John Latimer said.

"No, John, no one did," Hannah said. She turned her back on him on the pretense of watching Blanche Carter tinker with the steam engine.

Red stepped into the silence that followed and helped the distressed Latimer save face. "I'm sure grateful to every one of you for your help," he said. "Just don't take any undue risks. As I said already, at the first sign of trouble, hightail it for the Kline place." He dropped his voice, making sure they knew the gravity of the situation. "Dave Winter and his gunmen are not the kind of rannies you want to face off against. And Hannah, that also goes for you."

The woman said, "The wind is from the north. I wish I had my balloon and a few bombs."

Red grinned. "If I know Winter, he'd shoot you out of the sky, and besides, one of your bombs might blow up the stage and everyone in it."

Hannah made a face. "Please, take care."

Red nodded. "On this ride, I plan to be nothing but careful."

* * *

Red Ryan rode into a glowering dusk. From horizon to horizon the sky looked like a sheet of lead and to the south lightning shimmered. There was a sharpness to the smell of the air, an ozone tang that heralded the thunderstorm to come, and here on the plains it would come with sledgehammers. Red's slicker was stashed in the coach, as was his shotgun, and he berated himself for a considerable lack of foresight.

His eyes on the empty land ahead of him, the Colt on Red's hip gave him little reassurance. If he accidentally rode in on Dave Winter and his boys, they'd chop him into little pieces and feed him to the coyotes.

The trouble was that he had no plan of action, just a vague notion to scout the outlaw location, study on it for a spell, and then come up with something brilliant.

But Red knew that wasn't about to happen. He was smart enough, sure, but wasn't known for his brilliance. After he reported back to the others, maybe those Yale professors would hatch a foolproof plan. They were clever, right? Must be if they worked in a university.

Lulled somewhat by that thought and the steady fall of the American mare's hooves on the grass, Red took his eyes off the menacing sky and thought about Blanche Carter. She was a fine-looking woman and no mistake, she'd slept with him. Well, slept beside him, which was almost the same thing. Maybe when they got to Fredericksburg they might . . .

What the hell was that?

It sounded like a groan, and it came from ahead of him.

Red drew rein, suddenly worried that in the darkness he'd been riding around in circles. But as Hannah had said, the wind was out of the north, and he'd kept his back to its chill, so he reassured himself that he was still heading south. The sky flashed a dazzling blue, and distant thunder banged as Red swung out of the saddle and drew his Colt.

There it was again, the sound of a man in considerable hurt. Maybe he was trying to get to his feet and the effort pained him. Maybe he was one of Winter's men. Maybe he . . .

The hell with maybes.

"Who's there?" Red said, two homely words dropping into the immensity of a vast wilderness. Then, "I'm with fifty Texas Rangers here, all well-armed and determined men."

For a moment there was silence.

Then an answering voice came out of the gloom, each halting word rasped with the effort it took to speak.

"Y'all are Red Ryan, the shotgun guard. And ah kinda figured you didn't have a lick of sense. Right about now there probably ain't fifty rangers in the whole of Texas."

The Texan accent was unmistakable, and so was the voice of the man saying it.

"Ranger Adams, is that you?" Red called out.

"Who the hell else would it be? I'm straight ahead of you, Ryan. I'm shot through and through, so don't step on me with them big feet of yours."

"Be like stepping on a wounded rattler, I reckon," Red said.

"You got that right."

Red gathered up the mare's reins and walked forward. After a few paces lightning shimmered, and he made out the still form of a man lying on his back on the grass. Red took a knee beside Adams and saw immediately that the front of the young ranger's shirt was covered in blood.

Adams opened his eyes and said, "Looks bad, huh?"

"I can't see where you were hit," Red said.

"My right shoulder is all smashed up. The bullet went clean through from back to front, but I was able to keep up with the stage for a distance and I even got off a few shots." He managed a wan smile. "Then I got burned across the side of the head, and that knocked me out of the saddle. But I'm not kicking about it. The bullet saved my life, because when Dave Winter galloped past he took one look and figured me for coyote bait."

"How many men does Winter have?" Red said.

"Too many, Ryan. You can't tackle him by yourself, and them professors won't be much help."

Driven by a keening wind, the thunderstorm moved closer and lighting scrawled across the sky like the signature of a demented god. The air was edged and smelled of ozone every time a sizzling bolt splintered the night.

"Ryan, Winter and his boys saw the stage coming

and waited," Adams said. "They didn't talk. There was no palaver, just shooting. I got hit in the first volley, and then we started running, and then I was hit again and what happened after that is almighty hazy."

"Buttons?" Red said, fearing the answer. "What happened to Buttons?"

"I don't know," the ranger said. "The stage was going hell for leather, and that's the last I remember. I can't recollect if the driver was hit or not."

Red nodded. "You're in bad shape, Adams," he said. He shook his head. "Wish I could, but I can't say otherwise."

"I don't need you to tell me what kind of shape I'm in, Ryan. I'm all shot to pieces."

"I'm taking you back to the others," Red said.

"What others?" Adams said. His face was ashen, and he spoke through gritted teeth, obviously in considerable hurt.

"Hannah Huckabee and the professors, those others," Red said.

"My brain isn't working right, Ryan," Adams said. "I thought you meant the stagecoach others."

"I can't blame you none for being confused, Ranger, ventilated the way you are an' all," Red said. "Maybe Owen or one of them other eggheads knows something about doctoring. Fix you right up." Red sighed. "Adams, I have to lift you onto my horse, and it's going to hurt like hell. But there's no other way."

"Then get it done, Ryan," Adams said. Lightning flashed, and thunder roared right after it. "Hell, on that big American hoss, I'll be the tallest lightning rod on the prairie for miles around."

"Yeah, and as if that ain't bad enough, the damned rain has started," Red said. "It never rains but it pours, ain't that the saying? Well, let me get ahold of you. Glad you ain't no bigger'n a nubbin."

When Red lifted him, he figured Adams hurt bad, judging by the ranger's sharp, sudden intakes of breath. But Adams had sand and allowed himself to be manhandled into the saddle without a word of complaint. Red's regard for Texas Rangers in general and Tim Adams in particular went up several notches.

"Hold on now, we got some walking to do," Red said, taking up the reins. "And it's fixing to storm bad."

Adams was slumped over in the saddle, his arms around the horse's neck.

Red watched the sky continually split apart by lightning, while thunder crashed, and the rain fell around him in torrents, drumming on the crown of his plug hat.

He turned his head, and yelled above the tumult, "Adams, all things considered, this ain't a night for a stroll."

But the ranger was unconscious and made no answer.

Chapter Twenty

From the ruined, but partially roofed, officers' quarters, Buttons Muldoon gloomily stared out at the raging thunderstorm and attendant rain that hammered across the old Fort Mason parade ground. Behind him, sitting with their backs to a wall, another eight men were crammed into what had once been a junior officer's modest parlor but was now a rubble-strewn wreck. There were two Mexican peons, Mr. Chang and Professor Edward Drinker Cope of Yale, Professor Thomas Anderson also of Yale, Professor Algernon Makepeace of Oxford, and Professor Oscar Turner of Princeton. All four were battered and bruised after the beatings they'd taken when Dave Winter decided he didn't like highfalutin' professors telling him how outraged they were at his conduct.

The eighth man was a Mexican, their morose guard, a gunman that Dave Winter had referred to as Tijuana. Buttons had heard the name before, and everything he'd heard about its owner was bad. Tijuana was a killer and rapist who, at the age of thirteen, was said to have murdered his farmer parents for their horse, saddle, and fifty-three pesos in savings.

Winter's orders to the man had been to the point: "Tijuana, if one of these sorry-looking clowns tries to escape, shoot him in the belly. Make him feel sorry, huh? But don't shoot them all, at least not yet. I need them to dig for Len Blackburn's buried treasure." And all Tijuana had answered was an unsmiling, "*Sí, señor.*"

The Apache girl had been with Buttons and the others for a short spell, but Winter's men had carried her off, and judging by the roars of drunken laughter now coming from the former adjutant's office where they'd taken her, Dahteste was now dancing with the devil.

Thinking about the girl filled Buttons with despair and a sense of helplessness. He was unarmed, and the Texas Ranger who might have helped was dead, shot out of the saddle by Dave Winter. He turned his head, pretending to look around the lamp-lit room, but as he expected, the Mexican gunman stared right at him. Tijuana had pegged Buttons, short, stocky, and belligerent, as the man most likely to make a move, and he was ready for him.

A streak of forked lightning followed by a peal of thunder seemed to shake the foundations of the room and that's when Buttons saw it . . . a flicker of alarm in the Mexican's black eyes.

Damn it all, it seemed that one of the most feared gunman on the frontier was himself afraid of thunder. Many men who often rode the open prairie had witnessed a lightning strike that killed both a horse and its rider and they had learned to fear thunderstorms. Tijuana could be one of them.

Buttons's nimble brain worked, coming up with a plan, discarding it, coming up with another. The storm was roaring its way north and would soon be directly overhead. He smiled to himself. What he needed was a bolt of lightning and a big bang at the same time . . . so long as it wasn't the big bang of Tijuana's Remington.

For his scheme to succeed, Buttons had to stand by the door and look out as he'd been doing, but he had no way to explain his plot to the others. One of the peons was very sick, but the one who'd tried to run from the ranger was game and he might help if the plan didn't work and everything fell apart. The Celestial he didn't know about, but Mr. Chang was smart enough to realize what his fate would be if he remained a prisoner of Dave Winter. The four professors were out of it. They'd tried to stand up to Dave Winter and paid the price and were too weakened from their beatings to help.

Buttons was aware that what he aimed to do would be dangerous and had only a slim chance of working . . . but it was better than what was facing him . . . no chance at all.

He stared into the relentless, rain-riven darkness and waited for a thunderbolt . . . and waited . . . and waited . . .

Lightning lit up the sky and thunder rumbled, but distant, as though the storm, out of spite, had decided to make a detour around Fort Mason. Buttons turned his head slightly and glanced at Tijuana out of the corner of his eye. The gunman sat with his back to the wall and was as alert as ever. With a pang of disappointment, Buttons saw that the man was riding out the storm just fine.

But a couple of tense minutes later Buttons's big moment finally came.

BOOM!

An explosion of thunder so close that Buttons almost jumped out of his skin. Then, without a moment's hesitation, he let out a high-pitched shriek and fell to the ground, twitching horribly.

Fear spiked at Buttons Muldoon as he lay on the rough wood floor. In a few more seconds he'd be either dead or alive. His fate was in the hands of the gods . . . and how a ruthless Mexican gunman would react. In his later years when he lived on the Mogollon Rim (1923), he'd tell Zane Grey that his life balanced on the head of a pin that night, and that he never wished to face the like again.

Buttons quit twitching and played dead. He heard the measured *chink* . . . *chink* . . . *chink* . . . of Tijuana's spurs as the Mexican crossed the floor. Then the footsteps stopped.

Buttons braced himself. He planned to turn on his left side and then dive for the gunman's legs and bring him down. Uneasy seconds ticked past. He heard the coarse laughter of Winter and his men, and then a girl's scream. He closed his mind to what was happening in the adjutant's office. He had to concentrate on the matter at hand . . . downing the Mexican.

But Tijuana was as smart and wary as a lobo wolf.

He kept his distance and bent from the waist, his Colt in his hands. He pushed the muzzle into the back of Buttons's neck and said, his grin thinning out the words, "Thunder doesn't kill a man. Only the lightning does that. So . . . I'll count to three, one, two, three, understand? If you don't get on your feet in that time, I'll blow your stupid gringo head off. One . . ."

"All right, damn you, I'm moving," Buttons said.

Tijuana, real name Marco Antonio Suarez, laughed . . . and died with that laugh on his lips.

A fieldstone weighing close to thirty pounds that had been used in the original construction of the building crashed into the back of the Mexican's head, wielded by the manacled hands of the peon Juan Perez.

Tijuana fell without a sound and was already dead from a shattered skull when he hit the ground. One of the most deadly and notorious gunmen in the West, a desperado with fifteen kills to his credit, fell to a little Mexican peasant who weighed about a hundred and twenty pounds.

Buttons jumped to his feet and recognized the Mexican, the peon who'd fled from Tim Adams, standing in the middle of the floor, staring down at the man he'd killed.

"Hell, you did good," Buttons grinned. "Little man, you are a mucho hombre."

The Mexican stared at him with blank brown eyes, having no idea what the hell the gringo had just said.

Buttons had no time to explain. He quickly stripped the dead man of his Remington and gunbelt and buckled it around his own waist. He crossed the floor, picked up the Winchester propped against the wall, and then said, "Right, let's get out of here." Sounds of drunken merriment still came from Winter's men as he added, "Hurry . . . Professors, on your feet."

Cope, one eye swollen shut, helped his groaning colleagues stand.

Mr. Chang grinned at Buttons and tapped his temple with a forefinger. "Mr. Muldoon, you very clever man." Then to the peon, "And you very brave."

Before he was thrown into the Patterson coach back at Fort Concho, the Mexican had never seen a Chinaman before, and he backed away, a little afraid of Mr. Chang.

"Mr. Chang, he doesn't know what you said to him, but I think he caught your drift," Buttons said. "Now let's light a shuck."

He herded his charges to the door and led them outside into the fierceness of the storm. As the cartwheeling rain instantly soaked him to the skin, Buttons yelled to Mr. Chang, who had his head bent against the wind, "It ain't a fit night for man nor beast."

Mr. Chang nodded and put his mouth close to Buttons's ear. "Shakespeare say that hundreds of years ago. Like Muldoon, he very wise man."

"Damn right I am," Buttons said, his eyes fixed on the storm-tattered murk ahead of him.

Chapter Twenty-one

The storm had passed, and the night sky showed stars as Red Ryan led his horse into the camp he'd so recently left. Tim Adams was unconscious, and Red lifted him from the saddle and laid him gently on the wet grass before he hollered, "Hello the camp!"

Somehow the professors and the women had managed to erect the tent in the storm, and its sides and roof bulged as people moved around inside. The flap flew open and Sir Richard Cope, fully dressed except for his collar, stepped into the night. He took time to glance at the sky before he said, surprised, "Mr. Ryan, you're back so soon?"

"Yeah, I am, and with Ranger Adams," Red said. "He's shot through and through and in mighty bad shape."

"My God," Owen said, as he finally saw the unconscious man lying on the ground near the animal. "There's blood all over the horse."

"That's the ranger's blood," Red said. "Let's get him into the tent."

Owen was joined by Hannah Huckabee and the others, and they gently carried Adams into the tent.

"Dave Winter shot him and left him for dead," Red said. "Winter and his boys went after the stage, but I don't know if Buttons Muldoon outran them or not. Somehow I doubt it."

Professor Edwin Harcourt said, "Step aside, everybody, let me take a look at the ranger. I've had some medical training. Miss Carter, bring the medical kit from *Aurora*. The rest of you, please clear the tent."

When Red stepped outside, Hannah joined him.

"Red, Mr. Chang is well able to take care of himself, but I'm so worried about Dahteste," the woman said. "If anything happens to her at Dave Winter's hands I'll never forgive myself."

"There's nothing that's your fault, Hannah," Red said. "Men like Winter are a force of nature, they just happen. You can't blame yourself for a thunderstorm or big snows or floods. They just come about and there's not a damn thing you can do about it."

"I brought her here," Hannah said. "I insisted Dahteste leave Fort Concho and come with me."

"And she was glad you did, Hannah," Red said. "When you told her, it was the first time I'd seen her smile."

"Maybe she'll be all right," Hannah said. "Maybe those bandits will treat her right. Tell me she'll be all right, Red."

"I don't think they'll abuse her, Hannah," Red said. "Women are respected in Texas."

"Even Apache women?"

"Sure thing, even Apache women," Red said, his belly in knots.

And not only am I a liar, I'm a damned liar.

When Professor Harcourt came out of the tent, his face was grim.

"Well?" Owen said.

"I've stopped the bleeding, but the damage to Ranger Adams's shoulder is both extensive and serious. I'm afraid he needs a better doctor than I am," Harcourt said.

"Then we must return to Fort Concho forthwith," Owen said.

"Not with the Abe Patterson and Son stage in the hands of outlaws," Red said. "Besides, Fredericksburg is closer, and there's bound to be a doctor there." Red smiled, "Professor Owen, your big lizard can't walk, so it isn't going anywhere."

"It's a dinosaur," Owen said glumly. "And Professor Cope can make it walk . . . just dig it up and walk away with it."

"Professor Cope is with the stage," Red said. "If he's still alive, about now I reckon digging up old bones is the last thing on his mind."

To Red's surprise, Owen looked genuinely concerned. "Mr. Ryan, do you think that Professor Cope and Professors Anderson, Makepeace, and Turner are in real danger?"

"Do you want it straight?" Red said.

"No . . . no, I don't, but tell me anyway," Owen said.

"If I was a betting man, I'd wager the farm that they're already dead."

"Oh, my God," Owen said. "Don't let it be so."

Blanche Carter had been standing close, waiting for a lull in the conversation between Red and Owen, and now she stepped into the silence. "Red, what will you do now?" she said.

"Finish what I started, Blanche. I'll do my shotgun-guard duty as I see it and go after Buttons Muldoon and the fare-paying occupants of the Patterson stage."

"Alone?"

"Seems like. I've got a Texas Ranger who's all shot to pieces, a man with a coward label pinned on him, two women, and three elderly professors to go up against Dave Winter and a dozen of the worst hard cases in Texas." Red shook his head. "In a gunfight we'd last about two seconds."

"Red, you're only one man," Blanche said.

"And a damned good one at that," Red said. "Who knows? That might be enough."

Blanche smiled. "You won't be alone, shotgun guard. I'll be with you."

Red opened his mouth to object, but the woman said, "Before you say no, I want to show you something."

"What?"

"I want to show you *Aurora*'s claws."

Blanche stopped at the tent to pick up an oil lamp. When she came outside again, she said, "Ranger Adams is asleep. That's good, because where there's sleep there's no pain."

"I don't think he'll be able to shoot a rifle off that shoulder for a long time," Red said. "And maybe it will slow his gun hand."

Blanche smiled. "That's a man's way of looking at it, I suppose."

The thunderstorm now a memory, Red and the woman walked to the steam wagon under a canopy of stars, and the night air smelled fresh and clean, washed by the rain. A fitted canvas tarp covered *Aurora*'s driver's compartment, and there was a similar one a few feet behind it. Blanche handed the lamp to Red and began to undo the straps holding that cover in place.

"You'll see why the army is interested in testing *Aurora* as a fighting machine," Blanche said. "My father engineered the cradle."

Red smiled. "You're showing me a baby?"

"No, I'm showing you a Gatling gun."

Blanche pulled back the canvas, and Red held the lamp high as he looked inside. "Well I'll be, that's a big gun," he said.

Brass and blue steel gleamed in the lamplight as the woman leaned into the compartment and threw a lever. Immediately, the Gatling slowly rose until it was two feet above the top of the steam wagon, held by a greased steel cradle that supported its weight. Blanche climbed the light metal ladder fixed to *Aurora*'s metal side that gave access to the gun and stood behind the weapon.

She held a handle at the breech end of the big gun

and said, "Red, this is the crank handle that fires the Gatling. The weapon can shoot in all directions except directly behind it."

"Because it would shoot up the steam engine, huh?" Red said.

"That's correct," Blanche said. "The army told my father they could probably build a turret that would allow the gun to turn one-hundred-and-eighty degrees, but they haven't yet tested *Aurora*, so who knows?"

Red stood for a few moments admiring the Gatling, a magnificent firearm with six rotating barrels, then said, "What's that thing on top of it?"

"This? It's the ammunition hopper," Blanche said. "You pour the shells in there and then start cranking."

"Do you have ammunition?"

"Yes, a thousand rounds of .45-70 in boxes, thanks to the army," Blanche said. "An officer brought the shells with him, but then postponed the test."

"I don't know how useful the big gun might be," Red said. "You can't drive and shoot at the same time, Blanche."

"I can't shoot it," the woman said, shocked. "I thought you could."

"No. I'm a shotgun guard," Red said. "I use a Greener, not a Gatling."

Then a voice from the gloom. "I can shoot it."

Red turned, and John Latimer stepped toward him. "I've fired a Gatling before," the man said.

"Where?" Blanche said.

"In India during the Afghan War. The British army had several batteries of Gatlings, and officers were invited to try them. I jumped at the chance to shoot two hundred rounds a minute. It was fun." Latimer shook his head. "But later in the war I saw hundreds of dead Afghans who probably didn't think the Gatling was fun."

"Come up here, Mr. Latimer," Blanche said, "Familiarize yourself with the gun again."

"Why? Do you think you'll need it?" Latimer said.

"Miss Carter thinks we can use it against Dave Winter," Red said.

"He'll hear us coming and run, surely?" Latimer said.

"Winter won't run," Red said. "Running is not in the man's nature."

"Unlike mine," Latimer said.

"You said it, not me."

"Mr. Latimer, try the gun, see if you remember," Blanche said.

Latimer climbed the ladder and tested the Gatling, swinging it around, moving it with the cranking handle. "I remember," he told Blanche, smiling. "I remember it well. It's a formidable weapon, but it does tend to jam when it gets dirty."

A moment later Red Ryan found himself looking down the business ends of six barrels as Latimer aimed the big gun directly at him.

"How do you think it would feel to be shot by a gun that fires two hundred rounds a minute, Mr. Ryan?" he said. "How many bullets would hit a man before he dropped?"

"Latimer, my answer to your first question is . . . mighty unpleasant. To the second . . . how the hell should I know?"

"A lot. That's the answer to my second question," Latimer said. He swung the Gatling away. "You're a cool customer, Mr. Ryan."

"I knew the big gun wasn't loaded," Red said. "If it was, I would've drawn down on you when you started swinging it in my direction."

"There are no rounds in the chambers, Miss Carter?" Latimer said

"Not as far as I know," Blanche said.

"But you can't be certain?"

"No, I'm not certain."

Latimer smiled at Red. "Let that be our little mystery, huh, Mr. Ryan?"

Red shook his head. "Latimer, even for an Englishman, you are one strange ranny."

"When your man Winter comes, I'll shoot the gun," Latimer said. "I guess we must hope that he comes right at us and gives me an open field of fire."

"When he comes? What makes you so sure he'll attack us?" Red said.

"He must come. By now he knows we're here."

"Buttons won't tell him anything."

"Perhaps not, but I'm certain that under torture someone will," Latimer said.

"Maybe you can shoot the big gun, maybe you can't," Red said. "The question is . . . if an attack comes will you stand?"

"You'll find out, won't you, Mr. Ryan?"

"Yeah, I guess I will, Mr. Latimer," Red said.

Chapter Twenty-two

Buttons and all but one of his charges came in at first light.

"The sick Mexican died," he said. "We left him out there. We can give him a decent burial later."

"Where's Winter?" Red said.

"Probably right behind us."

"Then we're in for a fight," Red said.

"Seems like," Buttons said. "Cope and the other professors have been beaten pretty bad, and they're done. We can't depend on them in a battle. But we can give the Mexican a rifle. He helped us escape, and the little feller's got spunk. I don't know about the Chinaman."

"What happened, Buttons?" Red said.

"I'll tell you later. We killed one of Winter's men, and my guess is he'll be right on top of us soon."

"Mr. Muldoon!" Hannah Huckabee called out, running toward him. "Dahteste? Where is she?"

"Miss Huckabee . . ." Buttons's words choked in his throat.

"Where is she?" Hannah said. "Tell me!"

"Miss Huckabee . . ."

Hannah looked stricken. "Dahteste is dead, isn't she?"

"Maybe . . . or she wishes she was . . . I don't know."

"Did they . . . what did they do to her?" Hannah said.

"I don't know," Buttons said. "They took her away with them, and later I heard her scream. It doesn't bode well, Miss Hannah. It just doesn't bode well for Dahteste, and I'm real sorry."

Hannah's pith helmet was tipped low against the morning sun, and her eyes were in shadow. "If Dave Winter harmed Dahteste, I'll find him, and I'll kill him," she said.

It was no idle boast. Red Ryan could tell by her voice, each word like the clang of an iron sword.

"Miss Huckabee," Buttons said, "I reckon that before this day is done, you'll get your chance."

John Latimer stepped beside Red. "Mr. Ryan, how will they come?" he said. "Straight at us, or will they try a flanking movement?"

"Latimer, right now all Winter knows is that he's chasing Buttons, a Chinaman, a couple of Mexicans, and a bunch of professors, but when he sees us, I don't think he'll be impressed," Red said. "So, in answer to your question, he'll come straight at us, shooting. That's Dave's way of doing things."

Latimer nodded. "Good, then we'll position the steam wagon broadside to the trail Mr. Muldoon and the others made, hoping that's the way Winter will arrive. But Miss Carter will remain in *Aurora* should the machine need to be redeployed."

Buttons was tired and irritable from his long walk and from what had gone before, and he was outraged. "Here, who made you the boss, Latimer? I ain't taking orders from a coward, and a Limey coward at that."

Latimer smiled. "Fine, then tell us what to do, Mr. Muldoon. We don't have much time."

Buttons looked at Red, who said, "If you got a plan, let's hear it."

"Damn it all," Buttons said, "I say we stand on this ground. Right here."

"That's a good start, Mr. Muldoon," Latimer said. "How should we deploy?"

Buttons said, "How should we what?"

"Where should we take up our fighting positions to meet Winter's charge?" Latimer said.

Buttons looked baffled, and Red said, "Somebody better come up with a plan right quick. I'm sure I saw the sun glint on a rifle barrel to the south of us."

"Well, it's downright obvious, ain't it?" Buttons said. Then, pretending exasperation, he added, "You tell him, Red."

"Latimer, Blanche stays in the driver's seat. Where do you want the rest of us?" Red said.

"I'll be with the Gatling," Latimer said. "Picket the remaining horses, Mr. Ryan, and you and the rest take cover behind the steam wagon. Arm anyone who can fight with the rifles stored in *Aurora*, and here, Mr. Muldoon, this is yours." Latimer handed Buttons his gun and belt. "Thank you for the loan."

"Think nothing of it," Buttons said, scowling, smarting at his poor showing as a general.

"Mr. Ryan—"

"Call me Red, for God's sake. Folks who could soon die together should be on first-name terms."

"Red, when I get behind the gun, cover me as best you can with the canvas tarp," Latimer said. "There's always a chance that Dave Winter knows what a Gatling gun looks like, and that could make him shy."

"Anything else?" Red said.

"No, that's it, except for one thing," Latimer said. "Red, you're going to ask Hannah to play a very special role, and it won't be easy."

Red was suspicious. "What won't be easy?"

"The asking won't be easy. She might not like your suggestion one bit."

"And if she doesn't like it, she might shoot me, huh?"

"With Hannah, all things are possible."

"And what kind of suggestion might it be?"

Latimer told him, and Red exclaimed, "Are you out of your mind?"

"No, I'm quite sane. We have to bring Winter into the Gatling," Latimer said. "Bring him in any way we can."

All seven professors, even those who'd been beaten by Winter and his boys, armed themselves with sporting rifles, but Red Ryan doubted their effectiveness as a fighting force. The professors took cover behind the steam wagon that was now broadside to the tracks Buttons and the others had left earlier. Thanks to the rain, the tracks were faint, but Red knew Winter would be a good enough scout to follow them . . . or at least he hoped that would be the case.

Latimer took his place behind the big gun, and Red covered him with the canvas, allowing just enough of a crack for him to see what was happening. Mr. Chang, armed with a knife, stuck close to Latimer, for some Oriental reason appointing himself the Englishman's bodyguard.

Red sought out Hannah, took her aside, and told her what he wanted. "Blanche can't do it, because she has to stay with the steam wagon," he said. Then, feeling an explanation was necessary, "Winter has to come in. He has to charge straight at us. We need bait, Hannah."

Hannah raised an eyebrow and said, "My dear Mr. Ryan, the last time I put my bosoms on display was at the Czar of Russia's birthday ball. It was a contest between me and another twenty women and I won, though I was blue with cold. The Czar said he was very impressed and presented me with a golden egg. I later donated it to the Washington Ornithological Institute and to this day they call it a 'blue tit's egg.'"

"Sorry, but I'm not the Czar of Russia. You'll be displaying them on the cheap today," Red said.

"Well, I value my life more than a golden egg," Hannah said. "All right, I'll do it. Was this your idea?"

Unwilling to land Latimer in more trouble, Red said, "Yeah. It was my idea."

"I might have known," Hannah said.

"I'll tell you where and when," Red said. "All we can do now is to wait for Dave Winter to make the next move."

"I'll live through this, Red," Hannah said. "If Winter has harmed Dahteste, God won't let me die until I kill that sorry piece of trash."

Red's face showed his concern. "Hannah, don't take on too much. Dave Winter is no bargain."

"Neither am I, shotgun man," Hannah said. "Neither am I."

Red Ryan had been right when he said he'd seen the light of the rising sun glint on metal. What began with dots in the distance soon took form as fourteen riders, strung out in a skirmish line. Because of the earlier rain, the horsemen raised no dust as they came on at a determined canter, and Red swallowed hard. Fourteen skilled gunmen were a handful and could well be an unstoppable force. The Gatling gun might tip the scales, but if it didn't . . . well, he and the others were already dead.

Blanche Carter sat in *Aurora*'s red velvet driver's seat and Hannah, Buttons Muldoon, and Red stood beside the steam wagon's V-shaped front. One of the professors coughed, loud in the morning quiet, and the Mexican peon muttered a prayer in a language no one around him understood.

Winter's men came on . . .

Red's eyes narrowed, his mind working.

For God's sake stop, Winter. Take a look before you charge.

Then alarm bells clamored in his head. Damn them, they were coming straight in at a gallop . . .

Red was about to raise the alarm when Winter, at

a distance of a hundred yards, suddenly lifted a hand and drew rein, his men following suit.

Dave Winter prospered in a dangerous business because he was a careful man, and the presence of the huge steam wagon had made him cautious. What the hell was it?

As Red watched, Winter held out a hand and the man next to him passed over a brass ship's telescope. The outlaw put the glass to his eye and scanned what he saw in front of him, the machine, the tent, and the people around both. It seemed to Red that Winter lingered on himself and Buttons, whom he no doubt recognized, and finally Hannah.

"Latimer, get ready," Red said. "The ball is about to open."

He took Hannah's arm, and both of them walked forward. After fifteen yards, Red stopped and said, "All right, Miss Huckabee, the one with the carroty hair is Dave Winter. Bring him in and someday I'll buy you another golden egg."

Hannah had already unbuttoned her safari jacket and unlaced the front of her bodice. Now she pulled the bodice down and bared her breasts. Later Red Ryan would say, "If any woman could flaunt her assets, it was Hannah Huckabee."

Smiling, Hannah jiggled, cupped her breasts in her hands, bent forward and pursed her lips as though offering a kiss, moved her hips in a mighty suggestive fashion and, in short, made a whore of herself on the Texas plains. Mr. Chang would later comment on her performance, "Sometimes Miss Huckabee can be very naughty lady."

Hannah's show worked, because cheers, jeers, and laughter went up from Winter's men, and a couple of riders broke ranks to take a closer look. Winter collapsed the telescope and waved his men forward. He'd seen enough to convince himself that there was no real danger from a bunch of professors and a stagecoach driver. Red he dismissed as just another Texas waddie who used his six-gun to string wire. And he badly wanted the woman with the big tits.

To Red's relief, Winter and his boys advanced at an unhurried, menacing walk, taking their time, giving the men taking cover behind the big machine time to realize just how futile their resistance would be.

Seventy-five yards . . . Hannah still flaunted her charms.

The grinning outlaws continued their advance.

Sixty yards . . .

Fifty . . .

Red yelled, "Latimer! Now!" and threw himself on top of Hannah, flattening her into the damp ground.

Before the woman could utter the outraged cuss that was on her lips, the Gatling cut loose, shooting over them, making a noise like a brass bedstead dragged across a knotty pine floor.

Bullets zipped over Red's head and he heard a few rifles and revolvers firing, but the dominant weapon was the Gatling. Designed to put an end to warfare because of its terrible firepower, that day the big gun was a grim reaper that cut men down in swathes.

After a few moments, Red looked up . . . and beheld a scene of carnage and chaos.

Men and horses were down, screaming and kicking

in their death throes, the stream of lead from the Gatling's six barrels chopping them to the ground like a gigantic meat cleaver. Red saw a bloodied gunman stagger to his feet and curse his defiance. His Colt bucking in his hand, he was scythed down where he stood, his life blood exploding around him in a scarlet cloud.

"Get the hell off of me," Hannah said. After Red rolled away, she looked up at the murderous butchery the Gatling had wrought and whispered, "Oh, my dear God in Heaven."

In the space of a few seconds, more than half of Winter's men had been cut down, and the rest, most of them wounded or riding bloody horses, were looking to get the hell away from there, several already streaming back across the prairie. John Latimer had been a trained soldier of a great empire, and in Richard J. Gatling's gun he'd found his calling. His eye was unerring, his aim true, and the slaughter he'd brought down on Dave Winter and his men had been as quick and devastating as the wrath of God.

Red drew his Colt and fired at Winter, who was shrieking curses as he vainly tried to rally his remaining men. Red missed with several shots, but Winter realized the hopelessness of his position and he, too, turned his horse and fled the unequal fight.

After the clattering clamor of the cranking Gatling ended, a church-like silence again descended on the prairie, and gunsmoke drifted like the spirits of the slain.

Winter's butcher's bill was high.

He had lost eight men, all of them dead, including

one terrifyingly wounded man without a lower jaw who'd been put out of his agony and misery by Red. The dead included a man Buttons identified as Bean Gosford, the bandit chief's second-in-command and a known killer.

There were no casualties on Red's side. The surprise attack with the Gatling had been so successful he doubted that very few of Winter's men had managed to get off a shot.

Red helped Hannah to her feet, and when she saw the direction of his eyes, she pulled her safari jacket closed. A couple of professors moved among the dead, searched for signs of life, but found none. Professor Cope dispatched a couple of wounded horses, and when he looked at Red his face was ashen.

"A terrible business, Mr. Ryan," he said.

"I hope I never see its like again," Red said.

"It was necessary, I suppose," Cope said. "We had no alternative, did we?"

"We were fighting for our lives," Red said. "It doesn't get any more necessary than that."

Cope nodded. "Yes . . . that's what I'll tell myself."

"Red, did Winter make a clean break?" Hannah said.

"Yeah. I don't think he got hit. He has the devil's own luck, does ol' Dave."

Hannah nodded. "When I find him, his luck will run out."

Chapter Twenty-three

"Latimer, you done good," Buttons Muldoon said. "You played a man's part this morning."

"As it happened, there was very little risk to me," Latimer said. "But thank you, I appreciate the compliment."

"Did Hannah speak to you?" Red said.

The Englishman shook his head. "As far as she's concerned, firing the Gatling wasn't an act of atonement. In Hannah's eyes, I still have a lot to prove."

Buttons said, "Latimer, it takes a heap of forgiving and forgetting to restore a man's reputation. It's been nigh on fifty years since Moses Rose hightailed it from the Alamo, and Texas hasn't forgiven him yet."

Latimer smiled slightly. "Then I've got plenty of time to work on it, haven't I?"

"Seems like," Buttons said.

"What the hell . . ."

Buttons and Latimer followed Red's gaze . . . to where Hannah Huckabee had just saddled a professor's discarded horse and was preparing to mount.

"Hannah, hold up there!" Red yelled.

He reached her just as the woman stepped into the saddle. She wore her Colt and knife, and Mr. Chang handed her a rare Allen & Wheelock single-shot .44 rifle, Sir Richard Owen's personal long gun.

Red decided it was time to be strict and put an end to this female foolishness.

"Miss Huckabee, you are a passenger of the Abe Patterson and Son Stage and Express Company, and I am its representative," he said. "I forbid you to leave here without my permission."

Hannah's determined face did not change expression.

"I must find out what happened to Dahteste," she said. "If she's been harmed, or worse, I'll go after Winter and I'll kill him."

"Then go after him with the rest of us," Red said. "Me and Buttons will help you find him, and we'll help you kill him."

Hannah shook her head. "No, Red, this is something I need to do by myself. It's a personal matter. If I don't catch up with Winter, I'll meet you in Fredericksburg."

"Hannah, wait a moment!"

Blanche Carter hurried to the other woman. She held up a thin chain with an attached silver medal. "It's St. Christopher, the patron saint of travelers. He'll help protect you."

Hannah smiled. "I'm sure he will, Blanche."

Hannah sat a tall horse, and she bent low to let Blanche fasten the chain around her neck. "There," Hannah said. "I feel safer already."

Red was beside himself. He tipped his plug hat at a

fighting angle and said, "No, this won't do. I won't have it. Miss Huckabee, the Patterson and Son Stage and Express Company, of which I am a representative, is better protection than a medal. I order you to get down from that horse, instanter!"

Hannah laughed, kicked her mount into motion, and called out over her shoulder, "See you in Fredericksburg, shotgun man."

With wide, unbelieving eyes, Red watched Hannah Huckabee gallop into the distance, and he was thunderstruck. "Blanche, Buttons, she refused to obey a direct order from—"

"I know, a representative of the Abe Patterson and Son Stage and Express Company," Blanche said.

"Yeah, that's right," Red said. "This has never happened before."

"Shotgun man, you never met a woman like Hannah Huckabee before," Blanche said.

Mr. Chang giggled. "Mr. Ryan try to tame wrong gal. Get kick in teeth."

Red and the others used the rest of the morning readying the steam wagon for the trip to Fredericksburg. Texas Ranger Tim Adams, conscious but in pain, was settled on the seat beside Blanche, the tent was taken down, and everybody ate a quick breakfast of bacon and bread.

"We're pulling out now, Adams," Red said, taking back the sandwich that the ranger had refused to eat. "Once we get to Fredericksburg, the doctor will fix you right up, you'll see."

"I'm a burden to you and all the rest, Ryan," Adams said. "You'll make quicker time if you leave me here."

"And that's not going to happen," Red said. "We're all in this together, and we'll stay together. That's the Patterson and Son policy, all written down and legal."

"I saw Hannah Huckabee leave," Adams said.

Red nodded. "She's gone after Dave Winter."

"A tad overmatched, ain't she?" Adams said.

"I tried to tell her that very thing, but she wouldn't listen," Red said.

Adams managed a smile. "Ryan, she's an obstinate, headstrong girl. Best not to stand in her way. What a ranger she'd make."

"Yeah, she would, she'd make a crackerjack ranger. That is, if she could learn to take orders."

"Wait, Ryan, before you go, I have something to say," Adams said.

"Say it. I'm listening."

"You saved my life. I could've died out there on the grass."

"Think nothing of it," Red said.

"I owe you," Adams said.

Red smiled. "Well, if you ever catch me robbing a bank, let me go with the loot and we're even."

"I can't see you robbing a bank."

"Me neither. But maybe I'll call in the favor one day."

"Anytime. I've never been beholden to a man before."

"Like I always say, there's a first time for everything," Red said. "Now don't wear yourself out with more ranger talk. We got a long trail ahead of us."

* * *

Red mounted the American mare, and Buttons and the professors settled into the rear compartment in front of the blue pagoda where the Mexican and Mr. Chang were seated. The Gatling, which no one wanted to look at, was again stored in its compartment out of sight.

There was no question of burying the dead, bloody heaps of mangled men and horses where black flies already buzzed. Despite his misgivings on the matter, Sir Richard Owen agreed with Red to let nature run its course and leave it to the buzzards and coyotes to take care of the dead.

"Damn it all, Mr. Ryan, I feel responsible for all those deaths," Owen said, his hands kneading a handkerchief. "After all, they were coming after my colleagues who were here because of the Bone War."

"Dave Winter was responsible for the deaths of those men, Professor Owen, not you and not the Bone War," Red said.

"And Miss Huckabee, what about her?" Owen said. "I gave her my rifle. I hope it helps."

"Hannah is fighting her own personal war," Red said. "I don't know how that will turn out."

"It will turn out well, I hope," Owen said.

"Yeah, we all hope that it turns out well," Red said.

Chapter Twenty-four

Hannah Huckabee followed the tracks that had been left by Dave Winter's men on their way north. The beautiful Texas morning, the limitless prairie and infinite sky, reminded her of just how precious was life and how she might well be throwing hers away bracing a man whose gun skills were said to be so much deadlier than her own.

She had no idea if Dahteste was alive or dead, but either way, Dave Winter had to face a reckoning. And she had to bring it about. It would be so easy to feel lost, trapped, and Hannah battled her own fears as she drew rein and looked around her at the vast wilderness. Someone, somewhere, had once told her, "You're never alone if you're with a cigar," and she heeded that advice. She took a slim, black cheroot from her case and lit it, letting the fragrant smoke soothe her.

After a while, Hannah kneed her horse forward. Ahead of her was Dave Winter, the dreadful ogre who was growing even more dreadful with every passing hour.

No matter, she owed it to Dahteste. She had it to do.

By mid-afternoon the tumbled ruins of Fort Mason came in sight. Buzzards glided in lazy circles above the fort, and Hannah felt a dreadful sense of foreboding, as though something terrible had happened in this place.

She drew rein and studied the demolished layout of the fort, especially those buildings that still had standing walls. The Patterson stage was parked to one side of what had probably been the parade ground, and the six horses of the team were scattered around, grazing.

There was no sound from the sun-splashed ruins, and nothing moved. She laid the Allen & Wheelock, hammer back, across her mount's withers and then kneed the horse forward again.

The tall gelding immediately tossed its head, jangling the bit, and danced a little jig of alarm. Hannah spoke soothing words to her restive mount and pushed it ahead, fighting small battles of will with the horse as she made her way onto the parade ground.

Around her, everything lay in ruins, but a small building to her right still had all four of its walls standing, and even the door, though badly warped, was still in place. The big horse whinnied and backed away. It wanted nothing to do with the structure that looked as though it had once been an administrative office of some kind.

The horse smelled or sensed death or both, and with a feeling of dread Hannah dismounted and let the gelding back off, its reins trailing. Her rifle at the ready, she advanced on the building, the two front-facing windows reflecting the sun flare like rectangles of fire. Somewhere close she heard a bird sing, trilling notes that fell into the hush like a rush of water, and then a flutter of wings followed by a silence that closed in on her once again.

Hannah swallowed hard and tightened her grip on the Allen & Wheelock.

The door hung on leather and brass tack hinges and Hannah raised her booted foot and kicked it in. The door slammed against the wall with a bang that reverberated around the compound, and she leveled the rifle, ready to shoot at anything male that moved.

Nothing. The stillness mocked her. How could complete silence be so loud?

Once the office had partitions, but those were long gone, and what remained were four fieldstone walls. And what had once been Dahteste lay curled in a corner, her naked body already showing signs of decay and something else . . . bruises and cuts all over her arms and legs and a deeper, deadlier one across her throat.

Hannah closed her eyes and then opened them again. But the horror was still there. It was all too real. Now she had to face reality and think the unthinkable, the way of Dahteste's appalling death.

Dave Winter and his men had used her unmercifully, enjoying both rape and torture. And at the end, when they tired of her, Dahteste's throat had been cut and she'd been thrown away, tossed into a corner like garbage along with the cigar stubs and empty whiskey bottles.

To Winter, Dahteste had not been a human being,

but a . . . thing . . . to be used for his own amusement and then disposed of.

Hannah fought back tears, knuckles white on the rifle. Winter was not fit to live. By God, she'd kill him, slaughter him, like he'd slaughtered Dahteste.

Hannah Huckabee stripped to the skin and bathed in the shallow stream that ran close to the fort. She dressed again, putting her clothes on her damp body, her pith helmet and goggles on ringlets of wet hair. After she buckled on her Colt and picked up her rifle, she walked to the grave she'd made for Dahteste. Beyond tears now, she stood in silence at the cairn of piled fieldstones for a long time. And then she said, "Please forgive me, Dahteste."

The quietness enfolded her, birds sang, and under her tomb of rock, Dahteste lay still.

"Forgive me," Hannah said again.

Afterward, she mounted her horse and rode away from Fort Mason, and in the distance, she heard the dull thrum . . . thrum . . . thrum . . . of the approaching steam wagon.

Hannah was not an expert tracker, but she figured there was no need. It seemed logical that Dave Winter would head for Fredericksburg, where he could rest up and scheme his next plan of action.

She decided to spend the night on the prairie and with luck ride into the settlement around noon the next day.

The moonless night had drawn a black curtain across the plains when Hannah dismounted and unsaddled her horse, letting it graze on what was good grass. From a pocket of her safari jacket she retrieved a thick slice of sourdough bread and some fried bacon, the breakfast she hadn't eaten that morning. A cold camp is a cheerless place, and after she'd eaten, Hannah hugged her legs and laid her head on her knees. Soon the steady chomp of her grazing mount and the soft whisper of the wind in the grass lulled her to sleep. A pair of hunting coyotes wandered close to the sleeping woman, but they feared the human smell and it drove them away. Hannah dreamed of Dahteste in a white buckskin dress, her jet-black hair circled by a wreath of pink wildflowers. The girl rode a spotted pony, following a great buffalo herd that kicked up enough dust to haze the sun. Dahteste stopped and then, smiling, turned and waved.

Hannah woke with a start, and for a fleeting moment she looked around for Dahteste and the great buffalo herd, but now, in the bleak dawn, she saw only grass and the uncaring sky.

A sadness in her that was almost a pain, Hannah touched the St. Christopher medal that Blanche Carter had given her. It brought her a small comfort. Then she caught up her horse and again rode south.

Chapter Twenty-five

"She took time to bury the Apache girl," Buttons Muldoon said. He shook his head in wonder. "That's a lot of rock."

"And that's a lot of grief," Red Ryan said.

"I guess Winter was long gone and Miss Huckabee went after him," Buttons said.

"Looks like," Red said. "I guess she figured he'd head for Fredericksburg."

"There's law there," Buttons said.

"Yes, I'm sure there is," Red said.

There was nothing more to be said, and a silence fell between the two men. Then Buttons said, "My team is scattered to hell and gone, I'll round them up, and the Patterson stage will be back in business."

Professors Richard Owen and Edward Cope, their feud forgotten, at least for a while, shared a concern for the welfare of Hannah Huckabee.

"Mr. Ryan, does she really plan to have it out with that thug Winter, or will she just inform the law in Fredericksburg?" Owen said.

"I think Hannah is her own law," Red said. "Yeah,

Professor, if she finds him, she'll have it out with Winter."

"But she's only a slip of a girl," Owen said. "What chance does she have against a dangerous ruffian like this Dave Winter person?"

Red considered that for a few seconds and then said, "None at all. Let's hope that she doesn't catch up with him, not now, not ever."

"Perhaps our fears are unfounded," Professor Cope said. "Miss Huckabee is an adventuress, well acquainted with precarious situations. I'm sure she's aware of how dangerous the Winter gunman is and will leave the law to deal with him."

"I sure hope you're right," Red said.

It took Buttons the best part of an hour to collect a team that had decided an easy life on the open prairie was preferable to hauling the Patterson stage all over God's creation. As a result, he was all cussed out and hoarse before the team was hitched and ready to go.

While Buttons was on his horse hunt, Red checked on Ranger Adams, who looked awful.

"You look awful," Red said.

"Thanks, and the same to you, Ryan," Adams said. "I can't smell the wound, and that's a good sign. It means there's no gangrene."

"Hurts like hell though, don't it?" Red said.

The ranger managed a weak smile. "Ryan, it's sure a pleasure for a sick person to be around you."

Red ignored that and said, "We'll be in Fredericksburg tomorrow and get you to a doctor. Say, Adams, what do you want us to do with the Mexican? As you know, we buried the one who died."

"Where's the black Madonna?"

"Still tied to the back of the stage. Got a few bullet holes in her, but nothing too serious." Adams didn't answer right away and Red said, "He saved lives here at the fort, including the life of Buttons Muldoon, a man I set store by."

"Yes, Professor Cope told me that, and he says Juan Perez stood his ground during the Winter attack."

"Is that the little feller's name really Juan Perez?" Red said. "Funny, you never think of Mexicans having names, unless it's something like Mexican Bob or such."

"They all have names," Adams said. "It's just that Americans never care to find out, I guess." He moved a little and winced in pain. "Damned shoulder," he said.

"I think you should let him go," Red said.

Adams frowned, the pain nagging at him. "Let who go?"

"Juan Perez."

The ranger didn't hesitate. "Yeah, he acted like a white man, and I guess he's earned his freedom. I'll return the Madonna to them New Mexicans the next time I'm up that way."

"I'll go tell him." Red said.

Adams closed his eyes and drowsily said, "Yeah, you do that . . ."

"Give him your horse, Mr. Ryan," Professor Cope said. "He can't walk home."

"Professor, that's an expensive mare," Red said. "I guarantee that Juan Perez has never seen a hoss like that in his life, unless there was a Mexican lancer officer on its back."

"I know. And give him this. I passed the hat and we all put in something, even your driver."

Red counted the money. "There's two hundred dollars here."

"Yes, another small way of thanking the man who saved our lives," Cope said.

"Professor, an American hoss and two hundred dollars isn't small," Red said.

"Neither," Cope said, "is my life."

Red sought out the little Mexican, who'd helped Buttons with the team and was now sitting beside the big driver sharing beef jerky, the other supplies running low.

Red held the saddled mare by the reins and stopped in front of the Mexican. "Juan Perez," he said.

The little man rose to his feet and said, *"Sí, señor."*

"Here, this is for you," Red said, holding out the money.

Perez hesitated, suspecting that this was some kind of gringo trap.

"Take it," Red said, shoving the notes and silver into the man's hand. He passed Perez the mare's reins. "And this is yours."

The Mexican stared at him with confused eyes. "Damn it, learn to speak American," Red said. Then slowly, "El caballo is yours."

Perez, now looking thoroughly frightened, dropped the reins and the money and backed away.

"What are you trying to tell him?" Blanche Carter smiled at the Mexican and frowned at Red. "Are you abusing the poor man?"

"Hell no," Red said. "I'm trying to tell him that the money and horse are his, a gift from the professors for helping them escape from Dave Winter."

"I can speak a little Spanish as it's spoken in Spain," Blanche said. "Will he understand?"

"He doesn't savvy much," Red said. "But try him."

Juan Perez understood.

As Blanche spoke to him, his expression changed from fear to apprehension to wonder to delight and ended with a smile.

"He understands," she said.

"I figured that," Red said.

Perez probably never heard the saying that he who hesitates is lost, but he acted on it. He stuffed the money in a pocket, shook Red's hand, and then vaulted onto the horse. Yipping like an Apache, he lit a shuck across the long grass and was soon gone from sight.

"There goes a happy man," Blanche said.

Red nodded. "He may not have the Madonna, but an American horse and two hundred dollars will make him a big man in his village. And, damn it all, I reckon he deserves it. The little runt had sand."

Buttons Muldoon stepped beside Red and handed him the Greener shotgun. "Time to roll," he said. "I got seven professors who want to ride in the stage and only room enough for six. That Sir Richard feller and Professor Cope finally agreed to ride in the steam wagon with the . . . with Latimer." He looked at Blanche. "You got enough wood to take you to Fredericksburg, lady?"

"Yes. If I keep the steam pressure low enough, I can make it," Blanche said.

"Hitch up a team to that thing and it will take you anywhere you want to go," Buttons said. "It's cheaper to burn hay than wood."

Blanche smiled. "Mr. Muldoon, you may be right."

"Damn right, I'm right," Buttons said. Then to Red, "Excuse me, but when you've finished making calf eyes at Miss Blanche, the Patterson stage is in need of a shotgun guard."

Chapter Twenty-six

The oil lamps were lit in Fredericksburg when Hannah Huckabee rode in on a tired horse. The town was settled by German farmers and had none of the saloons and whorehouses of the Texas cattle towns, although their several beer halls did a lively business. It was a clean, well-ordered settlement of stone and plaster houses, churches, and schools. The county seat of Gillespie County, it had a sheriff who spoke German and broken English and attended Lutheran services every Sunday.

Fredericksburg was a straitlaced town, a civilized town, a peaceful town . . . and not a good town in which to kill a man.

Hannah rode along the main street, lined with a large variety of stores on each side, past some warehouses ,and then drew rein when she spotted a large, white-painted building with a sign above the double doors that read:

LANGE LIVERY
~ Horses for Rent ~
ENGLISH SPOKEN

Hannah dismounted and led her gelding inside. The stable was clean, smelled of horses and leather, and only two stalls were occupied, one with a bay nag, the other with a tall Thoroughbred stud that couldn't have cost less than two hundred and fifty dollars . . . unless it had been stolen.

A kid who looked to be about twelve or thirteen 'ing a bucket and a shovel. He smiled at Hannah and said with a slight accent, "I'll take care of your horse, ma'am. Fifty cents a day and oats are fifteen cents extra."

"Expensive," Hannah said.

"That's because we're the only game in town," the kid said.

Hannah smiled. "At least you're honest about it. I want the oats."

The kid had never seen a woman like Hannah Huckabee before. From her boots to the top of her pith helmet she was a strange, exotic visitor to a very unremarkable town, and as the boy unsaddled her horse he looked at her from the corner of his eye, wondering who and what she was.

"That's a beautiful horse," Hannah said about the Thoroughbred.

"Came in yesterday," the kid said. "It was lathered up some."

Trying to sound disinterested, Hannah said, "Who is the owner?"

"He didn't leave his name. He brought in the horse and paid for oats, same as you, ma'am."

"Is that his saddle?" Hannah said, pointing to one of two saddles thrown over the partition between stalls. "It looks as valuable as the horse."

The boy nodded. "Yep, nice saddle. Got lots of silver on it. I'll take your horse back and rub him down. If you're lookin' for a hotel, try the Alpenrose Inn just up the street a ways. Mein Vater always says they serve the best rouladen in town."

"Thank you, I'll try it," Hannah said.

The kid led her horse to a stall, and Hannah took a quick look at the fancy saddle. Inlaid on the cantle were two silver letters: DW.

Hannah Huckabee had only seen Dave Winter at a distance, but she believed she could recognize him by his red hair and beard and black frock coat. There were no brothels in Fredericksburg, so the chances were that he was in one of the beer halls. But which beer hall out of so many? There was only one way to find out, and that was to try them all.

After checking into the Alpenrose Inn and being shown to her comfortable room, Hannah left her rifle behind and then returned to the lobby and walked into the street.

She turned down a dozen offers by eager young men to buy her a drink as she made her round of the beer halls and gardens. After an hour of fruit-less searching, she had one more to try, the Munich Keller, set in a grove of ancient oaks on the outskirts of town. Call it woman's intuition, call it wishful think-ing, but Hannah was convinced that Dave Winter was inside. She was sure she could feel the man's vile presence reach out to her like a poisonous cloud.

Standing in shadow, she checked the loads in her Colt and then removed her pith helmet and goggles. She took a scarlet ribbon from her safari jacket pocket and tied her hair back, then, holding the hat in her left hand at waist level, she hid the short-barreled .45 behind it. The door of the beer hall was open, and Hannah stood just outside the entrance and studied the patrons at the tables. An older couple faced each other and silently drank beer. Three young men and a blonde girl about the same age argued loudly about the merits of their favorite Gilbert and Sullivan operetta and two men sat at tables by themselves. One was a pipe-smoking gent in broadcloth who read a newspaper, a beer stein on the table in front of him, and the other was . . . Dave Winter.

It had to be!

There was no mistaking the man's red hair and beard and the mad-dog glitter in his eyes when he looked around him.

Winter sat quietly, drinking beer, keeping to himself. Fredericksburg was a settlement filled with rubes and pumpkin rollers, but he didn't want to draw attention to himself, not when he was concocting a plan to rob the bank on his way out of town. He did want the young, yellow-haired girl at the next table, but couldn't have her because of the bank robbery thing, and that was a disappointment. But he'd get over it.

The *Fredericksburg Pioneer Press* would later claim that Dave Winter recognized Hannah Huckabee as soon as she walked into the beer hall. But that was not the case. In fact, he didn't look up until she stood at his table and even then, he didn't peg her.

Winter smiled. "Well, well, well, what have we here? Sit down, girlie, let me buy you a beer. My, but what big brown eyes you have."

Hannah pitched her voice loud, almost to the level of a shout.

"Her name was Dahteste. She was sixteen years old," she said.

Now the people at the other tables were looking in Hannah's direction.

"What the hell are you talking about?" Winter said.

"I'm talking about the girl you raped and murdered. I'm talking about how you threw her body aside like a piece of worthless garbage. She was nothing to you, Winter, just a thing to amuse you, and when you finished with it, you destroyed it. Except she wasn't an *it* . . . she was Dahteste, and she was an Apache girl, and she was sixteen years old."

Winter felt the eyes of the other people on him, including the proprietor, who'd just stepped from behind the bar. "I want no trouble here," the man said. He was big and blond and German.

"Damn you, I never heard of her, but she was an Apache, you say," Winter said. "Who cares what happens to an Apache? Besides, I bet she begged for it, the slut."

Hannah took that last like a series of blows. "Get on your feet, Winter. Draw your gun and get to your work," she said. "After tonight you'll never abuse another woman."

"Here, this won't do," the proprietor said. "I've sent for the law."

"How do I get you to draw, Winter?" Hannah said.

"You damned yellow-bellied coward, are you so afraid of me?

"I've been threatened," Winter yelled. "My life is in peril. All here present bear witness that this crazy whore called me out."

"You lowlife piece of trash, skin the iron," Hannah said. "Or are you just going to stand there and piss yourself from fright?"

Winter roared his rage, and his criminal instincts took over. He had to silence the bitch before she said too much. He went for his gun.

But Hannah had the advantage on him.

She just lowered the pith helmet and fired. At a range of about four feet, the bullet ran true and crashed into the middle of Winter's chest. The man staggered back, knowing he was dead, but he badly wanted to take the woman with him. His eyes losing their focus, he got off a shot. A miss. Hannah fired again. A second hit and another chest shot. Winter's jaw hung slack, the gunman unable to believe this was really happening to him.

Hannah Huckabee made a believer out of him.

"For Dahteste," she said, as she emptied her revolver into Winter's chest and belly.

His eyes wild, the big gunman stood for a second and then fell dead on the timber floor.

A few moments later, the sheriff of Fredericksburg, looking stern, took the still-smoking Colt from Hannah's hand.

Chapter Twenty-seven

Red Ryan said, "Miss Hannah Huckabee is a fare-paying passenger of the Abe Patterson and Son Stage and Express Company, and I'm its lawful representative. As such, I demand that you release her at once."

"And that goes double, Sheriff," Buttons Muldoon said. "I'm the stage driver and he's the shotgun guard and we're both representatives, so stick that in your pipe and smoke it."

"Yes, you do that, Sheriff," Mr. Chang said, scowling. "You smoke pipe."

"I haven't charged her with anything," Sheriff Herman Ritter said. He picked up a wanted dodger and tossed it across his desk to Red. "Can you read, shotgun guard?"

"I can read," Red said, "Let me see the dodger."

Red glanced it over and said, "Dave Winter. Wanted for rape and murder. Dead or alive." He looked up from the dodger. "And there's a thousand-dollar reward."

"Sheriff, it's obvious to me and should be to you

that Miss Huckabee done the community a service," Buttons said. "So why are you holding her?"

"Took me a while to find the dodger," Ritter said. Then, his blue eyes on Red, "I'm confiscating Winter's horse, saddle, and traps, the proceeds to go to city law enforcement."

"You mean to you," Buttons said.

"I enforce the law," Ritter said. "If Miss Huckabee leaves a forwarding address, I'll see that she gets the reward."

"She's an adventuress and doesn't have a forwarding address," Red said.

The sheriff smiled. "I'm sure she has somebody somewhere."

He rose, took a key from a hook on the wall, and walked back to the cells. He returned with Hannah, who looked tired. "I leave this lady in your charge, gentlemen," he said.

Ritter sat at his desk, opened a drawer, and produced a Colt and a knife. "These are yours, I think, Miss Huckabee," he said. Ritter smiled. "And let me tell you that you are the most beautiful and most deadly woman I've ever had in my jail."

"You're very gracious, Sheriff," Hannah said. "Supper last night was excellent, as was breakfast."

"We aim to please," Ritter said.

Hannah slipped the gun into her holster, the knife in its sheath.

"Dahteste" . . . she looked at Red and swallowed hard . . . "Dahteste can rest in peace now."

"Hannah, you did good," Red said. "If ever a man needed killing, it was Dave Winter."

"I know he did," Hannah said. "And I killed him."

She was very pale and she shivered, as though she'd been fighting to stay strong but the events of the previous night had come back to haunt her.

She stepped to Red. "Hold me, Red. Don't say anything, just hold me for a while."

Red took the woman in her arms and held her close.

Ritter and Buttons looked on, silent. Mr. Chang smiled.

After a while, Hannah stepped away and said, "Thank you, Red. I feel better now."

"Anytime," Red said, grinning.

"So, how are you feeling?" Red Ryan said.

"The doc says I'll make a full recovery," Texas Ranger Tim Adams said. "But I tell you what, Ryan, I don't intend to lie in this bed much longer."

Adams lay in a cot in a recovery room behind Dr. Steve Morgan's surgery. He was attended by a middle-aged German nurse with hard eyes who would either cure him or kill him, as the ranger had told her on several occasions.

"I heard gunfire last night," the ranger said. "Anyone I know?"

"Yeah, it was someone you know. Hannah Huckabee killed Dave Winter in the Munich Keller beer hall last night," Red said.

Adams's silence was proof of his shock. Finally, after a while he said, "Why? How? I mean . . ."

"Hannah adopted an Apache girl, and Winter raped and killed her," Red said. "She followed him here to Fredericksburg and shot him."

"I remember the Apache girl, but I didn't know what happened to her after Winter shot me," Adams said.

"No, you were out of it for a spell," Red said. "Do you recollect the big fight between us and Winter's boys?"

"I heard it. I was in the tent, but there was a lot of shooting."

"A Gatling in the steam wagon made the noise," Red said. "John Latimer knew how to use it, and use it he did. Winter saw his men chopped up and lit a shuck, and Hannah tracked him to here."

"The English coward came through for you, huh?" Adams said.

"I don't think he's a coward," Red said.

"Then I'll take your word for it, Ryan." Adams winced as he pulled himself higher on the pillow. He was pale but seemed much stronger. "So, Winter was here in Fredericksburg when Miss Huckabee caught up with him. I have to ask the question . . . how come she's still alive?"

"She called him out in a beer hall, and when Dave went for his gun, she shot him," Red said. "Five times, according to what I hear."

Adams shook his head. "Don't that beat all, one of the fastest gunmen in the West killed by a girl."

"Yeah, but she's some girl," Red said.

"Ain't she though," Adams said. Then, after a moment, "There will be no charges, of course."

"According to the sheriff here, a man called Herman Ritter, Hannah will get a thousand-dollar reward. Winter was wanted, dead or alive."

"I know Ritter," Adams said. "He's a fair man."

"Oh, I almost forgot, Buttons sent you these," Red said. He reached into his pocket and produced a small red-and-white-striped paper bag. "Peppermint humbugs."

Adams smiled and took the bag. "Tell Buttons thanks."

"He says peppermint humbugs are good for folks with a misery," Red said.

"What about all those professors?" Adams said. "Bring me up to date."

"Well, even as we speak, Sir Richard Owen is hiring men to dig his big lizard out of the ground," Red said. "He's hiring a wagon to carry it back to Fredericksburg, and Professors Marsh and Harcourt are going with him. Professor Cope and his colleagues suspect treachery and plan to stay in town to keep an eye on Owen."

"And the steam wagon?" Adams said.

"Blanche is nursing her sick father at the hotel, and they'll wait here until the army decides to test it," Red said. "Hannah Huckabee, John Latimer, and Mr. Chang will stay with the Patterson stage all the way to New Orleans."

"When are you leaving?" Adams said.

"From the old Butterfield depot building at eight sharp tomorrow morning," Red said. "Buttons likes to put on a show when he leaves a town, and the old stage depot is as good a place as any to start."

The door to the room opened, and the nurse stepped in, carrying a basin of water and a sponge. "Herr Adams, it is time for our bath," she said. She ran a hostile gaze over Red's plug hat, stained buckskin shirt, and the Colt holstered at his waist. "You," she said, "may go."

Red nodded. "Oh, I left the Madonna with Sheriff Ritter, and he said he'd guard her with his life. Well, good luck, Ranger Adams."

"And you too, Ryan. Good luck."

The chatty desk clerk at the Alpenrose Inn looked at the register, gave Hannah Huckabee her room key, and said, "You've become quite famous in Fredericksburg, Miss Huckabee. Haven't you?" The man was small, balding, and wore a pair of round glasses on the end of his nose.

"I don't want to become famous for killing a man," Hannah said.

"But he wasn't just any man, he was Dave Winter, the most dangerous desperado in the West. I heard he'd three of his scoundrels with him, all armed to the teeth, but they fled when you walked into the Munich Keller with a six-gun in one hand and a bowie knife in the other and told them to get to fighting or go away."

"There was no one with Winter," Hannah said. "He sat at a table alone."

For a moment, the clerk looked disappointed, but

then he cheered up and said, "Well, the story I heard is better. Can I get you anything?"

"Yes, send up a bathtub and hot water," Hannah said. "Oh, and Pears soap. Accept no substitute."

"Yes, for you, Miss Huckabee, I will do that with pleasure." The clerk looked serious. "By the way Dave Winter is to be buried today at three o'clock in Der Stadt Friedhof."

"What is that?" Hannah said.

"Oh, in English it means the city cemetery."

"Thank you," Hannah said. "Don't forget the tub."

Two city gravediggers laid Dave Winter in an unmarked grave. But before they could shovel dirt on the hastily hammered-together pine coffin, Hannah Huckabee stopped them.

"Mr. Chang," she said. "Please do as I asked."

The little Chinese bowed his head, lifted his robe, pissed, and his urine drummed on the lid of the coffin. When he'd finished, he adjusted his robe, bowed to Hannah again, and stepped away.

Hannah stood at the edge of the grave, looked down at the wet coffin, and said, "Her name was Dahteste, and she was sixteen years old."

Then she and Mr. Chang walked out of the cemetery without a backward glance.

Chapter Twenty-eight

"I'm sorry we couldn't finish what we started that night on the prairie," Blanche Carter said. "My father pretty much takes all my time and attention."

Red Ryan smiled. "There's always a next time."

Blanche nodded. "Yes, of course. There is always a next time."

She tiptoed, kissed Red on the cheek. "Now I must get back to the hotel."

Hannah Huckabee watched the woman leave and said, "There goes another adventuress. I'm so glad I met her."

"I sure can't disagree with that," Red said. "She does adventurous things."

The thanks to Red Ryan and Buttons Muldoon from the professors was prolonged and profuse. There was much handshaking, backslapping, talk about lives saved and villains slain, and Sir Richard Owen hinted in confidential tones that he might name his latest find a Ryanosaurus.

Farewells were said, backs slapped once again, and

then the Patterson stage left Fredericksburg with a sound of rolling thunder, and Buttons, looking like an old pagan god, cracking his whip to supply the lightning. Teutonic voices raised in cheers as the stage hurtled across the city limits and then rocked headlong into the wilderness.

Up on the seat, Red sat with his shotgun across his knees and grinned, "You gave them a show, Buttons."

"Damn right, I gave them a show," Buttons said. "One them squareheads will never forget."

Hannah had refused to sit inside with Latimer, despite his prowess with the Gatling gun, and Mr. Chang and took her accustomed place on top of the stage when they left Fredericksburg. The brim of her pith helmet dropped over her eyes several times as Buttons's shenanigans bounced her around, but now it felt wonderful to be rolling across the vast prairie again, under a limitless sky. The sense of freedom it gave her was exhilarating.

Buttons slowed the team to a trot, turned his head, and said, "Miss Huckabee, according to the map, we got ten miles of good level grass ahead of us and then we ford the Perdinales River and get into hilly country. A few miles beyond that and we can change horses at the Mullen's Creek station."

"Is the river deep, Mr. Muldoon?" Hannah said.

"Not at this time of the year, but flash floods can happen at any time, so we need to be careful."

Red explained, "First you see rainclouds, then there's a downpour, and then the flood. Anybody standing in its path gets swept away."

"Thank goodness the sky is clear," Hannah said.

"Let's hope it stays that way," Red said.

As it happened, the stage forded the shallow Perdinales without much difficulty, there was no flash flood . . . but Mullen's Station no longer existed.

"Apaches," Buttons said as he looked bleakly at the ruined cabin, barn, and corrals. And to Hannah, "The Mescalero and Chiricahua broke out last year and played hob all over this part of Texas, a lot of white folks killed."

Red climbed down from the stage and scouted around the place. When he returned, he said, "Two graves back there. Looks like the army dug them."

"I was here once before a couple of years back," Buttons said. "I didn't like Pete Mullins much, or his wife, and the grub they served tasted like it had been cooked in year-old axle grease." He shook his head. "They didn't deserve to be killed by Apaches, though."

Buttons decided to rest the team for an hour and then continue on to Austin, where there was a Patterson depot. "Get there by sundown, I reckon," he said. "Red, in the meantime, boil up some coffee, and, Miss Hannah, there's some bacon if you'd like to try it."

"I'm so tired of bacon I'd rather wait and get a proper meal in Austin," Hannah said.

"Then the Driskill Hotel on Sixth Street fits the bill," Buttons said. "It claims to be the finest hotel south of St. Louis, and maybe it is."

"Good, it will be nice to wear a dress again," Hannah said. "If my luggage has survived."

"It's all there, Miss Hannah," Buttons said. "Seen to it my ownself."

"You're a treasure, Buttons," Hannah said, smiling.

"It's all part of the service," Buttons said.

"Mr. Muldoon take good care of passengers," Mr. Chang said, bowing.

"And don't you forget it, Chinaman," Buttons said.

Why Buttons thought Mr. Chang would forget it, is not known.

Hannah studiously ignored Latimer and busied herself helping Red gather wood for a fire. The Englishman followed Hannah with his wounded brown eyes but made no attempt to talk to her.

But on that day came the small beginning of what would turn out to be John Latimer's redemption.

Chapter Twenty-nine

"Riders coming in from the south," Red said.

Buttons Muldoon used his lifted hat to shade his eyes against the sun, stared into the shimmering distance, and then nodded. "Four of them, coming in at a walk."

Buttons took the shotgun from the stage and tossed it to Red. "Keep it handy. They look friendly, but this close to the border, you never know."

Red lifted the lid of the steaming coffeepot to check its progress, but he kept eyes on the riders. "Looks like they're going to stop by for a visit," he said.

"They might be sociable folks, but they might not," Buttons said. "I don't plan on making any judgments until they're closer."

It was Hannah who first recognized two of the riders as women. "Two females all right," she said. "And they don't look happy."

"Hard to say," Red said. "Buttons, keep a sharp eye."

"And you, Red."

The reason for the women's unhappiness became obvious a short time later. They were young, mounted on nags, and had their hands tied in front of them. Their two male companions each held a lead rope and they looked well-fed and prosperous. They rode good horses and wore ditto suits, with celluloid collars and striped ties and bowler hats. The older of the two affected yellow kid gloves.

Red saw no sign of revolvers but suspected shoulder holsters under the suit coats.

Both men drew rein, and the older said, "Good day to you. I am Mr. Telfer, and this is my business associate, Mr. Miles."

Red nodded. "Pleased to make your acquaintance." His eyes went to the women, both young, pretty, and Mexican.

Hannah stared hard at the visitors, not liking what she saw. Near her, Latimer seemed perplexed, trying to make sense of what was happening, and Mr. Chang looked on, his face inscrutable.

"Smelled your coffee from a ways off," Mr. Telfer said. His eyes moved to Hannah, and his gaze explored her body. "Ah, maybe we can do business here today," he said. He looked around at the ruined station. "Not an ideal location, but I'm sure we can reach an amicable agreement."

Buttons spoke for the first time. "What kind of business?"

"We deal in commodities, sir," Mr. Miles said. "Yes, I say commodities. In our case indentured servants. May I ask if the young lady in the strange costume is a servant? And if she is, would you consider selling her?"

Hannah said, her anger flaring, "She's not for sale, and you don't deal in servants. You're nothing but a damned slave trader."

Mr. Telfer fixed a small, humorless smile on his mouth. "My dear lady, slavery was abolished in this country during the late War Between the States, and even indentured servitude is not at all what it once was." He waved a hand in the direction of the Mexican women. "In five years, these señoritas will be freed with a considerable sum of American dollars. They can then return to Mexico, marry and" —his smile widened—"live happily ever after."

"Who will hire them as servants?" Hannah said.

"Why, whatever business or respectable home needs their services," Mr. Telfer said.

"Like the brothel business?" Hannah said. "Houses of prostitution?"

Mr. Telfer's face stiffened. "Young lady, why do you care what business needs them? They're only Mexicans, for heaven's sake."

"I care. Why are their wrists tied?" Hannah said.

"For their own protection," Mr. Telfer said. "It wouldn't do for them to wander off into the wilderness and die of starvation or get eaten by wild animals, now would it?"

To everyone's surprise, Latimer spoke up, his voice clipped. "I've listened to what you have to say for yourself, and I believe that you, sir, are a bounder," he said. "Untie those women at once." And he surprised everybody a second time when he took a Remington derringer out of his coat pocket and pointed it at Mr. Telfer. "I mean now!"

"How dare you!" Mr. Telfer said. "These women are my property. I bought them in Durango for a considerable price to sell for a small profit in San Antonio or Austin." He scowled. "I'm a respectable businessman, and you are heavy-handed, sir, and a foreigner to boot. I'm sure the Texas Rangers would love to have words with you."

"That's telling him, Mr. Telfer. The impertinence of the fellow is beyond belief," Mr. Miles said. "It's obvious we're not welcome here, so we'll ride on."

"Not with the women, you won't," Latimer said.

"Are you threatening us?" Mr. Miles said.

"I'll tell you once again, and then I won't repeat myself," Latimer said. "Free those Mexican girls."

Mr. Telfer's hand reached under his coat, but he froze when he heard the hammers of Red's Greener click back and looked into muzzles as big as train tunnels. "You heard the man," Red said. "Drop those lead ropes."

Mr. Telfer hesitated, and Mr. Miles looked angry. So did Buttons Muldoon.

"You're not riding out of here with the two Mexican women," Buttons said, his eyes blazing. He had his gun in his hand. "Drop the lead ropes like my shotgun guard told you. Now, the next few seconds will be almighty tense, and things will play out much better for you gents if no mistakes are made."

"Damn you," Mr. Telfer said. "Damn all of you to hell."

John Latimer sprung another surprise. "Hannah, use your knife to cut those women free." He looked at Mr. Telfer. "Now, give me your wallet."

"No, and be damned to you," the man said.

"Give me your wallet, and yours too, Mr. Miles," Latimer said.

"Go to hell," Mr. Miles said.

"You insist on making me repeat myself," Latimer said. There was a half-smile on his lips. "I won't have it. It's very rude."

He raised the Remington and put a .41 caliber ball into Mr. Miles's shoulder.

Two events followed the sharp crack of the derringer . . .

Mr. Miles shrieked like a stuck pig. And Mr. Telfer hurriedly produced his wallet.

"I will not stand idly by while women, children, or animals are abused," Latimer said. "I will not tolerate it. Now your wallet, too, Mr. Miles, if you please. Thank you. And now you may dismount."

Latimer removed money from the wallets and gave it to the Mexican women, who cried and thanked him and made such a fuss that he found it mildly embarrassing. He helped the grateful women, girls really, into the saddles of the horses recently vacated by Mr. Miles and Mr. Telfer and said, "Go home. And good luck."

Red Ryan shook his head. "Seems like we give every Mexican we meet money and a horse. Maybe we should make it part of the Patterson stage's official policy."

Buttons smiled. "Not a bad policy at that."

After he watched the Mexican girls gallop away, Latimer turned his attention to Mr. Telfer and Mr. Miles. "You can ride the ponies you gave the women. Mr. Miles, I suggest you seek medical attention for your wound as soon as possible."

"San Antone is nearest," Buttons said, never taking

his incredulous eyes from the Englishman. "But you boys probably know that already."

The two men climbed onto the bare backs of the nags and Mr. Miles looked at Latimer and said, "When I see you again, and I will, I'll kill you."

"You may try at your earliest convenience," Latimer said. He gave an elegant bow. "I'm at your service."

Buttons Muldoon slapped John Latimer on the back and grinned, "Damn it all, you never cease to surprise me, Limey. Where the hell did you get the stinger?"

"I took it from the vest pocket of a dead man after the Gatling gun fight. He had no further use for it, and I thought it might come in handy."

"You were right to shoot that ranny," Red said. "I'm sure he was reaching for a hideout."

Latimer smiled. "So am I. I've seen shoulder holsters before."

Hannah Huckabee retained a coolness that revealed itself by her tone of her voice as she said, "You did well to free those women, John. It was the act of an English gentleman."

"Thank you, Hannah," Latimer said. "You are very kind."

An awkward silence followed . . . stretched . . . until Red snapped it. "Well, the coffee's on the bile," he said. "Find yourself a cup, ever'body, and let's have at it."

Chapter Thirty

Its side lamps glowing yellow in the gloom, the stage rattled to a halt outside the depot in Austin. The two-story building was a holdover from the old Butterfield days that had been renovated and pressed into service by Abe Patterson.

A gray-bearded oldster stood on the porch outside the main door, peered into the gloom, and said, "Is that Buttons Muldoon, and if it is, who's that with ye?"

"It sure is me, and this is Red Ryan, my shotgun guard," Buttons said.

"Ach, I know him. I'm talking about the lady that's with you."

"Her name is Miss Hannah Huckabee, and she's a paying passenger, Rush. So be civil," Buttons said.

The old man touched the visor of his threadbare Confederate kepi and said, "Right pleased to make your acquaintance, ma'am."

Hannah smiled. "And I you, Mr. . . ."

"Sanford, ma'am. Rush Sanford at your service." Then to Buttons, "I never expected to see you here,

Muldoon. This far south, you're a long way off your regular routes, ain't you?"

"A Texas Ranger commandeered the stage to carry a couple of prisoners here to Austin," Buttons said. "Now one of them prisoners is dead, another lit a shuck, and the ranger is wounded and laid up in Fredericksburg. Ain't that a kick in the butt?"

"Best to steer clear of the law when you can," Sanford said. "At least, that's been my experience."

"Yeah, been mine too," Buttons said.

"You can change your team here," Sanford said. "I got bunks in the back for whoever wants them. Save you money on a hotel. That goes for you too, Red. Shoot anybody real recent?"

"Not real recent, Rush," Red said.

"Too bad," Sanford said. "There's coffee in the pot. Unhitch and then come inside."

Red climbed down from the seat and then held out a hand for Hannah, who joined him on the porch. "Shall we look at the accommodation?" she said.

"Don't expect much," Red said. "But Rush Sanford makes good coffee."

The back room of the building had half a dozen bunks but no pillows or blankets. The place smelled of ancient sweat and rising dampness, and Hannah made a face. "I prefer to spend the night in a hotel," she said.

"I don't blame you none," Red said.

"But I will sample Mr. Sanford's coffee," Hannah said.

The coffee was as good as Red had promised, and

Sanford said the secret was in the Arbuckle if it was treated right.

After Hannah finished a second cup, she asked Mr. Chang to collect her luggage from the stage and accompany her to the nearest hotel.

"Good you have an escort, Miss Huckabee," Sanford said.

Hannah smiled. "Are the streets in Austin that dangerous for a lady?" she said.

The oldster nodded. "Right now? Yes, they are."

He walked away as though unwilling to say more, and Hannah wondered at that.

But Red heard what Sanford said, and since Latimer and Mr. Chang had elected to bed down in the depot, Red volunteered to take over the escort duties.

He said, "If the streets are really that dangerous, which I doubt, you're better off with me, Hannah. It's my duty as a representative of the Patterson and Son Stage and Express Company to see you safely to your hotel."

Mr. Chang didn't seem to mind. "Good idea. Man good with gun walk with more confidence," he said. "Mr. Ryan good with gun."

Carrying what luggage she needed, Red escorted Hannah in the direction of the Regency Hotel that Sanford had recommended for ladies of good breeding.

The coming of the Houston and Texas Central Railway had turned Austin into a boomtown with three-story buildings, gas street lighting, a streetcar line, and a population exceeding ten thousand. Red steered Hannah through a crowd of traders, construction workers, students, businessmen of every stripe, and here and there tall, taciturn ranchers in from the range. Hannah, who'd spent time in some of the greatest capitals in Europe, was nonetheless impressed with Austin, and she told Red that the town was "the Paris of the prairie."

But Red had his reservations, and he was wary.

There were a lot of blue-uniformed policemen in the street, some of them mounted, and it seemed that every woman that passed was escorted by at least two men. There was tension in the air, and the crowded streets were unnaturally quiet, everyone talking in low voices . . . as though the city was gripped by a nameless fear.

Red dismissed the thought, guessing that the events of the past few days had put him on edge, but he couldn't shake the feeling that something was not quite right with the city of Austin.

The Regency was a three-story stone building with a pleasant façade and an etched-glass double doorway. Inside, the furnishings were red velvet and gold, and the rugs on the wood floor were thick and added to the genteel silence of the place. The desk clerk, a balding young man in a high celluloid collar with a slightly disdainful air, spoke in a brusque tone as he welcomed Hannah and asked her to sign the register.

"Will you be alone?" the clerk asked,

"Yes, quite alone. My servant has found other accommodation," Hannah said.

"Then rest assured that the Regency has first-class

security, and you need have no fear . . ." He glanced at the register . . . "Miss Huckabee. There are armed policemen constantly patrolling the street outside, and there's a bell on your bedside table that will raise the alarm in the very unlikely event that you feel in the least uncomfortable."

Hannah smiled. "I'm armed. I don't ring bells."

The clerk managed a smile that lasted about half a second and said, "Then all will be well."

As though he was making small talk, Red said, "I noticed that there's a great many policemen in the street. Are you expecting trouble?"

The clerk's Adam's apple bobbed as he said, "No. No, there's no trouble in Austin."

"Tell him the truth, damn it."

Red turned to see a man at his elbow, a bearded giant in a caped, tweed overcoat, and a brown bowler hat who looked to be around forty years old. He had an S-shaped pipe clamped between his teeth, and when he removed it to speak, a gold signet ring gleamed on the little finger of his left hand.

"The police are on the street because people live in terror of the Servant Girl Annihilator, a monster who has murdered seven women already and is on the lookout for more," the man said. "He attacks women while they're sleeping and chops them up with an axe. Skulls split wide open, that kind of thing." He stuck out his hand. "Rufus T. Proudfoot of the Pinkerton Detective Agency. I've been in town a few days investigating the murders."

Red shook his hand and said, "Red Ryan, shotgun

guard with the Abe Patterson and Son Stage and Express Company."

"And your lovely companion?"

"Miss Hannah Huckabee. She's an adventuress."

Proudfoot's shrewd eyes took in Hannah's safari clothes and pith helmet and goggles and said, "And indeed she looks like one. It's a real pleasure to meet you, Miss Huckabee."

Hannah dropped a little curtsey. "Likewise, I'm sure."

"Are you staying in Austin for a while or just passing through?" Proudfoot said.

"Passing through," Hannah said. "I'm bound for New Orleans."

"On the Patterson stage," Red said.

"New Orleans is a wonderful town, Miss Huckabee. You will not be disappointed," Proudfoot said. "Business or pleasure?"

"A little of both," Hannah said. "I'd hoped to gather supplies for a balloon trip around the world I'm planning. But recently I've thought to begin my trip in London or Paris and head east across Europe and into Asia and beyond."

"Ah, around the world in eighty days, I'll be bound," Proudfoot said. "Haven't we all read Mr. Verne's wonderful book?"

Hannah said, "Unlike Phileas Fogg, I'm in no hurry, so it will take longer than eighty days. I do very much want to visit the African continent and spend some time in Cathay again."

"Wonderful!" Proudfoot exclaimed. "Africa, the

Dark Continent, mysterious Cathay, you are indeed an adventuress."

The Pinkerton got his key from the clerk and looked at the one in Hannah's hand. "Ah, we're both on the third floor. Tonight, you'll be quite safe as you slumber, Miss Huckabee. I'm both armed and a light sleeper."

Proudfoot took out a gold watch as big as a pie plate and said, "It's six-thirty now. Miss Huckabee. I know this is short notice, but perhaps I could interest you in supper tonight?"

"Yes, I'd like that," Hannah said. "I've grown tired of bacon and beans."

"Then I'll meet you here in the lobby at eight?"

"Yes. Eight will be fine."

Proudfoot touched the brim of his hat. "It was a pleasure to meet you, Mr. Ryan."

"You too," Red said, disliking the man and more than a little jealous.

"So why did she agree to have supper with him?" Buttons Muldoon said.

"She told me after all that's happened she wanted to do something normal, something civilized, she called it," Red Ryan said.

Buttons shook his head. "By times, womenfolk have strange notions."

"Miss Hannah have stranger notions than most," Mr. Chang said. "One time she have dinner with John L. Sullivan, the famous pugilist. Mr. Sullivan got drunk on champagne, and Miss Hannah carried him home. Next day, Mr. Sullivan send her three dozen roses."

Red's interest perked up. "I've heard of him, the Boston Strong Boy." He shook his head. "When I was a booth fighter, I never boxed him, though. Probably just as well."

"Just as well for who?" Buttons said.

"For me," Red said. "From what I hear, Sullivan is a handful."

Without appetite, Red used his fork to push around the tough beef and mushy beans on his plate. Rush Sanford wasn't much of a cook.

"Buttons, you heard about the Servant Girl Annihilator?" he said.

"Yeah, Rush told me about him," Buttons said. "It's a bad business. One of his victims was an eleven-year-old girl."

"Hannah Huckabee is our passenger, and it's our duty as representatives of the Abe Patterson and Son Stage and Express Company to keep her safe while she's in Austin," Red said.

John Latimer was stretched out on a cot and now he sat up and said, "Red, do you think Hannah is in real danger?"

"No, I don't think so. The Pinkerton has a room in the Regency Hotel on the same floor."

"Unless the Pinkerton is the killer," Latimer said.

"He was brought in a few days ago by the mayor to

investigate the murders," Red said. "They all happened before he arrived."

"Miss Hannah will only be in town tonight," Buttons said. "I reckon she'll be safe enough with the Pink."

He didn't know it then, but terrifying events would soon prove Buttons Muldoon very wrong.

Chapter Thirty-one

"The venison was to your liking?" Rufus T. Proudfoot said.

"Yes, indeed it was, and the dessert figs were wonderful," Hannah said. "I'm quite surprised that a frontier town has such exquisite cuisine."

"Yes, it always comes as a surprise to visitors. More wine?"

"Just a little."

Proudfoot poured the red zinfandel and said, his face revealing nothing, "You're an adventuress, Miss Huckabee, and you've recounted some of your adventures, especially those with the wild Cossacks on the Russian steppe, that had me on the edge of my seat with excitement."

"Well, thank you, Mr. Proudfoot," Hannah said. She opened the tiny purse that matched her evening dress and produced a silver cigar case. She extracted a slim cheroot and held it up to her companion. "May I beg your indulgence?"

"Please do," Proudfoot said. "I was about to have a pipe."

The man tipped the candelabra so that Hannah

could light her cigar, and then he looked around the crowded restaurant and dropped his voice to a whisper.

"You are no stranger to danger, Miss Huckabee, and you have a pistol that you know how to use. Is that not so?"

"Yes, it's so," Hannah said. "I was taught to how to use a revolver by my late uncle. He was an adventurer and a crack shot."

Proudfoot saw the question on the woman's face, and said, "I'm about to ask you to embark on yet another adventure, one that will involve considerable risk to yourself."

"I'm not sure that I want to hear this, but go on," Hannah said, smiling. She took a sip of wine. "Now you intrigue me, Mr. Proudfoot."

The Pinkerton reached inside his jacket and produced a folded piece of paper. "First read this, Miss Huckabee."

"What is it?" Hannah said.

"It's a list of the victims of the Servant Girl Annihilator."

"This is hardly after-dinner reading," Hannah said.

"I know, and I apologize for that. But before I tell you about the perilous adventure I propose, I really think you should see this."

Hannah frowned. "Well, if you insist."

She took the paper, unfolded it, and read the meticulous copperplate:

Mollie Smith, 25, colored servant girl. Killed by an axe as she slept.
Eliza Shelly, age unknown, colored servant girl.

Dragged from her bed and then killed outside house with an axe.

Irene Cross, colored servant girl, killed by a knife while she slept.

Mary Ramey, 11, raped and killed by an axe. Her mother Rebecca seriously wounded while trying to save her daughter.

Gracie Vance, colored servant girl, dragged from bed and killed by knife and axe. Orange Washington killed during attack on Gracie Vance. Lucinda Boddy and Patsey Gibson seriously wounded.

Susan Hancock, white woman, dragged from bed and murdered by an axe.

Eula Phillips, white woman, murdered by an axe. Decapitated. Her husband James seriously wounded.

"Well, that was not a very pleasant experience, Detective Proudfoot," Hannah said. "Why did you insist on me reading it?"

"Because the Annihilator will kill again, and soon more names will be added to that terrible list," Proudfoot said. "He has to be stopped. His pattern is to allow a week to elapse between murders, and Mrs. Phillips was killed six days ago. He will strike tonight or tomorrow night. He'll be forced to it, Miss Huckabee. The need to kill will drive him."

Hannah allowed herself a slight smile. "Mr. Proudfoot, I think I know where this conversation is headed, and I feel the need for a brandy and coffee."

"Coming up." The Pinkerton grinned.

"I must warn you, I'm not a cheap dinner companion," Hannah said.

"I know. Thank goodness for an expense account."

They both laughed, and after the brandy and coffee arrived, Proudfoot said, "Now, do you wish to know about the adventure I have in mind for you?"

Hannah smiled, and the candlelight tangled in her auburn hair and gleamed on the swell of her breasts. "No, let me tell you, Detective."

"Please do," Proudfoot said, smiling.

"You're going to ask me to walk the streets alone and shake my bustle, bait for the woman killer," Hannah said. "The only thing is, there are several things wrong with that plan, the most obvious being . . . where the hell do I hide a .45 in this dress? In my corset?"

Disapproving heads turned in Hannah's direction, and she whispered, "I was a little loud there, wasn't I?"

Proudfoot smiled. "Who can blame you? But no, Miss Huckabee, you will not walk the streets, you will go to bed in your hotel room. In other words, just do as you would normally do when visiting a strange city."

"And when the Annihilator comes in, I plug him. Is that the case?"

"You won't need to shoot him, because you won't be alone. I'll have armed men in the next room ready to intervene at a moment's notice," Proudfoot said. "And, of course, I'll be one of them."

Hannah swirled her brandy, sniffed, tasted, and then said, "It's quite ordinary. I'm surprised."

The Pinkerton smiled. "I'm sure that somewhere in this town there's better. I'll use all my detective skills to track down a fine brandy. That is, after . . ."

"After tonight," Hannah said.

"Yes, after tonight."

"Mr. Proudfoot . . ."

"Call me Rufus."

"Oh dear, do I have to?"

"I have an unlovely name, but I try to make the best of it."

"Then Rufus it is," Hannah said. "You know your plan isn't going to work. The killer isn't going to walk past a hotel desk clerk, climb the stairs to the third floor, and attack me in my bedroom. And that's if he even comes at all."

"There won't be a desk clerk. Between the hours of eleven at night and seven in the morning, the Regency front desk is not manned. The hotel owners figure everyone will be asleep, or they're trying to save money, take your pick. The murderer is quiet, and he's daring. He's already entered several homes and dragged screaming women from their beds and axed them to death outside, and all the work of a moment. He then disappears. To where, no one can tell."

"But the Annihilator doesn't even know I'm in the hotel," Hannah said.

Proudfoot's face drained of all expression. His voice strangely hollow, he said, "By now he knows, Miss Huckabee. Trust me, the fiend already knows, and he's already whetting his axe."

"Rufus, what a singularly strange and frightening thing to say." Hannah drank more brandy, this time without complaint.

"I was given a good description of the killer and spent the past few days following every lead," Proudfoot said. "I tracked down a suspect who fits the bill, and if it is indeed him, he'll strike tonight. By the way, the city authorities, from the mayor on down, want the killer dead. There are no ifs, buts, or maybes on that. I've been ordered to kill him so that his shadow no longer falls on the earth."

Hannah was silent for long moments and then said, "As a woman in a man's world with everything to prove, I can't claim to be an adventuress and refuse a dangerous adventure when it's offered. And if I can save another female life, then that is an even greater incentive. But I must make a condition, Rufus."

"Name it, dear lady," Proudfoot said. "I will make any concession within reason."

"There are only two men I'll trust to be in the adjoining room, Red Ryan, shotgun guard, and Buttons Muldoon, driver, of the Patterson stage."

"Ah, Red Ryan I met in the hotel. He seemed competent enough. What about the Muldoon fellow?"

"Fear doesn't enter into Buttons's thinking. He and Red are more than capable, and they've proved their valor many times," Hannah said. "Their bravery is not in question."

"And where can I find these paladins?"

"I expect we'll find them at the Patterson stage depot," Hannah said.

"Then, if you're ready, let's put our proposition before them," Proudfoot said.

Chapter Thirty-two

"Are you out of your mind, Pinkerton?" Buttons Muldoon said. "Only a crazy man would say what you just said."

"Miss Huckabee is a fare-paying passenger of Abe Patterson and Son Stage and Express Company, and as such I am responsible for her safety. I will not let her be used in this way," Red Ryan said. "No, it's out of the question."

"Red, I want to do it," Hannah said. "If I can get rid of this murderous fiend and save another woman's life, then my duty is clear. And I very much want you and Mr. Muldoon to protect me tonight. But if you refuse, then Detective Proudfoot says he can hire some likely lads."

"All of them stalwarts, I assure you, Miss Huckabee," Proudfoot said. "Well-armed and resolute citizens of this fair town."

"Hannah, let me be in that adjoining room," John Latimer said.

"No, John," Hannah said. "I won't trust you with my life, and there's an end to it."

"I would willingly sacrifice my life for you, Hannah," Latimer said.

"No, John. And please do not mention it again."

"Hannah, are you sure you want to go through with this?" Red said. "It's dangerous, and Proudfoot had no right to ask you to do it."

"Yes, I want to go through with it. My mind is made up. I have it within my power to save the life of another woman, or a young child, and I can't—and I won't—turn away from that responsibility."

Mr. Chang said, "As Miss Huckabee say, if she can do good things for other people, it is not a choice, it is a duty."

"Miss Hannah could get her head chopped off with an axe, you crazy Chinee," Buttons said.

Mr. Chang smiled. "You and Mr. Ryan brave men, Mr. Muldoon. You can prevent such an unfortunate end to Miss Huckabee's illustrious career."

"Pinkerton, you don't even know if the killer will show up," Buttons said.

"I'm pretty sure he will," Proudfoot said. He consulted his huge watch and said. "It's ten o'clock. Time Miss Huckabee was tucked up in bed."

Red and Buttons exchanged glances, and Rush Sanford said, "Don't anybody ask me for help. I'm too damned old to be facing down an axe murderer."

Red's sigh seemed to come all the way from his toes. "All right, we'll do it," he said. "I'm agin it, but I'll do it for Hannah's sake."

"Damn tomfoolery if you ask me," Buttons said. "The killer isn't going anywhere near the Regency Hotel tonight, anyway. But nobody cares what I think."

Then to Proudfoot, "Is there a back door to the hotel?"

"Good question, Mr. Muldoon," the Pinkerton said. "Yes, there is, and that's the door you and Mr. Ryan will use. I will already be there, waiting for you. The room adjoining Miss Huckabee's is number 27." He consulted his watch. "Give us thirty minutes to get ready and then come to the Regency. One last thing, I want this killer dead."

"Question is, what does he want?" Buttons said.

Proudfoot frowned. "He wants Miss Huckabee. That I can guarantee."

The balding desk clerk was just going off duty when Hannah Huckabee and Rufus Proudfoot arrived in the lobby.

"All quiet tonight," the clerk said. "It seems that all the guests are asleep." He hurried toward the door as though anxious to leave. "Well, good night to you, Miss Huckabee. I'll be here at seven sharp tomorrow morning, should you need anything."

After the clerk left, the Pinkerton saw Hannah to her room and said, "For obvious reasons I won't say good night, but keep your revolver handy."

"Trust me, I will," Hannah said. "Now that it's happening, I don't feel as brave as I did in the restaurant."

"It's a fearful thing I'm asking you to do," Proudfoot said. "Hannah, if you wish to back out now, I won't blame you. And no one else will, either."

"I'll stick," Hannah said. "I've come this far, and I'll see it through."

The Pinkerton placed his hand on Hannah's slim shoulder. "You're a brave woman, Hannah. The bravest I've ever known."

"Thank you," Hannah said. "Well, let's get this adventure underway."

"Mr. Verne would be proud of you," the Pinkerton said.

Hannah smiled. "I'd rather be in a balloon." She closed the door but didn't turn the key in the lock, and Proudfoot stood in the hallway for a long time, his head bent in thought, his heart racing. He heard Hannah preparing for bed as he reached into his coat and drew his Shopkeeper Colt from the shoulder holster and thumbed a round into the revolver's empty chamber. Satisfied, he re-holstered the Colt and remained outside Hannah's door a while longer, his face grim, before he made his way downstairs.

The key to Room 27 hung on a hook on the rack behind the desk, and Proudfoot took the key and walked through a darkened hallway to the back door. Behind him, in the lobby, the slightly-out-of-tune grandfather clock chimed into the dead silence, like eleven silver coins dropping one by one into a cracked pewter bowl.

Red Ryan and Buttons Muldoon were already waiting outside. The Pinkerton held up the key. "Room twenty-seven," he said. "Let's go. Quietly now."

Red carried his shotgun and Buttons his holstered revolver, but what suddenly gave Proudfoot pause was the tall, slim figure of John Latimer emerging from the gloom. "And you are?" the Pinkerton said.

"My name is Latimer. I'm a friend of Miss Huckabee."

"He's all right," Red said. "He wanted to come along with us, and he's handy with a gun."

"You can vouch for him?" Proudfoot said.

Buttons said, "Like Red said, he's all right. He was once engaged to be married to Miss Huckabee."

"A lifetime ago," Latimer said. "But yes, we were engaged to be married."

Proudfoot nodded. "Good to have you along, Latimer. Are you armed?"

"I have a derringer."

"Good. If you tangle with the murderer, stick it in his face and pull the trigger. It will get the job done. Now follow me."

The four men returned to the lobby, walking carefully through darkness. Buttons, prone to hay-fever attacks when he was excited, sneezed, and Red, irritated, jabbed the butt of the Greener into his ribs.

"I can't help it," Buttons said. "A man can't hold in a sneeze."

And Proudfoot said, "Shh . . ."

The stairs were in darkness, and Buttons said to no one in particular, "Watch where you walk."

Slowly, carefully, the four men climbed the stairs, a single, creaking step at a time. Once in the hallway, Proudfoot whispered. "Room twenty-seven. Let's go."

"I don't like this," Buttons said. "I don't like this one bit."

"Shh . . ." Proudfoot said again.

The Pinkerton halted at Room 27 and opened the door. It creaked on its hinges, and for a moment Red thought his heart had stopped. One by one the four men filed into the room, and Proudfoot stood by the door of the adjoining room and whispered, "Now we wait . . ."

Buttons, in distress, held his nose, squeezing hard, trying to stifle a sneeze. Red glared at him.

Proudfoot was breathing noisily in short little gasps.

Red felt his belly tying itself in knots, and his mouth was dry. He put his Colt in his left hand, dried his sweating gun hand on his pants, and then passed the revolver back to his right again.

Outside a woman laughed in the street, a man's droning voice said something to her that made her laugh again, and then there was silence.

The room was so quiet, Proudfoot's watch could be heard *tick, tick, tick*ing in his vest pocket. Sweat trickled down Red Ryan's back, and beside him Buttons gave a little series of gasps as he held back a sneeze. Time seemed to stand still, the four men in the room standing motionless in place. Then, from Hannah's room her brass bed creaked, accompanied by a soft, thumping sound as she pounded her feather pillow into place. Then the hush descended again.

Buttons took his hand from his nose, looked at Red, and smiled and nodded.

Then two events happened that opened the ball.

Buttons let out a rip-roaring, "Aaach-oooo!"

And a moment later a gunshot hammered through the hotel . . . followed by the shriek after hysterical shriek of someone in mortal agony.

Chapter Thirty-three

"Ryan, kick the door in," Rufus Proudfoot yelled.

Red raised his booted foot, kicked hard, and the door that separated the rooms slammed open wide in a shower of wood splinters, and the four men burst into Hannah's room.

Red was the first through, and he took in the situation at a glance.

Hannah Huckabee had her back to the wall to his right, a look of horror on her face. She held her Colt in her hand, smoke trailing from the muzzle.

A man lay writhing, twisting, convulsing on the floor, screaming in pain like a wild animal. His feet were bare, and beside him, its blade honed to a razor edge, lay a wicked-looking hand axe.

Hannah ignored Latimer and ran to Red, and he held her close, feeling her body tremble through the thin silk of her nightgown.

As voices were raised in the hallways, Hannah said, her voice rising, "He came into the room and tried to drag me out of bed. I had my gun hidden under the pillow and managed to shoot him. He was growling like a mad dog, snarling at me . . ."

Red made comforting noises, his eyes on the thing that twined and untwined like a wounded serpent on the floor, its screams reverberating through the witching hour quiet of the hotel.

"Son of a bitch is gut-shot," Buttons Muldoon said. He made a face and pressed the palms of his hands over his ears against the shrill clamor of the man's screeches and said, "That's why he's squealing like a stuck pig."

Proudfoot stepped to the man and held him down with an elastic-sided boot on his chest and said, "Finally met your match, didn't you, Ernie? Your murdering and raping days are over, my friend."

The man cried out louder, his face twisted into a grotesque mask of torment. He opened his mouth and tried to talk, but he gagged on his own blood.

Proudfoot said, "Ah, yes, that's what I wanted to see, Ernie, fear in your eyes. Was there fear in little Mary Ramey's eyes as you raped her? Was there, Ernie?"

The man shrieked and tried to twist away from the Pinkerton boot that pinned him like an insect to the floor.

Proudfoot said, "Mary Ramey was just eleven years old, Ernie. A child. Just a child. You split her head open, Ernie. Yes, that's what you did, didn't you?"

The Pinkerton reached into his coat and drew his Colt. "I'm sending you to hell, Ernie. Enjoy the ride, huh?"

The killer's shrieks abruptly cut off as Proudfoot's bullet crashed between his eyes.

After the racketing roar of the Colt faded into a ringing silence, Proudfoot said, "His name was Ernie Miller, and he was the desk clerk of this hotel."

At breakfast, in Mom's Kitchen, Buttons asked, "Here, Pinkerton, did you know he was the Annihilator all along?"

"No. He was one of three men that fit the description I was given, and he was the last one I investigated," Proudfoot said. "Ernie Miller was a loner. He had no known relatives or friends and spoke to nobody but the residents of the Regency Hotel. I dug deeper and discovered that he'd lived with a whore named Bessie White who he abused regularly. A doctor who treated Miller told me he blamed Bessie for the syphilis he'd contracted."

The Mom's Kitchen waitress refilled coffee cups, and the Pinkerton waited until she left the table to attend on the other early-morning breakfasters before he spoke again.

"Bessie White vanished, and Miller told his doctor that she'd gone to live with a maiden aunt in Philadelphia," Proudfoot said. "The doctor suspected that Ernie killed her and dumped her body somewhere. Bessie White was probably the Servant Girl Annihilator's first victim, but there's no proof of that. Putting it all together, I was convinced I had my man." The Pinkerton smiled. "And you know the rest."

"Rufus, why did he go barefooted?" Hannah said.

"He'd creep up on his victims while they were asleep, and bare feet are silent." Proudfoot smiled. "Ernie

Miller had never attacked an armed female before, and Hannah, you took him by surprise when you cut loose with your revolver. The Pinkerton Agency hires female detectives, and I was always against arming them, but after last night, I've changed my mind."

"A woman detective is an adventuress," Hannah said. "She should be given a revolver and taught how to use it."

Red Ryan said, "Proudfoot, how come Miller was able to get into Hannah's room without being seen?"

"I thought Miller had left the hotel, but he'd waited outside in the dark, watching through the window," the Pinkerton said. "When he saw me come down the stairs and head for the back door, he thought I was leaving. Ernie saw his chance and was determined to take it, but I think he stood outside for a while, anticipating the exquisite thrill of his next murder, and only then did he silently make his way upstairs. Little did he know that instead of a terrified victim he'd come up against an adventuress who carried a gun and could get her work in quickly."

"I nearly wasn't quick enough," Hannah said. "When he grabbed me by the hair and raised the axe, I thought I was dead. And I would be dead now if I'd put my revolver on the bedside table and not under my pillow."

Proudfoot leaned forward like a cloak-and-dagger conspirator and said in a low tone, "I do apologize, because I have yet another favor to ask, Miss Huckabee."

"Then ask it if you must," Hannah said. "So long as it doesn't involve madmen, axes, and darkened rooms."

"Well, it does in a way," the Pinkerton said. "Did

you happen to see those three gentlemen standing outside the hotel after the . . . ah . . . incident?"

Hannah shook her head. "No, I did not. For a while afterward, I was very distressed and didn't notice much of anything."

"Well, one of them was the mayor and with him was the chief of police and a representative of the town's leading citizens," Proudfoot said. "They request that you do not take the credit for killing the Annihilator. To put the minds of the women of Austin at rest, they wish the credit to go to the city police. They want them to know, or to think, that the constabulary can protect them."

"Rufus, what kind of woman would I be if I went around boasting of a killing?" Hannah said. "Yes, let the police take the credit for ending the madman's reign of terror, and welcome."

"The mayor will be relieved to hear that," Proudfoot said. "And so too will the chief of police and the women of Austin."

"Glad I could be of help," Hannah said.

The Pinkerton nodded. "Miss Huckabee, you're the bravest woman I've ever met, a heroine in every sense of the word."

Hannah looked at Red's plate. "Are you going to eat that last sausage?" she said.

Chapter Thirty-four

"We picked up a fare-paying passenger for New Orleans," Buttons Muldoon said. "And you'll never guess who he is."

"No, I don't think I can," Red Ryan said.

"Try."

"I don't know. President Arthur?"

"No. Try again."

"Lillie Langtry."

"Better than that. Are you ready for this?"

"I'm ready."

"Sage Barnard."

"The Cajun gambler we met in Galveston that time?"

"Yeah. The time he shot Flynn Mayfield in the Ruby Saloon."

"What the hell is Barnard doing in Austin?" Red said. "He always stays east of the Brazos."

"I asked him that very question," Buttons said. "He said Texas is the best place to outrun a losing streak. Plenty of room, he said."

"And did he?"

"Well, he paid his fare in advance. That ought to tell you something."

"I hope he gets along with John Latimer and Mr. Chang," Red said. "They'll be spending five hundred miles of open prairie together."

"I heard that when he's in drink, Sage becomes a mite testy and ain't above shooting folks," Buttons said. "That's what I heard one time, but I don't know if it's true or not."

"I hope we don't find out," Red said. "There's been more than enough killing on this trip already."

"Truer words were never spoke," Buttons said. "I'm looking forward to some quiet times."

"And so am I," Hannah Huckabee said. She joined Red and Buttons on the porch of the stage depot. "Are we ready to go?"

Buttons consulted his watch. "It's eleven-thirty. After all that's happened, the Patterson stage for New Orleans now leaves at noon."

"Did you say your farewells to the Pinkerton, Hannah?" Red said.

"Yes, I did. Rufus says we may meet up again in New Orleans, but I don't intend to linger, so that's unlikely to happen," Hannah said. She was again dressed in her tan safari clothes and pith helmet but wasn't wearing her gun. "I've finally decided that my around-the-world balloon trip will start from London or Paris. Mr. Chang favors Paris because he enjoys French cuisine, but we'll see."

Rush Sanford walked onto the porch. "Sacked up some grub for you, Buttons," he said. Then, scratching his beard. "Did you hear? The police shot the woman killer last night. A couple of officers caught him red-handed trying to climb through the window of a servant girl's bedroom on Pecan Street. Good work by the police, huh?"

Buttons nodded. "Yeah, good work."

"Excellent work," Red said.

"I'm glad it's over," Hannah said. Then, turning to the elegant man who'd just joined her, "I don't think we've met. I'm Hannah Huckabee."

Sage Barnard bowed over Hannah's hand and gave his name. "I'm enchanted," he said. "Are you destined for New Orleans?"

"Yes, I am."

"Then the journey will seem much shorter in the company of such a beautiful traveling companion," Barnard said.

Hannah smiled. "Mr. Barnard, you are very gracious."

Barnard was the typical gambler/gunman of the frontier, a tall, handsome man with sky-blue eyes dressed in a black broadcloth frock coat and spotless white linen. His clothing was expensive, conservative, and beautifully tailored. His only concession to conspicuous jewelry was a gold watch chain and his silver gambler's ring. He wore no belt gun but would have one out of sight and handy.

Hannah thought Barnard very attractive, but there was an air of danger, of an inclination to violence, about him that troubled her. She'd been around men like him before, the American mercenaries, most of them ex-Confederates, who found employment with Chinese warlords and could explode into terrible violence at any moment, powder kegs with fast-burning fuses that had only to be lit.

Sage Barnard would be right at home among them.

Red Ryan introduced John Latimer to Barnard and the two shook hands, a pair of young men sizing up each other and finding no reason for antagonism or disrespect. Mr. Chang never shook hands with anyone, but he bowed, and Barnard bowed in return.

Red Ryan, watching, thought, *So far, so good.* The last thing he and Buttons needed on this trip was friction between the passengers.

The death of the Servant Girl Annihilator had put Austin in a festive mood, and people in the crowded streets cheered as the Patterson stage made its dramatic exit from the town, Buttons Muldoon handling the ribbons and whip with his usual élan.

Hannah Huckabee took up her accustomed place on top of the stage, and Red Ryan sat with his shotgun between his knees. He and Buttons expected that this would be a quiet trip, especially since Rush Sanford told them that the stage stations along the route had avoided the recent Apache troubles and were functioning normally.

"We got five hundred miles of flat country ahead of us, Miss Huckabee," Buttons said to Hannah. "So, maybe I can find time to teach you the ways of a horse team."

"I'd like that, Mr. Muldoon," Hannah said loud, talking above the rumble of the coach wheels and the jangle of horse harness.

Red grinned and said, "It's plain sailing all the way to New Orleans."

Unfortunately, events would prove him wrong.

Chapter Thirty-five

"My dear Captain Bentley-Foulkes, my frigate didn't cross the Atlantic for the sole purpose of picking up a man accused of cowardice in the Afghan War," Commander John Pickering said. "I mean, the Admiralty is extremely parsimonious and has better things to do with its money."

"My information was that John Latimer wrote to the War Office and demanded a court-martial," Rupert Bentley-Foulkes said.

"And so he did," Pickering said. "And the War Office contacted the Admiralty and their lordships contacted Admiral Kent of the home fleet and Admiral Kent discovered that the steam frigate *Hephaestus,* commanded by yours truly, was bound for New Orleans on a courtesy visit. Admiral Kent than contacted the War Office and the War Office then contacted Latimer and told him to present himself at the Port of New Orleans and surrender to me." Pickering, resplendent in the blue and gold of Her Majesty's navy, smiled. "We British take good care of our heroes. We take good care of our cowards as well."

Bentley-Foulkes and Pickering sat in a bar on Bourbon Street, the open doors and windows doing little to alleviate the stifling heat of the day. Outside, a loaded dray rumbled past and Bentley-Foulkes waited until it passed before he said, "What are your plans for Latimer?"

"Plans?" Pickering said, looking puzzled. "I don't have any. I could clap him in irons, I suppose, and lock him up in the hold, but since his cowardice hasn't yet been proven, I'll probably let him have free run of the ship. After all, he's still a British army officer."

"And if he doesn't show up?"

Pickering shrugged. "Then he doesn't show up, it's no concern of mine. I'll report to my superiors that Latimer either changed his mind or was killed by savages. Another glass of rum with you?"

"No, I must be leaving," Bentley-Foulkes said. "I wish to thank you again for meeting with me."

The commander waved that off. "One officer to another, it's just professional courtesy, old boy. But why your interest in Latimer, an obscure army captain who disgraced himself in a meaningless skirmish in a now-forgotten little war?"

"I haven't forgotten. Latimer's dereliction of duty cost the life of my brother," Bentley-Foulkes said. "I want to see justice done and the coward shot."

"I rather fancy that to see justice done, you'll have to return to England and attend Latimer's court-martial," Pickering said. "After so many years have passed, it promises to be a very dull affair. And even if he's found guilty, I doubt the chap will face a firing squad. A sharp rap on the knuckles and a 'Don't do that again,' is more likely."

"That will not be the case," Bentley-Foulkes said. "Latimer will pay for his crime." He rose to his feet. "Good day to you, sir."

"And you, too, Captain," Pickering said. "We'll be docked for another week, so stop by the ship for lunch and I'll show you around. The *Hephaestus* is a new armored frigate and one of the most powerful fighting ships in the world." He grinned. "There's nothing better than a courtesy visit to show the Americans a thing or two about the power of the Royal Navy and the future of warfare at sea."

"Yes, yes, of course," Bentley-Foulkes said, distracted. "Jolly good."

Commander Pickering nodded, then, as the young man turned to leave, he said, "I hope you find the justice you're looking for, Captain."

"The navy ship has no orders to wait for John Latimer to surrender himself," Rupert Bentley-Foulkes said. "Colonel Grierson at Fort Concho was misinformed by someone in London, some junior Admiralty clerk I suppose."

"And if he doesn't appear?" former lieutenant Granville Wood said.

"Commander Pickering said he'll be written off as having changed his mind or dead, killed by savages."

"Are we savages?" John Allerton said, his young face earnest.

"No, we're not," Bentley-Foulkes said. "We're judges."

Brack Cooley, a dark, brooding figure, looked out the window of Bentley-Foulkes's hotel room into busy Lafayette Square, where children played with hoops and fashionable ladies with white parasols promenaded with their gentlemen.

Without turning, he said, "How do we play it?"

"At all costs we must make sure Latimer doesn't board the warship," Bentley-Foulkes said. "If he does, we'll have lost him."

"I can kill him anytime you say," Cooley said.

"I want him to have his court-martial first," Bentley-Foulkes said.

"And then I kill him," Cooley said.

"And then you execute him, yes."

"Kill, execute, it's the same thing," Cooley said. "Either way Latimer ends up dead."

"We must get to him shortly after he leaves the stage," Bentley-Foulkes said. "There's an old coaching inn on Broad Street, and the proprietor says that's where the Patterson and other stages stop. Lieutenant Allerton will take a room at the inn and keep the place under observation, so we can grab Latimer when the opportunity arises."

"Just remember that Red Ryan is riding shotgun," Cooley said. "We've got to make it look good."

"If the worse comes to worst, you can handle Ryan, can't you, Mr. Cooley?" Bentley-Foulkes said.

"Sure, I can, but I'd rather he didn't get involved. He's good with the iron, and in my business that kind of man is best left alone. No profit in it."

"Well, we'll cross that bridge when we come to it," Bentley-Foulkes said. "The main thing is we kidnap

Latimer shortly after he leaves the stage and then bring him to justice."

"As I told you already, I can take care of Ryan," Cooley said. "I just don't like complications, and he's a complication."

"You will kill him, Mr. Cooley, and that will simplify matters considerably," Bentley-Foulkes said. "Until then, we must be discreet."

"I'll earn my money, Englishman," Cooley said. "Don't worry about that. When you decide Red Ryan has to go, then he's a dead man."

Bentley-Foulkes said, "On open ground not too far from here, Lieutenant Wood stumbled on an abandoned slave warehouse that's situated well away from prying eyes. I'll show it to you, since you must bring Latimer there."

Wood smiled and said, "It's supposed to be haunted by the ghosts of dead slaves, and that's why everybody shuns the place. The good folks of New Orleans are superstitious."

"Ghosts or not, the court-martial of Captain John Latimer will be held there," Bentley-Foulkes said. "If he's found guilty of cowardice in the face of the enemy, he will then be shot."

Cooley nodded. "And I'll do the shooting."

"Yes, you will. As I told you before, Mr. Cooley, I won't have the blood of a coward on my hands.

"Hell, it doesn't bother me none," Brack Cooley said. "I've shot cowards afore."

Chapter Thirty-six

Singer's Station had the reputation of being the worst stage stop in central and east Texas, but Buttons Muldoon had no choice. Thanks to the recent Apache trouble, intact stations were few and far between, and since the day was shading into evening, hot food and a roof overhead seemed a better proposition than spending yet another night on the prairie. Besides, he could change horses for the last eighty-mile leg of the run into New Orleans.

Red Ryan had his reservations. Jeb Singer made his own rotgut whiskey that he sold by the jug, and all manner of trash frequented the place: outlaws on the scout, wolfers more treacherous and wild than the animals they hunted, thieves, vagabonds, border ruffians, the dangerous dregs of the frontier. Only a year before, two Texas Rangers, men Red knew and liked, had been murdered in the place, and their killers had never been found.

Hannah Huckabee had proved that she could take care of herself, but bringing a woman into a snake pit like Singer's Station was always a risky business.

After Red voiced his concerns to Buttons, the driver said, "Counting Latimer and Barnard, there's four of us men. I reckon nobody is going to give us trouble." He turned and looked at Red. "The team needs changed. They're all tuckered out. Jeb Singer may be a rogue, but he knows horses."

"The Patterson stages usually don't stop at Singer's place," Red said.

Buttons nodded. "I know, but the old Butterfields did, and it's used by the Cloverleaf stages out of Austin and Houston."

"I rode shotgun for the Cloverleaf only once and vowed to never work for them again," Red said. "It's a two-by-twice outfit that's lucky to get any passengers at all. Their old stages kept breaking axles and it took us three days to cover a hundred miles."

"The Cloverleaf is owned by a syndicate in El Paso," Button said. "They have no interest in spending money on stages and good teams. Dallas Stoudenmire and Doc Manning are shareholders and all they care about are the profits. Abe Patterson calls the Cloverleaf a disgrace to the staging business."

"And so is Singer's Station," Red said.

"Trust me, we'll be just fine," Buttons said. He turned his head. "Are you listening to this, Miss Hannah?"

"Yes, I am," Hannah said.

"Singer's Station isn't as bad as Red makes out," Buttons said.

"I hope not," Hannah said. "But I must confess, it will be a relief to get off this stage for a while."

Red shook his head. "Damn it all, I got a bad feeling about this that I can't shake."

"You're just weary, Red," Buttons said. "Once you

get some coffee in you, you'll be as right as rain. Trust me."

"I sure hope so," Red said. He slid his Colt from the leather and put a round in the empty chamber under the hammer.

Buttons pretended not to notice.

Singer's Station consisted of a collection of long adobe buildings with sod roofs and doorways so low even a man of medium height had to duck his head to enter. There was a small barn for harnesses and tack and a larger stable that could house up to twenty horses at a time. The main accommodation and passengers' dining room had a few bunks and a single window that wasn't glazed. The flooring was hard-packed dirt and there was no stove, but a fireplace was used for cooking, and two large coffeepots simmered day and night. There were no shelves or cupboards, and in one corner stood an open sack of flour, a bag of salt, and a side of bacon. The room smelled of horses, man-sweat, bad whiskey, and pipe tobacco. Washing facilities were outside the door: a basin, a piece of tan-colored soap, and a much-used towel. A hand-lettered sign was nailed into the wall above the basin that read:

For DRIVER *and*
MESSENGER *only*

When Hannah Huckabee saw the run-down place, she thought she'd died and gone to hell.

Buttons and Jed Singer shook hands, and the

proprietor, a tall, cadaverous man with a beard down to his waistband, said, "After you change the team, you gonna eat and run, or is it your intention to spend the night?"

Red saw Hannah's shocked face and said quickly, "We'll eat and then be on our way."

Buttons seemed surprised and opened his mouth to object, but a sidelong glance from Red silenced him, and he bit his tongue.

"Fried bacon and pan bread and coffee is tonight's bill of fare," Singer said. He seemed tense, his black eyes never at rest. "Sit at the table. My wife will be with you shortly. Buttons, I'll help you change the team."

Reluctantly Hannah sat, joined by Red, who felt the tension in the air, the atmosphere stretched as tight as a fiddle string. John Latimer and Mr. Chang, who looked as though someone held a dead fish under his nose, joined them, but Sage Barnard remained outside smoking a cigar.

A shadowy corner of the room was cordoned off by a blanket that hung from a post driven into the adjoining walls. From behind the blanket a man grunted like a rutting hog and then gasped and fell silent. A few moments later the blanket was pulled back, and one by one, three big, uncurried men stepped out, one of them buttoning his pants. Behind them a tall, thin, careworn woman with gray in her hair adjusted her skirt and stepped to the table.

As though nothing unseemly had happened, she said, "I'm Mrs. Singer. Your grub will be right up."

"Just coffee for me," Hannah said.

Red looked around the table and said, "And I guess that goes for the rest of us."

The woman shrugged. "Suit yourselves."

And there, matters might have rested, had not the three men caught sight of Hannah, dramatically pretty in the glowing lamplight.

Red had voiced his reservations about bringing Hannah into the place, and very soon he'd be proved right.

The biggest of the three men, like his companions dressed in buckskins and knee-high moccasins, with a belted Colt and ivory-handled knife at his waist, bellowed a laugh and then said, "Boys, we just spent three dollars on Singer's scrawny old lady when we could have had this purty little gal." He smiled, showing bad teeth. "What do you say, missy? Want to leave the Chinee and them other nancies and share a jug with some real men?"

"No, I certainly do not," Hannah said. She frowned. "And why don't you take a bath now and again? I can smell you from here."

Red shook his head and sighed, "Well, that just about tears it."

The big man's bearded face showed shock, then anger. "We was prepared to be sociable about it, lady, you being the purtiest thing west of the Trinity, but now we'll do it the hard way. Git behind that there curtain and be nice or us three, we might just take it into our heads to do some cuttin' on you."

He took a step toward the table but stopped when two events happened . . . Latimer got to his feet and

Sage Barnard walked into the room. "You heard the lady," Barnard said. "She doesn't want anything to do with you. Go away and behave yourself."

"Well, well, what do we got here," the big man said. "I declare, it's a fancy gambling gent on his high horse."

Barnard smiled. "I don't want to upset anybody, and I sure as hell don't want to kill somebody. So just back off, and I'll buy you a drink. I can't say fairer than that."

"I buy my own drinks, mister," the man said. He seemed confident, ready to kill, but a glint of uncertainty had come into his eyes. He didn't know who the hell the gambler was, but it was obvious he'd been up this particular trail a few times before. But he pulled himself together and said, "Now stand aside afore I decide to get rough."

"You go get him, Ezra," one of the big man's cohorts said, grinning, his reptilian eyes glowing. He licked his thick lips. "I say we take both the fancy man and the whore behind the curtain."

"You heard my brother," the man called Ezra said. He pulled his knife and beckoned with his other hand. "Come here, Nancy. We got plans for you and your little lady."

Barnard seemed relaxed, confident, but to his right Latimer's face stiffened. "Sir, are you determined on this disgusting course of action?"

Ezra was taken aback. "Enough of the fancy talk. You, gambling man, git the hell over here and bring the woman with you. Or you'll die right where you stand."

Red slowly got to his feet, his hand away from his gun. "I think I should inform you that John Latimer and Sage Barnard, the gentlemen in question, are fare-paying passengers of the Abe Patterson and Son Stage and Express Company, and I am its representative. I will not allow them to be abused in this way by backstabbing lowlifes like you."

"You shut the hell up," Ezra said. "Damn you, I'll shut you up my ownself."

The two other men, big, bearded and as mean as curly wolves, one with a grotesquely knife-scarred face, sided Ezra.

"All right, enough talk, let's take them," Ezra's brother said.

The three men reached for their guns as they advanced on Latimer and Barnard, but it was the Englishman who opened the ball.

He'd palmed his derringer as soon as he'd gotten to his feet, and now he extended his right arm and at a range of five feet fired at Ezra. The shot was within the belly gun's capability, and the bullet ran true. Ezra's eyes crossed as he looked at the hole that had suddenly appeared above the bridge of his nose, staggered back, and thudded to the dirt floor like a toppled oak.

For a split second the two others were shocked into immobility. And a split second was all a draw-fighter like Sage Barnard needed. He shucked iron from a shoulder holster and fired, a killing shot that took Ezra's brother in the chest and dropped him. The other scar-faced man, facing two targets, decided that

Barnard was the more dangerous and fired. But he hurried the shot and heeled the Colt. This was a common mistake a practiced shootist never made. The scar-faced man exerted excessive forward pressure with the heel of his hand and forced the sight up as he triggered his gun, resulting in the round going high and left. The bullet neatly drilled Red's plug hat but did no other damage. A Remington derringer holds two rounds, and Latimer's second shot was a hit that staggered Scar-face. The man stumbled back, cursing, and raised his revolver again. Barnard and Red fired at the same time, and two bullets slammed into the man's chest. Hit hard, his mouth sagged open, and he dropped without a sound.

Sage Barnard, long schooled in the belief that it's never a good idea to leave a wounded but vengeful man on your back trail, looked over the three huge bodies sprawled on the floor.

After a few moments of study, he turned to Red and the others and said, "All three of these boys are on a stony lonesome." He shook his handsome head. "Once they'd decided to draw and get their work in, I sure thought they would've done a sight better."

Red nodded and said, "Mistakes were made." He looked at Latimer through a drift of gunsmoke and said, "You stood well. You stood like a man." Then, after a moment's thought, "Latimer, I reckon the men who branded you a coward were fools."

Hannah Huckabee stood up and said, "Was I a fool?"

"Only you can answer that question," Red said.

"John, have I been a fool?" Hannah said.

"You were told what happened in India, or a version of it," Latimer said. "I want you to judge me on that, not on what happened here."

"I need time, John," Hannah said.

"You've had time, Hannah," Latimer said. "And your mind is already made up."

"I can change my mind," Hannah said. "Isn't that a woman's prerogative?"

"So I've heard them say," Latimer said.

The cabin door burst open, and Buttons Muldoon and Jed Singer rushed inside. "What's all the shooting about?" Buttons said before he saw the three dead men sprawled in the dirt floor. He turned to Red. "What the hell?"

"They pushed it," Red said. The question hadn't left Buttons's face and he said, "Two of them were brothers, and I don't know who the other man was." He wanted to say, "They'd had Mrs. Singer but wanted Hannah," but to spare Jed Singer's feelings he didn't, saying only, "They wanted Hannah."

Jed Singer looked down at the dead men. "Two of them are the Rayner brothers, Ezra and Isa. The other man is Fulton Driscoll. They got by wolfing and the occasional murder and robbery. You killed three of the sorriest pieces of trash in Texas." He shook his head. "Pity, because they were good customers of mine."

Buttons said, "Red, did you do for the three of them?"

"I helped shoot one of the brothers. Latimer and Barnard got their work in and did the rest."

Buttons looked at Latimer in surprise. "You done for two of them?"

"One of the reasons I came up through the ranks of the British Army was because I was a good marksman," Latimer said. "Most times I hit what I aim at."

Buttons smiled. "Well, I'll be. Latimer, you pistol-shootin' son of a gun, you can march in my parade anytime."

Mrs. Singer stepped around the dead men and laid a tray with steaming tin coffee cups on the table. Jed held out his hand, and she dropped three silver dollars into his palm. "That's all?" he said.

"Tonight, it was all they had or it's all they thought I was worth," the woman said. "Take your pick, Jed."

Hannah Huckabee listened to the exchange with growing horror. Enraged, she said, "Singer, you make a prostitute of your own wife? What kind of man are you?"

"This isn't a big-paying business we're in," Singer said. "To keep the wolf from the door, we got to make money any way we can."

"You're a disgrace," Hannah said. "I can't believe that you treat your wife like a thing to be bartered for money when the lusts of men need satisfied."

"Woman, why don't you mind your own damned business," Mrs. Singer snapped. "We're poor folks and we do whatever it takes to make ends meet. A high-falutin lady like you won't understand that, but it's a fact of life on the frontier."

Hannah was shocked, unbelieving. "You don't mind being used as . . . as a whore?"

"If that's what I must do, then no, I don't mind a bit."

Jed Singer smiled and kissed his wife on the cheek. "That's telling her, Lucy. Humble as it is, you're all that holds this damned place together."

"Then, if that's your attitude, I won't stay under your roof a moment longer," Hannah said. "Mr. Muldoon, isn't it time we were back in the stage?"

"Yes, go right ahead and leave," Singer said. "Me and Lucy will bury your dead and keep their guns and horses as payment." He looked at Red. "Have you any objections?"

"None," Red said. Then, "Hannah, you didn't drink your coffee."

"I don't want any. Do you?"

Red hesitated a moment, took a cue from Hannah's frowning face, and then said, "No, I guess not."

But Buttons, his hunger getting the best of him, was having none of that. "Mrs. Singer," he said, "can you quick fry me up some bacon and wrap it in pan bread? I'll take it with me."

Once outside, Red said to Hannah, "Don't judge people like the Singers too harshly. Like many other poor people in Texas, they do what they have to do to survive."

"But for a man to sell his wife . . ."

"He doesn't have much else to sell," Red said. "And Lucy Singer knows that."

"You think I judge people too harshly?" Hannah said.

"Yes, I do. First it was John Latimer and now it's Mrs. Singer. Hannah, where does it end? With me? With Buttons? With Mr. Chang? All three of us?"

Hannah was silent for a few moments, then said,

"Now. It ends now. You're right. Who am I to judge anyone?"

"Well, I don't know about the right or wrong of the thing, but it seems to me that it's up to God to do the judging. You haven't walked in Lucy Singer's shoes, so how could you judge her?"

"Red, I'm a rich adventuress, and up until recently I thought I was a unique, wonderful person," Hannah said. "Now I'm not so sure what or who I am. I have the ability to judge everyone else, but I don't know how to judge myself. Red, who am I?"

Red smiled. "You're Hannah Huckabee. That's good enough for me."

Chapter Thirty-seven

Buttons Muldoon expected a trouble-free ride to New Orleans, especially since Hannah Huckabee elected to ride inside the stage for the first time since leaving Fort Concho.

"Miss Hannah and Latimer seemed to have kissed and made up," he said to Red.

"I don't know that they're on kissing terms, but at least she and Latimer are being polite to one another," Red said.

"Well, it's a start," Buttons said.

"Maybe they'll pick up where they left off before that business in India," Red said. "I guess we'll see, huh?" Then, his eyes on the trail ahead, he said, "The new team seems to be pulling all right."

Buttons nodded. "They're doing just fine." He smiled. "Jed Singer knows horses. We'll change again at Horseshoe Bluff. If old Silas Brown is still running things, the grub will be a sight better."

After an hour of travel on level ground, the stage entered a stretch of shallow, rolling hills and then encountered wagon ruts that crossed their path then headed east, ending at an isolated cabin barely visible in the distance, half obscured by a stand of wild oak and stunted juniper.

"What the hell is that doing out here?" Buttons said.

"Beats me," Red said. His eyes on the cabin. "I never expected to see a homestead out here."

Buttons drew rein on the team. "I was sure there was nothing between the Singer place and the Horseshoe," he said. "I reckon that's an abandoned cabin. Looks run-down enough."

"Seems like," Red said.

Buttons took up the reins to drive on, but stopped when a single shot rang out. "What the hell?" he said, as a thin cloud of white gunsmoke drifted through the tree trunks.

"That came from the cabin," Red said.

"Where did the bullet go?" Buttons said.

"Whoever fired the shot wasn't shooting at us," Red said.

"What's going on, Ryan?" Sage Barnard said, his head sticking out of the stage window.

"I don't know," Red said. "The shot came from the cabin but wasn't aimed at us."

"Well, I reckon I'll go find out," Buttons said. "There's something mighty strange going on here."

He urged the team into motion and then followed the wagon ruts in the direction of the cabin. The stage rolled down a slight grade and passed over patches of bottlebrush, hawthorn, and red burning bush. It seemed that a wagon hadn't come this way in some considerable time.

The cabin was square, without a corral or outbuildings, a drab, cheerless place that had no right to be there, a wreck adrift in an endless sea of grass.

Buttons told Red to stand by with the shotgun and then halted the stage. He stood in the box and yelled, "Hello the house."

A minute ticked past and then a weak man's voice from inside the cabin called, "In here."

"I'll go find out," Red said.

"No, wait," Buttons said. "It could be a trap." Then, yelling, "State your intentions. We're careful men out here."

Again, there was a long pause before the man inside spoke again. "Help me. I'm shot."

"I'll talk to him," Red said. He climbed down, took the shotgun from Buttons, and walked toward the cabin. Sage Barnard joined him, looked at Red, and said, "Are all your stage journeys so eventful?"

Red smiled. "Some are, some are not. But now when I study on it, most are."

"Well, this one sure is," Barnard said. He had a short-barreled Colt in his hand.

"I wouldn't jump to conclusions," Red said. "We don't know what's happened here yet."

"Nothing good, I'll wager," Barnard said.

The cabin's front door was ajar on its rawhide hinges. Red pushed it open with the barrel of the Greener and then stepped inside. He saw a single room with a dirt floor, a bed with a colorful patch-work quilt against one wall, and a few spare furnishings, including an easy chair in front of a stone fireplace. A vase containing wildflowers spoke to a woman's presence.

A middle-aged man, gray at the temples, sat propped up against the far wall. There was blood on the front of his shirt, and beside him lay a single-shot squirrel rifle.

He looked up at Red with pained eyes and said, slowly and painfully, "Renegades . . . took my woman . . . took my milk cow . . ." He pushed an empty tin money box with his foot. "Took two hundred dollars . . . every penny we had."

Red kneeled beside the man and examined his wound. After a while he said, "Mister, I won't piss in your boots and tell you it's raining. It looks bad."

"Figured that. I took a Winchester bullet to the chest and knew I was done for. Name's Bill Morton. Maybe you could do me a kindness and put that on my grave marker."

The man knew he was dying, and Red said nothing to soften the blow. "Red Ryan," he said. "Shotgun guard with the Abe Patterson and Son Stage and Express Company. Glad to make your acquaintance."

"Likewise," Morton said, trying his best to smile.

Sage Barnard said, "Who were these renegades?"

"Four of them. A couple of white men dressed up like Mexicans and two Apaches," Morton answered. "They said they'd come up from the Sierra Madre and crossed the border a week ago. That's all they told us before they cut up rough and shot me and grabbed my woman."

The little cabin suddenly became crowded when Hannah, Buttons, John Latimer, and Mr. Chang stepped inside.

Hannah immediately went to the wounded man,

smoothed his hair back from his fevered forehead and, as Red had done earlier, studied Morton's wound.

"Mr. Chang," she said, her voice small.

The Chinese kneeled beside the man and his slender fingertips explored the wound. He looked at Hannah and shook his head.

Morton saw that and said, talking directly to Hannah, "Me, I never had much. Worked as a laborer all my life and never owned nothing but the clothes I stood up in. But I worked harder and saved money, and two years ago I brought Effie, my bride, out here. Figured I'd buy stock and start a ranch. But we had a bad winter, and then the Apaches played hob. And now the renegades took my woman and my last two hundred dollars." This time Bill Morton did manage a smile. "Seems like everything went to hell real fast, huh?"

Hannah said, "Don't try to talk. Save your strength." Mr. Chang, bring the canteen from the stage."

"Miss Huckabee take good care of the sick," Mr. Chang said.

"The pain is all gone," Morton said. "That means I'm dying, don't it?"

Hannah said, "I think it's time you made peace with your Maker, Mr. Morton."

"Done that already. I've always been on speaking terms with God," the man said. Then, "Shotgun guard . . . I . . . I . . . can't see you."

Red kneeled again. "I'm right here."

Morton's bloody hand reached up and grabbed Red by the arm. "Save my Effie. She's a good woman."

The man's voice faded as his breathing faltered. "Shotgun guard . . . save her . . ."

Bill Morton gasped then closed his eyes.

Mr. Chang brought the canteen to a dead man.

"We couldn't save Dahteste, but maybe we can save Effie Morton," Hannah Huckabee said. "I'm all for trying. Does anyone else feel the same as I do?"

Buttons Muldoon said, "Them renegades got a head start. I say we head for New Orleans." He looked at Red with pleading eyes. "Red, there's already been enough distractions on this trip. The last thing we need is another."

"Those boys won't have gotten far," Red said. "They're dragging along a milk cow, and since the chances are they don't drink milk, they probably plan to butcher her and eat fried liver for supper tonight."

"I don't like to think of a white woman in the hands of border scum like those outlaws," Sage Barnard said. "It's mighty hard to turn our backs on her and just ride away like nothing happened."

"I have a schedule to keep," Buttons said, looking miserable.

"What's more important, Mr. Muldoon, your schedule or a woman's life?" Hannah said. "Remember Dahteste."

"It's mighty hard to forget her, Miss Hannah," Buttons said.

"There's still four hours of daylight," Red said. "We have to make a decision soon."

"Then I'll leave it to the passengers," Buttons said,

"To keep it official, like, I'm putting it to a vote. All those in favor of heading directly for New Orleans raise your hands."

No hands were raised.

Buttons shook his head and, resignation in his voice, he said, "Then it's unanimous. We go try to save Mrs. Morton."

"I'll go," Red said. "And Barnard, I'd be beholden to you if you agree to come along."

"Red, I'll join you," Latimer said.

"And me too," Hannah said.

"No. There's four of them, and when I track them down, it will call for close-up and sudden work," Red said. "Apart from me, the only one among us with that kind of speed is Barnard."

The gambler smiled. "Sure, I'll come," he said. "It's been a while since I tracked down a pack of killers. Makes a man hanker for the good old days before the West got so civilized."

"I reckon the men we're going after don't fit into the civilized category," Red said.

"I agree with you there, Ryan," Barnard said.

Hannah frowned. "But—"

"No buts," Red said. "Hannah, you've done enough. Leave it to the men this time, huh?"

"Four hours of daylight, Ryan," Barnard said. "High time we were making tracks."

"You want I can cut a couple of horses out of the team, if'n you can ride them without bridles," Buttons said. "Trouble is, they're young and don't know too much."

"We'll walk," Red said. "Keep to the long grass and

injun up on them boys. I have a feeling they're not far away and maybe spending time with the woman."

"Then, Red, and you, too, Mr. Barnard, be careful," Hannah said.

Red shook his head and grinned. "Being careful isn't going to get the job done, not on this trip. Ready, Barnard?"

"I'm always ready," the gambler said.

Chapter Thirty-eight

The tracks of the four renegades and the lumbering milk cow across the late summer grass were easy to read, and Red Ryan and Sage Barnard covered three miles in the first hour, Red setting a brisk pace. They walked in open country, here and there occasional stands of scrub oak and piñon, and a few cottonwoods growing on the banks of dry streambeds.

In the middle of the second hour, the pace of the pursuers slowed a little. Neither Red's boots nor Barnard's elastic-sided congress gaiters made for cross-country walking.

Finally, Barnard stopped, wiped off his face with the large white handkerchief he'd taken from his pocket, and said, "Ryan, I reckon those boys are setting a faster pace than I expected."

Red was also glad to stop. "They'll camp soon," he said, taking out the makings. He started to build a cigarette. "Getting on to sundown earlier than I thought, too."

Barnard waited for Red to light his smoke before he held out his hand for the tobacco sack and papers.

He deftly rolled his own cigarette, passed the makings back to Red, and then said, "Give me ten minutes and we'll hit the trail again. As you say, those four can't be that far away. This past half hour I thought the tracks looked a sight fresher."

"They are," Red said. "We're catching up . . . slowly."

Then, through a cloud of blue smoke, Barnard said, "How many men you killed since you became a shotgun guard, Ryan?"

"A few," Red said. "I don't like to boast of it." Then, "You?"

"Seven before our run-in with the Rayner brothers," Barnard said. "All of them in saloons. Bad whiskey and sore losers are a bad combination." He shrugged, a typically Cajun gesture. "Goes with the gambler's vocation, I guess."

"Buttons Muldoon and me saw you kill Flynn Mayfield in the Ruby saloon in Galveston that time," Red said. "We were pretty new to stagecoaching then. Well, I was. Buttons had been driving for a spell."

"Did we talk?" Barnard said.

"No. It wasn't exactly what you'd call a social occasion."

"Flynn Mayfield was a fool," Barnard said. "He fancied himself a shootist, but he'd never shaded anybody with a reputation. Called himself the new John Wesley Hardin, but he didn't even come close."

"He drew down on you, Barnard," Red said. "I saw that."

The gambler nodded. "Mayfield had been notified, but blunders were made."

Barnard took a last draw on his cigarette and crushed out the butt under his heel. "Well, shall we resume our delightful promenade?"

"Suits me," Red said. "I wish I could say the same for my feet."

The day was slowly shading into night, and scarlet banners streamed in the sky when Red and Barnard saw a fire glimmer in the distance directly ahead of them.

Trusting to the growing darkness to conceal them, the two men advanced slowly on the camp, set among an isolated thicket of piñon and brush. The dusky blue twilight was tinged with pale bronze from the sky, and the air smelled faintly of coffee and broiling meat. The grass underfoot made a soft swishing sound as Red and Barnard stepped closer to the camp.

Then Red stopped and waved Barnard into a crouch. The thickest brush grew to his right, and it would offer cover, but it was too dense to penetrate quickly and Red dismissed it as an attack route. For a long minute or two, he studied the layout of the camp. Men passed in front of the fire, dark silhouettes in the gloom. He saw no sign of the woman.

Damn it, there was no cover, no way to walk closer unseen. The only option Red had was to get down on his belly and crawl. This was no time and place for foolish bravado. He dropped on his front and motioned for Barnard to do the same.

But the gambler had other ideas. His gun held low, close to his leg, he straightened from his crouch, walked forward like a man out for a Sunday stroll, and when he was just a few yards away he said, "Howdy, boys."

The reaction was immediate.

Four men, two in the garb of Mexican vaqueros but wearing Stetson hats, and a pair of Apaches in their usual shirts, breeches, and headbands, scrambled to their feet and, guns drawn, faced their unexpected visitor.

Red silently cursed Barnard but got to his feet and stepped closer to the camp on the gambler's right.

He held his shotgun, unwavering muzzles pointed in the direction of the foursome, and said, "Fine evening, ain't it."

The renegades didn't like that one bit. They didn't like it that two men had walked up to their camp unnoticed, and they didn't care for the scattergun. Later Red would say that they should have gone to their pistols right away, but instead they wasted time on palaver. It would prove to be a fatal mistake.

One of the white outlaws, a tall man with a large dragoon mustache, stepped forward and said, "What the hell do you want? There's nothing here for you."

The Apaches had picked up their rifles. The cow carcass, freshly butchered, lay at the far side of the camp. Lumps of meat were broiling on sticks suspended over the campfire.

"There is something here for us," Red said. Where was Effie Morton? "We want the woman."

"What woman?" the man with the mustache said.

"The woman you took from the Morton cabin after you killed her husband," Red said.

"Are you the law?" the man said.

"No, we're not the law. We just want the woman," Red said.

"The woman is over there, by the trees," the mustached man said. "Go over and have at her if you want. She ain't much to look at."

"Bring her over here," Red said.

The renegade turned his head, his eyes never leaving Red. "Jake, bring her over here," he said to the other white man.

The man called Jake was short and stocky, and his eyes were reckless. "To hell with you, Frank. I want that woman for my ownself."

Frank said, "You can share her with this gent, Jake." He said to Red, "Does that sound fair to you, mister?"

Then Sage Barnard spoke, his voice angry in the quiet. "The hell with this! You all know this is headed for a shooting, so cut the chitchat and strike up the band." He raised his Colt and fired: two quick shots that slammed into the Apaches. One dropped, the other got a shot off with his rifle at Barnard. Red ignored the Indian and concentrated on Frank and Jake, who'd drawn and were shooting at Barnard. Red triggered the Greener and Jake took two barrels of buck in the belly that just about cut him in half. Red dropped the shotgun and drew his revolver. Barnard was hit and was down on one knee, but he fired steadily at Frank, who took several bullets before he fell to the ground. The surviving Apache swung his rifle on Red, and both men fired at the same time. But the Indian had been shot earlier by Barnard, and he was unsteady on his feet. His bullet went wild, but Red scored a hit and the man staggered, tried to work the lever of his old Henry, but didn't have the strength. Red fired again and again, and the Apache dropped.

A gray pall of gunsmoke hung in the camp as Red rushed to Sage Barnard, who was lying on his back, his Colt still in his hand.

The gambler looked into Red's face and said, "Damn it all, Ryan, it's bad. I can't believe it, but I reckon I'm done for."

Barnard had a chest wound, dead center, and could not be expected to live.

"Where's the woman?" he said.

"She's fine," Red lied. He hadn't seen Mrs. Morton yet.

"That's good, made it all worthwhile," Barnard said. He smiled. "Saving a lady in distress and all."

"You did well," Red said. "That was some shooting."

"No, it wasn't," Barnard said. "I could use more practice. I was too slow on the shoot."

"You were faster than I could ever be," Red said.

Barnard was silent for a while, the light in his eyes fading. "I'm leaving soon, Ryan," he said. "Take off my boots. There's a good fellow."

Red did as the gambler asked.

"Are . . . they . . . off?" Barnard said.

"Yeah. They sure are."

"That's good," the gambler said, "It's how a man should die."

Barnard smiled . . . then all the life that was in him fled.

Red felt a pang of regret. He'd asked Barnard to accompany him and was indirectly responsible for the man's death. Not only that, but Sage Barnard was a fare-paying passenger of the Abe Patterson and Son Stage and Express Company, the first Red had lost to outlaws. He would have to explain his dereliction of duty to Abe Patterson and accept whatever punishment the old man saw fit to impose on him. It would not be a pleasant meeting, because Abe was a stickler about passenger safety.

Red rose to his feet. That was for the future. Right then his responsibility was to the living. He had to comfort Effie Morton.

But the woman had gone.

Red searched around the area of the camp and found nothing. Then, snagged on a thornbush he discovered a scrap of blue cloth, likely torn from the woman's skirt. Fresh tracks led through the underbrush toward the open prairie, and he followed them.

After a few yards, the tracks lost themselves in darkness and Red called into the gloom, "Mrs. Morton! Effie Morton!" There was no answer. Perhaps the woman stood out there too afraid to respond, thinking that he was one of her kidnappers.

"Mrs. Morton, this is Red Ryan, shotgun messenger with the Abe Patterson and Son Stage and Express Company, and I'm here to rescue you," Red yelled. "The renegades who took you are all dead. You heard the shooting, huh?"

The ensuing silence mocked him.

Red tried again, louder. "Mrs. Morton! Effie!"

No answer. Nothing but the crackle of the campfire and the whisper of the wind in the long grass.

Red returned to the fire, where a coffeepot simmered on the coals. He found a cup and drank coffee that was black, bitter, and scalding hot. Around him lay the bodies of five men, unmoving in death, all of them gunned down in the space of a couple of minutes. And this for a woman who'd walked into the prairie and was now out there alone in the darkness.

Red built a cigarette, smoked, called out again for Effie Morton, smoked another. Then he dropped his head and dozed, wakened constantly, and again and again shouted the woman's name and as before was rewarded by silence.

Just before sunup, Red saddled one of the renegades' picketed mustangs, a hammer-headed steel gray, and let two of the others loose. He drank more coffee, and at first light swung into the saddle and went in search of Mrs. Morton. After two hours of riding in ever-increasing circles around the camp, he had found nothing, and a rising wind had erased any tracks. It seemed that Effie was a small woman, and she'd left no mark on the land. She could be anywhere, hiding in the long grass, not wanting to be found. Probably, after seeing her husband killed and the ordeal she'd suffered, she was no longer in her right mind.

As late as 1904, a couple of cowboys reported seeing, at some distance away, a ragged woman walking across the range. They tried to reach her, but she vanished from sight. Mrs. Effie Morton or the ghost of some long-dead prairie wife? The mystery woman was never seen again, so we will never know.

* * *

Red Ryan brought Barnard back to the Patterson stage across the back of a mustang. To the shocked, questioning faces that greeted him, Red said, "There was a gunfight, and Sage Barnard got hit." Then, so they'd know that it was something of great importance, "He didn't die with his boots on."

Buttons Muldoon read the emptiness in his shotgun guard's expression and said, almost gently, "And Mrs. Morgan?"

Red shook his head. "I don't know. She wandered off into the prairie, and I don't know where she is." Red continued to sit the mustang and said, "Barnard dead, four other men dead, and the woman gone. I did real good, didn't I?" His eyes found John Latimer. "Mister, now I know how you feel."

Buttons said, "We buried Bill Morton, and Sage Barnard can lie beside him. They'll keep each other company."

Red swung out of the saddle. "Yeah, we'll do that, and then we'll head for New Orleans. I plan to get drunk."

Chapter Thirty-nine

New Orleans in the 1880s was a bustling metropolis built on swampland between the Mississippi River and Lake Pontchartrain, its crowded, bawdy streets dedicated to debauchery and every kind of vice.

Brack Cooley, bored, restless and on the scout for any kind of distraction, was drawn to the French Quarter with its cast-iron balconies, hidden, mysterious courtyards, and stucco buildings stained by time and weather. The exotic sights, sounds, and smells of Bourbon Street that he had experienced nowhere else attracted him like a moth to the flame.

The open carry of firearms in the city was prohibited and the law was strictly enforced by the police. Cooley shoved his Colt into his waistband, covered by his frock coat, and he had a small fighting knife in his boot. He didn't expect trouble, but he was by nature a prudent man.

After walking through the streets for an hour, the day had become hot and humid, and a café with a court shaded by a magnolia tree beckoned to him. Cooley took a seat at a ridiculously small iron table, ordered coffee from a pretty Creole waitress, and lit a cigar.

He was unhappy with Rupert Bentley-Foulkes. This thing had dragged on too long. He could have shot John Latimer any time between Fort Concho and Austin, and it would be over with by now, and he'd be busy spending the other five hundred dollars that the Englishman had promised him. Now the business was being drawn out again. Instead of plugging the cowardly son of a bitch, Bentley-Foulkes wanted him captured and then taken to stand trial. Court-martial, the Englishman called it. The sun was warm on Cooley's shoulders, and he forced himself to relax. Ah well, it would be over soon, a couple of days at the most, and then he'd enjoy New Orleans until his money ran out.

To his surprise, the coffee was not served by the young waitress he'd ordered from but by a stunningly beautiful older woman, dressed like Cooley had never seen before. She was tall, slender, and wore a black dress, split at the front to reveal a scarlet petticoat underneath. Around her black hair was a turban of the same color. From her neck hung an elaborate necklace of hammered silver that matched the light gray of her eyes. She moved with effortless elegance, a gliding walk with a minimal swing of her hips, just enough to accent their shapely fullness but no more.

The woman laid the cup and saucer on the table, sat in the chair opposite Cooley, and then said, "I knew you would come here today, big man."

Cooley smiled. "And how did you know that?"

"I dreamed of a death bringer, a killer of turbaned,

dark-skinned men, who will come to New Orleans. Is that one you?"

Cooley shook his head. "No, lady, I've never shot a black man, wearing a turban or not. Dead or alive, they don't bring much of a reward, hardly worth the cost of the ammunition it takes to kill them. I'm a businessman. I keep my eye on the bottom line."

"And I saw a ship, a great iron warship. Do you sail on such a ship?"

"No, I sure don't," Cooley said. "Being a sailor is not in my line of work."

"But I know that you are not a good man," the woman said. "Why would I see you in a vision?

"Sorry to hear that you think I'm a bad man," Cooley said. "Because you're a mighty pretty lady. As for seeing me in a vision, I don't know anything about that."

"I don't understand its meaning, therefore my vision disturbs me," the woman said. "Why did I see the iron warship with its great blue cannons?"

"Beats me," Cooley said. Suddenly he felt uneasy. Did this strange woman know he was contracted to kill John Latimer? No, that was impossible.

The young waitress returned, bowed low, and laid coffee on the table in front of the older women. The girl bowed again and left.

"Who are you, lady?" Cooley said.

"My name is Antoinette Baudet. In New Orleans I am called a Voodoo queen." She paused, sipping from her coffee. "Do you know what Voodoo is?"

"No idea," Cooley said.

"Then it is best you do not know. I saw you in my vision. I knew you would come to me today."

"I have a vision," Cooley said, grinning. "I see you and me sitting in a saloon sharing a bottle of whiskey and getting to know each other real well. I'd be good to you . . . Antoinette."

The woman shook her head. "A Voodoo queen cannot lie with a man. Such a thing would destroy my power and end my visions. Do you understand?"

"Sure, I understand," Cooley said. "But spend a little while with me, and you'll change your mind."

The woman ignored that and said, "God hasn't given me the understanding of why I was chosen to warn you, but this much I will say . . . beware of the man who has killed dark-skinned men and beware of the great iron ship. Somehow they are joined together and walk hand in hand." Antoinette Baudet shook her lovely head. "That is all I can tell you, because it remains a great mystery."

The woman rose and walked away from Cooley, stepping into the busy street. He sat where he was for a few moments, thinking, and then went after her. But Antoinette Baudet had vanished into the crowd.

"Where were you today, Mr. Cooley?" Rupert Bentley-Foulkes said.

"Walking around town, seeing the sights," Cooley said.

"Please stay here in your hotel room. The Patterson stage could arrive any time now."

"This Latimer feller, did he ever kill men with dark skins?" Cooley said.

"What an odd question," Bentley-Foulkes said.

"Well, did he?"

"Latimer was an officer in the British army and served in the Afghan war in India against men with dark skins," Bentley-Foulkes said. "Before his act of cowardice, he fought in several skirmishes against Afghans, and yes, I'm sure he killed some."

"Them Afghans, did they wear turbans on their heads, huh?" Cooley said.

"Some Afghan tribesmen wear turbans and others round hats against the heat of the desert sun and most have long hair," Bentley-Foulkes said. "Why do you ask?"

Cooley knew he had to explain his sudden interest in Latimer and Afghan men. After a few moments of thought he said, "I met a fortune-teller this morning and—"

"Plenty of those in New Orleans," Bentley-Foulkes said.

"Yeah, I guess there is. Well, anyway, she told me to beware of a man who has killed dark-skinned men wearing turbans."

Bentley-Foulkes smiled. "And you think she meant John Latimer?"

"Maybe so."

"Latimer is a coward. You have nothing to fear from him."

"She told me she saw a great iron ship. Strange that, huh?"

"There's a British frigate docked in the harbor.

That's the ship she saw. Everybody in New Orleans knows it's there, so she didn't need a crystal ball to tell you that."

Cooley nodded. "So, I guess she was a faker."

"Fortune-tellers usually are," Bentley-Foulkes said. "Mr. Cooley, you're not having second thoughts about executing Latimer, are you?"

"When I take a job, I see it through," Cooley said. "I'll capture him, and then I'll kill him for you."

"Capture, Mr. Cooley," the Englishman said. "Keep that word uppermost in your mind. Take him at gunpoint. I want Latimer to stand trial."

"Justice has to be seen to be done, right?" Cooley said.

"Yes, since the only verdict that can be passed on Latimer is guilty as charged," Bentley-Foulkes said. "I'd consider any other verdict as a stab in the back."

Chapter Forty

The old coaching inn on Broad Street that doubled as the Patterson stage depot was a two-story stucco building with corrals around back and an adjoining open area where stages could be parked, washed, and cleaned out. The inn boasted twelve guest rooms, a restaurant, and bar. The proprietor was a former Butterfield driver by the name of Gil Hooper who walked with a limp after taking a road agent's bullet to his right leg years before. It was Hooper's considered opinion that the coming of the Texas and New Orleans Railroad was the worst thing that had ever happened to his fair city of New Orleans, and he prophesied that the clanging of locomotive bells would sound the death knell of the stagecoaching industry.

Sitting in a rocker on the inn's front porch, Hooper told Buttons Muldoon that very thing, but it was something Buttons had heard the old man say many times before, and he was only half listening.

Hooper realized he didn't have the Patterson

driver's full attention, and he changed the subject
from railroads to Red Ryan.

"I haven't seen him in a while," Hooper said. "Nor
you, come to that, Buttons."

"Yeah, we pretty much stick to the northern routes,"
Buttons said. He decided not to go into details. "We're
in New Orleans because we brung in a feller who's
meeting a ship here."

"City's full of damned sailors," Hooper said.
"Drinkin' and whorin', pretty soon they're gonna give
New Orleans a bad name. And talkin' of drinkin' and
whorin', how is Ryan?"

"He's doing just fine," Buttons said. He laid back in
his rocker, a schooner of beer in his hand, and studied the young man sitting in a chair not far from him.
He didn't look American, the clothes were all wrong,
a much tighter, tailored fit. A foreigner of some kind
then. A moment later, when the man ordered coffee
and a beignet from one of Hooper's waiters, Buttons
pegged him as an Englishman since he sounded just
like Latimer. A tourist, probably.

"I'm glad to hear Red's still above ground," Hooper
said. He had a gray beard and blue eyes and was missing most of his teeth. "Shotgun messengers don't last
long in Texas."

Buttons nodded. "How many did you go through
in the old Butterfield days, Gil?"

"Lost four in my time," Hooper said. "Tom Barnes
got shot by road agents and so did Kit Johnson.
Comanches done for Micah Rawlins and then there
was a kid, I don't remember his name, but he got his
neck broke when the coach overturned when I was

following the old Ox-Bow Route up in the New Mexico Territory." Hooper shook his head. "I felt real sorry for that kid. Me and six passengers didn't even get a scratch."

"How it goes sometimes," Buttons said. "I mind the time—"

"Drinking beer early, ain't you, Buttons?" Red Ryan said.

"It's never too early to drink beer. Where are the passengers, Red?"

"Former passengers," Red said. "Howdy, Gil."

"Good to see you again, Red. Glad you ain't been shot," Hooper said, extending his hand.

Red shook hands with the old driver and then said to Buttons, "Hannah is still in her room, and John Latimer and Mr. Chang left after breakfast. Latimer said something about talking to the captain of the British warship in the harbor."

"Giving himself up?" Buttons said.

"Seems like. That's what Mr. Chang told me is happening. He's going along to make sure Latimer isn't clapped in irons."

Buttons eyes were again drawn to the young Englishman, who rose quickly from his chair, leaving his coffee and beignet untouched. He stepped off the porch, hurried into the street, and was soon lost among the passersby.

Buttons wondered at that and then dismissed it. The Patterson passengers were delivered to their destination, and that was his only concern. He took a pull on his beer and relaxed. Life was good.

"Pull up a rocker and sit down and relax, Red," Buttons said. "It's about time you gave yourself a rest."

"Maybe later," Red said.

Gil Hooper said, "Ryan, sit for a spell and watch the world go by. If a man insisted always on being serious, and never allowed himself a bit of fun and relaxation, he would go mad or unstable without knowing it." The old driver winked. "You know who said that?"

"I've no idea," Red said.

"The ancient Greek historian Herodotus. That old boy knew what he was talking about."

That last didn't surprise Red in the least. Western men were voracious readers and since books were comparatively rare on the frontier, they devoured every volume they could lay their hands on, from dime novels to the classics. Many could quote Shakespeare chapter and verse and often did when the occasion demanded. Gil Hooper was no exception,

"Well, since you put it that way, Gil, I guess I'll sit for a while," Red said. "They say it's good for the digestion."

Chapter Forty-one

The ironclad HMS *Hephaestus* was a three-masted, steam-driven frigate of thirty guns, the equivalent of five artillery batteries, and before the introduction of the *Dreadnought*, was one of the most powerful warships afloat.

But to Mr. Chang she was an intimidating sight.

"I think it best that Mr. Latimer stay away from warship," he said. "It looks like gray ghost." He shook his head. "You enter ship, you never come back."

John Latimer smiled. "It's just a ship. You stay here on the dock, Mr. Chang. Wait for me."

"I gladly wait. British navy has no love for Chinese."

Latimer stepped to the marine sentry at the gangway and gave his name, rank, and reason for being there. The young marine seemed confused and said he must talk to the officer of the day. After a while, the officer of the day, also looking confused, yelled down to Latimer to come aboard.

After observing the protocols, saluting the ensign, saluting the officer of the deck, requesting permission to come aboard, and when this was granted, only then did Latimer step onto the quarterdeck.

"The captain will see you in his cabin," the deck officer said, a fresh-faced young lieutenant, and then after a pause, a hesitant "sir."

"Damn your eyes, Captain Latimer, no one wants anything to do with you, including myself," Commander John Pickering said, his weathered face red. "The War Office can't be bothered, the Royal Navy can't be bothered, and the army sure as hell doesn't want you back under any circumstances. You're a damned pariah, an outcast, a leper. More tea?"

"Please," Latimer said. "It's been a long time since I enjoyed navy tea."

"Biscuit?"

"No, thank you, sir. The tea will be fine."

"As things stand, you're a bloody nuisance, Captain," Pickering said. "And I've landed with you." Then, sugar tongs poised, "One lump, I think it was?"

"Yes, sir. One lump."

"After all, I can't clap you in bloody irons, can I?" Pickering said, dropping the sugar cube into Latimer's cup. "That's what I told . . . what's his name? Ah yes, Captain Bentley-Foulkes."

"Rupert Bentley-Foulkes is here in New Orleans?" Latimer said, surprised.

"Yes, he is, and he badly wants you to be stood up against a wall and shot. It seems that he blames you for the death of his brother."

John Latimer absorbed that and said, "I won't

trouble you with the story of how Lieutenant Bentley-Foulkes died."

"Please don't. Save it for the court-martial, if that's what you really want."

Latimer sipped his tea, deciding not to comment.

Pickering in turn seemed exasperated. "No one cares about the bloody Afghan War any longer. The queen, God bless her, thinks it was an embarrassment and wants it forgotten. No one remembers Bentley-Foulkes, a junior lieutenant who died in some obscure skirmish. The generals are all retired and busy attending regimental balls, and the last Afghan army of any size was crushed two years ago at the Battle of Kandahar. You're a relic, Latimer, an anachronism, and demanding a court-martial will upset the bloody applecart. Your trial will be disposed of quickly, you'll get a swift kick up the arse and dishonorably discharged, and then where will you be? Right back where you started, a disgraced officer without a pension who'll die in poverty, probably of starvation." Commander Pickering was silent for a few moments and then said, "Is that what you really want?"

"I thought it was," Latimer said. "I very much wanted to restore my reputation."

"You won't. You'll have inconvenienced the War Office and the British army, and that they won't forgive. Generals hate inconveniences." The commander made an effort to soften his tone and said, "Captain Latimer, can I give you a piece of advice?"

"About now, I can use some, sir."

"Don't even think about returning to England," Pickering said. "There's nothing there for you. Make a life for yourself here in America and forget you were ever an officer in . . . what the bloody hell were you in?"

"The Fifty-first Lancers."

"Ah, then there it is . . . forget you were ever an officer in the Fifty-first Lancers."

"It's bitter pill, sir," Latimer said. "A bitter pill to swallow."

"I realize that, Captain . . . or should I now say Mr. Latimer? I'm a blunt sailor, and I don't know how to soften the blow," Pickering said. "Just go in peace and become a bloody American and make your fortune."

"I'll think over what you said, Captain," Latimer said.

"Not for too long. The *Hephaestus* sails in three days," Pickering said.

Latimer stood. "Thank you for your hospitality and advice, sir," he said.

"I'll have the officer of the day escort you off the ship," Pickering said. When Latimer stepped to the cabin door, he added, "Latimer, do you consider yourself a coward?"

"No, sir, I do not," Latimer said.

Pickering nodded. "If it's any consolation, I don't think you are, either. Well, good day to you, Mr. Latimer. And jolly good luck."

Chapter Forty-two

"You came back, Mr. Latimer," Mr. Chang said. "I am so happy that you were not made a prisoner."

Latimer gave the Chinese a wan smile. "Nobody wants me, Mr. Chang. I have no one to surrender to, and that includes Captain Pickering."

"What will you do now?" Mr. Chang said.

"I don't know. Find a job of some kind. All I know is soldiering. Maybe I'll join the United States Army under an assumed name. My own is tainted, and it seems that it will remain that way."

Latimer was busy with his thoughts as he and Mr. Chang left the dock area and wandered more or less aimlessly. On Mr. Chang's suggestion, they finally decided to stop at a café on Canal Street. Their waiter told them they were close to the business and warehouse district, but the place would not get busy until later when the offices closed for lunch. The café was shady and offered relief from the growing heat of the day, and Latimer and Mr. Chang were the only customers.

After their coffee was served, Mr. Chang leaned across the table and said, "Growing up in the lawless streets of Shanghai gave me eyes in the back of my head, so trust me when I say that we're being followed."

"Followed? By whom?" Latimer said.

"Man I saw in Fort Concho. Big man and rough. Maybe gunman."

Latimer looked around him at the people passing by in the street but saw no one fitting that description. He shook his head. "I don't see him."

"No, not now. But he will be somewhere. Could be he is watching us right now."

"A robber, you think?" Latimer said. "He'll find slim pickings if he tries to rob me. Are you sure it was the man you saw in Fort Concho?"

"Not sure, Mr. Latimer. But pretty damn sure. He been following us since we left dock."

"We'll finish our coffee and head back to the coaching inn, that is, if we don't get lost," Latimer said. "If he continues to follow us, then we'll be on our guard. No matter how desperate a character he is, there's not much he can do in broad daylight."

The Chinese nodded. "Maybe so, but Mr. Chang uneasy. On tenterhooks, as Miss Huckabee say."

Latimer smiled. "Hannah always had a way with words."

"Could be that you and Miss Huckabee will get together again, now that captain of big iron ship doesn't want you," Mr. Chang said.

"I don't think Hannah wants me, either," Latimer said.

"Then that very sad."

"Yes, you're right, Mr. Chang. It is indeed very sad. Drink up your coffee. Let's see if the robber follows us."

"Ah, then you think he is robber?"

"No, I don't. But you do, and that's good enough for me."

They were being followed. Even as Latimer and Mr. Chang weaved their way along the busy sidewalks, the big man shadowed them closely but always staying back, waiting for an opportunity to do what? Rob them?

Latimer discounted that notion and the sudden thought formed in his mind that the man was somehow connected with Rupert Bentley-Foulkes. What was a career army officer doing in New Orleans at the same time as the gunman Mr. Chang was sure he'd seen in Fort Concho? Then the wild suspicion entered Latimer's head that Bentley-Foulkes was there for one reason . . . revenge. Did he blame him for the death of his brother? Family ties were strong among the British aristocracy, and the retribution motive was not out of the question.

John Latimer was now certain that he was the target of an assassination plot.

Brack Cooley's opportunity came when Latimer and Mr. Chang approached a narrow, paved alley hemmed in by balconied, three-story buildings on either side, the tallest with a dramatically angled fire escape.

Cooley hurried his pace, drew alongside Latimer,

and pushed him into the deserted alley. The Englishman threw a punch that the gunman easily brushed aside, pinned him against a wall with his muscular right arm and pulled his coat aside, showing the Colt in his waistband.

"Quit struggling or I'll kill you," Cooley said.

Mr. Chang came to Latimer's aid, but Cooley drew his gun and slammed it into the little man's head. Mr. Chang's skullcap flew off and he hit the ground hard, groaned, and lay still.

"You damned rogue!" Latimer said.

He tried to struggle free of Cooley's grasp, but the big man's strength was relentless. His face close to Latimer's, the muzzle of his revolver rammed into the Englishman's belly, he said through gritted teeth, "You come with me, Latimer, or I'll blow your damned guts out."

"Shoot me here and you'll bring the law down on you," Latimer said. "Or are you too stupid to realize that?"

Cooley smiled. "Latimer, you've had too much to drink," he said.

Before the Englishman could react, Cooley swung his revolver and slammed it into the side of Latimer's head.

Cooley grabbed the unconscious man and half-carried, half-dragged him out of the alley. He hailed a passing cab and gave the top-hatted driver an address in the business district. "My friend's had too much to drink," he said. "I'll take him back to work until he sobers up."

Falling-down drunks were not rare in New Orleans

and the cabbie didn't as much as raise an eyebrow as Cooley bundled the groaning Latimer into the hansom.

"Oh, you poor man, are you all right?"

Mr. Chang woke to a pounding headache and the sound of a woman's voice in his ears. He opened his eyes and saw the blurred face of a middle-aged New Orleans matron who was both comely and sympathetic.

"Thank you, dear lady, I will be fine now," Mr. Chang said.

"It looks like you took a nasty bump on the head," the woman said. "Did you fall?"

"Yes. I tripped on paving stone and fell. Chinese men seldom fall but sometimes miss their footing."

"You poor thing, then you're one of the unlucky ones. Let me help you to your feet," the woman said. "Oh, here is your little hat."

Still groggy, Mr. Chang bowed. "Lady is most kind."

"Can I help you get a cab?" the woman said. "Do you live nearby?"

"My name Mr. Chang. And I currently reside at old coaching inn on Broad Street. And yes, help in hailing cab would be most appreciated."

"You poor dear," the woman said. "Take my arm, and I'll help you to the street."

It took a couple of minutes to stop a vacant cab, and in that time the woman told Mr. Chang that her name was Mrs. Bell and that she was widowed, had two daughters, one a secretary, the other a domestic, and that she suffered from rheumatisms and a wandering womb, but the doctor said neither was very serious, and how glad she was to have met a Chinese gentleman because she'd never had the pleasure before.

For his part, though he was profuse in his thanks, Mr. Chang was glad to climb into the cab and leave the charming but loquacious Mrs. Bell behind.

Chapter Forty-three

"There was only one gunman at Fort Concho, and that was Brack Cooley," Red Ryan said. "And if it was him that took Latimer, then the Englishman is in a heap of trouble."

Buttons Muldoon said, "But Cooley is a bounty hunter. What interest would he have in Latimer? He isn't wanted by the law."

"I think I might have the answer to that question, or at least part of an answer," Hannah Huckabee said. Buttons and Red were in her room to hear what the badly shaken Mr. Chang had to say about the kidnapping. "Red, do you remember I told you I'd seen three men at Fort Concho who looked like British army officers? I think they're tied in with Cooley."

"Why?" Red said.

"They may plan to pay Cooley to kill him."

"I guess it's possible. Killing for hire is one of Cooley's specialties," Red said. "Mr. Chang said the British navy captain talked Latimer out of insisting on a court-martial. Maybe that didn't set well with those army officers, if that's what they are."

"Or maybe that's exactly what they wanted," Hannah said. "The officers would rather kill him themselves."

"They must be rannies who carry a grudge," Buttons said. "Hell, it all happened years ago."

"John's regiment was the Fifty-first Lancers. The lancers had won many battle honors in the Napoleonic wars and the Indian Rebellion of 1857 and then John Latimer committed an act of cowardice that brought disgrace to the regiment and the army. For many of the junior officers, that betrayal was like a knife to the back, and they bayed for John's blood." Hannah shook her head. "And, God help me, I was among them."

"So some of those junior officers are now here in New Orleans, and they plan to kill him," Buttons said. "Is that what we reckon is happening?"

"Or have Brack Cooley kill him," Red said.

"And if that's the case, John is probably already as good as dead," Hannah said.

"Well, now it's a matter for the law," Buttons said. "We'll let the New Orleans police handle it. Maybe organize a search."

"How interested will they be in the disappearance of one man, and a foreigner at that?" Hannah said. "Mr. Muldoon, I don't think the police will do much searching."

Buttons said, "Miss Hannah, John Latimer is no longer a passenger of the Abe Patterson and Son Stage and Express Company, so it's not our concern. Gil Hooper says two people have already signed up for a trip to Austin, so Red and myself will be leaving, starting out the day after tomorrow."

"Buttons is right, Hannah," Red said. "We're still working for the Patterson stage."

"Then can we conduct our own search?" Hannah said. "You're not leaving New Orleans just yet."

"Search? That's impossible, like looking for a needle in a haystack," Buttons said. "New Orleans is a big town."

"I guess it's worth a try," Red said. "I don't think we'll find him, but we should make the effort. We owe Latimer that much."

"New Orleans not so big," Mr. Chang said. "I have idea."

"Then spill your plan, Chinaman," Buttons said. "The white folk are all out of ideas."

"Not just yet. Bad to get hopes up only to have them fall. Sometimes plan just a list of things that do not happen." Mr. Chang rose from his chair, a small, frail figure with a bump on his head. "I leave now, see what I can do to save Mr. Latimer, if the honorable gentleman still alive."

After Mr. Chang left, Buttons said, "You can never figure what a Chinee is thinking. But one thing I hope he isn't thinking of is getting a gun and going up against Brack Cooley."

"I reckon that's not what he has in mind," Red said.

"Mr. Chang will do what he can," Hannah said. "I don't know what that could possibly be, but right now we need all the help we can get."

"I guess we can make a start by going back to where Latimer was taken," Red said. "Mr. Chang said it was a paved alley close to the business district."

"And follow tracks, Red? This ain't the Texas plains," Buttons said.

"We can ask around," Red said. "Maybe somebody saw what happened."

"Well, good luck with that," Buttons said. "Me, I'm gonna sit on the porch and drink beer until it's time for dinner. I ain't one for gallivanting all over New Orleans looking for a man who could be anywhere by this time, including out of town."

"I know, but let's give it a try," Hannah said. "I must find John. Suddenly it seems that I have so much to tell him."

Chapter Forty-four

The city of New Orleans was home to the largest Chinatown in the South. The Chinese influx began after the War Between the States when local planters imported hundreds of Cantonese laborers to replace slaves. But by the mid 1870s, the Chinese had abandoned the plantations and most found work in the factories of the business district. However, they also dominated the laundry industry in the city, and it was to one of those establishments that Mr. Chang directed his steps.

Although he'd be suspicious of whites asking questions, the laundry owner readily opened up to Mr. Chang, and told him that Chinatown was located at the end of Tulane Avenue and South Rampart Street.

"Speak to Huang Tian, the moneylender," the laundryman said. "Stop anyone in the street and you'll be directed to his office." Then, a warning. "Be respectful. Huang Tian is a rich man and he has many bodyguards." And a further caution of just one whispered word. "Triads."

Mr. Chang was more than familiar with the violent

and widespread Triad crime syndicate and knew that when he visited Huang Tian he must be on his guard and give the great man much veneration.

The day was still young, and Mr. Chang walked to Chinatown, ignoring the heat of the day. It took several inquiries and blank stares from other Chinese before a woman directed him to the moneylender's place of business, a nondescript, single-story building with a brass plaque over the door that read ENTER.

His heart racing, Mr. Chang opened the door and stepped inside into a carpeted reception area that displayed nothing that was Chinese. On the wall behind the male secretary's desk hung a generic seascape with a sailing ship that was neither inspired nor valuable.

The secretary, young, tough-looking, and dressed in European garb, greeted Mr. Chang with a notable lack of enthusiasm, his eyebrow raised over the visitor's traditional Chinese robes and pigtail. After a slight adjustment to the shoulder holster under his dark gray suit coat, the young man told Mr. Chang to state his business . . . and he spoke in English, surprising Mr. Chang greatly.

"I am here to talk with the esteemed lord Huang Tian," Mr. Chang said, bowing,

"On what matter?" the secretary said.

"I wish him to help me save the life of a friend."

"Many people ask Mr. Huang Tian for help, but most days he has none to give. Do you want to borrow money?"

"No. I do not. I only wish to save a life."

"I will tell him you are here," the young man said. "But I doubt that he will see you."

"I am Triad," Mr. Chang said. "Or I was."

"Where?"

"Shanghai. And other places."

"Show me."

Mr. Chang pulled up his left sleeve and showed the red dragon tattoo on his forearm and then the phoenix tattoo on his right.

"Once a Triad, always a Triad," the secretary said "There is no 'I was,' only 'I am.'"

"That was my impression," Mr. Chang said. "Young man has much understanding of the way of the Triads. It speaks a great volume about the worthiness of his upbringing."

The young man stared hard at his visitor for long moments and then said, "Wait here. I will talk with Huang Tian and ask if he is willing to meet with you."

Mr. Chang bowed.

After a couple of minutes, the secretary returned, and his face wore a slightly surprised expression. "Huang Tian will see you."

The young man quickly patted down Mr. Chang, looking for weapons, and took a small jade figurine from the pocket of his robe. "What is this?" he said.

"A gift for the great lord Huang Tian."

The man smiled, handed back the figurine, and said, "Follow me."

Mr. Chang was ushered into an office that would not have been out of place in Washington, D.C. The shelves on the walls held only rows of ledgers and bundled papers, and the rug underfoot was Persian, not Chinese, and incongruously, an 1866 model Yellow Boy Winchester and a holstered Colt hung in a gun rack beside the door. Mr. Chang observed silently that Huang Tian was a careful man.

The moneylender, and extortioner and opium smuggler, was a slender, middle-aged man with an immobile, closed face. He wore a dark business suit and a celluloid collar with a red and black striped tie and round glasses with tortoiseshell rims, and to Mr. Chang's relief he didn't in the least look intimidating.

But looks can be deceptive.

Huang Tian's voice was harsh and authoritative as he said, "We will conduct our business in English, since it is the language of commerce."

Mr. Chang bowed and said, "It is a great honor that you would meet with a person as worthless as myself."

"You are a Triad. No Triad is worthless. State your business," Huang Tian said.

"A gift, lord," Mr. Chang said. He took the figurine from his pocket, a small, jade dragon of exquisite workmanship and, as etiquette demanded, offered it to Huang Tian with both hands. "This was a gift to me from the Son of Heaven, the Emperor Tezong, and now I present it to you."

In fact, it was a present to Hannah Huckabee from a minor court official in Peking, but Mr. Chang decided that the importance of his mission called for a certain amount of exaggeration.

Hung Tian, recognized the Chinese court workmanship and took the little jade dragon at face value. But, as was the custom, he refused the gift three times before accepting it. Then he said, "You are a Triad, and you have given me a gift that was touched by an emperor's hand. Now tell me what I can do for you. If it is within reason, I will grant your request."

And Mr. Chang told him.

When he was finished speaking, Hung Tian thought for a few moments and said, "The Chinese who work in this city's business district are invisible because the white Americans do not see them. They never notice how the little yellow people glide here and there, busy with the burdens of the day's tasks, making no sound, troubling no one. But what they don't understand is that those same little people are aware, watchful, they see and hear everything and forget nothing."

Mr. Chang nodded. "Yes, great lord, that is so."

"If your friend was taken at gunpoint to somewhere in the business district, or any other district, it is almost certain that Chinese eyes saw him. I will make inquiries. Come here at this time tomorrow. Perhaps I will have news for you then."

"You are most kind, great lord," Mr. Chang said, bowing.

Huang Tian waved a hand. "Go now." Then, "If it was not the case that you are a Triad and if you did not have the good breeding to bring me a gift, you would not leave here with a head on your shoulders. Coming here to ask a favor of me was an impertinence."

"Huang Tian is most merciful," Mr. Chang said, swallowing hard.

"No, little man. Mercy is a trait I do not possess," the moneylender said.

Chapter Forty-five

Following Mr. Chang's directions, Red Ryan and Hannah Huckabee found the alley where John Latimer had been abducted. On both sides were apartment blocks, but knocking on doors turned up nothing. No one had seen or heard anything, and the usual advice was, "Go talk to the police and stop bothering folks."

"So where do we go from here?" Hannah said. She wore a brown afternoon dress with white collar and cuffs and a defeated expression.

"Beats me," Red said. "Buttons was right, I can't pick up any tracks." He smacked his lips. "My mouth tastes like it's full of dry mud. Let's go get a drink."

"We could talk to the police, I suppose," Hannah said, as though she hadn't heard.

"Yeah, we could," Red said.

"But you don't think it would do much good."

"A big-city police department? They probably investigate scores of crimes every day, and like you yourself said, the kidnapping of a grown man, and a visiting

Englishman at that, would be far down on their list of priorities."

"Red, do you think John is still alive?" Hannah said.

"I don't know, Hannah. I really don't know. I can't even guess."

"I think Brack Cooley means to kill him."

"Or those officers you spoke about do."

"I'm sure they hate him."

"Well, that's a pretty good reason to kill somebody."

"If you kidnapped someone off the street, where would you hide him?" Hannah said.

"In New Orleans? Ask a native and they'll probably give you a thousand different places," Red said.

"We're close to the business district, Red. Wouldn't that be an obvious place, among all those offices and warehouses?"

"Obvious to you, fairly obvious to me, but was it obvious to Brack Cooley?"

"I don't know, but let's take a look around the place."

"Hannah, that's a heap of ground to cover in this heat," Red said. "And I need a beer, and my mouth needs a beer."

"There will be time enough for beer after we make a search," Hannah said. "Just put one foot ahead of the other and follow me."

"It's a wild-goose chase, Hannah."

"Perhaps, but John Latimer's life is at stake, so it's worth a try."

Red's sigh came all the way up from his toes. "All right, lady. Lead the way. I swear, if I run into Brack Cooley I'm going to—"

"Hang him up by his heels ," Hannah said.

Red managed a smile. "Yeah, something like that."

Commerce in nineteenth-century New Orleans began and ended with the Mississippi River. Planters needed access to the water to move raw goods like cotton, indigo, and sugarcane to the port. The merchants and shippers constructed wharves and warehouses on the river, and industrialists built businesses to support them, including metal foundries, rope makers, and victualers. Thus, the business district had many layers, and as Red and Hannah walked from the river in the direction of Lake Pontchartrain, they passed first warehouses, then factories and plants, and finally two- and three-story office buildings.

They saw no sign of John Latimer and at least a hundred places where he could be hidden.

The district was crowded with workers from brawny laborers to men in ditto suits and celluloid collars, as well as many silent, usually overburdened Chinese. Goods wagons crowded the clamoring streets, and the constant noise from the factories provided a clanging, clanking, steam-hissing background.

It was unfortunate for Red and Hannah that they overlooked a narrow alley between two corrugated iron warehouses that ended with a dilapidated timber building dating back to the 1850s with a faded sign above its double doors that read:

SLAVES
AT AUCTION
Jas. Beck, *Prop.*

As it was, as the day faded into evening, the disappointed pair gave up the hunt and hailed a cab that took them back to the coaching inn and the schooner of beer that Red so badly needed.

It would be much later before Red and Hannah realized that for a few moments during their search, John Latimer had been only a stone's throw away.

Chapter Forty-six

John Latimer regained consciousness and discovered two unpalatable truths. The first was that he could not move his arms or legs, the second was that he was in some kind of barn that smelled of decay and many years of disuse.

As he grew more lucid, he realized that he was hog-tied, his ankles and wrists tied tightly with rope, and that he was in some kind of cage with a dirt floor, iron bars in the front, and a padlocked timber door. As his eyes grew accustomed to the gloom of the place, he made out a couple more cages and an open area and, dusty and cobwebbed, what appeared to be a preacher's podium.

But he quickly understood that was not the case. No matter how sinful they may be, a preacher's flock was not kept in barred and padlocked cages.

Prisoners had been held in the barn. But what sort of prisoners? And why the large and substantial podium? Then it dawned on him. It was an auctioneer's podium, and he'd been locked up in a place where slaves had been held in cages and then sold, and it hadn't been used since the end of the Civil War, hence the smell of rot and abandonment.

He'd been knocked on the head, rendered unconscious, and was now trussed up and thrown in a pen like a rat in a trap. Was Rupert Bentley-Foulkes about to take his revenge?

The answer to that question was not long in coming.

A padlock rattled on the outside doors, and one of them opened and, after a few moments, closed again. From his position on the floor, Latimer saw two men step toward him. One was the man who'd clubbed him, the gunman Mr. Chang called Brack Cooley. The other man, slim, tall and refined-looking, he didn't know, but he had the bearing of a soldier . . . and a suspicion began to form in Latimer's mind that he was now just moments away from being shot.

The door to his cage was unlocked, and a grinning Cooley opened a pocketknife and cut the rope that bound Latimer's ankles. He kicked the recumbent man in the ribs and said, "Someone wants to talk with you, Latimer. On your feet."

Latimer's "Go to hell" earned him another kick, and Cooley, a big man and strong, hauled him to his feet and dragged him out of the cage. He was pushed in front of the soldierly man, who had already taken his place on the podium. "Is your name John Latimer?" the man said.

"I rather fancy that you already know it is," Latimer said.

"Yes, your name is John Latimer, formerly a captain in the Fifty-first Lancers. I am Captain Rupert Bentley-Foulkes of the Eightieth Regiment of Foot."

"I heard Lieutenant Tom Bentley-Foulkes mention you," Latimer said. "You were his brother."

"I was his brother. He is dead."

"I know."

"And you were responsible for his death."

"As his commanding officer, yes, the responsibility was mine."

"Do you know why you have been brought before this court?"

"What court? I see only you and a gunman thug."

"Latimer, you are charged with cowardice in the face of the enemy. The officers who will sit in judgment of you will join the court tomorrow. In addition to that duty, Lieutenant Granville Wood will act as trial counsel and Lieutenant John Allerton for the defense. Both these gentlemen were officers in the Fifty-first. Do you know either of them?"

"No."

"Then that is all to the good," Bentley-Foulkes said.

"I don't recognize this court," Latimer said. "As far as I'm concerned, you and the rest of your cohorts are a common lynch mob."

"I suggest you keep a civil tongue in your head, Latimer," Bentley-Foulkes said. "This is a very serious matter indeed, and if you are found guilty, you will be shot."

"I imagine that is a foregone conclusion," Latimer said. "Bentley-Foulkes, your brother was an insubordinate fool who threw his life away. It's he who should be facing a court-martial."

"And that is very unlikely since my brother is dead and his body was never recovered. Two months later my mother died of a broken heart, Latimer, and her death was also a result of your . . . as your judge I must say alleged . . . cowardice."

"I am sorry to hear about your mother," Latimer said.

"Yes, shed crocodile tears for her. She means nothing to you."

"She does, more than a man like you can realize," Latimer said.

"Mr. Cooley, take the prisoner away," Bentley-Foulkes said. "Latimer, your court-martial will commence tomorrow at dawn. If found guilty, which I don't doubt, you will be shot at dusk."

Latimer's feet were again tied, and Cooley's farewell was a grin and another kick in the ribs. The outer door opened, closed, the padlock rattled, and he was left to the growing darkness without food or water, his only companions the restless rats that rustled in the corners.

Chapter Forty-seven

Huang Tian had seen to the matter personally, not because it was of great importance—it wasn't—but his righteous wrath must be witnessed by all in Chinatown as a terrible thing.

Fifty dollars loaned out at forty percent interest was not a large sum, but refusal to repay was a monumental affront, and an example had to be made . . . and now the laundryman Long Yu was paying the price.

Naked, bloody from the beatings he'd taken, the wretch hung by his thumbs from the ceiling of his own premises while his wife and daughters wailed, and his sons stood apart, their heads lowered, fearful that they might be blamed for their father's failings.

The moneylender's armed men, all of them Triad, had ordered the attendance of many neighbors to witness the disgrace and suffering of the scoundrel Long Yu and to see what a dreadful thing was the displeasure of the great and powerful lord Huang Tian.

As the Triad amused themselves by spilling hot candle wax on Long Yu's trembling, tortured body to hear him scream, the laundryman's wife could bear it no longer. She rushed into the living quarters and returned with a tin box that she opened and then, bowing low, offered to Huang Tian.

The lord did not deign to count the money himself but passed the money box to one of his men. The amount was a hundred and ten dollars. Huang Tien then took the money and threw it to the crowd and a shrieking scramble for bills and coins followed.

When the hubbub died down, Huang Tien warned Long Yu's wife that if there was a next time, depending on how merciful he felt at the time, her husband would lose a hand or his nose.

At this, Long Yu's wife was very afraid, and she swore that it would never happen again, and Huang Tien said, "See that it doesn't." And then to his men. "Make him feel a little more pain and then cut him down."

Long Yu's screams followed Huang Tien as he left the laundry and stepped into the street under a haloed moon, a good omen that pleased the money-lender. Flanked by a pair of his gunmen, Huang Tien lingered for a while, and this was fortunate for a humble laborer named Sun Wen. After the lamentable violence that had taken place inside, Huang Tien was eager to reveal his benevolent side to the people around him and take time to listen to a petitioner.

But Sun Wen was not asking a boon. He had information to impart and secretly harbored the hope that he might be rewarded.

As his bodyguards scowled at Sun Wen's boldness and the calculating look in his eye, Huang Tien inclined his head and listened attentively to what the man, speaking in a whisper, had to say.

And when Sun Wen had finished talking, Huang Tien's satisfaction was obvious to all. Loud enough that everyone could hear, he said, "Sun Wen," displaying a common touch by the use of the insignificant laborer's name, "you have done me a great service, and it will not go unrewarded."

Inside Long Yu shrieked as his more grievous wounds were treated by his wife and daughters, but outside the people were hanging on the great lord's every word.

"Come with me, Sun Wen, and we will talk further," Huang Tien said.

The two men moved off some, standing in darkness, and the moneylender said, "You will go to a man called Chang. I will tell you where to find him. You will impart to him what you have told me. Come back and tell me the good tidings have been delivered and I will reward you. If you fail to deliver the news to Chang, for the sake of your family, never come back. Do you understand?"

Sun Wen was afraid because he seldom ventured far from Chinatown, but he nodded and said, "Yes, I understand."

Huang Tien then told the man where Chang could be found and sent him on his way.

It was a long walk to the old coaching inn through deserted streets under the light of the strange moon, and Sun Wen was relieved when he reached his destination. But the inn was in darkness since the midnight hour had passed a long time before. Where to find Mr. Chang?

Sun Wen stood on the hotel porch and looked through the glass doors into the darkened lobby. He saw no one, and nothing moved but the pendulum of the grandfather clock against the far wall. The little Chinese swallowed hard and fought his growing fear. He could not fail Huang Tien, since, as was known to all in Chinatown, the great lord's reward for failure was death in its most painful forms.

Mustering his courage, Sun Wen tried the door handle. It turned in his hand, and when he pushed, the door creaked open. The little man stepped inside and the *tick . . . tock . . . tick* of the grandfather clock welcomed him.

Then, not the clock, but disaster, struck.

Daisy, Gil Hooper's little calico cat, had free run of the inn, but that night, for reasons known only to herself, she'd decided to bed down in the middle of the lobby floor, and Sun Wen, shuffling forward in the gloom, stepped on her tail. The hissing, screeching, howling bedlam that followed woke Hooper from his shallow sleep, and the old man jumped out of bed, grabbed his rifle, and hurried downstairs, dressed only in long johns.

He saw a shadowy figure in the lobby and yelled, "Stay right where you're at, or I'll drop you where you stand!"

Sun Wen, who spoke no English, didn't know what the man was saying, but the rifle in his hands made his intent clear. The Chinese raised his hands and screamed, "Mr. Chang! Mr. Chang!"

There was a commotion on the stairs, and Red Ryan and Buttons Muldoon, both wearing pants and hats, but no boots, hurried down the steps, demanding to know what the hell was happening.

"This Chinee attacked my Daisy," Hooper said. "Probably planned on eating her. I aim to plug him fer a damned cannibal."

Now thoroughly frightened, Sun Wen thought about making a run for it, but his fear of admitting failure to Huang Tian was even greater and he yelled again, "Mr. Chang! Mr. Chang!"

"Gil, no," Red said. "He's here to see Mr. Chang."

"At this time of the night? Only whores and burglars are awake at three in the morning."

"Two in the morning," Buttons said absently. And then to the Chinese, "You want to see Mr. Chang?"

Sun Wen answered with a string of Cantonese, and then he nodded and said, "Mr. Chang."

From the staircase Hannah Huckabee said, "What's happening?

"This feller wants to see Mr. Chang," Red said. "Apart from that, I don't know what the hell he's saying."

Hannah stepped down into the lobby and a few moments later Mr. Chang joined her. He took in the situation at a glance and said, "I will speak to him."

"No, step aside," Gil Hooper said. "I want to drill him. He wanted to eat my cat."

"Not yet, Mr. Hooper, I want to hear what humble Chinese man has to say," Mr. Chang said.

Then followed a short conversation in Cantonese between the two Chinese. Hannah had some knowledge of the language and said to Red, "His name is

Sun Wen, and he says he knows where John is being held." After a while she continued, "He's in the business district in an old barn where slave auctions were once held."

"I didn't see an old barn," Red said.

"Neither did I," Hannah said. "But this man says it's there. His wife saw a drunk white man being carried into the place."

"Anything else?" Red said.

"I'm listening," Hannah said. Then, when the Chinese stopped talking, she said, "No, that's it. Just the drunk white man."

"Mr. Latimer struck over the head by Brack Cooley," Mr. Chang said. "If he was unconscious, he could be mistaken for drunk man." He patted Sun Wen on the shoulder, said something in Cantonese, and the little man, after a last look at mean old Gil Hooper and his rifle, scampered out of the lobby into the night.

"Mr. Chang, you're a sore disappointment to me," Hooper said, "I should've plugged that damned cat bandit."

"He very useful, bring news from Huang Tian, who very great Chinese lord and knows all," Mr. Chang said. "I think I can now lead way to Mr. Latimer's place of captivity."

"Mr. Chang, are you sure?" Hannah said. She wore a pink robe, and a pink ribbon tied back her hair, and Red Ryan was amazed that anyone could get out of bed at two in the morning and look that lovely.

"I am sure," Mr. Chang said, "I can find the way."

"Red, what do you think?" Hannah said.

"If the little Chinese is telling the truth, the slave barn is worth a visit," Red said.

"A man sleeping off a drunk or John?" Hannah said.

"There's only one way to find out," Red said. "We must be in the business district and ready to search at first light."

Hannah turned to Gil Hooper. "Coffee and an early breakfast, Mr. Hooper?"

"That can be arranged," the old man said.

"Plenty of drunk white men in New Orleans," Buttons said, looking sour. "Could be another wild-goose chase, and I've got a schedule to keep."

"But will you come with us, Mr. Muldoon?" Hannah said. "We need your stalwart bravery in the face of danger."

"Damn right I will," Buttons said, pleased. "I wouldn't miss this shindig for the world."

Chapter Forty-eight

At dawn, John Latimer was again kicked and dragged out of his cage. Brack Cooley frog-marched him in front of the podium where Rupert Bentley-Foulkes was waiting, his face stern. Two other young men were also present, and Latimer assumed that they were the two lieutenants who would sit in judgment of him.

"Captain Latimer, you know why you're here," Bentley-Foulkes said. "Let's not drag this out any longer than we need to. How do you plead?"

"I need a drink of water," Latimer said.

"You will get water before your execution," Bentley-Foulkes said. "I will not send a man to hell thirsty. Lieutenant Allerton, please enter a plea for the defendant."

"Not guilty," the young man said. He looked as though he'd just sucked on a lemon.

"Very well then, let the trial commence," Bentley-Foulkes said. "We will return to the events of the twenty-third of June, 1879, on the Indian Northwest Frontier. Captain Latimer, you will now tell the court about that day and the death of Lieutenant Thomas Bentley-Foulkes of the Fifty-first Lancers at the hands of a small party of Afghan tribesmen."

"Go to hell," Latimer said. "This trial is a farce and you know it, Bentley-Foulkes. Shoot me and get it over with, you damned scoundrel."

Bentley-Foulkes shook his head. "I will see justice done," he said. "Lieutenant Wood, read the official report of the action."

"The only official report was mine, and it was given verbally," Latimer said.

Wood ignored that and said, "This report was later submitted to General Sir Frederick Roberts by a member of his staff."

Bentley-Foulkes said, "Let it be entered into the record. Proceed, Lieutenant Wood, but it's a lengthy document, so just cover the main points."

"Yes, sir. On the twenty-third of June, 1879, Captain Latimer led a scouting patrol of nine lancers into India's Northwest Frontier of which Lieutenant Thomas Bentley-Foulkes was a supernumerary, having volunteered for the reconnaissance in the hope of getting to grips with the enemy."

"Indeed, he did," Bentley-Foulkes said, smiling. "Carry on, Lieutenant Wood."

"Certainly, sir. Captain Latimer sent his command into an abandoned village to ascertain if there were any Afghan tribesmen present, and then sat his horse at some considerable remove while his order was carried out."

"That's a damned lie," Latimer said. This earned him a slap from Cooley.

"Carry on, Lieutenant," Bentley-Foulkes said.

"Yes, sir. A large force of Afghans attacked the patrol from the cover of an adjoining thorn-tree patch, and Lieutenant Bentley-Foulkes and his lancers were quickly overwhelmed. At this point Captain John Latimer had already fled the field and took no further part in the action." Then, after a short pause. "The bodies of a sergeant and three privates were later recovered from the abandoned village, but the remains of Lieutenant Bentley-Foulkes were never found. It is thought the officer's body was carried away by the Afghans and burned."

"The facts seem to speak for themselves," Bentley-Foulkes said. "Lieutenant Allerton, have you anything to say on behalf of Captain Latimer? Confine your remarks to the events of the twenty-third of June."

"Yes, sir. Captain Latimer said he discharged his revolver into the ranks of the Afghans, killing several. But it was only when he saw that his men were already dead did he retreat."

"Sir, we only have Captain Latimer's word for that," Lieutenant Wood said. "May I remind the court that he is not a gentleman and as a consequence is not bound by truth?"

Lieutenant Allerton, warming to his task, said, "Captain Latimer is the son of an impoverished country parson who had ten children that he could ill afford to feed and clothe. That is why his oldest son, twelve-year-old John, went for a soldier and joined the army as a drummer boy. Through dint of hard work and obedience to orders, he quickly moved through the ranks and was commissioned a second lieutenant when he was twenty-three years old. The trial counsel is correct that Captain Latimer rose from humble beginnings and is not a gentleman. It is the opinion of the defense that he should therefore not be held to a gentleman's code of conduct."

Lieutenant Wood said, "May I remind the court that, apart from Lieutenant Bentley-Foulkes, the lancers who died were not gentlemen, but by God, sir, they fought and died as though they were. Should we not expect the same behavior from their commanding officer?"

"A point well taken, Lieutenant Wood," Bentley-Foulkes said. "Now, let us consider the military events in India that led up to the twenty-third of June and the death of the gallant Lieutenant Thomas Bentley-Foulkes . . ."

John Latimer, his head reeling from a lack of water and food and his ribs throbbing from the kicking they'd taken from Brack Cooley, listened in growing disbelief and horror to the travesty of justice unfolding around him. He would be found guilty, that was inevitable . . . He just wished it would soon be over.

Chapter Forty-nine

Two cabs clattered to a halt in the industrial section of the business district. Red Ryan and Hannah Huckabee, dressed in her safari clothes and pith helmet and goggles, climbed out of one, Buttons Muldoon and Mr. Chang from the other. But not before Buttons gave the cabbie a piece of his mind about his sloppy work with the lines and the poor job he'd made of harnessing the horse in the first place.

For his part, the cabbie seemed unimpressed and told Buttons to go to hell, adding, as he looked askance at the few coins in his palm, that in the past he'd received a better tip from a nun who'd taken a vow of poverty.

Buttons was all for arguing the case, but Red dragged him away and reminded him why they were there.

"Sorry, Red, but he didn't even have a checkrein on his horse," Buttons said. "Depending on the horse, that can be a disaster."

"We're looking for two corrugated iron buildings

with an alley between them," Red said. "For now, that's more important than a checkrein."

"Nothing is more important than a checkrein," Buttons said. "But I'm looking, I'm looking."

Thanks to the directions given to Mr. Chang, they tracked down the corrugated iron warehouses, two vast buildings with a narrow, graveled alley running between them. The slave-auction barn was on about an acre of rubble-strewn, open ground about a hundred yards from the end of the alley. It was a windowless structure with double doors to the front and a sagging, shingled roof. There was no sign of life around the place, no tethered horses or wagons.

"It looks like it's deserted," Hannah said.

"Seems like," Red said.

"Wild-goose chase, if you ask me," Buttons said. "But nobody ever asks me."

A huge, rusted iron steam boiler lay to their right, and Red suggested they take cover behind it while he scouted the place. "Hannah, do you have your revolver?" he said.

"In my pocket."

Buttons opened his sailor's coat and showed the Colt in his waistband.

"All right, shuck those guns, and if you see me fogging it with Brack Cooley on my heels, cut loose," Red said.

"At who?" Buttons asked. Then, seeing the look on Red's face, "Just a little stage-driver humor there."

Hannah smiled and so did Mr. Chang.

"All right, let's get it done," Red said. "When I come back, one way or another, we'll make our plan."

"Red, I don't want John to get hurt," Hannah said.

"We won't know if that's possible till we get in there," Red said.

"Hell, we don't even know that he is in there," Buttons said.

"Well, I aim to find out," Red said.

"Red, be careful," Hannah said.

Red nodded, left the cover of the boiler, and angled across open ground toward the back of the barn. The sun was higher in the sky, but the morning was not yet oppressively hot. The factories and workshops that ran twenty-four hours a day hammered and clanged in the background, and a steam whistle intermittently shrieked like a banshee. Red was sweating as he reached the rear of the building and then dropped to the ground, watching, listening, waiting. Nothing moved, and there was no sound from inside . . . or was there?

The barn had a single, padlocked door at the back that had sagged on its hinges and was slightly ajar on the top and one side. Red wasn't certain, but thought he'd heard the drone of a man's voice from somewhere inside the building. He drew his Colt, rose to his feet, and stepped closer to the door. There! Now he heard it plain, a man with a cold, clipped English accent talking angrily to someone. The voice didn't sound like John Latimer's, but Red was sure the man was inside, and with others. He touched his tongue to his dry top lip. The joker in the deck was Brack Cooley . . . was the gunman in the building? The answer to that was "probably" . . . but around a man like Cooley, uncertainty could get you killed.

On cat feet, moving slowly, Red made his way along the windowless side of the barn, thumb on the hammer of his up and ready Colt. In the distance he heard the steady pound of a steam hammer in one of the factories and closer, insects made their small sounds in the grass. He reached the corner, wiped sudden sweat off his forehead with the back of his gun hand, and then darted his head around for a quick look at the front of the building.

He took in what there was to see in an instant.

The barn had a double door and was open slightly, the padlock and chain dangling. Red ducked behind the corner again and stood with his back against the rough timber wall. Through those doors was the path inside . . . the way to rescue John Latimer from his captors.

It sounded easy, but it wasn't. Red did a quick mental calculation.

Pull open the door . . . two seconds.

Run inside . . . a second, maybe two.

Assess the situation . . . two seconds.

Fire!

He would give Brack Cooley at least five seconds to respond to the intrusion. Five seconds when all the gunman needed to draw and shoot was a fraction of just one.

Red realized he was up against a stacked deck.

There had to be a better way.

And maybe there was . . . if Hannah Huckabee was once again willing to lay her life on the line.

* * *

"It's a lot to ask, Hannah," Red Ryan said, once more behind the cover of the steam boiler. "And I'm asking it."

"Red, I say we go to the police, let them handle it from here," Buttons Muldoon said.

"By the time the police got here, if they even came, John could be dead," Hannah said. "Red thinks he's in the barn with Cooley and the others. We just can't take a chance on them shooting him out of hand."

"Then you'll do it, Hannah?" Red said.

"I don't see that I've any choice."

"There is a choice," Buttons said, stubborn as ever. "Let the law handle it."

"No. I want John Latimer out of there, and I want him out now . . . not later today or tomorrow or the next day, I mean now," Hannah said.

"Miss Huckabee make up her mind, nothing can change it," Mr. Chang said.

Buttons shook his head. "In all my life, I've never won an argument with a woman, and I'm losing this one. Red, what do you want me to do?"

Red told him, and Buttons said, "You know you and me are both dead, don't you?"

"It can work, Buttons," Red said. "Trust me on this."

"Red, we're talking about Brack Cooley here, remember? There ain't anybody in the world faster with the iron than ol' Brack, an' that's a natural fact."

"I know it is, Buttons. Neither of us can match his speed on the draw and shoot, but together we just might."

"And pigs will fly," Buttons said.

"If Hannah plays her part, I can do it myself," Red said.

"I won't let you do that, Red," Buttons said, "even if I miss my chance to stand at your grave and say, 'Well, I told him so.'"

Red smiled. "You're true blue, Buttons. I knew you wouldn't let me down."

Buttons growled and muttered to himself, and Hannah said, "Let's do it now before I lose what little courage I have left."

"Remember, you're lost, alone, trying to find your beloved, and crying bitter tears," Red said. "Sob for all you're worth, Hannah, like a widow woman at a funeral."

"As a general rule, I don't cry," Hannah said.

"Just think of taking advice from Buttons Muldoon and the tears will come," Red said.

Red Ryan retraced his steps to the rear of the barn, this time with Buttons in tow. They made their way to the corner of the wall and waited. Red drew his Colt, and Buttons did the same.

"How are you holding up, old fellow?" Red whispered.

"I want to sneeze. But since you ask, I'd rather be driving my coach."

Red nodded. "I guess that goes for both of us." He glared at Buttons. "For God's sake don't sneeze. It almost got us all killed in Austin."

"You're a man prone to exaggeration, Red," Buttons said. "I just nearly got Miss Hannah killed."

Chapter Fifty

". . . and then Captain Latimer was ordered to take out a patrol and investigate the abandoned Afghan villages in General Sir Frederick Roberts's line of march," Lieutenant Granville Wood said. "And we've already covered what followed in some depth."

"Yes, we have," Captain Rupert Bentley-Foulkes said. "Lieutenant Allerton, have you anything to add for the defense?"

"No, sir," Allerton said. "As trial counsel has stated, we've already covered that in depth."

"Now, gentlemen, I must ask you for your verdict," Bentley-Foulkes said. "Lieutenant Wood?"

"Guilty as charged, sir."

"Lieutenant Allerton?"

"Guilty as charged, sir."

"Captain Latimer, you have heard the verdict of this court-martial," Bentley-Foulkes said. "You have been found guilty of cowardice in the face of the enemy. Have you anything to say before sentence is passed?"

"Go to hell," Latimer said. "And take your back-stabbing lackeys with you."

"The sentence of this court is that you be taken thence from this place and shot," Bentley-Foulkes said, his face like stone. "And may God have mercy on your soul. Mr. Cooley, do your duty."

"John! John Latimer! Are you in there?"

"Hannah!" Latimer yelled. "Run! Get away from here!"

"Who is that woman?" Bentley-Foulkes said, alarmed.

Latimer tried to run for the door, but Cooley stepped in front of him and threw a straight right to the Englishman's chin. Hands tied, unable to defend himself, Latimer took the full force of the blow, staggered back, and fell to the ground.

"Yes, John, It's me. It's Hannah! I've been searching all over New Orleans for you."

"Mr. Cooley, bring that woman in here," Bentley-Foulkes said. "She's Latimer's whore and as guilty as he is."

Cooley grinned. "I'll get her."

He pushed open the barn door and stepped outside . . . just as Red and Buttons rounded the corner.

Cooley's face changed from a grin to a scowl. "Damn you, so that's it!" he yelled.

He went for the Colt in his waistband.

Cooley determined, rightly, that of the two men facing him Red Ryan was the fast gun. But in making that decision, he seriously underestimated Buttons Muldoon. Buttons was not fast, but he was sure, and both he and Red had the advantage of commencing the gunfight with their revolvers in their hands.

But Cooley was good, very good. Lightning fast on the draw and shoot.

He got off the first shot and fired at Red. A hit. Red took the bullet low on his left side, and it staggered him, but he shot back. Missed. Buttons now joined in the action and, at a range of just ten feet, fired at Cooley, a deliberate shot that hit the gunman high in the gut. And in that instant, Cooley knew he was a dead man. Enraged, he fired at Buttons. But with the amazing alacrity shared by many short, stocky men, the driver was already diving for the ground, firing as soon as he hit dirt. His bullet went wild, but Red had now steadied himself and fired. A center-belly hit that made a shocked Cooley bend from the waist, doubling up around the bullet's entry wound. Shot through and through, bleeding, aware that he'd been hit hard, Red nonetheless continued to stand his ground and got his work in. He snapped off two fast shots at Cooley, both hits, one smashing into the bicep of the gunman's right arm. Game as they come, Cooley attempted to switch his gun from one hand to the other, but his strength was gone, and his Colt thudded to the ground at his feet. Another bullet from Buttons's gun crashed into Cooley's chest, and the big man dropped to his knees, done. After a single, unbelieving look at Buttons, he fell on his face, dead before his nose hit the grass.

Red kneeled, his head bowed, and Buttons ran toward him. "No, Buttons!" he yelled. "Get Latimer!"

But Hannah had already rushed into the barn, her short-barreled Colt in her hand. Behind her, Mr. Chang had pulled his knife.

Rupert Bentley-Foulkes saw Hannah and yelled, "No! No! Kill him! Kill Latimer!"

He reached under his coat and drew a .476 Enfield revolver, ignored Hannah, and fired at the still-prostrate Latimer.

Hit, the Englishman groaned, and Hannah yelled, "Damn you!"

She triggered a shot at Bentley-Foulkes, and the man staggered off the podium and slammed into the wall behind him. Bleeding from a chest wound, he again ignored the woman, intent on killing Latimer. He raised his Enfield, and he and Hannah fired at the same instant. Bentley-Foulkes's bullet kicked up a startled exclamation point of dirt inches from Latimer's head. Hannah's bullet crashed into Bentley-Foulkes left shoulder, and her next shot dropped him.

Dying, the Englishman raised himself up on an elbow and said, "I killed him, you bitch."

"And I killed you," Hannah said, her face ablaze with anger. She emptied her Colt into Bentley-Foulkes, and the man died with his handsome, refined face in ancient slave dirt.

"Give me an excuse," Buttons Muldoon said, his gun in his hand. "Any excuse to plug you two damned scoundrels."

But Lieutenants Wood and Allerton wanted no part of this fight. They raised their hands, and Wood said, "It's over. We surrender."

"Damn right it's over," Buttons said. "You damn yellow-bellied cowards."

As Hannah kneeled beside the still-conscious

Latimer, Buttons forced the two young men into the cage where the Englishman had been held and turned the key in the padlock.

"You'll stay there until the law arrives," Buttons said. "But if Red Ryan looks likely to die, I'll come back and kill you both."

Chapter Fifty-one

Red Ryan and John Latimer spent two weeks lying in adjoining beds in a ward in the New Orleans Charity Hospital being cared for by nuns, who were aware, as Red told them several times, that they were nursing a representative of the Abe Patterson and Son Stage and Express Company and that he took no sass. The nuns ignored that and gave him plenty of sass because he was a difficult patient, especially when Buttons Muldoon left for Austin with four passengers and a temporary shotgun guard.

John Latimer, suffering from a wound in his lower back, was visited every day by Hannah, and they talked about renewing their engagement.

During the second week, Hannah visited with plans for their future.

"John, when you're stronger, we'll travel to Paris and start our balloon journey around the world from there," she said. "And with Mr. Chang as your valet."

"I've nothing to offer you, Hannah," Latimer said. "All I own are the clothes I wear . . ."

"And right now, you ain't even wearing those," Red said.

"The only thing I was ever any good at was soldiering, and now that's gone," Latimer said. "I've never done anything else, except some saloon swamping when I first arrived in Texas."

"We'll make out just fine, you and I, John," Hannah said. "You don't have to offer me anything when we have the whole world to share."

"Listen to the lady, Latimer," Red said. "She makes sense. That is, if you don't mind going up in the air in a balloon. It would scare the hell out of me."

"After what I've been through recently, I don't think anything can scare me ever again," Latimer said.

"Then it's settled," Hannah said, smiling. "We can get married in Paris."

"The hell you will," Red said. "As soon as Buttons gets back, you can get hitched right here in New Orleans. Me and Buttons love weddings, and Buttons always cries. We'll especially love yours, and he'll cry a lot."

"Hannah? What do you think?" Latimer said.

"That's fine by me. Red will be best man and Buttons will give the bride away."

"Sure thing," Red said. "All right, Latimer, now's the time to haul off and kiss her."

And he did.

* * *

Red was recuperating in the coaching inn when Buttons got back from Austin. After he'd seen to his horses and had a schooner of beer in hand, he joined Red on the porch.

"How are you feeling?" Buttons said.

"Better," Red said. "I was shot through and through, but Cooley's bullet didn't hit any of my vitals. Still hurts like hell, though."

"Can you ride the coach?" Buttons said.

"Sure, I can."

"Glad to hear it."

Red had to ask the question. "How was your hired shotgun guard?"

"Right nice feller, neither smoked not drank. He'd gotten religion and kept preaching at me about death and Judgment Day. Said if I don't repent and lay off whiskey and whores, I'm surely gonna be one of the damned."

"Cheerful kind of feller, huh?" Red said.

"That he wasn't." Buttons took a pull of his beer, wiped foam off his mustache with the back of his hand, and said, "How is Latimer?"

"Just fine. Him and Hannah are getting hitched, and we're invited to the wedding."

"Good. I'm right partial to weddings. I always cry at weddings."

"You're giving the bride away, so be on your best behavior," Red said.

"When are the nuptials?"

"Next week."

"Good, I'll have lined up some passengers by then. We got schedules to keep."

Buttons stared out into the street for a while and then said, "Well, tell me."

"Tell you what?" Red said.

"Are we wanted men?"

"Nope," Red said. "It took the law a long time to make up their minds, and for a spell, men in them blue police coats visited me in the hospital to warn me that there could be some hangings. But in the end, they decided that we'd acted in self-defense and dropped all charges."

"What about them two youngsters I locked up?"

"Gone. Hannah says they're probably headed back to England."

"Good riddance," Buttons said. "They surrendered " —he snapped his fingers—"just like that. Damn yellow-bellied cowards. Of course, Latimer was a coward, but he redeemed himself." He locked eyes with Red. "But no more cowards are allowed on the Patterson stage. That's a new rule I just wrote down on my last trip."

Red smiled. "Sounds like a good rule to me, Buttons."

"Damn right it is. And no more adventuresses and their Chinamen. I wrote that down as well."

"I'll keep that in mind," Red said.

"When I get a chance, I'll show ol' Abe Patterson my new rules and see what he thinks," Buttons said.

"He'll give you a pat on the back, Buttons," Red said.

"Damn right he will," Buttons said.

* * *

Hannah Huckabee thought it appropriate that she and John Latimer be married on the dock where their life together was beginning and no longer ending. Captain John Pickering was in favor of the idea and volunteered the services of his ship's chaplain to perform the ceremony.

Red Ryan and Buttons Muldoon, freshly bathed and shaved, were in attendance when the chaplain made the happy couple man and wife, and Captain Pickering, a little the worse for wear from rum, got so carried away by the occasion that he ordered a joyful five-gun salute to celebrate the union.

Unfortunately, the cannonade caused great consternation in New Orleans when the word quickly got around that the British had declared war on the city and had bombarded the dock area.

The constabulary arrived, and after the matter was explained and official congratulations were made to Hannah and Latimer, the tipsy Captain Pickering received a stern warning from the mayor and the chief of police that further broadsides would be punished to the fullest extent of the law that could, and probably would, end up with the confiscation of his warship. Nor was the lawman impressed by the groom's best man in his buckskin shirt and plug hat or with the stagecoach driver, acting as father of the bride, saying in a loud aside to one of his officers that they looked like "a pair of desperate characters."

That afternoon, after seeing Hannah and John Latimer off on the train for their honeymoon, Buttons decided that chiefs of police would no longer be carried on the Patterson stage, and he wrote down that new rule in his book.

Chapter Fifty-two

Over the next couple of days Buttons Muldoon lined up passengers for a trip as far as Austin, a reverend and his wife, and a young mail-order bride who would be meeting her rancher husband-to-be for the first time.

Despite nagging discomfort from his wound, Red Ryan was riding shotgun and was looking forward to the trip.

The Reverend Thaddeus Mosley, a small, timid man with frightened eyes, was taking over a leaderless flock following the sudden death of their pastor, and this would be his first stage journey.

"As you may expect, my dear wife and I are nervous about this trip," he told Buttons as they stood on the porch of the coaching inn. "Lavinia is of a delicate constitution, and I fear the journey will be too much for her. I'm convinced that she is already quite undone."

Buttons slapped the little man on the back and said, "Hell, Reverend, there's nothing to worry about.

I've got a good coach, fine horses, and the shotgun messenger is the best in the business."

"Oh dear, shotgun messenger," Mosley said. "I don't like the sound of that."

"Well, here he is right here," Buttons said. "Speak to him your ownself."

Red held his Greener in the crook of his arm and shook hands with the little man. "Glad to have you and your wife aboard, Reverend," he said.

"The reverend is nervous about the shotgun, Red," Buttons said.

"Nothing to be nervous about, Reverend," Red said. "As a representative of the Abe Patterson and Son Stage and Express Company, I can assure you that you'll be riding in the safest coach in all the Western routes."

"As I already told the driver, my dear Lavinia is a delicate flower, you understand," Mosley said.

"And so are you, Reverend, but me and Red will soon toughen you up," Buttons said. "By the time we reach Austin you'll be chewing baccy and cussin' like a cavalry trooper."

Mosley managed a weak smile. "Mr. Muldoon, I doubt that very much, since I'm not inclined to tobacco and cussing. Ah, here is my bride."

Lavinia Mosley was a large woman, somewhere in early middle age, with small, blue eyes in a round, rosy face shaded by a blue poke bonnet. Buttons later claimed that she'd dress out at around three hundred pounds.

"Who's the driver? You?" she said to Buttons. Her voice was harsh and loud with the habit of command.

"Thaddeus booked this trip without consulting me first." She glared at her spouse. "He'll never do that again."

On hearing that last, the little reverend seemed to shrink so much that suddenly his clothes appeared several sizes too big for him.

Buttons gave a little bow. "Indeed, dear lady, I am your driver, and your husband made an excellent choice. You just can't go wrong with Abe Patterson and Son."

"Oh, we can't," the woman said. Then she did something that shook Buttons to the core and left Red with his mouth hanging open. Her hand shot out, she grabbed Buttons by the front of his sailor's coat, and pulled him in so close to her that their noses almost touched. "Get one thing straight, driving man, I don't like to be bounced around inside a stagecoach. On uneven ground you'll drive slow, real slow, understand?"

Red came to the rescue. "Mr. Muldoon always does, Mrs. Mosley. As a representative of the Abe Patterson and Son Stage and Express Company, he is very mindful of the comfort of the ladies."

Lavinia pushed Buttons away from her. "See that you are." Then, her voice rising several notes, she said her husband's name. "Thaddeus!"

"Yes, my dear?" the reverend said.

"It's hot. Bring me a mug of beer." She nodded to Buttons. "A big one like he's got."

"But Lavinia . . . the doctor . . ."

"Don't tell me what the doctor says. Just do as I tell you," the large woman said.

Mosley was already scuttling for the door as he threw over his shoulder, "Yes, my dear."

Lavinia stared at a rocker, seemed doubtful of its proportions, and spread her bulk out on the swing that Gil Hooper kept for courting couples. The old man would later confide to Buttons that the swing was never the same again.

By contrast, Helen Corbin, the mail-order bride, was a quiet seventeen-year-old, short, plain, with dark brown eyes and brunette hair tied in a severe bun. She'd told Buttons, who had a way of getting people to talk about themselves, that as a baby she'd been left on the steps of an orphanage and raised by the Sisters of Charity. As far as she knew, her husband-to-be was twenty years older than she was, but she was eager to swap the orphanage for life as a rancher's wife. The girl carried all her belonging in a single carpetbag, and her dress was frayed and much patched by the thrifty nuns. Red noticed that she had good teeth and a nice smile, and he figured the rancher would be very pleased with her.

The three passengers elected to spend the night in the coaching inn since their departure was scheduled for daybreak the following morning.

But disaster struck that evening . . . and Buttons Muldoon thought he might lose them all.

Shortly after five, a J. D. Kinnear stage pulled in front of the inn with a badly wounded driver, a dying passenger, and a dead shotgun guard, a family man named Roberts who Red knew and liked.

The driver's name was Charley Mays, almost eighty years old and a legendary name on the frontier. As Buttons and Gil Hooper helped Mays down from the stage, it was obvious that the old man would not live much longer.

"Charley, what happened?" Hooper said.

"Road agents. About ten miles west of town." Then, his milky eyes staring into Hooper's face, "They've killed me at last, Gil."

Hooper sent for the police, and he and Buttons carried Mays into the inn. Red and another man, a corset drummer by the look of his samples, lifted the now-dead passenger out of the stage and laid him out on the porch.

"Buttons, help me with the guard," Red said,

"Do we know him?" Buttons said.

"Sure, we do. That's Dave Roberts up there."

Buttons nodded. "Now I recollect. He owned a restaurant in El Paso for a spell."

"And before that he was a deputy marshal for Judge Parker, then he signed on with big Jim Kinnear as a messenger." Red shook his head. "Well, he ain't nothing now, is he?"

"Nothing but dead," Buttons said. "God rest his soul."

Before he died, Charley Mays told the police that there had been three road agents, all wearing flour sacks over their heads. They had opened up on the stage without warning, killing Roberts in the first volley. He said one of them had been riding a palomino horse, but apart from that, he had nothing else to offer. Mays died with the name Anna on his lips, and there was later much speculation about who "Anna" was. Some said it was Charley's mother's name, others that it was the name of a sweetheart, but to date no one has ever solved the mystery.

The New Orleans police formed a posse and went out after the stage robbers, who'd taken a strongbox containing ten thousand dollars in coin and notes, but they rode back empty-handed just before midnight with a casualty of their own, a posse member who'd suffered a heart attack during the search.

Meanwhile Red and Buttons had troubles of their own. As they had feared, the Reverend Thaddeus Mosley, his formidable wife in tow, demanded a guarantee of their safety or a full refund of their fares plus hotel expenses. Helen Corbin looked frightened, but seemed content to let the Mosleys do the complaining.

"Well," Lavinia said, her balled fists on her broad hips. "We're waiting for an answer."

"My dear lady," Buttons said, "I can assure you that the safety of its passengers is a major concern of the Abe Patterson and Son Stage and Express Company."

Red said, "Those road agents have ten thousand dollars to spend. They're probably headed for Mexico even as we speak."

"Probably?" Lavinia said. "Is that all you can give me . . . probably?"

"This is so distressing," the Reverend Mosley said. "Lavinia, I fear we face a most singular danger with road agents on the rampage. Perhaps we should postpone our journey until the miscreants have been found."

"And what about your wayward flock, Thaddeus?" Lavinia said, her thick eyebrows lowered. "What about the wayward souls of the Austin First Apostolic Church who will sin without regard to man or God until your arrival?"

"I'll pray for them, my dearest."

"Pray for them? You'll do nothing of the sort," Lavinia said. "Grow a backbone, Thaddeus."

"But my sweet . . ."

"You, shotgun man . . . what a disreputable occupation that is . . . you heard my husband," the woman said. "Give me your guarantee that we will come to no harm from road agents. Speak now, don't shilly-shally."

"As a representative of the Abe Patterson and Son Stage and Express Company, you have my guarantee," Red said.

"And mine," Buttons said.

Lavinia, with a look of disapproval, turned on Helen and said, "Now, you bold-faced thing, what is your decision?"

The girl, who at that moment looked far from bold-faced, said, "If the driver and the guard say it's safe to travel, then I'll take their word for it."

"And I should certainly hope so," Lavinia said. "Be guided by your elders and betters, missy."

Thaddeus Mosley said, "My dear, I really don't think . . ."

"Oh, do be quiet, Thaddeus," Lavinia said. "I'll do the thinking for both of us."

"As you always have, my dear," the reverend said, shrinking into his clothes again.

"Then we accept your guarantees, driver and shotgun man," Lavinia said. "For your own sakes, I hope you're right."

The following day, four hours and a horse change out from New Orleans, Buttons drew back on the lines and said, "Red, you see what I see ahead of us?"

"Sure do. Three road agents, flour sacks over their heads, one of them riding a palomino hoss. Sound familiar?"

"Yeah, it sounds familiar," Buttons said. He shook his head. "Well, here we go again."

"Seems like," Red said.

Lavinia Mosley stuck her head out of the stage window and yelled, "You there! Why have we stopped when you know that my husband has a flock waiting and time is of the essence?"

"Looks like road agents ahead of us," Red said. "Stay in the coach, ma'am."

The Reverend Thaddeus Mosley's wail of fear ended any further discourse, since Lavinia turned her wrath on her timid spouse: "Don't sit there whining. Do something."

Red figured that about then Thaddeus had shrunk

into his clothes so much he probably looked like a scarecrow made from a broom.

"Red, how do you want to play it?" Buttons said.

"We won't stand still for them," Red said. "I prefer a running fight, so whip up the team and charge right at them."

"You sure?" Buttons said.

"You got a better idea?" Red said.

"Nope."

"You up there, drive on," Lavinia yelled. "The reverend is quite undone, though he's ready to answer any call to arms."

"Buttons, you heard the lady, the reverend is loaded for bear," Red said. "Have at it."

His face grim, Buttons hoorawed as he whipped up the team and the rocking, bouncing stage streamed a dust cloud as it hurtled toward the outlaws. One of the bandits, the man riding the palomino, raised his rifle and snapped off a shot that split the air between Red and his driver. Startled, Buttons yelled, "Damn, he's good!"

Red made no answer. The distance between himself and the road agents was closing fast, and now all three of them were firing. Red braced himself and raised the shotgun. He needed to get within scattergun range . . . if he lived that long.

The outlaws had obviously been up this road a time or three. Wary of the shotgun, they pulled off to the side of the trail a good distance and let the stage pass, firing their revolvers as Buttons urged the team to a greater effort. Bullet after bullet splintered into the thin wood of the Concord, and Red cut loose with both barrels at the nearest rider, missing at that range, but keeping the man honest. Then the stage was through with flat, open ground ahead.

The road agents immediately gave chase, firing as they came.

Lavinia Mosley stuck her head out of the window again, the jouncing stage making her chins bounce. "Slow down, you lunatic!" she yelled. "You'll kill us all!"

Red heard that. Buttons didn't, but he had no intention of slowing down the team anyhow.

The bandits were closing fast, and Red knew his situation was deteriorating, getting downright dangerous. He watched the man on the palomino ride wide and thumb off a shot, not at the coach but at the team, trying to drop one of the leaders. The bandit missed, but he might not miss a second time. Red reloaded the Greener, sliding a fresh, red cartridge into the chamber.

Then, a calamity that Buttons Muldoon would later claim aged him ten years in a split second. He yelped as a bullet burned across the backs of his gloved hands and the reins dropped from his suddenly numb fingers. Red saw the danger. He gripped the shotgun in his left hand and grabbed the lines with his right, hauling with his considerable strength. The team responded by swinging abruptly to their left and the stage followed, yawed violently, and tilted over on two wheels before righting itself broadside to the oncoming riders. The team was experienced and savvy and stopped on a dime, but Buttons lost his footing in the jolting halt and went over the side in a cussing tangle of whip and reins.

There are times for talking, for smoothing things over, but during a gunfight is not one of them, and nobody knew that better than Red Ryan. He took up his shotgun in both hands and immediately looked for a target. He found it in the first rider who rode up on the stage. The bandit and Red saw one another at the same time and fired in the same instant. Both men hurried the shot, and the road agent's bullet went an inch wide of Red's head. A scattergun at close range is forgiving of a hasty trigger finger, and two barrels of buckshot slammed into the bandit and blew him out of the saddle. Red dropped the Greener and drew his revolver. A shot came from his right on the other side of the stage and a man screamed. Then another and a third. A moment later the rider on the palomino decided that things weren't going so well, and it was time to get the hell out of town. He came from behind the team, favoring his left arm that hung uselessly by his side, and set spurs to his mount.

For a moment there, Red had been scared and a scared man is not a forgiving man.

He threw himself across the top of the stage and drew bead on the fleeing rider. It was a long shot for a Colt revolver but Red was determined to try. He held his breath, squeezed the trigger, and cut loose.

The bandit kept on going . . . but after fifty yards he stood in the stirrups and toppled out of the saddle. When he hit the ground, he raised dust.

At times Red had seen Buttons Muldoon irritated,

peeved, distressed, unhappy . . . but he'd never seen him angry . . . never seen him in a black, killing rage like he was that morning on the south Texas plains.

His Colt hanging by his side, he walked to the man who'd ridden the palomino. Red saw Buttons say something to the man, who answered and then pulled off his flour sack mask, revealing a mop of yellow hair, and raised his hand in a gesture of supplication, begging for mercy. But that day Buttons Muldoon had none. He pumped three bullets into the bandit and then turned and stepped away from him. He didn't look back.

Buttons collected the palomino, and when he led the horse to the stage, his face was like thunder. He'd taken off his gloves and the backs of his hands were bloody.

"Not one to hold a grudge, are you, old fellow?" Red said.

"That sorry piece of trash said his name was Pete Skyler and he said he'd nothing to do with the holdup that killed Dave Roberts and Charley Mays," Buttons said. "He was a damned liar and a thief, and a liar will steal and a thief will kill and I'm sick of his kind."

Red patted the palomino's neck and said, "Nice-looking hoss."

Buttons nodded. "Round up the other two, Red, and tether them to the back of the stage. We'll sell them and send the proceeds to Dave's widow. God knows, she'll need the money with with a passel of young 'uns to raise."

The stage door opened, and the Reverend Thaddeus Mosley was pushed outside. "My husband will help you with the horses," Lavinia said. "Won't you, Thaddeus?"

The little man shrank, his neck ringed by the celluloid collar that seemed a bunch of sizes too big for him. "But, precious, I don't know anything about horses," he said. "And . . . and . . . Lavinia, there are dead men everywhere."

"The shotgun guard will teach you about horses," the big woman said. "And dead men can't harm you, Thaddeus. God knows, you've buried enough of them. The sooner you bring in the horses, the sooner we can leave this wasteland." The slim figure of Helen Corbin was propelled though the door. "She'll help too," Lavinia said. "The bold-faced thing."

Chapter Fifty-three

To Red Ryan's relief, the Abe Patterson and Son stage reached Austin without further incident, though his recent wound ached. "And no wonder," Buttons Muldoon said, "jumping all over the coach like a jack in the box."

The Reverend Thaddeus Mosley was greeted by the open arms of his flock, a small throng certainly, but Lavinia, who'd expected a multitude and was visibly disappointed by the small turnout, brightened considerably when one of the woman informed her that chocolate cake and ice cream would be served at that night's welcoming social. Helen Corbin, the blushing bride, met her tall, rancher husband and apparently neither found cause for complaint.

"All's well that ends well, huh?" Buttons Muldoon said to no one in particular as he and Red sat with old Rush Sanford drinking beer on the front porch of the Patterson stage depot.

"Seems like," Red said. The reverend has his flock, and that nice Miss Corbin gal has her husband."

"And the town's quiet, now the crazy axe murderer is no more," Sanford said. "Say what you want about him, but he sure gave Austin some snap." The old man sighed. "Ah well, no use crying over spilt milk, I always say."

A silence followed that statement that neither Red or Buttons seemed anxious to fill, but then the tall, narrow-shouldered man that stepped onto the porch did the filling for them.

"Good evening, gentlemen," he said. "I'm looking for the driver of the Patterson stage."

"You found him," Buttons said. "What can I do for you, mister?"

The man wore a plum-colored frock coat, a top hat of the same shade, and a brocade vest. A trimmed mustache covered his top lip. "Ah, then we're well met, my good fellow," the man said. "I am Professor—"

"Hold it right there, stranger," Buttons said. "Don't say another word. The Patterson stage don't carry professors. I wrote that down in the rule book quite recent on account of how our experience with professors ain't exactly been agreeable."

The man smiled. "Well, that's no problem. I'm not really a professor. It's just something I call myself. My name is Octavius Ashton, purveyor of Professor Ashton's Blood Renovator, guaranteed to cure scrofula, consumption, gout, dyspepsia, insomnia, heart disease, baldness, dementia, nervous prostration in women, and much more. In short, if you got it, my medicine will cure it."

"It takes care of all them miseries?" Button said.

"Every single one, and many others that I don't care to mention in polite company. Shall we say those maladies that plague a man after he's spent too many nights with Venus."

"Then I'll take a bottle," Buttons said, brightening. "How much?"

"Alas, I have none on hand, and that is the reason I'm here," Ashton said. "My medicine wagon burned up in a fire and with it all my supplies. Now my only recourse is to make the journey to San Angelo where my brother Nehemiah resides. He has assured me he has the monetary wherewithal to finance a new wagon and the ingredients to make more of my miraculous elixir."

"San Angelo, up Fort Concho way, is on one of our routes," Buttons said, looking disappointed. He studied Ashton from his patent-leather shoes to the top of his hat. "Here, do you have the money to pay?"

"Yes, I do," Ashton said. "My brother has agreed to pay for myself and two more passengers, my assistants, a man and a woman who are the stars of my gaslit medicine show that has been enjoyed by most of the crowned heads of Europe."

"For all three of you, that will be sixty dollars, including meals," Buttons said.

"And that price is most satisfactory," Ashton said. "And meals included. Now there's luxury for you."

Buttons rose to his feet and extended his hand. "I am Mr. Muldoon, and the redhead over there wearing the plug hat and fancy buckskin shirt is my guard, Mr. Ryan. We'll leave tomorrow morning at seven sharp, rain, hail, snow, or shine. The Patterson stage always gets through."

"Bravo!" Ashton said. After he dropped Buttons's hand, he added, "You are most gracious, Mr. Muldoon. Being driven by you will be a great pleasure. And I'm certain my assistants will agree."

"Likewise, I'm sure," Buttons said. "The Abe Patterson and Son Stage and Express Company will make sure that your journey is a pleasant one, and we always make special arrangements for the ladies."

"Until tomorrow morning then," Ashton said.

"Yeah, until tomorrow morning," Buttons said. "And if you come across a bottle of that there blood renovator, give it here, huh?"

I surely will," Ashion said. It's very precious, you know, but I may have a bottle stashed somewhere. If not, I'll mix up a batch for you just as soon as we arrive in San Angelo. It will make a new man of you, Mr. Muldoon."

After the man left, Buttons said to Red, "Now that was a right nice feller. Three fares. That ought to please the company."

Red nodded. "I guess it will." Then to Sanford, "Rush, you'll make sure that Mrs. Roberts gets the money we raised on the horses."

"Depend on it, Red," Sanford said. "And I'll throw in a little bit extry from me."

"Good man, Rush," Buttons said. "You're true blue."

"Least I can do," Sanford said. "Dave Roberts was a good man."

"A sight better man that the one who killed him," Buttons said. "And that's a natural fact."

* * *

The following morning dawned rainy and gray, and Red Ryan sought out Buttons, who was drinking coffee and eating a bacon sandwich in the depot dining room.

Rush Sanford, who was doing the cooking, nodded to Red and held up a strip of bacon on a fork. "Want some?" he said.

Red shook his head. "No thanks, Rush. I've kinda lost my appetite. Happened quite recent."

"I'll take it, Rush," Buttons said. "Then to Red, "What's up with you?"

"Your passengers are here," Red said.

"Then let them wait in the stage," Buttons said. "It ain't seven yet." He opened up his sandwich and said, "Put that strip right in there, Rush. There's a good man." He chewed for a while and then said, "Is the gal pretty, like Hannah Huckabee?"

"Nope," Red said. "She's nothing like Hannah Huckabee."

Buttons's face fell, but then he brightened. "Well, we can't all be purty folks like Hannah Huckabee and you."

Red smiled. "Well, thank you for the compliment, Mr. Muldoon."

"Hey, what do those two do that help the medicine man? I mean, do they sing or dance or what? Maybe they could entertain us at the stage stops, huh?"

"I don't know, Buttons. I think folks would just want to look at them," Red said.

"Why would they look at them? I mean, I don't catch your drift. Do they get nekkid, or something?"

"I don't think so," Red said. "I wouldn't want to see them get nekkid."

"Now you got me all confused," Buttons said. He stuffed the remainder of his sandwich into his mouth, chewed, swallowed, and said. "Well, let's go take a look, huh?"

"Hold on, I'm going with you," Rush Sanford said. "If the woman takes her clothes off, I want to be there and see the sights."

When Buttons, Red, and Rush Sanford stepped onto the porch, three people were waiting, Octavius Ashton and his two assistants. The man smiled and said, "Well, good morning, gentlemen. May I introduce my fellow passengers and assistants?" He pushed the woman forward. "This is Miss Cleora Sackville, known to her legions of admirers the world over as the Amazing Bearded Lady. And here, standing only three-and-a-half foot tall, every inch of him muscle, is the one, the only, Mongo, the Mighty Midget. Bend the poker for the gentlemen, Mongo."

The dwarf, for that's what he was, held a thick iron poker in his hands and then, grunting, he bent it double and then proceeded to tie it into some kind of bizarre sailor's knot. Miss Cleora, who sported a thick beard that fell all the way to the top of her breasts, jumped up and down, clapped her hands, and yelled, "Huzzah! Huzzah for Mongo the Mighty!"

Ashton beamed and said, "Mr. Muldoon, aren't they wonderful? Between them, I can assure you that they sell many bottles of my remedy."

Buttons, who looked like he was suffering a sudden attack of indigestion, nodded. "Yeah, yeah, wonderful," he said.

"Now, Cleora, Mongo, into the stage," Ashton said. "Get settled, and don't squabble."

Once the pair were seated inside, Ashton stood at the door and then turned and said to Buttons in a conspiratorial whisper, "I should tell you that Miss Cleora gets very sick when she rides in a coach, and I must warn you that she can be very amorous at times. Mongo now, well ,he will become violent when he doesn't get his own way. As strong as he is, he can be very dangerous, especially if he attacks you when you're sleeping." The man smiled. "I've got the scars to prove it."

"I'll bear that in mind," Buttons said.

Ashton smiled. "But apart from their little peculiarities, they are pleasant travelling companions, though it's prudent to have a sick bucket handy for Miss Cleora. Oh, and they both sing and dance, so they can entertain you along the way. Now there's something to look forward to, Mr. Muldoon."

After Buttons climbed into the driver's seat, Red grinned at him and said, "Well?"

"Well what?"

"Don't we get the strangest people on the Patterson stage?

Buttons shook his head and sighed. "Here we go again."

"Seems like," Red said.

Chapter One

"Guess you heard the good news, Sheriff." Deputy Jimmy "Hawkeye" Hauk hitched up his belt as they began their morning foot patrol along Main Street. The sunrise in Blackstone, Wyoming Territory, always revealed a few drunks who'd passed out in the alleys between the many saloons along Main Street. Some just needed help going home. A few were actually dead from time to time, which required much more attention on the part of Sheriff Trammel and his deputy. "Word is they're hanging Madam Peachtree down in Laramie some time in the next month or so."

"Pinochet," Sheriff Buck Trammel corrected him. "Her name is Pinochet, and yeah, I read about it in the *Bugle* same as you."

"Pinochet," repeated Hawkeye, as if he was trying it on for size. "Anyway, you got any plans to head down there and see her swing? After all, you're the one who brought her in."

"And the reason why she's swinging." The big man shook his head. "Never was much for witnessing hangings myself, though. Too much of a spectacle for all the wrong reasons."

"After what she done to you?" Hawkeye said. "All them times she tried to have you killed? Hell, she almost had the entire town destroyed while gunning for you."

Trammel had no desire to relive the complexities of the Madam Pinochet matter with his talkative deputy. He genuinely liked Hawkeye and had come to rely on him. He admired the way the young man handled a gun. He wasn't trigger happy, but he wasn't afraid to shoot when the time came. He was brave and even-tempered, and Trammel was glad to have him at his side.

But if the boy had one failing, it was that he couldn't keep his mouth shut. He'd been born in Blackstone and had never lived anywhere else. He knew everyone and they knew him, but Trammel couldn't call him a gossip. Hawkeye was proud of his new position and the knowledge it gave him. He wasn't old enough yet to know when to talk and when to keep his mouth shut. It was the kind of practical knowledge only years could give him and he didn't have enough behind him yet. Only experience could teach such lessons.

Lessons that Buck Trammel had learned long ago. The hard way.

"They hit us with everything they had." He decided to boost the younger man's ego. "But we fought them off anyway, didn't we? You and me."

The young man stood taller. Even though he was

almost six feet tall, Hawkeye barely reached Trammel's shoulder. "Yes, sir. We most certainly did."

Both men looked up when they heard screams coming from farther along Main Street. The town's main thoroughfare was lined with dozens of saloons, gambling dens, and kitchens that all catered to various crowds. Trammel knew the scream could have come from any of them.

When he saw Adam Hagen step out of the Pot of Gold Saloon, he knew the scream must have come from there. Trouble always had a knack for finding Hagen.

The gambler and new proprietor of the saloon lit a cigarette as the lawmen approached him. His red brocade vest and white shirt were as fresh as if he had just put them on, though Trammel imagined his duties at the Pot had probably kept him up all night. "Morning, gentlemen. And what a morning it is! The crispness of the mountain air. The calmness of a town just beginning to shake off the dust of a good night's sleep. The—"

"That scream came from your place, didn't it?" Trammel had no time for the gambler's fancy talk. He knew Adam Hagen to be an elaborate man . . . in his words, in his dress, and in the saloons he had recently acquired. The two men had saved each other's lives several times on the trail from where they'd first met in Wichita to Blackstone. They had once considered each other friends.

That was in the past as far as Trammel was concerned. Their friendship ended the moment Hagen had decided to take Madam Pinochet's place as the territory's chief vice merchant.

Hagen shrugged. "And what if it did? One is apt to hear a scream or two from a house of ill repute from time to time."

Hawkeye spoke out of turn. "The sheriff told you he'd leave you alone so long as you kept things to a dull roar around here. That scream's not part of the bargain."

Hagen smiled at the young man. "Would you look at that? Pin a star on a gadfly and watch him turn into Wild Bill Hickok." He looked up at Trammel. "Has he even begun to shave yet?"

Trammel wouldn't be baited. "You're going to tell me where that scream came from, or we're going to kick in every door in the place."

"The change I've witnessed in you since coming to Blackstone is especially fascinating" Hagen frowned. "A few months ago, you were in a lookout chair at the Gilded Lily in Wichita minding drunks and drovers. Now you're the pious lawman of Blackstone." He looked away. "Guess the old saying about beggars and horseback still holds true."

Trammel felt his temper begin to rise. He didn't like Hagen bringing up their former association. He didn't like Hagen at all. Not anymore. "I asked you a question."

Hagen sighed as another scream came from the Pot of Gold, this one louder than the last.

Trammel took a step closer to Hagen, looming over him. "What room?"

"Let it burn itself out, Buck. It's just one of my

customers getting rambunctious. I'll handle it myself when he's done."

Trammel pushed past him and stormed into the saloon. Hawkeye was right behind him.

From the boardwalk, Hagen called out, "Room Twenty, damn you. But don't kill anyone this time. Death is bad for business."

Trammel ignored the stares he and Hawkeye drew from the men at the gambling tables and standing at the bar. Every working girl in the place ignored their potential customers and looked up in the direction from where the screams had come. They knew that, one day, the screams might be coming from them.

Trammel took the steps two at a time as an unholy shriek came from room twenty. He used his bulk to barrel through the door, splintering it from the jamb.

A large man had one of Hagen's girls pinned against the wall by the neck. He held a knife to her eye. Both of them looked at Trammel as the door slammed open and he stepped inside.

The man's knife twitched. "Take one more step, law dog, and I swear I'll—"

Trammel tomahawked the man's knife hand away from the woman as he yanked him away from her. The assailant's grip broke, and the woman ran toward Hawkeye as Trammel threw the big man back onto the bed, causing it to collapse beneath his weight.

Hawkeye drew his pistol and held it on the man as he shielded the young lady from further harm. "Don't move, mister. You're under arrest."

The panicked working girl bolted from the room,

knocking Hawkeye out of the way, sending his pistol toward the ceiling.

The attacker bellowed as he clumsily lunged off the collapsed bed at Trammel, his knife held high in his right hand.

Trammel sidestepped the lunge, grabbed the big man's right hand, and pushed the arm farther back. A sickening crack made the man scream as his shoulder broke. The knife dropped to the bed as he spilled onto the floor.

Trammel put his foot on the back of the screaming man's head, pinning him to the ground. "Tell me it's over and I'll let you up."

Hawkeye grabbed the knife off the bed and tucked it into his belt.

Hearing no response, Trammel applied more weight to the back of the man's neck. "Is it over?"

"You broke my arm!"

"I'll do more than that unless you come along peacefully."

"Fine!" the man yelled as best he could. "It's over."

Trammel grabbed a handful of greasy hair and pulled the man to his feet. The sheriff was about to lead him toward the door when the man's left arm swung around wildly and broke his grip. Trammel staggered back with a handful of the man's hair still in his hands. He launched himself into Trammel, knocking him back against the wall.

The attacker staggered back and threw a left hook that Trammel easily dodged.

By then, Trammel's rage had already boiled over. The sheriff buried a straight right hand into the man's belly, doubling him over. He snatched him by the back of the neck and his britches and threw him through the closed window.

Trammel and Hawkeye looked out the window to see the man had hit the ground and rolled down the small embankment that ran behind all of the establishments along Main Street. His legs were still moving, but barely.

"Looks like he's still movin'," Hawkeye observed. "So he's still alive."

"Yeah." Trammel spat blood out the window in the man's direction. "Let's go get him."

As they turned to leave the room, Adam Hagen was standing in the doorway. "Was that really necessary? Do you know how long it's going to take me to get that window replaced?"

Hawkeye hurried past him, but Trammel took his time. "The girl's fine, by the way."

"I know she's fine," Hagen said. "I just checked on her before I came in here. But you still owe me the cost of a new window, Trammel."

"He pulled a knife on me," the sheriff said as he pushed past him into the hallway. "You remember how much I hate knives, don't you, Adam?"

"And do you know how much a new window will cost me? I'm a businessman now, Buck," Hagen called after him as the sheriff walked down the stairs. "I don't have to be the only one making money here. You could have your share, just like I offered, you know. It's not my fault you're so damned stubborn."

Trammel didn't dignify it with an answer as he went down the stairs to retrieve his prisoner.

* * *

Trammel and Hawkeye ignored the injured man's pleas for a doctor as they practically dragged the man all the way back to the jail.

He screamed when they dumped him onto a cot in one of the cells and slammed the door shut. "I need a doctor, damn you!"

"Seems like everyone we dump in here needs a doctor." Hawkeye grinned. "Maybe we're gettin' what you might call a reputation for being rough?"

"That's a reputation I can live with." To the prisoner, Trammel said, "We'll see about getting you a doctor as soon as we've finished our patrol. You interrupted us while we were in the middle of making it, so you'll have to wait."

The man slumped on the cot, his ruined right arm lying limp on the cell floor. "You'd better get me a doctor damned fast, boy. You don't know who you're dealing with."

Hawkeye laughed as he turned the key in the cell door. "Where have we heard that one before?"

"Don't know how many times you heard it," the prisoner said, "but this time, it holds water." He glared up at the sheriff. "I know who you are, Trammel. So do a lot of people."

Trammel knew his name had appeared in the papers a few times as a result of the Madam Pinochet incident. He hadn't been happy about all of the attention, but gunfights and shoot-outs on main streets were big news back east and elsewhere, so he had no choice but to go along with it and wait for it to die down.

"The longer you keep talking, the longer it'll take for you to get a doctor to look you over." He elbowed his deputy. "Come to think of it, we haven't had our coffee yet, have we, Hawkeye?"

Hawkeye played along. "Can't remember that we have."

"I don't know about you, but I'm no damned good until I've had that first cup to start the day. We'd best get ourselves some before we resume our patrol."

"Sounds good to me, boss."

They ignored the man's threats as they left the cells and shut the door leading to the office behind them.

Hawkeye sheepishly laid the keys on Trammel's desk. "Boss, we just had some coffee not half an hour ago."

Trammel sometimes forgot how gullible the young man could be. "That was just for his benefit. You stay here and keep an eye on him. I don't think he'll give you any trouble in his condition, but keep an eye on him just the same. I'll go fetch Doctor Downs right away to take a look at him. His arm's broken, and he probably busted a few ribs when he fell out that window. Don't want him dying on us if I can help it. Get started on writing up the report in the meantime."

Hawkeye eagerly pulled up a chair and took the paper from the bottom drawer of his desk. The boy's spelling was horrible and his grammar was even worse, but he enjoyed writing up reports, so Trammel let him.

The sheriff scooped up the keys from the desk as he left. "I'll lock the door on my way out. Best to keep it that way until I get back. That drunk might have friends, and if he does, it'd be best if we faced them down together."

"I'll be too busy with this here report to do anything else," Hawkeye said. "Say, boss. What did Mr. Hagen mean back there? That stuff about beggars and horses."

Trammel knew Hagen had a unique ability of saying something that could stick in your mind all day. He knew he had fallen prey to it from time to time. "It's an old saying. 'Put a beggar on horseback and he'll ride to Hell on account of he doesn't know any better.'"

Hawkeye looked more confused than ever. "Well, you ain't no beggar and Blackstone sure ain't no Hell."

Sometimes, Trammel admired the way the boy's mind worked. "I'll be back with the doctor as soon as I can."

Chapter Two

Trammel enjoyed how Emily Downs's kitchen always smelled like baked bread and coffee. The widow's mother-in-law was a dour old woman who had lost her ability to speak after the sudden death of her son more than a year before, but she hadn't lost her ability to cook.

Trammel was enjoying some of that fine coffee while he sat in the kitchen waiting for Emily to come down from dressing. Upon being named sheriff of Blackstone, he'd rented a room in her house rather than in the run-down hovel that came with the job at the Oakwood Arms or at the Hagen-controlled Clifford Hotel.

Trammel's predecessor—Sheriff Bonner—had used a room at the Oakwood and, given how he'd been shot in the back as he fled his debts, Trammel decided to make his lodgings elsewhere. Mayor Welch, who owned the Oakwood, was annoyed at the loss of income, but the town elders applauded the sheriff for finding much cheaper lodgings at Doctor Downs's place.

Trammel looked out the window as he sipped his coffee. He ignored the black-clad widow's vacant stare from her perch in the chair next to the stove. Her expression never changed, whether she was at church or sitting outside enjoying the sunshine at her daughter-in-law's orders.

But he always felt there was something extra in the way she looked at him. It was as though she could see through all of the fame and glory he had received for bringing Madam Pinochet and her allies to justice. It was like she could see into his very soul and all of the many sins he had committed in his thirty years. He didn't know if that was the case, but if it was, he doubted she'd ever get bored, for there was plenty to see.

"Good morning," Emily Downs sang as she entered the kitchen. She gave her mother-in-law a kiss on the forehead, which garnered no response from her.

"And good morning to you, Sheriff Trammel," she said with false propriety. They were on a first-name basis when they were alone, but kept to formal titles when others were around.

"And a good morning to you, Doctor Downs," he answered.

She had chestnut-brown hair and bright eyes that were even more captivating in the gentle light of the morning. Her simple dress did an adequate job of disguising the curves of her body of which Trammel had become so fond.

"I trust you slept comfortably."

She turned her back to her mother-in-law to hide her blush as she had spent a good portion of the night in Trammel's bed. "Most comfortably, thank you." She lifted the coffeepot from the stove. "More coffee?"

He smiled. "Thanks."

"I understand you've already had a busy morning."

Even though he had been the sheriff of Blackstone for several months, the speed with which news spread around the small town at all hours of the day and night still fascinated him. "How the h—?" He remembered the widow was there and caught himself. "I mean, how did you know? You just got up."

"I heard the screams coming from Main Street and imagined it was something that required your attention. Am I right?"

He chose his words carefully for the widow's sake. "Someone got rough with one of the dance hall girls at the Pot of Gold. Hawkeye and I had to take care of it. You might need to check on the girl involved."

Emily filled her own cup and set the pot back on the stove. "And the man who attacked her? I trust he needs attention, too, thanks to you."

"When you get around to it."

"Is he still alive?"

"Fell out a window," Trammel said. "Busted up some. He'll probably keep until you tend to the girl. She's more important."

Emily strategically moved the kitchen chair so her back wasn't to her mother-in-law and she wasn't sitting too close to her boarder, either. "How bad is he?"

Trammel shrugged. "He fell out a second-story window and rolled down the embankment. His right arm is broken, and I'd be surprised if his ribs weren't cracked, if not broken. His lungs work fine, though and he's not bleeding much."

"Imagine that," she chided. "Only a half-dead patient for once. You're getting benevolent in your old age, Sheriff."

He couldn't really argue with that. In his time in Blackstone, Trammel had developed a reputation for being rougher than he had to be with some characters, which had led to a drop in crime since the Madam Pinochet incident. His size had usually been enough to discourage most men from stepping out of line, but now that he had some notoriety behind him, men tended to do what he said.

He also knew notoriety was a double-edged sword, and it would only be a matter of time before someone decided to test it in an effort to gain some notoriety for themselves.

He would worry about that if and when it happened. For now, he was content with the morning's work while enjoying the widow's coffee and Emily's company.

"The Pot of Gold is Adam's new place, isn't it?" she asked.

"Opened last week," Trammel said. He knew what was coming next. It had been a bone of contention between them for months.

"Did you have a chance to speak with him yet? About mending fences?"

Trammel sipped his coffee. "The opportunity to do so didn't present itself, Doctor. Besides, the fence between us is just fine as it is."

She lowered her cup. "I wish you boys would figure

out a way past your differences. You were friends once, Buck. Good friends."

"That was then. This is now. He works his side of things and I work mine." He saw no reason to explain himself, especially in front of the widow.

Hagen had decided to hold on to Madam Pinochet's ledger of illegal actions in the territory. He had also expanded her opium trade against Trammel's wishes. While there may not be any laws against opium in Wyoming or in Blackstone, he hated the practice. In his time as a policeman in New York City and later, with the Pinkerton Agency, he had seen what smoking the sticky tar could do. He had seen good men brought low by the desire to hitch a ride on the dragon's back one more time.

Opium may not have been illegal, but that didn't make it right. Hagen's desire to peddle flesh was bad enough in Trammel's eyes, but he knew if Hagen didn't do it, someone else would. Robbing men of their souls was something Buck Trammel would never tolerate.

"Friendships in this life are so hard to come by," Emily went on. "Especially good friendships like the one you had with Adam. Maybe you could be a good influence on him if you were close to him again."

Trammel laughed as he got up to pour himself another cup of coffee from the stove. "The die for Adam Hagen was cast long before he left Blackstone and only hardened in the years since. There's no amount of praying or cajoling that'll make him change unless he wants to. Or has to, if it comes to that." He poured his coffee. "And if it comes to that, it'll probably be thanks to me." He held out the pot to her. "More coffee before we head out to tend to your patients?"

She drained her cup and gently placed it back in the saucer as she stood. It was a delicate motion, but sounded as loud as a judge's gavel in the quiet of the kitchen. "I'll get my shawl and bag. I'd appreciate it if you'd escort me to the jail to see the prisoner, Sheriff. After that, I'd like to look in on that poor girl he assaulted."

Trammel shut his eyes as she left the kitchen. He knew her tone well enough to know she was upset. He felt the widow's constant glare upon him as he set the coffeepot back on the stove. Her eyes were as vacant as they were alive.

He finished his coffee in two swallows and smiled at her as he set his cup aside. Her look never changed.

He held the back door open for Emily as she appeared with her shawl wrapped around her shoulders and her husband's old medicine bag in her hand. "Can I carry that for you?"

She walked past him into the chilly morning. Trammel sighed as he quietly shut the door behind him.

Out on the boardwalk and still out of view of anyone who might see, she swung her bag and hit him in the side.

Trammel stifled a yelp. "What the hell was that for?"

"For being pigheaded," she said without breaking her stride. "I swear, Buck Trammel, you're a tough man to love sometimes."

Trammel smiled as he caught up with her. She had told him she loved him several times since they had become a couple, but he never tired of hearing it. He easily matched her pace with a little swagger to his step. "So you love me, huh?"

He yelped again when she pinched his side. "Don't get too cocky on me, Sheriff. I might not be a real doctor, but I know all the right places that hurt."

He rubbed the spot where she'd pinched him. "Yes, ma'am."

Connect with Us

Visit us online at
KensingtonBooks.com
to read more from your favorite authors, see books
by series, view reading group guides, and more.

Join us on social media

for sneak peeks, chances to win books and prize packs,
and to share your thoughts with other readers.

**facebook.com/kensingtonpublishing
twitter.com/kensingtonbooks**

Tell us what you think!

To share your thoughts, submit a review,
or sign up for our eNewsletters, please visit:
KensingtonBooks.com/TellUs.